"No one writes Victorian romance like Mimi Matthews, and her Belles of London series just keeps getting better! No-nonsense Lady Anne has renounced marriage and devoted herself to two things— her band of equestrienne friends and her widowed mother still locked in deepest crepe-veiled mourning. But a dashing former suitor blasts back into Anne's shuttered world, bringing passion and change in his wake, and Anne must decide if she will embrace life or remain safe in her chrysalis. *The Lily of Ludgate Hill* made me smile from beginning to end."   —*New York Times* bestselling author Kate Quinn

"I've long been a devoted fan of Mimi Matthews, and with *The Lily of Ludgate Hill*, the delightful continuation of her Belles of London series, my admiration of her work has only increased. Her command of historical detail is faultless. . . . I loved Anne and Hart; was instantly and completely consumed by their tangled past and seemingly impossible future."

—Jennifer Robson, international bestselling author of *Coronation Year*

"Mimi is truly a national treasure. All of her books are filled with such delicious chemistry and heart, and her writing is superb. This one is another winner. Highly recommend."

—#1 *New York Times* bestselling author Isabel Ibañez

"Mimi Matthews is a master at combining rich historical detail with an emotionally tender love story. Watching Anne come into her own while Hart's long-denied flame for her nearly burns him alive was absolutely delightful. I loved *The Lily of Ludgate Hill* and I hope this series never ends."   —Harper St. George, author of *The Stranger I Wed*

"It is truly a wonder how Matthews can consistently craft fresh romances featuring unique, multidimensional characters who face huge obstacles to their relationships."   —*Booklist* (starred review)

"Absolutely enthralling: an endearing, novel-reading heroine who's in dire danger; a swoon-worthy war hero with a scandalous past; and secrets, lots of secrets. Mimi Matthews's *The Belle of Belgrave Square* is a thrilling, emotion-packed read from start to finish. I loved it!"

—*USA Today* bestselling author Syrie James

"Combines deception, risk, and a resourceful heroine to create an intoxicating, suspenseful romance. Highly recommended."

—*Library Journal* (starred review)

"A grand cross-class romance, a twisty mystery, and emotional internal struggles combine to excellent effect. . . . Fans and new readers alike will root for this well-earned love story."

—*Publishers Weekly* (starred review)

PRAISE FOR

The Siren of Sussex

"What I love about Mimi Matthews is that in the crowded field of historical romance she always finds new and interesting slants for her plots and characters. That, along with her wonderful writing and meticulous research, makes every book she puts out a rare treat to enjoy and savor. Highly recommended!"

—*New York Times* bestselling author Kate Pearce

"Unflinching, tender, and moving, the delicately crafted *The Siren of Sussex* might just be my favorite work from Mimi Matthews; it certainly is one of my favorite historical romance reads this year."

—*USA Today* bestselling author Evie Dunmore

"Lush, seductive, original—*The Siren of Sussex* drew me in from the first page and wove its magic. A fresh, vibrant, brilliant Victorian romance, making it an unforgettable read."

—*New York Times* bestselling author Jane Porter

"The best book I've read in a long time: gorgeously written, thoughtfully considered, swoonily romantic, and unafraid to examine issues of class, race, and gender."   —National bestselling author Olivia Dade

"A moving love story and a vivid re-creation of Victorian life, *The Siren of Sussex* by Mimi Matthews is a treat of a book for the historical romance lover."   —Award-winning author Anna Campbell

"Impeccably researched, brimming with passion and chemistry, and a loving tribute to Victorian fashion and horsemanship, *The Siren of Sussex* is a page-turning, powerful, and endearing love story about two people rising above the pressures of society to follow their hearts. A five-star fantastic read!"
     —*USA Today* bestselling author Syrie James

"A tender and swoon-worthy interracial, cross-class romance in Victorian London . . . Readers will delight in this paean to women's fashion and horseback riding."   —*Publishers Weekly* (starred review)

"Romance aficionados who love fashion and animals will delight in this tender romance and will be excited to see Evelyn's friends in future installments."   —*Library Journal* (starred review)

"Matthews brings the Victorian era to vivid life with meticulously researched details and an impossible romance made believable and memorable."   —*Booklist* (starred review)

"Readers should expect emotional heft and fascinating historical detail. . . . Matthews explores cultural identity conflicts, exoticism, and the difficult position of a merchant catering to the whims of a privileged class, all within a tender, empowering love story."
     —*Shelf Awareness* (starred review)

Also by Mimi Matthews

BELLES OF LONDON NOVELS

The Siren of Sussex
The Belle of Belgrave Square
The Lily of Ludgate Hill

The Muse
of Maiden
Lane

MIMI MATTHEWS

BERKLEY ROMANCE

New York

BERKLEY ROMANCE
Published by Berkley
An imprint of Penguin Random House LLC
penguinrandomhouse.com

Copyright © 2024 by Mimi Matthews
Readers Guide copyright © 2024 by Mimi Matthews
Excerpt from *Rules for Ruin* copyright © 2024 by Mimi Matthews
Penguin Random House supports copyright. Copyright fuels creativity, encourages diverse
voices, promotes free speech, and creates a vibrant culture. Thank you for buying an authorized
edition of this book and for complying with copyright laws by not reproducing, scanning, or
distributing any part of it in any form without permission. You are supporting writers and
allowing Penguin Random House to continue to publish books for every reader.

BERKLEY and the BERKLEY and B colophon are registered trademarks of
Penguin Random House LLC.

Library of Congress Cataloging-in-Publication Data

Names: Matthews, Mimi, author.
Title: The muse of Maiden Lane / Mimi Matthews.
Description: First edition. | New York: Berkley Romance, 2024. |
Series: Belles of London
Identifiers: LCCN 2024014775 (print) | LCCN 2024014776 (ebook) |
ISBN 9780593639276 (trade paperback) | ISBN 9780593639283 (epub)
Subjects: LCGFT: Romance fiction. | Novels.
Classification: LCC PS3613.A8493 M87 2024 (print) |
LCC PS3613.A8493 (ebook) | DDC 813/.6—dc23/eng/20240401
LC record available at https://lccn.loc.gov/2024014775
LC ebook record available at https://lccn.loc.gov/2024014776

First Edition: November 2024

Printed in the United States of America
1st Printing

Book design by Daniel Brount

For Asteria.
And for all creatures who are lights in times of darkness.

Many a night I saw the Pleiads, rising thro' the mellow shade,
Glitter like a swarm of fire-flies tangled in a silver braid.

—"LOCKSLEY HALL," ALFRED, LORD TENNYSON, 1842

One

*S*tella Hobhouse raced down the gaslit corridor, the voluminous skirts of her white silk and crepe ball gown clutched in her gloved hands, and the swelling notes of Strauss's "Lava-Ströme" waltz chasing at her heels.

She was well aware of the ironclad rules that governed the lives of ladies. Those rules were somewhat less rigid among fashionable society than they were in Fostonbury, the suffocatingly restrictive Derbyshire village that she and her pious clergyman brother, Daniel, called home. But one rule remained as inflexible in London as it was across Britain entire: a respectable female *did not* color her hair.

Only actresses and—Stella blushed to admit to herself— prostitutes would resort to such tawdry tricks. A young lady of Stella's station would never reduce herself to purchasing a bottle of Circassian gold hair dye. Not even one procured through the post.

Great God, what had driven her to do it?

And what on earth had possessed her to copy, of all things, the exact shade of gilded auburn hair portrayed in the Whistler painting she'd seen on display in the Berners Street Gallery? The very painting that had been recommended to her by the handsome artist she'd encountered sketching at the British Museum?

It was a question she'd been asking herself ever since she'd entered the Earl of March's grand gothic ballroom and spied that very same man—a person she'd never expected to see again in her life—seated in his wheeled chair at the edge of the polished wood floor. He'd been dressed, not in the plain suit and carelessly knotted cravat he'd worn at the museum, but in flawless black-and-white eveningwear. She'd realized, all at once, that he was a guest here. Not just an eccentric artist who loitered about museum portrait galleries, but a *gentleman*.

Mortification had rushed over her in a mighty flood, drowning out all rational thought. Her only instinct had been to flee the ballroom before he saw her. And that's precisely what Stella had done: fled.

She ducked into a dimly lit anteroom at the end of the corridor. Music drifted after her, rising and falling, a waltz she was meant to be dancing with some gentleman or other. Resting her back against one of the shadowy, silk-papered walls, she pressed a hand to her corseted midriff, willing her nerves to steady and her breath to calm.

It wasn't as though she'd committed a crime. It was only a bit of playacting. A chance to be someone else for a change. To experience the world as a young lady whose hair hadn't turned completely gray at the age of sixteen.

Aside from her best friend, Lady Anne Deveril, only Anne's mother, the Countess of Arundell, and Anne's beau, Mr. Hartford, were aware of what Stella had looked like before she'd dyed it. There was no one else in attendance at the house party who knew her. Even if there were, Stella doubted very much that they'd recognize her. As a young lady with gray hair, possessed of modest breeding and little fortune, she was often dismissed and ignored. No one ever saw her. Not really. Indeed, no one seemed to notice her at all.

But tonight, she'd drawn every eye. Anne had called her luminous. Ethereal. And for the first time in her life, Stella had felt that way.

Until she'd seen *him*.

And it *was* him, whatever his manner of dress. He had the same inky black hair. The same turn of countenance, with sharply hewn features and a mouth that curved with equally sharp humor. A *dangerous* countenance. It was the face of a gentleman who saw too much. A face from which nothing—and no one—was hidden.

Stella exhaled an uneven breath. It wouldn't do, this ridiculous surge of schoolgirlish embarrassment. She was two-and-twenty. A steady, sensible young lady, not some green girl prone to fits of the vapors.

She must compose herself and return to the ball.

It was the only practical course. Lord March's house party was a week in length, and would be filled with Christmas festivities. She couldn't very well hide the entire time. Besides, there was a good chance the gentleman wouldn't recognize her. He'd met her only once before, and then just briefly.

Perhaps she'd overreacted?

But of course she had!

There was no way the gentleman would remember her. They'd been in each other's company for fewer than five minutes that day at the museum and had exchanged no more than a handful of words. He'd doubtless forgotten her the moment she was out of his sight.

To be sure, Stella felt a little foolish now she thought of it rationally.

Straightening from the wall, she smoothed her skirts, steeling herself to return to the ballroom. It was then she heard it: the unmistakable rattle of wheels drawing ever closer down the length of the marble corridor. The sound came to an abrupt halt outside the door of the anteroom where she was hiding.

A gentleman's deep voice broke through the shadows. "Good lord," he said in cheerful amazement. "It *is* you."

❖

Teddy Hayes rolled his wheeled chair into the dim interior of the anteroom. He wasn't about to wait for a gilt-edged invitation. Not after he'd spent the last three months excoriating himself for not discovering the mysterious young lady's name on the last occasion they'd met.

He'd been so thunderstruck by her then, so jaw droppingly dazzled, that it hadn't even occurred to him to ask until after she'd gone. By then, it was too late. There had been no one around who could enlighten him. No fashionable acquaintances who might know her identity.

Such was the price of being new to London.

Teddy was a visitor here. A guest, not a member of polite society. Aside from the small circle of friends that his older sister, Laura, and her husband, Alex Archer, surrounded themselves with, there was no one to whom Teddy could apply for information. Love his relations as he did, he was reluctant to ask them for help in such matters. Some things were private. Especially when it came to the subject of silver-haired goddesses he'd encountered in the British Museum.

"Why did you run away?" he asked.

The young lady stood with her back to the wall. Her white pearl-and-crepe-festooned skirts bowed out in front of her in an arc of petticoats and crinoline. "I did no such thing," she said stiffly.

It was the first she'd spoken since he'd entered the room. She had a soft, even voice, with a hint of velvet at the back of it. The kind of voice that could soothe as easily as it could seduce.

Teddy's blood thrummed with an unexpected pulse of heat.

He instantly dismissed the feeling. He hadn't gone after her because he was attracted to her. Not as a man, anyway. His interest was purely artistic. "You did," he said.

The same moment he'd clapped eyes on her from across the crowded ballroom, she'd spun on her heel and disappeared out the doors in a flurry of glittering skirts. He'd been left staring after her in dismay as the orchestra struck up the opening waltz, wondering for all of fifteen seconds whether he'd been mistaken.

"I felt a little faint," she replied, a trifle defensively. "I needed air."

"And you're taking it here?" He cast a dubious glance around the anteroom as he wheeled himself to the nearest lamp. It sat upon a low inlaid walnut table beside one of the damask-upholstered settees. Striking a friction match, he lit the wick. The room was at once bathed in a soft halo of light. "You might at least have opened a window."

"It's storming outside," she replied as he turned his chair to face her. "In case you hadn't noticed."

Teddy examined her in the glow of the lamp. She looked different than she had that day at the British Museum. He should know. The memory of her had been etched into his brain for months.

It wasn't because she was the most beautiful woman he'd ever seen—though she *was* beautiful. It was because she was different. And not just an oddity in her manner, or in the style of her dress or coiffure. She was *strikingly* different.

When he'd encountered her that day in the King's Gallery, her hair had been uniformly silver—the color of fine platinum or sterling. When coupled with her silver-blue eyes and the tender gravity of her manner, it had given her the look of a shimmering, vaporous spirit, newly alighted from the heavens to engage with lowly humankind.

She'd reminded him of one of the mythological Pleiades—the seven sisters the Greek god Zeus had famously transformed into stars to grace the night sky. Teddy had never in his life seen a woman who better embodied the myth. As an artist, the sight hadn't failed to make an impression on him.

"I notice everything," he said.

The young lady's throat worked on a delicate swallow. She edged toward the door. "I beg your pardon. I must return to the ballroom. My friends will be wondering—"

"I trust you're not afraid of me?"

She stilled. Her lips compressed in a vaguely affronted line. "Indeed, I am not."

"You appear so."

"If I do, it's only because I don't know you."

"We've met before," he reminded her. "It was some months ago. You were in the King's Gallery of the British Museum admiring a Van Dyck drawing."

"I remember," she said frostily.

His mouth quirked. Naturally, she did. He'd offended her then. Been too blunt. Too free with his opinions. It was a failing of his, one made worse by the virulent strain of scarlet fever he'd contracted in his youth. The illness had left his legs partially paralyzed, but had done nothing to curb the sharpness of his mind. Indeed, his sister often remarked that the more Teddy felt constrained by his disability, the less of a guard he was willing to set on his tongue.

It wasn't deliberate. He didn't mean to be rude or unkind. But he knew firsthand how short life could be, and how suddenly it might all come to an end. The time one had left was too precious to squander. He had no patience for mincing words.

"I recommended a painting to you," he said. "Mr. Whistler's new piece—*The Woman in White*. It was on display at the Berners Street Gallery at the time."

She blushed to the roots of her hair. Her *auburn* hair. It was now the same shade as the titian-haired lady depicted in Whistler's painting. "I could hardly forget," she said. "It doesn't follow that I know you. We haven't been introduced. Not properly."

"That's easily remedied." He wheeled a half turn closer to her. "My name is Edward Hayes. Most everyone calls me Teddy. And you are?"

"Stella Hobhouse," she blurted out, "but that isn't the point—"

"Stella," he repeated. A pleased smile tugged at his mouth. "Like a star." Surely it was a sign? He was meant to find her again.

She drew herself up with offended dignity. "I did *not* give you permission to use my Christian name."

"Why shouldn't I when it's so beautiful?" He wheeled nearer. "By the by . . . what happened to your silver hair, Stella?"

Her mouth fell open. "Why that's . . . that's none of your business!"

"You dyed it, I suppose." He frowned. "I wish you wouldn't have."

"How dare you, sir? To presume to make personal remarks about my—" She broke off. "Is this how you address ladies of your acquaintance?"

"With honesty and candor? Indeed, it *is* how I address ladies. It's the same way I address gentlemen. I see no need to insult you by dancing about with euphemisms."

"It's not an insult. It's decorum. Politeness. There are rules—"

"Yes, I've heard of them. I suppose that's how it must be in London. But we're not in London any longer. We're in Hampshire." His smile returned. "And house parties are wild places, I'm told."

She stared at him, the expression in her silvery blue eyes both intrigued and appalled. "How is it that you come to be here at Sutton Park? Do you know Lord March?"

"I don't," he admitted.

"Then what are you doing at his house party?"

"I'm not here by choice," he said. "My sister and brother-in-law were invited. As I traveled with them from France, they thought it best I accompany them."

It had been the only way to set Laura's mind at ease. He'd been in his chair for nearly five years, the first several of which she'd been his caregiver. It was a difficult role for her to relinquish. Never mind that Teddy was better now than he'd been in ages. She still worried about him to an excessive degree.

"They told me there would be great opportunities for sketching." He cast a grim glance at the rain beating down upon the windows. "I'm reserving judgment."

She inched toward the door. "Your relations are acquainted with Lord March?"

"Only slightly. My brother-in-law is arranging to purchase a new strain of the earl's roses for our perfumery in Grasse. Hayes's Perfumes. Perhaps you've heard of us?"

Again, she stilled, her curiosity seeming to get the better of her. "Hayes's Lavender Water?" She brightened with recognition. "Is that *you*?"

For once, Teddy was grateful for the negligible fame that his late father's perfume business brought to the family name. "It's partly me. I inherited half of the company when my father died. But it's my sister and brother-in-law who run it. My interests lie elsewhere."

"You're an artist," she said.

"I am." He paused. "May I ask you an impertinent question?"

She huffed a reluctant laugh. "Haven't you already?"

His smile broadened. "Tell me, Stella—"

Her chin dipped. She shook her head. "Please don't call me that."

"Tell me, Miss Hobhouse," he amended. "Would you object to my painting you?"

Two

✦

Stella had thought herself beyond shock. However, at the gentleman's outlandish request, she was scandalized anew. "Paint *me*?" She stared at him. "In a portrait, do you mean?"

"Yes, exactly that." He sat across from her in his wheeled chair, just as strikingly handsome as she recalled him being during their brief encounter at the museum.

More striking now, owing to the elegance of his dress.

His eveningwear was impeccably cut. And his gleaming black hair, formerly rumpled, was combed and pomaded into perfect order. It framed a lean face, characterized by high cheekbones, a firmly chiseled jaw, and clever blue-gray eyes set beneath a pair of uncompromisingly straight ebony brows. An austere face, softened only a fraction by a disturbingly sensual mouth.

Mr. Hayes, or *Teddy* Hayes as he'd so boldly introduced himself, was without a doubt the most singular man Stella had ever encountered. And it wasn't because he was in a wheeled chair—though that was rare enough in fashionable society. Most people had a fear of illness and infirmity. Invalids were meant to hide themselves away, to be coddled and cared for, their physical frailties kept firmly out of sight of able-bodied strangers. Unless, of course, the invalid was taking the waters in Bath or Harrogate, or out for an airing in the park.

No. Mr. Hayes's singularity wasn't on account of his chair. It was entirely owing to his manner.

He was both unrepentantly cheerful and remorselessly direct. It was a quality she'd first observed when they'd met in the King's Gallery. That earnest demeanor. That blunt way of speaking. One would think he saw nothing at all wrong in cornering an unmarried young lady in a darkened room and shamelessly propositioning her.

Had he no scruples? No decorum?

Stella's older brother, Daniel, would be outraged by the man's impertinence. So would Anne, come to that. Stella herself was somewhat less offended. Stunned, yes, but not at all inclined to swoon.

Mr. Hayes wasn't, after all, a complete stranger anymore. And not only because he'd introduced himself, but because he'd admitted to being part owner of Hayes's Lavender Water. The famous British brand was one of the most respectable scents a lady could wear. In her younger days, when her meager funds had stretched to affording her the little luxuries of life, it was the very fragrance Stella had often used to splash her unclothed body after a bath.

Good gracious. The very thought!

It was *that* which made her cheeks heat with uncontrollable warmth.

As for his suggestion that he paint her . . .

"On no account," she said. "I'm no artist's model."

Mr. Hayes was undeterred. "All the better. I've no use for an experienced model to pose for me. I require a particular look. A certain unique quality. Until I saw you at the museum, I despaired of finding it."

In other words, he wanted an oddity.

A knot twisted in Stella's stomach. No lady enjoyed being thought unique because of her most damning flaw.

"You wish to paint a lady with gray hair," she said flatly. "There are hundreds about. Thousands, even. You can take your pick."

"There are none like you." His keen gaze swept over her, from the spun-glass aigrette she wore in her hair to the hem of her white silk-and-crepe skirts. "None that I've seen."

She made a scornful sound. "That I can well believe. It isn't often a lady of my age—" She stopped herself.

What in heaven was she doing engaging with him on the topic of her *hair*? She should have left the instant he first remarked on it, not lingered to indulge his prurient interest! Not even an artist could be forgiven for discussing a lady's person in such candid terms.

"It isn't your youth." He rolled his chair another turn of the wheels toward her. "It's not even the color of your hair, though it is stunning."

Stunning.

The word reverberated in the shadowed anteroom. It echoed back at Stella, both in her ears and in her heart, a balm to her injured pride. She knew she shouldn't encourage him, but . . .

"What, then?" she asked.

"Why, you're a shining star, Stella," he said. "Hasn't anyone ever told you so before? It's *that* quality I need to paint."

Stella's breath caught at the compliment. She'd been praised so rarely in her life, and never for her beauty. And to be called a shining star, of all things!

Mr. Hayes had uttered the words effortlessly, but not at all frivolously. There was a seriousness behind his eyes at odds with his easy demeanor. *Need* to paint, he'd said. Not want. This endeavor meant something to him. A great deal, unless she was mistaken.

He rolled closer to her. "I have a fascination with light, you see. There's an art to translating it to canvas. It's present in the works of Turner and Constable. And in modern pieces, like Whistler's. I can show you, if you like, when we return to London."

Her heart quivered in unwilling anticipation. "You presume we'll see each other again."

"Naturally." He smiled, revealing a brief flash of even white teeth. "It's taken me three months to find you. I'm not likely to let you go."

Heat crept up her throat. She should be offended. But it was difficult to summon outrage when Mr. Hayes was so earnest.

She couldn't stop herself from blurting out the first thought in her head: "How peculiar you are."

His smile spread into a fleeting grin. "I shall take that as a compliment."

"You may take it how you like. But I shan't agree to your painting me, sir. My brother is a clergyman."

This time, Mr. Hayes's eyes smiled, too. "That's an odd non sequitur."

"It isn't. Not if you knew my brother. And if he knew of this—"

"Need he know of it?"

Her spine went rigid with reflexive indignation. "Do you suppose I go about deceiving the people I love?"

His smile faded, his expression becoming unsettlingly serious as he studied her face. "No. I don't suppose you do," he mused. "I expect you're loyal to a fault. Another reason you shine so very brightly."

She ducked her head, refusing to tolerate any more of his flattery. "Really, sir, this is all too much. You shouldn't opportune me so."

"I haven't a choice. You eluded me once. I can't risk you doing so again."

"This isn't the British Museum. This is a winter house party. We're both of us stuck indoors for the duration. I couldn't elude you if I wanted to."

"I'll wager you're capable of anything you set your mind to," he said. "I only ask that—"

"No," she repeated. "I could never."

He wheeled toward her. "But I *must* paint you. I shall run mad if I don't."

Stella couldn't suppress a flare of guilt. What could it really hurt to sit for a portrait?

But no.

She may be rebellious enough to color her hair, but that rebellion had to stop somewhere. Circassian dye was temporary. A painting would be forever.

"I am very sorry for it," she said. And before she could give in to temptation, before she could ask him anything else about his work (or worse, himself), she caught up her skirts and darted from the room.

This time, Teddy made no move to follow her. He remained in the shadowy anteroom, privately cursing himself for being so bloody eager.

Of all the offensive masculine qualities that ladies detested, eagerness was one of the worst. That's what Alex said. A gentleman was never supposed to reveal his hand. Never supposed to admit to wanting a lady's company more than a lady desired his. To do so was to put oneself in an immediate position of weakness. And ladies loathed weakness in a man, almost as much as they abhorred eagerness.

Teddy scrubbed his jaw in frustration. Unlike his brother-in-law, who had spent his early years earning his bread as a European sharper, Teddy was no cardplayer. He'd thought he could persuade Miss Hobhouse by conveying to her the simple truth. He'd dealt with her openly and honestly. He hadn't minced words about her loveliness or about his desperation to commit that loveliness to canvas. He'd laid himself bare.

Which was precisely why he was sitting here alone.

"Damn it all to hell," he muttered.

He wasn't accustomed to persuading gently bred ladies to sit for him. In the past, his portraits had been confined to his sister and aunt, and then, in time, to the wives of his friends. He'd painted other women, too. Though, not ladies, precisely.

During his years studying in Paris, an earnest young student at the renowned Montparnasse atelier of artist and teacher Charles Gleyre, many a prostitute had been willing to pose for a few sous. Teddy's portfolio was bursting with sketches of them. His fellow students could boast the same. Indeed, the professions of prostitute and artist's model were often interchangeable.

Such women were generally relegated to French brothels, but one could find them elsewhere on occasion, lingering in the streets or strolling through one of the newly completed public parks. Teddy had spent countless hours seated alongside the fashionable walks of the Bois de Boulogne, waiting for his muse to appear.

But when she finally had, it hadn't been in some Parisian park or brothel. It had been in London, in a stuffy gallery at the British Museum. A meeting that had arisen entirely by chance, when Teddy had least expected it.

And this time, the muse who had sparked his attention had been a true one. Not a passing fancy, sufficient to stimulate a sketch or two, but an out-and-out, flesh-and-blood Calliope, Clio, or Erato. A muse to inspire a masterwork.

He'd spent the past three months convinced that he'd never find her again.

"Teddy?" His sister's voice drifted from the hall. "Are you there?"

He sighed. Of course Laura would come after him. No doubt she thought he'd fallen victim to some mischief or other. "In here!" he called back.

Seconds later, Laura appeared in the doorway. She wore a ball gown of celestial blue figured silk, trimmed with goffered ribbons and blonde lace. A scrap of similarly trimmed blonde, in the guise of a matron's evening cap, was pinned atop her plaited coil of ebony hair.

At seven-and-twenty, she was only three years older than him. A negligible number, silently multiplied by the weight of Teddy's disability—and her own. Laura had contracted scarlet fever at the same time as he had. It had affected her lungs and had, initially, made breathing a struggle whenever she'd overexerted herself. She'd nursed Teddy through his illness, nonetheless. Indeed, she'd looked after him for so long, she couldn't help but think of herself as more akin to a mother than a sister.

Teddy loved her for it, even as he bridled under her concern. "I'm fine, before you ask," he said. "I was talking to a young lady."

Laura smiled as she came to join him. Her skirts rustled softly in a whisper of expensive French silk over sensibly starched petticoats. Years spent living on the continent had improved the quality of the fashions she wore, but her essential, no-nonsense British nature remained unaltered. "The auburn-haired girl I just saw racing down the corridor?"

"Yes." He scowled. "That is, no. She isn't auburn haired. She's the lady from the King's Gallery."

Laura's brows flew up. She'd listened to Teddy lament losing his muse for the past three months. She, of all people, knew what it had meant to him. "You found her! Oh, Teddy—"

"Yes, I found her, only to lose her again." He ran a frustrated hand through his hair, wreaking havoc with his carefully pomaded locks. "I've frightened her away."

His sister perched on the edge of a nearby chair. Her manner was immediately consoling. "You couldn't frighten anyone."

"I've scandalized her, then."

"She can hardly be scandalized easily if she's taken to dying her hair," Laura pointed out.

Teddy couldn't deny the truth in the statement. He knew enough of ladies—and of respectable society—to understand that dying one's hair was considered as unseemly as painting one's face. But Miss Hobhouse was surely an exception to the rule. She wasn't using cosmetics to gild the proverbial lily. Rather, the reverse. In coloring her hair, she was attempting to make herself ordinary. He recognized the fact, even if he couldn't entirely wrap his mind around it.

"I don't imagine she expected to see anyone here that she knew," he said.

"She must know someone," Laura replied. "How else could she have been invited?"

"I haven't the faintest idea."

"Did you at least catch her name?"

"Miss Hobhouse," he said.

He didn't share her first name. Stella, for star. It was too intimate. Too perfect. He wanted to hold it close, if only for a short while longer. It was a foolish, romantic impulse, and all of a piece with the rest of this infernal business. He'd been romanticizing his silver-haired stranger since the moment he'd first clapped eyes on her.

"She's the sister of a clergyman, apparently," he added.

"I see." A lengthy pause. "She's very pretty."

"She is," he agreed sullenly. "Much good that does me."

Again, Laura smiled. "Don't be so downhearted. She's here at Sutton Park, isn't she? You'll have ample opportunity to take her likeness over Christmas."

"*Take* being the operative word. She's not given her permission."

"There are ways to make allowances for that."

"Such as?"

"You could alter her face before you commit your preliminary sketch to canvas. That would be a way of respecting—"

"I want *all* of her," Teddy interrupted impatiently. "Her face. Her figure. Her silver hair. That's my star. It must be all or nothing."

Laura's forehead etched with concern. "What can I do?"

"Nothing."

"Nonsense. I can easily make her acquaintance. Once I do—"

"You can what? Facilitate a friendship between us?" Teddy scoffed. "No, thank you."

He may not be as independent as he'd like, but he was still a man. He wouldn't have his older sister acting as an intermediary with a young lady. Not this young lady, anyway.

"I shall simply have to try again on my own," he said. "I'll exercise more tact in future. Try not to scare her."

"You have an entire week to implement your strategy."

His mouth twitched. He knew when his sister was quizzing him. "Strategy, is it? You've been married to Alex too long. Where is he, by the way?"

"When last I saw him, he was talking with one of the gentlemen naturalists about soil acidity."

"A riveting subject."

"He seemed to be enjoying himself."

"I'll bet he is." Teddy's brother-in-law was in his element when he was gaining people's confidence. By the end of the evening, he'd no doubt possess all the botanical secrets of the realm. "What about you?" Teddy scanned his sister's face. "Are *you* enjoying yourself?"

Unlike her husband, Laura was accustomed to a quieter life. Before her marriage, she and Teddy had lived together in a smallish cottage in Surrey, all but isolated, under the questionable care of their aged aunt Charlotte. Even now, at their perfumery in Grasse, Laura and Alex kept much to themselves, enjoying their own company far better than they enjoyed the glamour and excitement of their regular jaunts to Paris and London.

Teddy was the one who craved excitement, to his constant frustration. Every adventure was an obstacle. And not all of the obstacles arose from the greater world around him. Some were created by his family—the people who loved him best. He felt their constraints as much as he felt the limitations of his chair. Worse, even, for those constraints had lately been more difficult to overcome.

"I'm longing for home," Laura said frankly. "Which is foolish, really. We'll be back soon enough, in the spring, when everything is blooming."

"You could return early," he suggested.

"And cut short our visit with Tom and Jenny in London? Or our trip to Devon after Christmas to see Justin and Helena, and Neville and Clara? Not to mention, this business with the roses for the perfumery." She shook her head. "No. We must remain in England through March. I'm resolved to be happy about it."

Teddy was acquainted with all his brother-in-law's childhood friends and their wives. Tom and Jenny Finchley, Justin and Helena Thornhill, and Neville and Clara Cross were as good as family to Alex and Laura. As good as family to Teddy, too. He'd been accepted into their ranks as easily as Laura had. It was a fact that Teddy meant to use to his advantage when the time came for Alex and Laura to return to France.

His sister didn't know it yet, but Teddy had no intention of returning home with them.

"You make it sound as though it takes an effort," he said.

"Not at all. I love dancing with Alex wherever we are."

"Dancing, yes." Teddy pulled a face. "A bit awkward with my chair."

His sister's blue-gray eyes lit with ready sympathy. She didn't pity him, but she comprehended the difficulties he experienced in making his way in the world. "You needn't have come to the ball. Lord March wouldn't have minded."

"*I* would have minded. I may not be equipped to dance, but they can very well make space for me in the ballroom. And if anyone is unsettled by the sight of me—"

"Indeed, they aren't," Laura protested, appalled by the suggestion.

Teddy suppressed a stab of irritation. His sister may want to sugar-coat his situation, but he saw no point in fooling himself. It was better to view his disability as pragmatically as possible. That meant acknowledging how others perceived him.

His chair was obtrusive, both physically and visually. Custom built for him in France, it sat upon a carriage axel, boasting a high-backed seat of well-padded wood, with two large, spoked wheels on either side, and a smaller wheel at the rear, which aided in turning. It was a decided improvement on the traditional Bath chair, which could only be pulled by a horse or pushed by an attendant, but there was no mistaking it for anything other than what it was: an invalid's chair. A cumbersome appliance for a man without the use of his lower limbs.

"Some are," he said. "People don't appreciate being reminded of their own mortality. It makes them uncomfortable."

"Silly of them."

"Yes. Quite." He forced a smile. "Fortunately, I don't exist to make anyone comfortable, excepting myself. And I like hearing the music and seeing the dancers. Besides, Miss Hobhouse has likely returned to the ballroom. She'll be dancing, too."

Laura gave him a doubtful frown. "You'll be content to watch her?"

Teddy shrugged. "It's enough," he said. "For now."

It would have to be.

Three

———✦———

Stella didn't go back to the ballroom. She was too flustered by her encounter with Mr. Hayes. The thought of him returning to sit on the edge of the dance floor, watching her in that all-too-perceptive way of his, made her insides melt into a puddle of warm treacle.

She was too used to being invisible. That was the problem. Her new auburn hair had already brought her some degree of attention—the comfortable kind of admiration she'd aspired to provoke as a girl. But to suddenly be seen in her entirety . . .

It made her feel naked. Wholly exposed.

When Mr. Hayes looked at her, it wasn't with simple masculine admiration. It was with something else. A sort of elemental recognition that Stella felt all the way to her core. She'd as soon parade through the ballroom in her altogether than go back now. No doubt the sensation would be the same.

I must paint you, he'd said. *I shall run mad if I don't.*

Her heart was still fluttering in response to the heated declaration over an hour later, when she was tucked safe in her upstairs room. Her ball gown, petticoats, crinoline, and corset lay on the bed behind her. Clad in her warmest wool dressing gown, she sat by the fire drinking a cup of milky tea.

She felt unmoored. Out of her depth. And it was only partially owing to her unsettling encounter with Mr. Hayes. Much of her uneasiness stemmed from the fact that she was far from home, cut adrift from the things that made her intrinsically who she was. Not only her gray hair, but her beloved horse, Locket, too.

Locket was a spirited mare with wildfire in her veins. Silvery white in color, she possessed the imposing size of her famous Thoroughbred sire, Stockwell, while still blessed with the elegantly contoured face and wide-set eyes of her crossbreed Arabian mother. Not many could ride her, excepting Stella. She was accustomed to exercising her daily—a necessary activity for both of their physical and mental well-beings.

When Stella had departed London, she'd been obliged to send Locket home to Fostonbury in company with her groom, John Turvey. It had been the kindest thing. The most sensible, too. It was Fostonbury, not London, where Stella would return at the close of the house party.

In her mare's absence, a certain hollowness had taken up residence in Stella's breast. She and Locket shared a special relationship. It was more than a partnership. More, even, than a friendship. It was a manner of mutual dependence. Stella couldn't be fully herself—happy, steady, brave—without Locket nearby. And Locket . . .

Well.

Without Stella's intervention, Locket wouldn't have much chance of living at all. Indeed, when Stella had first encountered the flighty mare, Locket had been on the way to the knackers.

"*You saved her life,*" Anne had observed once when she and Stella had been riding together in the early days of their friendship.

"*Rather, she saved mine,*" Stella had replied. "*I would never have been bold enough to come to London for the season if Locket wasn't with me.*"

Stella certainly didn't feel bold now, hiding in an upstairs room, nursing her tea while the ball continued below.

It was there Anne found her as the small, arch-top clock on the mantelshelf struck eleven.

"At last!" Anne entered, closing the door behind her. "I've had the devil of a time finding you."

She was still wearing her ball gown—a masterpiece of rich crimson velvet trimmed with black floral embroidery and red velvet roses. It had been commissioned from court dressmaker Ahmad Malik on the same occasion that Stella had ordered her own ball gown. Mr. Malik was known for his daring, yet intrinsically elegant, creations. It was how their dear friend, fellow horsewoman Evelyn Maltravers, had first met and fallen in love with him.

Auburn-haired, bespectacled Evie was a valued member of their small band of equestriennes. Mrs. Julia Blunt—formerly Julia Wychwood—was another. They were all of them horse lovers, and all of them excellent riders. They'd bonded together during the course of several unsuccessful London seasons, forming an unbreakable bond of friendship.

Stella hadn't seen Anne since they'd entered the ballroom this evening. Then, Hartford had promised to find Stella a suitable partner. Perhaps he would have done, too, if Stella had remained.

It was all beginning to sink in now. All this effort on her hair and her gown and she hadn't even danced one dance. What an extraordinary waste.

Though her heart wouldn't know it.

The single encounter with Mr. Hayes had fired her blood more effectively than a dozen waltzes with a dozen nameless, faceless gentlemen.

"I've been all over the house," Anne said, brushing a stray golden blonde lock from her brow. "First the ballroom, then the conservatory, and even the rose garden."

"I'm here, as you see," Stella replied.

Anne came to sit in the chair beside her. Her form-fitting velvet bodice was cut low off the shoulders. The crackling flames in the hearth cast shadows over the alabaster curve of her bosom and throat. "Are you ill?"

"No, no. Only tired." Stella gave her friend a brief, rueful smile. "I'm sorry I ran away."

"I should think so," Anne said with mock severity. "It isn't like you to shrink from a challenge."

"I suppose I wasn't feeling myself."

"Undoubtedly." Anne cast a speaking look at Stella's hair. She hadn't approved of Stella purchasing the Circassian dye, let alone using it. "I thought this masquerade was meant to make you more daring?"

"It isn't only the dye. You know how restless I get when I'm too long from Locket."

"Is that what's troubling you? Surely you have confidence in your groom."

"Oh, Turvey will feed her and water her well enough. But it's me Locket will be wanting. We've not been apart since I accompanied my brother to that dratted ecumenical conference in Exeter during the summer. And that was only a few days. I can't help but worry over how she'll manage now that I'll be gone a full week."

The house party extended through Christmas. Lady Arundell, Anne, and Stella wouldn't be departing until the following Monday.

"Dancing might have taken your mind off things," Anne said.

"It might have." Stella paused, adding significantly, "Under other circumstances."

Anne comprehended her meaning. She'd been present when Stella had first crossed paths with Mr. Hayes at the British Museum, and had seen firsthand how the encounter had disconcerted Stella.

"You had nothing to fear in the end," Anne said. "It turns out, the gentleman in the wheeled chair is perfectly harmless. He's only the brother of one of the guests. An aspiring artist, I understand. Apparently, he's lately returned from several years' studying in Paris under some famous painter or other."

"He studied in Paris?" Stella echoed in some surprise. She'd known Mr. Hayes resided in France, but she hadn't realized he was quite so cosmopolitan as that. She'd imagined his impertinence had arisen purely from the intensity of his fascination with her, not from the mere fact that he was accustomed to consorting with Parisian sophisticates and bohemians.

Was he truly a portrait painter, then? Not just an overbold gentleman intrigued by the appearance of a formerly gray-haired young lady, seeking to discompose her with nonsensical flattery, but a man who saw something of artistic merit in her face and figure?

"It goes a long way toward explaining his forward manner toward you at the King's Gallery," Anne said.

"Yes," Stella acknowledged, taking a thoughtful sip of her tea. "I suppose it does."

"So you see, you had no cause to flee. Indeed," Anne continued, leaning forward in her chair, "you'd have done better to remain. So much occurred after you went."

Stella caught the quiver of excitement underlying her friend's words. She came to immediate attention, her own troubles temporarily forgotten. "My goodness. What happened?"

"Oh, Stella." Anne's sherry-brown eyes glowed with warmth. "Hartford and I are going to be married!"

"*What!*" Stella hastily sat her cup on the small, inlaid rosewood table beside her, lest she spill what remained of her tea. "When?" she sputtered. "How?"

"There was such a to-do in the library. All manner of chaos with his family. But the long and short of it is that, once the others had gone away, Hartford proposed to me and I accepted." Anne's gaze held the shimmer of happy tears. "We're going to be ridiculously happy together."

Matching tears sprang to Stella's eyes. Crossing the short distance between them, she caught her friend up in her arms. The two of them hugged each other fiercely. "My dear, I'm so dreadfully pleased for you both."

"So am I. Pleased. Elated. Stunned." Anne uttered a shaky laugh. "What an evening! I still can't believe it's real."

"You do love him, don't you?"

"I do," Anne said. "God help me. And he loves me, too. He vows that he always has."

"Of course he has. How could he not?" Stella drew back to search Anne's face. She'd never seen her friend's countenance so full of joy. Not even when they were galloping their horses together in Rotten Row. "Oh, Anne. What a turn up!"

"I know. Only think—yesterday I was still in my blacks, today I'm in crimson velvet, and soon I shall be in white."

Anne and her mother, Lady Arundell, had been mourning the loss of the late Earl of Arundell for nearly seven years. Anne had only emerged from her blacks yesterday—a shocking event in itself. A betrothal was yet another happy alteration to her circumstances. One that must be universally acclaimed.

"Another wedding," Stella said. "Just as Julia predicted."

Anne laughed again. "Yes, she did, didn't she? I'd almost forgotten."

A newlywed herself, bookish, raven-haired beauty Julia had briefly returned to town a few months ago with her dour, battle-scarred husband, Captain Jasper Blunt, to attend Evie's wedding to Mr. Malik. The simple ceremony had been held at the home of Evie's uncle, Mr. Fielding, in Russell Square. It was there where Julia had remarked that one wedding generally prompted another. She'd given Stella a meaningful nudge as she'd said it.

Naturally, Julia had assumed Stella would be next. They none of them would have thought it would be Anne, their starchy, black-clothed leader who had long professed herself content with the single state.

Stella felt a twinge of sadness to think of it now. It wasn't because she had a particular longing to be married. It was because she wanted her freedom, and, rather ironically, marriage was the only way to se-cure it. Until such time as she was wed, she must live under her brother's thumb. Worse, she could now anticipate living under the thumb of her brother's future wife. And the reign of the sanctimonious Miss Amanda Trent didn't promise to be a comfortable one.

It was one of the reasons Stella had come to Hampshire—to thwart her brother's matrimonial plans. Without her to play chaperone, he'd be less likely to spend the holiday courting Miss Trent. Less likely to propose to her.

But Daniel's plans couldn't be thwarted forever. He would marry someone eventually. And when that day came, the hourglass of Stella's fate would effectively be turned over, and the sand would begin to run. She would no longer be needed at the vicarage. Possibly, no longer wanted.

The only solution was for Stella to find a husband of her own.

It was easier said than done.

She had but one viable prospect at present. Squire Smalljoy was a widowered parishioner of her brother's in Fostonbury. Though *viable* was overstating the case. The man was pushing sixty. One might better describe him as *willing*.

"*He won't mind your gray hair,*" Daniel had said.

As if that were the only consideration! What about compatibility? What about friendship? What about *love*?

Not to mention the fact that Stella would rather almost anything than end her days in Derbyshire, less than five miles from her brother, cursed to spend the rest of her life in the same deplorable state in which she'd entered it. A shadow. A secondary concern. And wed to a stodgy old farmer besides. A man who, on their marriage, would have rights to her meager funds. To her body. To her horse!

But Stella wouldn't sour Anne's moment with self-pity over her own situation.

"I expect it was inevitable," she said, smiling. "We're all of an age, and we *are* taking part in the London season. Marriage is the goal, is it not?"

"It never was for me," Anne said. "Not to any other gentleman but

Hartford, certainly. Once you've experienced true love, it's impossible to settle for anything less."

"Nor why should you?" Stella returned. No one should have to settle for a loveless match. Not even country girls with gray hair and no great fortune to speak of.

As ever, Anne appeared to comprehend the trend of Stella's thoughts. "You won't have to settle, either." She clasped Stella's hands, giving them a reassuring squeeze. "We've six more days left at Sutton Park. That's ample time to meet a suitable gentleman. If it's truly marriage that you want."

"What I want," Stella said, steering the conversation back on its proper course, "is to find but a fraction of the happiness you have, dearest. How well the state becomes you." She summoned back a smile, even brighter than before. "Now, tell me again how Mr. Hartford proposed. I long to hear every romantic detail!"

The following evening, after dinner, Stella and the rest of the guests repaired to the Earl of March's capacious drawing room. Papered in apple-green silk damask and furnished in grand rococo style, it was lit by a pair of magnificent Italian crystal montgolfière chandeliers. The whole of the room had been decorated for Christmas with pine boughs, garlands of holly and ivy, and a towering tree that glittered with blazing candles and gilded fruit.

A line of liveried servants awaited them, armed with trays of celebratory champagne, in anticipation of the earl's formal announcement of his grandson's engagement.

The news wasn't exactly a secret. The assembled company had already been buzzing with whispers all day, stealing covert glances at Mr. Hartford, the earl, and the earl's eldest son, Viscount Brookdale.

"I daresay people have already guessed what the announcement's to be," Stella said to Anne as they collected their glasses of champagne from a passing footman.

"It's not the engagement they've guessed at," Anne returned. "It's the source of the drama that embroiled the family last night in the library."

Stella's brows lifted in inquiry. Though her friend had referenced familial chaos, she'd yet to go into the particulars.

But Anne was no more inclined to explain now than she'd been in Stella's room last night. "It's not my secret to tell," she said.

Mr. Hartford stood on the opposite side of Anne, his hand resting rather possessively at the small of Anne's back. He was a tall, broad-shouldered gentleman, with seal-brown hair and blue eyes that were forever alive with droll humor. "If it *is* still a secret," he said mildly, "it won't be for long."

Stella looked between them. "What happened?"

"Do you see that gentleman standing next to my cousin?" Mr. Hartford asked.

Stella followed his gaze. Across the room, Mariah Spriggs, the stepdaughter of Mr. Hartford's uncle, Viscount Brookdale, stood near the doors with a handsome, dark-haired young man. The two of them were holding twin glasses of champagne, smiling at each other as they conversed.

Mr. Hartford lowered his voice. "That gentleman is Marcus Neale. My half brother."

Stella's eyes jolted back to Mr. Hartford in immediate understanding. He didn't have any siblings. Nor half siblings. Not that she was aware. Which meant—

"Exactly," Anne said, reading Stella's thoughts. "Mr. Neale was born on the wrong side of the blanket. His existence came as something of a surprise to the earl and Viscount Brookdale."

It was an understatement if Stella had ever heard one. The Earl of March may be a genial, absent-minded botanist, perpetually tottering about in soil-stained clothing with his white hair standing half on end, but his son and heir, Viscount Brookdale, had a reputation for being one of the most severe, straitlaced, and morally upright members in parliament. The fact that Lord Brookdale's equally moralistic late younger brother had sired an illegitimate child must have come as a profound shock.

"Has the earl acknowledged him?" Stella asked. "More to the point, has Lord Brookdale?"

"They will," Mr. Hartford said with unwavering certainty.

But not tonight, it appeared. Tonight was for happy news, not for scandal.

Separating himself from the assembled company, the Earl of March moved to stand in front of the room. He raised his voice above the murmurs of the fashionably clad guests still milling about. "Ladies and gentlemen. Esteemed guests. I ask you to raise your glasses on this, the happiest of occasions."

Stella obligingly raised her glass. She exchanged a giddy smile with Anne.

Anne was beaming. Beside her, Hartford wore a broad smile of his own. His face shone with warmth as he gazed down at his soon-to-be bride.

"I'm pleased to announce the engagement of my grandson, Felix Hartford, to Lady Anne Deveril, daughter of my dearest friend, the Countess of Arundell." Lord March lifted his glass high. The champagne sparkled like liquid gold in the blaze of candlelight from the chandelier above him. "A toast to their health and happiness, and to a long and fruitful marriage!"

Cheers erupted throughout the room, along with murmurs of appreciative surprise.

Stella took a deep swallow of champagne as guests came forward to congratulate Anne and her betrothed. In the happy commotion, Stella was nudged back by the growing crowd, further and further away from her friend, supplanted by the swell of well-wishers.

It was to be expected. This was Anne's moment to shine. The moment many a young lady dreamed about all her life.

Not Stella, of course. Not Anne, either, up to now. To be sure,

Anne had been the least romantic of all of Stella's friends, and the least prone to excess sentimentality. But judging by the turn of Anne's countenance—the shimmer in her eyes and the radiance in her cheeks—those jaded feelings had altered, now she was engaged herself. As for Stella . . .

Happy as she was for her friend, Stella felt herself as cynical on the subject of romance as ever. Withdrawing from the crowd, she wandered toward the bank of velvet-draped windows that lined the opposite end of the drawing room.

Perhaps it was sour grapes. She hadn't any prospect of romance in her own life, so she must disdain it in everyone else's. It was unworthy of her. The action of an embittered spinster, not that of a girl of two-and-twenty. She was meant to be eager and optimistic in the face of her future. If not forever, then at least for now. She should be enjoying her moment of auburn-haired freedom to its fullest.

That's why she'd colored her hair in the first place. To revel in the attention that would come her way once her silver tresses were temporarily no more.

Tipping her glass, she drained the remainder of her champagne. The vintage was an expensive one. Powerful, too. It fizzed in her veins. Emboldened by the feeling, she scanned the room for prospective suitors.

She was wearing another of Mr. Malik's creations: a dinner dress of pale violet glacé silk, cut low off her shoulders, with a heart-shaped neckline and double skirts trimmed in Maltese lace. A suave older gentleman, hovering at the fringes of the crowd with his wife, cast Stella an appraising glance as she passed.

Stella stiffened a fraction. She had no interest in married men, and—flattering as it was to be thought alluring—she found it offensive that any of them should be so shameless as to telegraph their interest in her.

She wasn't seeking a love affair. She wasn't even looking for love. Not any longer. With two seasons behind her and only five days of the house party remaining, she hadn't the time for girlish daydreams. On the contrary. Now was the time for ruthless pragmatism.

What she required was an eligible bachelor. Preferably, someone under the age of forty. A handsome face would help, but it wasn't a necessity. It was a handsome bank balance Stella required. Her future husband must be a man of property. A man with an estate where Stella and—more importantly—Locket could live out their days in peace.

It was that which was essential. Safety and security. Stella was resolved to be realistic about it.

She strolled on, covertly examining every gentleman she passed.

Or perhaps not so covertly.

Her frank perusals were met with varying degrees of interest and alarm. Perchance she was being *too* bold. But honestly, if a lady must wait for a gentleman to approach her, she could find herself waiting until doomsday. And this dratted Circassian gold dye wouldn't last forever. At the party's end, Stella's hair would revert to gray.

And so would her life.

She wasn't going to squander her all-too-brief chance, even if she must take the reins herself. She may have to settle for less than love, but she deserved a good man. A decent man. A man who, if she was very lucky, might make her heart beat the tiniest bit faster.

She'd nearly reached the window when she saw him.

Mr. Hayes was seated in an alcove on the opposite side of the Christmas tree, his wheeled chair arranged beneath a patinaed oil painting of a flock of Hampshire sheep dozing under a shade tree. He wasn't alone. A well-dressed lady and gentleman were with him, talking companionably. But Mr. Hayes wasn't attending to them. He was looking at Stella.

He met her inquisitive gaze with a slight smile.

Stella's heart gave a queer double thump.

Thus far, she'd been endeavoring to avoid him. It hadn't been difficult. Sutton Park was an enormous gothic pile of a house, and the party was a large one. On their first full day in residence, the guests had quickly clustered into factions, disappearing to play games or to conduct horticultural business. They'd only all been in one place at dinner. Stella had been seated near the top of the long, mahogany dining table, and Mr. Hayes at the bottom, her view of him obscured by towering silver candelabras and a long row of elaborate filigree epergnes, filled with exotic flowers cultivated from the earl's famous greenhouses.

She'd felt his presence nonetheless, on the other side of that sparkling wall of candlelight, silver, and foliage. That same strange crackle of awareness she'd felt when she'd faced him in the anteroom last night.

"You're a shining star," he'd said. *"Hasn't anyone ever told you so before?"*

The wondrous, bewildering compliment had played over and over in Stella's mind throughout the day, setting her stomach fluttering and her pulse beating hard at her throat. It was how she knew that she wasn't offended by his request to paint her. Not entirely. The truth was, she was altogether too intrigued by it.

And by him.

It was an interest she didn't dare indulge. That was precisely how silly young wallflowers got themselves into trouble—by melting at the first outrageous compliment to come their way. Young ladies who were so starved for masculine attention that they allowed themselves to be persuaded to do all manner of things harmful to their reputations. To cast off their modesty, their virtue. To become artists' models, for heaven's sake!

Stella refused to be counted among their number. She may be daring when the occasion called for it, but her reputation was worth more than that. *She* was worth more than that. It would be demeaning to entertain any sort of connection with a gentleman whose sole interest lay in her artistic possibilities—an interest seemingly fueled by the peculiar color of her hair. She had her pride, after all. It was the very reason she'd been avoiding him.

But there was no avoiding him now.

He'd seen her already, of course. No doubt he'd marked her the moment she'd entered the room. Hadn't he said he noticed everything?

She came to an uncertain halt, faced with a dilemma: to acknowledge the man or to ignore him. The latter course might be rude, but the former would surely be foolish beyond permission. To acknowledge Teddy Hayes would be to encourage him. And Stella had no desire to do that.

Did she?

Four

◆✕◆

Stella's dilemma was resolved by the timely arrival of Anne.

"There you are!" She materialized at Stella's side. "You're becoming as difficult to keep track of as Eris. Every time I avert my gaze, you disappear. I feared you'd gone back to your room."

Stella turned to face her friend, at once relieved and—to her shame—a bit annoyed. She nevertheless smiled at the comparison. Anne's adopted feral kitten—recently given over into Mr. Hartford's custody—was known for slipping into forbidden rooms, shredding the wall coverings, and climbing the draperies.

"Not so unpredictable as that," Stella said. "I only wanted a bit of air. It was becoming rather close."

"Don't think for a moment that you can fob me off with that nonsense," Anne replied. "You forget that I stood exactly where you are while Evie and Julia married. It's dreadful to be the odd person out when all of one's friends are pairing off." She took hold of Stella's gloved hand in a firm grip. "But I won't let you drift away. I mean to hold on to you, tight as ever."

Stella squeezed Anne's hand in return. "And I to you."

"One wouldn't know it by the way you keep vanishing."

"Hardly vanishing. I merely know when I'm surplus to requirements."

"You're nothing of the sort. This is a house party, not a honeymoon cottage. We Furies are meant to stick together."

Stella laughed despite herself. They had often been called that during her first season, when she, Anne, and Julia had ridden together in Rotten Row.

The next year, when Evie had joined their small band of equestriennes, the name had sometimes been changed to the Four Horsewomen. Though coined in a spirit of good-natured jest, both labels had ultimately served to single them out as oddities. But Stella and her friends hadn't received the appellations as such. The Furies were formidable women. And the Four Horsemen were a quartet to be reckoned with. In the end, as Anne often said, it was better to be powerful than to be popular.

"Only one Fury now," Stella said. "I shall be on my own."

"Rubbish. Furies are forever. And who says they can't be married? Marriage doesn't change a lady's identity—only her name."

Stella wouldn't know anything about that. She doubted she ever would. Chances were, she'd be taking the name of Hobhouse to her grave. It was either that or Smalljoy.

An involuntary shudder coursed through her.

Stella Smalljoy? Never. Not for any inducement. She would die, rather.

"Speaking of names . . ." Anne cast a discreet glance at the alcove. "I see you've found Mr. Hayes."

"I have."

"Have you spoken with him?"

Stella didn't answer. Not directly. She hadn't yet told Anne about Mr. Hayes's unseemly proposition. She was uncertain if she would. It was still too fresh. Too private. "I can hardly do so. We've yet to be introduced."

"That would have been easily remedied had you lingered a trifle longer at breakfast," Anne said.

"I never linger over breakfast. You know that."

Stella was accustomed to rising early in order to take Locket out for the first of the mare's twice-daily gallops. Intensive exercise was necessary to keep a horse of Locket's temperament in check. Stella often rode off in the mornings, with nothing but a cup of tea to sustain her.

It hadn't occurred to her to alter her habit while she was at Sutton Park. Breakfasts at country house parties were informal affairs, with the various dishes arrayed in warming trays on a server, and guests coming and going as they pleased. They filled their own plates and sat where they liked, unconstrained by the order of precedence.

Stella had joined Anne, Mr. Hartford, and Lady Arundell only briefly before marching off to the earl's stables, sketch pad in hand, to visit the horses. Their warm, snuffling breaths against her cheek had served to dull the ache of emptiness she always felt when she passed too many days out of Locket's company.

She'd remained for nearly two hours, first at the loose boxes and then at the rails of the paddocks, committing her impressions of the horses to paper with broad strokes of her pencil.

"Pity," Anne said. "Mr. Hayes arrived within seconds of your leaving. He remained at table for over a half hour with his sister and brother-in-law. That's them, standing next to him—Mr. and Mrs. Archer. Hartford introduced them to me."

Stella chanced another look in Mr. Hayes's direction. The pretty lady standing beside him was flanked by a tall, dashing gentleman with a roguish smile. They were both beautifully clad—she in an exquisite blue dinner dress, and he in an elegantly tailored black suit.

"They seemed pleasant enough people," Anne remarked. "Not at all vulgar."

"I shouldn't imagine they would be," Stella said. "Not even if they *are* in trade."

Anne's gaze drifted back in Mr. Hartford's direction. Her mouth curved in a mysterious half smile. "Indeed. Tradespeople can be quite congenial, I find."

Mr. Hartford emerged from the crowd to join them, a grin still on his face as he tossed a reply over his shoulder to another back-slapping well-wisher. "Thank you. We shall." His voice dropped to an amused murmur as he approached Anne. "Engaged less than twenty-four hours, and you've already abandoned me to the masses."

"You handle the masses beautifully," she replied. "I have complete faith in you."

"The congratulations are meant for both of us," he said. "Tedious, admittedly, but one must tolerate the formalities."

"Never mind all that." Anne took his arm. "You must introduce Mr. Hayes to Miss Hobhouse."

Stella flushed. "Really, Anne, it isn't necessary."

"It's necessary," Anne said firmly. "Our first meeting with him wasn't auspicious. There's bound to be awkwardness. An introduction will lessen it, and make your stay more enjoyable."

"An introduction, then, by all means," Mr. Hartford said. "Miss Hobhouse?" He proffered his free arm to Stella.

Stella moved to take it. She was grateful, at least, that he'd offered. Most newly engaged gentlemen wouldn't be so obliging to the spinster friends of their betrothed. "Thank you."

"Pray don't mention it." A gleam of kindhearted humor twinkled in his eyes. "Now I'm engaged to Lady Anne, I count the Furies as good as family."

Stella managed a distracted smile. It was impossible to give her full attention to Mr. Hartford or Anne when Mr. Hayes was gazing at her so steadily from his place across the room. She swallowed hard as they approached.

Mrs. Archer stepped forward to meet them, her husband at her side. She had the same ebony hair, straight ebony brows, and intelligent slate-blue eyes as Mr. Hayes. Not a traditional beauty, but lovely, nonetheless. There was an understated confidence in the way she carried herself, and a sympathetic softness in the curve of her quiet smile.

"Miss Hobhouse," Mr. Hartford said. "May I present Mr. and Mrs. Archer of Hayes's Perfumes? And this is Mrs. Archer's brother, Mr. Hayes."

Stella inclined her head. "Mr. Archer. Mrs. Archer." Her eyes briefly met Mr. Hayes's. Warmth suffused her midsection. "Mr. Hayes."

"Miss Hobhouse," Mr. Hayes said gravely.

It took an effort to avert her gaze from his. There was something fever bright in the way he looked at her.

Was it akin to an illness, she wondered, to want to paint a certain subject so badly? A sort of madness, as Mr. Hayes had claimed? One that obsessed the mind and riveted the senses, to the exclusion of everything—and everyone—else?

Stella didn't know. Though she enjoyed sketching herself, she'd never yet fixated on a single subject. Certainly not on a person. Her own sketches were largely limited to depictions of horses, or to simple country landscapes, not vastly dissimilar from the aged pastoral that hung above Mr. Hayes's head.

"Miss Hobhouse," Mr. Archer said, bowing. "You've already met my brother-in-law, I take it."

"I—" Stella stopped herself only to start again. "We, er, crossed paths at the British Museum some months ago."

Mrs. Archer smiled. "My brother no doubt importuned you with ravings about Turner."

Stella couldn't help but smile in return. "I believe Turner may have been mentioned."

"I should be surprised if he hadn't been," Mrs. Archer said. "There's no artist Teddy admires more."

"My brother-in-law is a painter," Mr. Archer explained. "A good one."

Stella had no choice but to look at Mr. Hayes again. It would have been impolite not to. Her heart once more lost its rhythm. "Oh?"

His gaze held hers. "A *very* good one," he said, without an ounce of humility.

Mr. and Mrs. Archer laughed. "It's true," Mrs. Archer said. "We're forever singing his praises."

"Miss Hobhouse is something of an artist as well," Anne volunteered.

Mr. Hayes's attention sharpened. "Is that so?"

Stella reflexively demurred. She wasn't in the habit of boasting about her accomplishments. "I only sketch a little."

"Beautiful sketches," Anne said. "As good as anything in a museum."

"*Anne*," Stella murmured, abashed.

"Well, it's true," Anne whispered back.

Seeing Stella's discomfiture, Mr. Archer was chivalrous enough to turn the subject. "Allow us to offer our congratulations on your engagement," he said to Anne and Mr. Hartford.

"Oh yes," Mrs. Archer agreed. "Such joyful news. We wish you every happiness together."

As Mr. and Mrs. Archer conveyed their good wishes, and Anne and Mr. Hartford received them, Mr. Hayes continued to command Stella's gaze.

"I'd like to see your sketches," he said.

Stella didn't doubt it. Most men who considered themselves experts in a field took great pleasure in offering unsolicited opinions on a lady's humble efforts. But Stella's efforts were far from humble. She may not have studied in Paris, but she was good at sketching. She required no man to validate her skill.

"I'm not inclined to share my work with strangers," she said.

"I'm not a stranger. We've met before, if you recall." A wry smile edged his mouth. "And not only in the King's Gallery."

Her cheeks heated, remembering their scandalous encounter in the anteroom last night. A swift glance in the direction of Mr. and

Mrs. Archer confirmed they hadn't overheard. The two of them were still conversing with Anne and Mr. Hartford.

Stella sunk her voice. "That's hardly a character recommendation."

Mr. Hayes shrugged. "I'm an artist. An extraordinary one. Character doesn't come into it."

She gave an involuntary huff of amusement at his unapologetic air of self-regard. "You were certainly extraordinary last night," she said. "Extraordinarily impertinent."

"Is that why you didn't return to the ballroom? Because of my extraordinary impertinence?"

"I needn't account to you for my whereabouts." The retort emerged more tartly than Stella had intended. She felt a twinge of conscience. She was rarely provoked into incivility. Altering her tone, she added, "I was tired."

"You'd only just arrived," he said. "You'd yet to dance a single dance."

"What's this about dancing?" Mrs. Archer asked as she and the others broke off from their conversation.

"We were speaking about the ball last night," Stella answered. It wasn't entirely a lie. "Such a pity it's over."

"Don't despair just yet," Mr. Hartford said. "My grandfather has called the village musicians back to Sutton Park for another evening of dancing tomorrow."

"Tomorrow?" Anne's face lit with delight. Tomorrow was Christmas Eve. "I thought the opening ball was the only dance Lord March had planned for the party?"

Mr. Hartford set a hand at Anne's waist. "That was before the announcement of our engagement. Now the news has been made public, Grandfather means us to celebrate to the fullest. The village musicians are in complete accord. They've agreed to forgo the warmth of their hearths on Christmas Eve in favor of the mulled wine and merriment on offer at ours."

Stella cast a sidelong look at Mr. Hayes as the conversation continued. Her pulse quivered. Another dance? That didn't trouble her. Dancing was a necessary precursor to meeting eligible gentlemen. She was eager for the opportunity. It was the whole reason she'd come.

No. What troubled her was the prospect of another encounter with Mr. Hayes.

Would he attend the Christmas Eve dance tomorrow just as he'd attended the opening ball? Would he sit in his wheeled chair at the edge of the ballroom, watching her? Judging her? Recognizing her as no better than what she was: a gaudily plumed ladybird soliciting a mate?

Tricking a mate, more like. For unlike the other young ladies in attendance, Stella's plumage was dyed. And Mr. Hayes knew it.

She had the sinking feeling that his unlucky presence at the house party was going to have a decidedly adverse effect on her future.

Five

⬥▸◂⬥

Teddy added a box of chalk to the growing pile of art supplies on the guest room's damask-draped four-poster bed. He'd already gathered a leather-bound sketchbook, soft lead pencils, Indian rubber for erasing pencil lines, and stumps—made of tightly rolled wash leather—for shading them. When combined with his drawing board and easel, it would be more than he could easily carry. But no matter. That was what Jennings was for.

The balding manservant bustled about the room. Part valet and part ham-fisted nurse, he was a hulking figure, well made for his work. Alex had hired him several years ago, in an act of kindness, not long after marrying Laura. Before Jennings, Teddy had been reduced to relying on a teetering old footman with scarcely the strength to lift him.

It was a grim reality that, in certain situations, Teddy must be carried. Though not entirely without feeling, his legs had long lost the strength to fully support his weight. He required assistance to climb up and down the stairs, and to attend to some of the essentials of life.

There wasn't anything dignified in it. Not so far as Teddy was concerned. In the beginning, he'd preferred to remain confined to his bed than submit to the humiliation. But for a man without use of his legs, life contained a series of unavoidable indignities. His chair was a necessary appliance, as was Jennings. Teddy endeavored to think of them in the same light. To do otherwise was to venture down a dark and miserable road. He knew that from experience.

It was especially dangerous thinking on a day like today—Christmas Eve Day—when the rain had stopped, and the sky was crisp with the promise of snow. A day when every other member of the house party had promptly dropped what they were doing in favor of venturing out of doors to gather Christmas greenery and mistletoe. Miss Hobhouse was no doubt among them.

Teddy, meanwhile, was confined to remaining indoors.

But he wouldn't allow himself to indulge in self-pity. Never mind that it was another lost opportunity with his muse. Just as the day before had been.

Miss Hobhouse had spent most of yesterday avoiding him. She hadn't been at breakfast, nor at afternoon tea. And when she'd at last appeared at dinner, looking stunning in a gown of pale violet silk, she hadn't addressed him at all.

The latter had, admittedly, been a disappointment. However, they hadn't been seated near each other at table. And afterward, amid the clamor that had followed the announcement of Mr. Hartford's engagement to Lady Anne, there'd been little opportunity for Teddy to get Miss Hobhouse alone. On the heels of their brief—and all-too-public—exchange in the drawing room, they'd separated off into smaller groups, with the rest of the guests, for an evening of cards.

Miss Hobhouse had made up a foursome with Lady Anne, Mr. Hartford, and Lady Anne's formidable, black-clad mother, the Countess of Arundell, while Teddy had been relegated to the opposite corner of the room, where he sat with Alex, Laura, and one of the other tradesmen in attendance—a rival lavender grower from Dorset, who hadn't the sense to beg off any card game where Alex was concerned.

The nurturing of business relationships between the earl and his botanical acquaintances may be the house party's raison d'être, but to everyone else in attendance, it was a party of pleasure. Especially now that there was a betrothal to celebrate. Games had taken up the whole of the evening. Not only card games, but games of charades, snapdragon, and blind man's bluff. It appeared that similar amusements would be enlivening the remainder of their stay at Sutton Park, punctuated by regular outdoor excursions.

It was dashed awkward for a man in Teddy's position.

One of his many leather traveling trunks sat on a silk upholstered bench at the end of the bed. He riffled through it with increasing irritation. "Where is my drawing board? I'm sure I brought it with me."

"You brought two of 'em, sir," Jennings said. "I put 'em in the dressing room with your canvases."

"Fetch the smaller one," Teddy said. "And I'll want my easel as well."

"Another day at the easel?" Alex's voice sounded from the doorway.

Teddy cast his brother-in-law a distracted glance. "As you see."

Alex strolled into the room, dressed in the same gray wool sack coat and trousers he'd been wearing at breakfast. He was a tall, athletically built man, with dark hair and a vaguely piratical countenance. A rogue, some might say. And many did, once they learned of his former career as a sharper. But he was a good-humored sort. Good-hearted, too, as Teddy and his sister could attest.

After breakfast, Alex and Laura had departed the table, along with several other of the more business- and botanical-minded guests, for a visit to the Earl of March's greenhouses. Teddy hadn't seen either of them since.

"Sometimes," Alex remarked, "it seems that Jennings spends more time hauling your art supplies about than he does hauling you."

It wasn't the first time Teddy's brother-in-law had made the droll observation. Teddy gave his usual reply: "He's paid well enough to do both."

Alex crossed to the bed. His gaze flicked over the chalk and pencils that lay atop the embroidered coverlet. "No paints?"

"Not today. I'm sketching something."

"Something? Or some*one*?"

Teddy stilled for an instant before resuming the search through his trunk for any other supplies he might require. "Laura told you." It wasn't a question.

"About your missing muse? She did. Why? Was it meant to be a secret?"

"Are you and my sister capable of keeping secrets from each other?"

Alex's mouth ticked up at one corner. "I like to think not."

"There you are, then." Teddy felt no rancor about it. It was merely the reality of life now his sister was married.

Laura and Alex had wed for love, but they'd been friends first, and were rather modern in their thinking when it came to the terms of their union. They ran the perfumery together, consulting each other on business matters both large and small. They were equally forthcoming with each other on personal matters.

"I'm not sketching Miss Hobhouse, by the way," Teddy added.

"Not yet," Alex returned. He had a flattering level of confidence in Teddy's abilities.

Teddy usually shared that confidence. But not today. He'd awakened with cramps in his legs—an unfortunate result of the change in weather. His lower limbs may not be strong enough to bear his weight, but the muscles still retained enough strength to cause him pain. They often contracted and twitched in the cold and the damp, sending a bone-deep ache through him that he had no power to alleviate.

Jennings had had to spend half an hour massaging Teddy's legs with the paralytic liniment that one of Teddy's doctors had prescribed in France. It was a mixture of beeswax, lard, turpentine, oil of lavender, and herbs, sometimes formulated with ether and laudanum.

Teddy had responded well to the treatment, despite Jennings's excessively rough handling. His cramps had eased within the hour. The pain had nevertheless served to sour his mood.

His precarious spirits had sunk even further when he'd spied from his window several of the guests tramping out across the grounds.

But of course, a Christmas party would devolve into outdoor pursuits. They always did, whether in London, Devon, or France. Why should Hampshire be any different?

"Not ever, the way things are going," Teddy said. "I made a poor first impression on her." He examined the nub of an old lead pencil, his brows notching in a frown. "I was too eager."

"You don't say," Alex remarked dryly.

Teddy scowled. "It isn't a laughing matter. I scared her off. And there's been no chance to repair the damage. Not when she's avoiding me. And not when everyone's out picking blasted mistletoe, and I'm stuck up here." He threw his pencil onto the bed in a burst of frustration. "I'll have to wait until the dance tonight. She won't miss that, I wager."

"You should have come with us to talk with the earl. He has more to offer than just that strain of tea roses he promised. Had you accompanied us—"

"To discover that the aisles of the greenhouse were too narrow to accommodate my chair? Or to find my wheels stuck in the mud while attempting to cross the grounds to get there?" Teddy uttered a derisive snort. "No, thank you."

"We would have made it possible for you."

"No. What you would have done is make me conspicuous."

It was always the case with outdoor pursuits. The ground was unsuited to Teddy's wheeled chair. Too uneven at the best times, and too perilous at the worst, with mud, snow, and clumps of grass and weeds barring his way, and no possibility of him rolling over them himself.

Instead, extra servants had to be employed to carry Teddy and his chair, or a special cart engaged to convey him. And all the while, the others would have to stand and wait, watching him with varying levels of pity and impatience as he was lifted here and carried there like a sentient sack of grain, his inability to walk delaying their pleasure.

It was a mortifying experience. One that Teddy had endured too many times before, both in England and while studying in Paris, when he'd made the mistake of joining some of his fellow artists at Atelier Gleyre on a jaunt to the French countryside to paint in the open air.

Teddy was unwilling to suffer the indignity again.

Alex's expression became unusually stern. "May I remind you that the perfumery is half yours? It would do you good to be more involved, even if you must occasionally draw attention to yourself to do so."

"I have no interest in the perfumery," Teddy said. "I never have, except as a source of income."

Alex picked up the sketchbook from the bed. He idly flipped through the first few pages. "Granted, it can't compete with art, but now that your time in Paris has come to an end—"

"By *my* choice."

"Yes. Because you're ready to take on more of the business."

Teddy flashed his brother-in-law a mystified look. "What the devil gave you that idea?"

"Laura mentioned you might have had a change of heart."

"If she did, it was nothing more than wishful thinking." Teddy returned to searching the trunk with a sardonic chuckle. "I? Take up an active role in Hayes's Perfumes? You know me better than that, and so does my sister."

Alex frowned. "You want to continue to paint, of course." Closing the sketchbook, he placed it back on the bed. "I gathered you would."

"Then why would you think—"

"Because you said you were done with Gleyre."

Teddy had spent the better part of two years at Atelier Gleyre. It had been a large studio, with more than thirty aspiring painters in attendance at any given time. Teddy had worked diligently alongside them. Had shared both his triumphs and disappointments. It had been his first experience with artists of greater skill. A humbling episode in his life, but a necessary one. His own skill had been challenged. Refined. Perfected.

"I'm done with Paris," he said.

Alex gave a humorless laugh. "What artist in his right mind can ever be done with Paris?"

"This one is. I'm ready to live in England again. It's time I came home." Finding a small box of oil pastels in the trunk, Teddy tossed it onto the pile. He doubted he would require it, but it never hurt to have alternatives to hand. The sketch he produced today would form the basis for his painting tomorrow. He intended to get it right.

"What about your sister?" Alex asked with deceptive calm.

Teddy's shoulders tensed. He recognized his brother-in-law's tone. Alex was generally a reasonable fellow, but when his wife's tender feelings were at stake, he could be as ruthlessly protective as a feral wolf.

It didn't prevent Teddy from answering with his usual frankness. "Laura may live where she likes."

"We have no intention of removing from France. I can't imagine we will, not in the near future. Not when the perfumery is doing so well."

"I'm not asking you to come with me," Teddy said.

Alex's gaze bore into him. "What do you intend? To live alone somewhere? Without family close enough to come to your aid should something happen to you?"

"I lived alone in Paris."

"And we kept an apartment nearby."

Teddy's jaw set. He didn't like to be reminded. "Not for the whole of the duration. You returned to Grasse in the end."

"We were still in France. A rail journey would have brought us to you."

"A lengthy rail journey."

"That's beside the point," Alex said. "Were you to remain in England, it would take us twice as long to get to you. Not to mention you'd be divided from us, not only by land, but by the entire width of the English Channel."

"Which takes only a few hours to cross by steamer ship." Teddy wheeled closer to the bed. He gathered his supplies into a neat pile. The orderly action helped to calm the surge of indignation that threatened to ignite his temper. By God, he wasn't a child! He was a man of four-and-twenty. He shouldn't have to argue for his freedom like a barrister in a court of law.

"You make it sound as though you and Laura never leave France," he said, "when, in fact, you've visited England every year since your marriage."

"*Every* year?" Alex repeated in exasperation. "We married but two years ago, Teddy. At the beginning of which, must I remind you, your health was something of a concern."

Teddy dismissed his brother-in-law's words. "I was thin, that was all."

"You'd all but wasted away up in your room. Your sister feared—"

Teddy sharply wheeled around in his chair. The muscles in his arms and back bunched hard with the effort. He'd spent a long while in building them. Hours each day expended in performing push-ups and pull-ups to strengthen his upper body, and stretching exercises to work the paralyzed muscles in his legs.

"Must you bring up all this ancient history?" he demanded. "I'm better, that's all that matters."

"Yes, you are. But—"

"Besides, most of that was melancholy. I have a purpose now—one you've so far encouraged. So long as that purpose remains, my health will continue to improve."

Alex's mouth set in a doubtful line. It was he who had first suggested that Teddy find an art teacher in France—one who could instruct him in the new styles that were emerging. Before then, Teddy had to content himself with his own imagination. He'd spent most of the time in his bedroom in Surrey, laid low by his illness, drawing the birds he spied through the window. Alex had prompted him to go out. To visit the seaside. To paint the tumultuous waves at Margate like Teddy's idol, the late artist William Turner, had.

That Alex was trying to constrain Teddy now rankled him in no small measure. But it was for Laura's sake. Teddy understood that. And he would no more hurt his sister than Alex would.

"You needn't mention it to Laura," Teddy said. "Not yet. I'll talk to her in my own time."

"When?"

"When we return from visiting Thornhill and Lady Helena."

"You still plan to accompany us to Devon after Christmas?"

"Naturally." The painting opportunities at the Thornhills' remote cliffside abbey were too plentiful to miss. Teddy intended to devote the entirety of the visit to working on his seascapes.

Afterward, he, Laura, and Alex were slated to travel back to London together, where they would spend the next several weeks visiting Tom and Jenny Finchley before boarding a steamer to Calais.

"I'll stay with you in Half Moon Street while I make my arrangements," he said. "I'll speak to Laura then, before the two of you return to France."

Alex's expression was dubious. "After which you expect she'll be content to just . . . leave you here alone?"

Teddy forced a smile. "I won't be alone. I'll have Jennings."

The manservant chose that moment to emerge from the dressing room. He had Teddy's easel in hand. "Here it is."

"Splendid," Teddy said. "You may carry it down, along with the rest of these supplies. Then you may come back for my chair."

"And then for you, sir?"

Teddy repressed a burst of impatience. By God, how he'd come to loathe his dependence! The fact that his body couldn't keep pace with the vigorousness of his mind. The fact that, absent his chair, he was wholly reliant on those around him. On Jennings. On Alex. On any servant strong enough to convey Teddy's uncooperative body from one place to another.

Try as he might, yearn as he did, freedom seemed to be forever just out of his reach. Freedom of movement. Freedom to make his own decisions. Freedom to paint the lady he longed to paint.

But no longer.

Henceforth, he was determined to take hold of the helm and steer his own course.

"Yes, Jennings," he said levelly. "And then for me."

Stella sat on the tufted velvet bench in front of the carved mahogany dressing table in her room as Anne's French lady's maid, Jeanette, combed out her hair. Anne had been generous enough to lend Jeanette's services to Stella before the Christmas Eve dance tonight, just as she had before the ball two nights before. Unlike Anne, Stella didn't have a maid of her own. When at home with her brother, she relied on one of the housemaids to assist her with her toilette.

"*Mon dieu*," Jeanette muttered as she attempted to get a blunt-toothed tortoiseshell comb through Stella's unusually sticky locks.

Unbound, Stella's hair reached nearly to her waist. It was normally thick and glossy, and shining with good health. If not for its natural gray color, it would have been considered her crowning glory. But not today. Not even with its new golden auburn hue.

Stella met the maid's frustrated eyes in the dressing table mirror. "Is it dreadfully tangled?"

"It's the bandoline, miss," Jeanette said. The maid had used the clear liquid gum solution to set Stella's coiffure on the night of the opening ball. It had left an unfortunate residue behind that had only worsened over the passing days.

There was but one way to be rid of it.

"Have we time to wash my hair before dinner?" Stella asked. "And, more importantly, to dry it?"

Jeanette looked at the mantel clock with a frown, appearing to perform a swift mental calculation. She nodded. "Yes, miss. Shall I call for hot water?"

"If you please," Stella said.

In the ordinary course of events, she washed her hair but rarely. It wasn't often necessary. Neither was it convenient. Washing one's hair in a basin was a tedious business that took more time than a young lady could spare during the season. Indeed, it had been many weeks since Stella's hair had last seen soap and water. But not ten minutes later, she stood in front of the wash basin, head bent over the bowl, while the maid lathered her wet hair with a bar of lilac perfumed toilet soap.

When Jeanette was finished, she rinsed the suds with warm water from the pitcher.

Stella raised a hand to her head. Her hair was still sticky. "Another good soaping, I think," she suggested.

"Yes, miss." Jeanette added another liberal application of toilet soap. This time she scrubbed twice as long.

Stella squeezed her eyes shut to protect them from the stinging lather. She was relieved when she felt the next deluge of warm water cascade over her hair. Until she heard Jeanette's gasp of horror.

"Oh, miss! I didn't mean to!" the maid cried, backing away. "I was only doing what you told me!"

Stella jerked her head up in swift alarm. "What is it? What's happened?"

But Jeanette would only stare, one hand covering her mouth.

Stella rushed across the room to the dressing table mirror, wet hair clinging to her face and neck. What she saw in the glass made her legs go weak beneath her. She sank unsteadily onto the padded bench.

"What shall I do, miss?" Jeanette asked, hovering about Stella in distress.

There was only one thing *to* do.

"Fetch Anne," Stella said tremulously. "Tell her she must come at once!"

Six

❖

"Circassian gold, my old aunt Sally," Anne said hotly. Wearing a hastily donned embroidered silk robe over her corset and petticoats, she stood behind Stella at the dressing table, staring at Stella's damp hair in pale-faced fury. "Any dye worth its salt must surely last more than three days."

"It was supposed to last a week." Stella's teeth chattered in response to the incipient cold. She'd been sitting in front of the mirror for nearly ten minutes, too much in shock to move in front of the fire.

"After which?" Anne prompted.

"The pamphlet said it would gradually fade to a strawberry sheen," Stella replied.

Anne scoffed at the pronouncement. "And you believed it?"

"Of course I did!" A hysterical note crept into Stella's voice. "How could they print it if it wasn't true?"

"There's no point in us arguing about what's already done," Anne said hastily. "Though I must say, these women promising Circassian beauty have a lot to answer for. They're no better than poison peddlers and quacksalvers, to my mind. Still"—she lifted a damp strand of Stella's hair to examine the unfortunate hue in the lamplight—"I suppose things could be worse."

"How could it be worse?" Stella's tone became shrill. "My hair is *green*, Anne!"

"It's not green. It's . . . Very well. It's green. But it shan't be for long. We'll simply wash it again." Anne briskly summoned her maid. "Jeanette? Go to the kitchens and have Cook make up a solution of borax, olive oil, and boiling water." She turned back to Stella, explaining, "Mrs. Beeton swears by the mixture in her *Book of Household Management*."

"Yes, my lady." Jeanette curtsied before scurrying from the room.

"She fears she'll be blamed," Anne said. "Silly creature. I don't suppose she's had much experience with hair dye."

Anguish welled in Stella's throat. She wouldn't have thought it possible to feel both shock and hysteria at the same time. The inevitable consequences of what she beheld in the mirror reverberated through her. Her hair was no longer auburn. It was no longer gray. It was the color of congealed pea soup.

"I shouldn't have done it," she said.

"It's rather too late for that now," Anne replied. "The best we can do is see this through to the other side."

Stella scarcely registered her words. She was too caught up in her own misery. "Daniel would say this is God's doing. He'd tell me I was being punished for the sin of vanity."

Anne gave an eloquent snort. "Rubbish. God has better things to do than hang about Hampshire turning ladies' hair green. This is deceptive beauty advertising, plain and simple. You're not the first female to fall victim to it. But you mustn't despair. We shall soon set it right."

"What if the borax doesn't work?"

"We'll try another hair wash recipe, and then another. We'll go through the whole store cupboard if we have to."

Stella met Anne's gaze in the mirror. Her eyes pooled with tears. "Someone will find out. They'll discover what a fool I've made of myself and carry the dreadful news straight back to London. Society will never forget it. And when Daniel learns—"

"No one will find out."

"How not? The house party has four days remaining. Even if we do manage to wash the green away, it will only be gray. That alone will cause remark. I've had auburn hair since I arrived in Hampshire. No one here knows my real color except for you, your mother, and Mr. Hartford."

And Mr. Hayes.

But Stella couldn't afford to think of Mr. Hayes in this moment. One gentleman's opinion meant nothing in comparison to the condemnation of the whole of society.

Anne chewed her lip. "I suppose we could dye it back. Do you have any of the Circassian gold left?"

Stella shook her head. "I used the entire bottle. I'd no notion I'd require another application."

"I wouldn't advise one anyway," Anne said. "Not after this debacle. Who knows but that it might not make your hair fall out entirely."

Stella emitted a strangled moan.

Anne grimaced. "Sorry. I'm not helping, am I?"

Stella dropped her face into her hands. "I shall have to hide for the rest of the house party. You shall have to tell everyone I died."

"We needn't go that far. There are caps and bonnets, after all. We'll simply disguise your hair, just as you do when you're riding in Rotten Row."

"I can't wear a cap at dinner. I can't wear a bonnet in the ballroom."

"Regrettably, no. You'll have to forgo those events." Anne set a consoling hand on Stella's shoulder. "I'm sorry, dearest. I know you'd hoped to meet someone during your stay."

Stella bleakly lifted her head. She was suddenly very tired. "It was a stupid plan, anyway, coming here in disguise. There's no way to hide who I really am. Not for long. Any gentlemen who thought me worth courting would find out the truth eventually."

"There's nothing wrong with who you are."

"What I am," Stella said, "is unmarriageable."

Anne pressed Stella's shoulder in a reassuring squeeze. "These are not subjects to contemplate when one's hair is green," she said wisely. "Let me first restore your beautiful gray, and then we shall discuss them."

"What if you can't?"

"Oh, ye of little faith." Anne gave her a bracing look in the mirror. "Don't you know by now? There's nothing I can't do."

On Christmas morning, Teddy awakened to find the windows of his room frozen over with a thick sheet of ice. The temperature had dropped dramatically during the night, and outside the grounds were blanketed in a pristine layer of snow. It covered the hills and pastures and clung to the branches of the majestic wych elm trees that flanked the house, sparkling like fine crystal in the cold winter sun.

It was too great an artistic opportunity to miss.

After spending a few brief moments with Alex and Laura, exchanging gifts and sharing a pot of chocolate in the privacy of their bedchamber, Teddy dressed, gathered his art supplies, and—with the aid of his manservant—took himself off to the secluded upstairs parlor the earl had given leave for him to use as a temporary studio.

There, Teddy set up his easel in front of a tall sash window. It gave him an unimpeded view of an aged oak sitting atop a snow-covered hill some distance away. A stark subject, with a hint of melancholy about it. The snow below the tree was bathed in a dazzling array of changing light.

Within two hours, Teddy's oil-painted depiction was well under way.

He'd cut his teeth on landscapes as a boy, forever painting some tree or bush or wildflower-blanketed meadow. After that, he'd graduated to birds. And then, eventually, to the sea. It was more satisfying to commit life to canvas, whether it was the raging waves or a song thrush in flight. A swirling snowscape was but a distant alternative, but it still had its lure.

Of course, it was nothing compared to a beautiful woman. To the elegant curve of a feminine cheek, the swell of a voluptuous hip, or the shimmer of sensual mystery in an otherwise ladylike gaze. It was that which most captivated Teddy's artistic attention now.

Regrettably, Miss Hobhouse had so far eluded him.

She hadn't been at dinner last night. And she hadn't attended the Christmas Eve dance, much to his irritation. He'd watched for her for nearly two hours before Laura had reported that she'd heard—via Lady Anne—that Miss Hobhouse had retired to bed with a nameless indisposition.

"*Don't be cast down,*" Laura had said to him. "*You're bound to see her tomorrow. Lord March will be hosting a grand Christmas tea in the drawing room. Miss Hobhouse is sure to attend.*"

Teddy doubted whether she would. His elusive silver star appeared a resourceful sort of girl. If she was set on avoiding him for the remainder of the house party, she'd likely succeed in her goal.

Drat it altogether.

He laid on a brushstroke with unneeded force. The thick layer of flake white paint globbed on the canvas, marring the careful shadowing he'd created on the snowbank. It was an amateurish mistake, completely unworthy of an artist of Teddy's skill. He uttered an eloquent French curse as he corrected his error.

"You'll be needing your tea, sir," Jennings said from his place near the fire.

Teddy continued painting, ignoring him.

But Jennings could never be ignored for long. He rose from his chair and crossed the length of the small parlor.

The earl had offered the room to Teddy at the dance last night. It had better light than the morning room where Teddy had sketched yesterday. It was also far more secluded. Located down an isolated corridor in the east wing of the house, the private parlor was set away from the guest rooms and the traffic of the common areas. Here, there would be no chance of Teddy's work being interrupted.

Unless that interruption was caused by his own bloody servant.

Jennings stopped in front of the window, blocking Teddy's light. "Did you hear me, sir?"

Teddy glanced up from his canvas with no little irritation. "What have I told you about disrupting my concentration?"

"Beg pardon." Jennings took hold of the back of Teddy's chair. "Mrs. Archer said as how I wasn't to let you forget to eat."

"Mrs. Archer doesn't employ you. I do." Teddy picked up another dab of paint from his light wood palette. "My brother-in-law may have hired you to begin with, but I pay your wages now. I won't be disturbed when I'm working." He shot a severe look at the man. "I'll thank you to let go of my chair."

"But Mr. Hayes—"

"I'll be joining the others for tea in the drawing room later."

"That's not for hours yet, sir."

"Then I shall wait," Teddy said. "If you're wanting your own tea in the interim, have it, by all means. I'll do very well on my own for the next hour."

Jennings reluctantly released his grip. "I shan't need more than ten minutes."

"*An hour*," Teddy repeated. "Two if you like. I'll not have you spending the whole of your Christmas waiting on me. I'm not Mr. Scrooge, for God's sake."

Jennings didn't appear to understand the reference. He wasn't much of a reader. "What if you need help while I'm gone?"

"I have access to the bell pull, don't I?"

"Yes, but—"

"Then we're agreed," Teddy said. "Now take yourself off before you cause me to make another mistake."

With a grudging grunt of compliance, Jennings retreated from the room. He would undoubtedly be back before the clock struck two. There was no persuading him to forget his duty to Alex and Laura.

As Teddy resumed painting, it occurred to him that he would do well to find himself another manservant when he settled in London. A man of absolute loyalty. One he could choose all on his own. Unfortunately, there was more skill required for assisting him than the average manservant possessed. Any mistakes in selecting the fellow would come to weigh on Teddy and Teddy alone. Who knows but that he might not find himself abandoned in his chair in an upstairs room or left to languish somewhere with no hope of summoning aid?

Teddy's jaw tightened to think of it. His wheeled chair gave him much-needed mobility, but he still required human assistance. And, in his experience, hired humans came in only two varieties: either painfully intrusive or intrinsically unreliable. Teddy couldn't risk landing with one of the latter, so—despite the man's shortcomings—Jennings it was and Jennings it would have to remain.

Returning his attention to his canvas, Teddy spent the next quarter of an hour adding a branch on his tree. He was just beginning the outline of another branch when his stomach uttered a distinct growl of complaint. Perhaps Jennings had been right. Teddy should stop to eat. He often forgot to when working. In the past, he had, at times, been too thin. It wasn't conducive to the active life he now envisioned for himself. For that, he must keep up his strength.

Setting aside his paintbrush and palette, he reversed his chair from in front of the easel and turned it in the direction of the bellpull across the room. In most circumstances, he could maneuver the wheels himself indoors. Especially now that he'd put on weight and muscle enough for the task. His only limitation lay in the terrain. Stairs were impossible, slick marble was a challenge, and thick carpeting was a bloody nuisance.

He muttered another curse as he laboriously rolled over the lush Aubusson that covered the parlor floor. His frustrated expletive was answered by a feminine gasp.

"Oh!" a soft voice exclaimed. "I thought this room was supposed to be empty."

Teddy's head jerked to the doorway. Every molecule in his body leapt to attention. He felt, all at once, as elementally alert as a vibrating tuning fork. He suppressed a smile. Suppressed hope. By God but there would be no eagerness this time. He'd be stoic and disinterested if it killed him.

"Miss Hobhouse," he said with a creditable degree of calm. "Happy Christmas morning."

Seven

※

S tella Hobhouse stood on the threshold, a brilliantly patterned blue-and-ivory cashmere shawl tangled about her arms, and a rather incongruous black crepe-and-lace matron's cap covering the entirety of her hair. Her pale, silver-blue eyes were wide with surprise. She clearly hadn't anticipated encountering him here.

But though she could have easily done so, she didn't run away. She remained, hovering on the threshold, her aura sparking with the same electricity as Teddy's own.

It took her but an instant to master herself. Her lush mouth compressed; her countenance rapidly composing itself into a ladylike mask. "Happy Christmas, Mr. Hayes," she said. "But it isn't morning any longer. It's past one."

He looked at the carriage clock as though noticing it for the first time. "Is it? Forgive me. I lose track of the time when I'm working."

She flicked a glance to his canvas, temporarily diverted. "You're painting?"

"The beginnings of a landscape, as you see. Not one of my best efforts."

A doubtful frown puckered her brow. "It looks quite good to me."

"From a distance, perhaps, but not when you view the brushstrokes at close quarters." He rolled his chair back a turn, giving her a better view. "See for yourself."

She hesitated. "I don't wish to disturb you."

"It's no disturbance," he said. "I was just breaking for tea."

There was a pause. A weighty one. Teddy's fingers curled tight on the wheels of his chair. He ruthlessly tamped down the urge to say something more.

"Very well," Miss Hobhouse replied at length. "If you're certain."

Hope surged in Teddy's breast, despite his best efforts to contain it. Restraining a smile, he motioned to the canvas, inviting her to look her fill. The gesture was deceptively nonchalant. It seemed to do the trick.

Miss Hobhouse slowly advanced into the room, as careful as a fox entering the secluded glen of a known hunter. Wariness shadowed her gaze, at war with a palpable curiosity. Curiosity about his work.

Or perhaps it was about him.

Teddy set a guard on his tongue. He wasn't going to be candid with her. Not this time. He wouldn't risk frightening her away.

She came to stand in front of his unfinished painting, studying the canvas for a long moment. The finely woven wool of her dark blue day dress caught the light, making the modest fabric gleam as sensuously as velvet.

Teddy watched her with rapt attention. She was a young lady comfortable with silences. Still and grave in her perusal, as he suspected she was in most areas of her life. It took an effort not to pepper her with questions. He had so many of them.

"How talented you are," she declared at last.

He swallowed an unreasonable swell of pride. She wasn't the first to compliment his work. Yet, her opinion held unusual weight. If he impressed her favorably enough, she might agree to let him paint her.

"I'm pleased you think so," he said.

"And yet so young," she added, still gazing at the canvas.

"I'm four-and-twenty. Older than you, I'd wager."

"Only by two years."

So, she was two-and-twenty. He'd guessed her age to be some-where thereabouts. But that wasn't what made him look at her with increased intensity. It was that their conversation had so rapidly es-calated to the personal. He didn't know whether to be encouraged by it or insulted.

Perhaps his unapologetic candor had inspired her own? Or perhaps . . .

Perhaps she was one of the countless females who regarded a gen-tleman in a wheeled chair as a variety of nonentity.

Teddy had met such women before. Ones who addressed him not as a man, but with the same degree of informality as they'd use with a boy in the nursery. After all, what harm could a crippled man do to a lady's virtue?

He hadn't thought Miss Hobhouse was such a lady. Not based on her behavior on the night of the ball. Then, she'd responded as any respectable young miss might when opportuned by an impertinent gentleman. She'd taken umbrage at his forwardness. She'd repri-manded him for using her given name. She had, ultimately, fled.

Teddy was nevertheless on his guard. "It's not the years that mat-ter in art. It's the experience of life."

She cast him an interested glance. "I suppose you've had a great deal of that experience, studying in Paris as you have."

Another irrational surge of hope caught him by the heart. She knew something about his life. Which meant she'd asked someone. Which meant she was intrigued by him.

He forced his fingers to loosen from the wheels of his chair. A man mustn't appear too eager, he reminded himself. Eager for ap-proval. Eager for admiration. Especially not where pretty girls were concerned.

Pretty? Ha! Who was he fooling? She was as shimmering as a

moonbeam. As bright as a star, even with that atrocious auburn dye marring her silver hair.

Not that the color was visible at the moment. Indeed, he couldn't see a single strand of Miss Hobhouse's hair. It was entirely masked by her cap.

He cleared his throat. "Paris. Ah yes. That provided a wealth of experience."

"You studied with a famous painter, did you not?" she inquired.

She *had* been asking about him, it seemed.

"I studied at the atelier of Charles Gleyre," he answered. "Are you familiar with his work?"

"I'm afraid I'm not. Should I be?"

"You definitely should. So should everyone. He's a brilliant artist in his own right, though he's largely retired from public life. He devotes himself to teaching now. He's instructed some of the most promising painters of the new age. Men like Mr. Monet, Mr. Renoir, and Mr. Whistler."

She abruptly looked away from him, turning her attention back to the canvas.

"Whistler," he reminded her. "The American artist who painted the piece in the Berners Street Gallery."

"Oh?" A faint flush of color seeped into her cheeks. She continued studying his landscape. "Is he a friend of yours?"

"Regrettably, no. He'd already left Gleyre's studio by the time I arrived. But I find much to inspire me in the way he works within the confines of a limited palette. Whites and grays and so forth. My own style differs greatly. Still, one can appreciate his genius."

Teddy had written as much in a letter of admiration he'd sent to Whistler last summer, not long after *The Woman in White*—then titled simply, *The White Girl*—had been rejected by the Royal Academy. The American artist had sent a cordial reply, acknowledging their shared connection with Gleyre, and expressing an interest in seeing Teddy's own work the next time they were both in London.

"Yes," Miss Hobhouse said. "I suppose he is quite talented in an unusual way."

Teddy nearly bolted straight up in his chair with excitement. "You don't mean to imply that you actually *went* there? That you *saw* Whistler's painting?"

Her gaze slid back to his. "I did," she confessed.

"And?"

"I've never encountered anything like it."

He rolled closer to her. Miss Hobhouse's reputed skill at sketching notwithstanding, she didn't strike him as being a learned critic of the arts. Chances were she had only a basic knowledge of the subject, of the sort conveyed to young ladies by their governesses in the schoolroom. Teddy nevertheless craved her opinion.

"You thought it ugly?"

"I thought it strange," she said.

"It is," he agreed. "But who's to say that strange is bad?"

A smile tugged at her mouth. Her eyes again found his. "You have an odd way of viewing things."

"Not odd," he said. "Not antiquated, either. Art is changing. It's no longer a matter of depicting something exactly as it is—some still life of fruit on a carefully draped table. There are other elements to consider. Light. Movement."

Her brows swept upward in disbelief. "Movement? In a painting?"

"Yes, exactly. It's the impression of a moment. The shimmer of the changing light on the water. The whisper of the breeze through the branches. The sensuality in the turn of a lady's countenance."

Miss Hobhouse visibly stiffened. "I don't think that's quite—"

"The elements. Nature. Human desire."

"Mr. Hayes, really—"

"Which is not to say that any of it's salacious. It's alive, that's what matters. And it's no longer . . ." He motioned with his hand, struggling for a way to describe it. "Earthbound," he managed at last.

Her brow creased. Some of the starch went out of her spine, her offense at his earlier choice of words momentarily forgotten. "It's no longer earthbound? Do you mean—"

"I mean that there are no limits. No boundaries. There are only feelings—the artist's own and those he evokes in the viewer. All the rest is . . ." He gestured vaguely again before trailing off with a grimace.

So much for guarding his tongue.

"I'm sorry," he said. "I get rather exercised on the subject."

"You needn't apologize for being passionate about something."

"For being ineloquent, then."

"You're not ineloquent." She motioned to a nearby chair. "May I?"

"Please," he said.

She sank down on the tufted seat, her full skirts pooling about her feet in a spill of sensible blue wool.

Teddy appreciated her sitting down. Many people didn't in his presence, preferring to loom over him in his chair. He despised having to crane his neck to look up at them. He'd much rather look a person in the eyes.

Had Miss Hobhouse intuited that? He suspected she had.

"Mr. Whistler's painting *did* make me feel something," she said, flicking a brief, rueful glance upward to her black-crepe-covered hair. "Obviously."

Teddy had noted the similarity of her hair color to that of the woman in Whistler's piece on the night of the opening ball, but he hadn't comprehended the reason behind that similarity. Not until this moment.

The realization struck him like a thunderbolt. "Is *that* why you colored your hair? Because of Whistler's painting?"

The guilty flash of embarrassment in Miss Hobhouse's eyes was as good as an admission.

"I don't know why he called it *The Woman in White*," she said, rather than answering him. "It didn't resemble any of the female characters in Mr. Collins's novel."

Wilkie Collins's wildly popular and sensational novel, *The Woman in White*, had been released but a few years prior, to enormous success. It was a common misconception that Whistler's painting was meant as an illustration from the story. Both the public and art critics had made the error, to Whistler's detriment.

"Whistler didn't name his painting *The Woman in White*," Teddy said. "You can blame that on the gallery owner. Apparently, he thought to capitalize on the success of Mr. Collins's novel."

"That was presumptuous of him."

"Unwise as well. All it's done is bring unwarranted criticism on the piece. He'd have done better to keep its original name—*The White Girl*—as Whistler intended."

Her brows notched in a thoughtful frown. "Still . . . I suppose the title is accurate. The painting *is* of a woman in white. The most arresting thing about her was her hair."

"And the light," Teddy said. "And the color."

"The absence of color, more like. There was so much white in it."

It was a valid observation on its surface. Whistler's painting depicted a fair-skinned lady in a white cambric dress. His mistress, in fact: the auburn-haired beauty Joanna Hiffernan. She stood on a white rug against a pale, curtained background, gazing out at the viewer with an enigmatic stare.

"I don't understand what it was all supposed to mean," Miss Hobhouse said.

"Why should it mean anything?"

"Why? Because art is *meant* to mean something." She gave him a doubtful look. "Isn't it?"

"Mean something how?" he asked. "Morally? Philosophically?"

"Yes, I suppose. To uplift or . . . or to educate."

"I reject that notion," he said emphatically.

A glimmer of amusement sparked in her eyes. "Naturally, you do."

"I'm not the only one. There's an entire class of artists who believe that art should stand alone. Whistler is among them. He says it's enough that a painting appeals to the artistic senses. It needn't be burdened with allusions to morality or politics or religion."

"Do you believe that?"

"I do. The French call it *l'art pour l'art.*"

"Art for art's sake," she translated. And then she laughed. It was a soft, husky sound. "My old governess would take issue with that idea. She used to say that all of my drawings should glorify God."

"Was it she who taught you to sketch?" he asked.

"I taught myself. Miss Callis only ever criticized my work. She didn't like that I gave my horses wings, or that I shaded them in outlandish hues. I keenly remember her rapping my fingers whenever I chose an inappropriate color from my paintbox."

"An inappropriate color?" He scoffed. "She sounds appalling, as well as ignorant."

Miss Hobhouse's smile dimmed. "I would certainly never have chosen her for myself. It was my older brother who employed her."

Teddy regarded her steadily. "Your brother the clergyman."

"Yes."

"What of your parents? Had they no say in your education?"

"My parents died long ago—my mother when I was born, and my father when I was but a child. He perished in a carriage accident traveling home from London. He was a barrister."

"I'm sorry to hear it." An eloquent wince flashed across Teddy's brow. "Not about his profession, I mean, but about—"

"I know what you meant." She smiled slightly. "Thank you. I'd like to say I remember them, but I suppose I was too young."

"Your brother has had charge of you ever since?"

"And of my education." She fidgeted with a crease in her heavy wool skirts. "I had a terrible time being rid of Miss Callis. Indeed, it seems I've spent the whole of my life deposing one tyrant after another. First my nurse, then my governess, and now . . ."

"Now?" he prompted quietly.

She gave him a rueful look. "My brother is contemplating marriage."

"Ah. His betrothed is of a tyrannical strain, I gather."

"She isn't his betrothed. It's one of the reasons I'm here."

His brows lifted in inquiry.

She hesitated before explaining, "The young lady is in town for Christmas. My brother had planned to invite her to stay with us. His plan was contingent on my being there. That's why I accepted Lady Anne's invitation—to frustrate my brother's aims. That, and . . . I'd hoped coming here might provide an opportunity to solve my own wretched problem."

"What problem is that?"

"The usual one. I've failed in my efforts during the London season. Twice failed, for this year was my second attempt at the business. If not for that sad fact, I mayn't have been so desperate as to color my hair."

"I see. You hope to marry." He'd already known that. It was why she'd been in town three months ago. Why *every* eligible young lady had been in town. Her words nevertheless provoked a pit in Teddy's stomach. Once she was respectably wed, he'd have no more chance of painting her. Not the way he wanted to. "If that's your ambition, I don't wonder that you'd rather I didn't paint you."

"I wonder that you'd wish to," she returned. "Do you mean to depict me like Mr. Whistler's *Woman in White*? As some stark, ethereal spirit the critics will write scathing reviews about?"

It was his turn to frown. "I don't know. I won't until I start with the preliminary sketches. Even then, my feelings can change. I've discarded entire canvases in the past when the piece wasn't going as I intended."

"Portraits of ladies?"

"Sometimes."

"Have you painted many of them?"

"A few."

She looked at him with that same cautious curiosity. "Why did you discard them? Was it because you couldn't accurately capture their beauty?"

"Not that," he said. "It was the light. It's *always* the light. Sometimes it eludes me."

"It might elude you with me, too."

"It won't."

"You're very confident."

"I've never been more so," he said. "You're made of light, Miss Hobhouse. It shines all around you. I've never yet met a lady who possesses one fraction of your brilliancy."

She held his gaze. "You're exceedingly persuasive when you wish to be."

"Not persuasive enough, I discern."

"As to that . . ." She furrowed her brow. But whatever she intended to say next was interrupted by the sharp sound of a stomach growling.

This time it wasn't Teddy's.

His mouth hitched in a swift grin. "Good Lord. Was that *you*?"

Her face flushed crimson. "I beg your pardon." She stood abruptly. "I'm afraid I haven't had my tea, either."

He pounced on the opportunity with instinctive speed. "Haven't you?" He rolled a half turn closer to her, all thoughts of remaining aloof and disinterested forgotten. "Then join me. I could use the company."

She backed up a step. "I don't think I—"

"It needn't spoil your tea in the drawing room."

She gave him a dubious look.

"The grand Christmas tea that Lord March is giving this afternoon," he reminded her.

She flushed. "Oh yes. That." Her fingers twined in the folds of her shawl. "I'm afraid I won't be attending. I've been . . . That is . . . I'm . . ."

"Then take tea with me," he said, ruthlessly pressing his advantage. "You'd be doing me a favor. My sister and brother-in-law are off with the others, and my manservant has gone down to the kitchens to enjoy his own Christmas repast. I'm on my own here. It's a bit awkward, truth be told."

Her attention dropped to the wheels of his chair. Her eyes lit in dawning comprehension. "Oh! I'm sorry. I-I didn't realize." Her shoulder set with a sudden resolve. An expression of determination came over her. "Yes. Of course, I'll join you. A cup of tea can surely do no harm."

Teddy's stomach sank. Too late, he recognized the conclusion she'd leapt to. She thought his reference to awkwardness had been about his chair, not about the mere fact that he was alone in a strange house, wanting for company. He opened his mouth to set her straight only to stop short.

To the devil with his pride! What did it matter why she remained, so long as she remained?

"Excellent," he said. "If you would be so kind as to ring the bell?"

Eight

─◆═◆─

Stella sat across from Mr. Hayes at the small table the footman had prepared for them by the parlor window. He and a maid had brought in a steaming pot of tea, a small plate of sandwiches, and slices of iced gingerbread and brandy-soaked fruitcake. After a bow and a curtsy, and a murmured "Will there be anything else, miss?" both servants had departed. Neither had batted an eye at leaving Stella alone, unchaperoned, with a young man. They hadn't regarded Mr. Hayes as a threat.

Stella wished she could feel the same. She'd been avoiding Teddy Hayes all morning. Indeed, she'd been avoiding everyone.

Anne had succeeded in washing the green out of Stella's hair last night. It had taken countless applications of borax and olive oil solution, and an equal number of rinses, before Stella had at last lifted her head from the wash basin to find her hair returned to its natural silver gray. Anne had promptly darted off to find Stella a suitable cap.

Alas, the sort of old-fashioned matron's cap that covered the whole of one's hair hadn't been easy to come by, especially not when they were attempting to keep Stella's altered hair color a secret from the other guests in attendance. The only one in possession of such an antiquated article had been Anne's mother. A black cap, naturally, given Lady Arundell's proclivities. It was more suited to an aged relic in deep mourning than to a young lady of Stella's tender years.

Stella had donned the cap this morning, nonetheless. She was grateful for it, but she knew full well how it made her look, and the questions it would engender. Only one gentleman would be bold enough to ask them. It had seemed imperative that she evade that gentleman's scrutiny.

In the end, all she'd done was delay the inevitable. Her very attempts at avoiding Mr. Hayes had led her straight to his door.

And then his painting had lured her inside.

It was unlike any landscape Stella had ever seen. Not an exact rendering, by any stretch of the imagination. It contained only the barest impression of the form of a tree, set against a snowbank of gleaming white. A blurred depiction, composed of small, unblended brushstrokes that rather miraculously managed to capture the changing effect of the morning light on the bark and across the expanse of the snow.

Some might call it an unfinished effort. A work unworthy of even a novice artist. But the whole of it inspired an odd ache in Stella's breast.

Was that how Mr. Hayes meant to depict her? Not as a duplicate of herself, but as an indistinct figure who would provoke that same queer feeling in others?

It was unnerving to think of.

It was also rather exciting.

He'd spoken of light and movement. Of paintings that served no purpose other than to stimulate the artistic sensibilities. "*Who's to say that strange is bad?*" he'd asked her.

Only everyone she'd ever met in her village in Derbyshire. Only the whole of fashionable London.

But Mr. Hayes didn't seem to care about any of them. He didn't appear to be influenced by anyone's opinions but his own.

"I intended to have my tea here alone," she informed him after the servants had gone. "Mr. Hartford said that no one ever came into this wing of the house. He said this parlor was private."

"Lord March assured me of the same," Mr. Hayes said. "He offered the room to serve as my studio for the remainder of my stay, so I might have a place to work in peace." He studied her face. "Why alone?"

"I beg your pardon?"

"Why not join the others in the drawing room for Christmas tea?"

Stella reached for the silver teapot to fill their cups. She would have liked to join the others, but there was no way to show herself in the drawing room without causing comment. With her cap on, she looked an absolute quiz. Everyone would know something was amiss.

It was a small miracle that Mr. Hayes had yet to remark on it. He'd glanced at the awful head covering often enough, and with a slight notch between his black brows, too, as though he couldn't quite discern what she was about in wearing it. It was only a matter of time before he broached the subject.

She'd hoped to get through the remaining three days of the party without encountering him—or any of the guests—in the house. Far better to see them out of doors, where she could justifiably cover her newly restored gray hair with a combination of a silken net and a bonnet.

As for the fact that today was Christmas, it would have to be enough that she'd honored the day with Anne and Lady Arundell earlier this morning. The three of them had shared a private breakfast in the small sitting room attached to the countess's bedchamber. Anne had surprised Stella with a ribbon-wrapped pair of new worsted riding gloves, and Stella had given Anne a framed sketch she'd drawn of Anne's golden stallion, Saffron.

"Sometimes I prefer being on my own," Stella said as she poured Mr. Hayes's tea. "What about you? Why aren't you celebrating with the others?"

"You weren't at breakfast yesterday, either, I observed," he said, not allowing Stella to turn the subject away from herself. "Nor at dinner last night. Nor at the dance." He paused. "You haven't, by any chance, been avoiding me?"

Her ungloved fingers slipped on the handle of the teapot. A gush of tea streamed from the spout, missing Mr. Hayes's cup and splashing onto the table. It soaked into the linen tablecloth in a swiftly expanding dark ring of Darjeeling.

Stella hurriedly sat down the pot. "Oh, how clumsy I am!"

Mr. Hayes seemed to take the spilled tea as confirmation. "So, you *were* avoiding me."

She exhaled a frustrated breath as she dabbed at the wet spot with her napkin. "Well, if I was," she muttered, "I've done an abysmal job of it. Rather than sharing a breakfast table together with dozens of other people, we're taking tea, just the two of us, in an otherwise empty room."

His mouth quirked. "Scandalous."

It was. Oh, but it was. Stella's thumping heart told her so.

That didn't mean she wished to draw attention to the fact. The less fuss they made over this situation, the better. And in the end, what damage could it really do? They were merely two guests at a respectable house party. Cordial and indifferent acquaintances brought together by chance. Surely any danger in their being of the opposite sex was outweighed by the obligations of civility?

He'd said he was on his own and desirous of company. It would have been churlish for Stella to dart off and leave him here, absent the assistance of a companion or servant.

But she recognized the danger. And not only the danger posed by his offer to paint her, but the very real danger posed by the mere fact of being in his presence.

It was too easy to talk with him. Too easy to share things she oughtn't. Good Lord, she'd already discussed coloring her hair, and told him about her old governess, and about her brother and Miss

Trent. Heaven only knew what else Stella would confide if she remained in his company much longer.

She finished blotting the spilled tea. "We've done nothing worthy of remark. The door is open. So are the curtains. And it's only tea and sandwiches."

"And cake," he added. "Don't forget the cake."

She glanced at him with a flash of humor. "Yes, I suspect the cake *is* taking things rather too far."

He smiled back at her. The movement lit his face, softening the sharp edges and making him appear at once more handsome and infinitely more dangerous. *This* was the countenance of a gentleman who could do more than persuade a lady to submit to his painting her. This was the countenance of a man who could persuade a lady to do *anything*.

Stella had to remind herself to resume her duties as hostess. She reached for the small silver pitcher on the tray. "Do you take milk? Or do you prefer lemon?"

"Milk, if you please," he said.

She added milk to both of their cups. It seemed a shame to pollute the Darjeeling. Its fragrance was as delicate as the finest perfume. The footman had told them it was the Earl of March's own special blend, made from the first flush of tea harvested in the spring.

"You needn't have avoided me, you know," Mr. Hayes said. "All I did was ask to paint your portrait. I'd never do you actual harm."

She sat down the pitcher. "The harm is in the temptation. By that measure, it's already been done."

"Then you *are* tempted to sit for me?"

"It makes no difference if I am. I couldn't possibly submit to such a thing. You must know that. Ladies don't pose for portraits."

"Rubbish," he said. "Loads of ladies do just that. Mrs. Polidori. Mrs. Millais. Not to mention the Queen."

"Isn't Mrs. Polidori Mr. Rossetti's aunt or some such thing? And

Mrs. Millais . . ." Stella helped herself to one of the thinly sliced cheese sandwiches. "Much as I may sympathize with her situation, one can hardly tout her as an example of a respectable lady."

Mrs. Millais's marriage to her first husband, the famed art critic Mr. Ruskin, had been annulled eight years ago, creating a shameful scandal. Her subsequent marriage to painter John Everett Millais had done little to quiet society's outrage, no matter that the pair were now properly settled with five children to their name.

"As for the Queen," Stella went on. "You can't compare the actions of the sovereign to that of an ordinary lady in private life."

"What about Mrs. Bowes? Mrs. Dickens? Mrs. Sutherland?" He rattled off a litany of examples.

Stella didn't know the half of them, but she recognized what they had in common. "Married ladies all. Their portraits were likely commissioned by their husbands. Or *for* their husbands."

"That doesn't mean young ladies of your class don't occasionally submit to being painted. Fathers commission portraits of their daughters all the time." He raised his teacup to his lips. The delicate, controlled movement served to emphasize the unmistakable strength in his hand. There were smudges of paint on his fingers, and calluses that were no doubt from maneuvering his chair. It was the hand of a gentleman who wasn't a stranger to hard work. One who could be as powerful as he was precise.

Stella's stomach fluttered. Forcing herself to look away, she ate in silence for a moment. She'd waited too long to sate her hunger. If she didn't pacify it now, she risked fainting. Such was the danger of corsets these days. Or, in any event, the danger of the new gowns she'd purchased from Mr. Malik before leaving London. They were as graceful as they were unforgiving, requiring that she lace her stays nearly a full two inches tighter.

The one she wore now was made of simple, untrimmed blue wool. But there was never anything simple about Mr. Malik's designs. They were tailored as artfully as a love letter to the female form, emphasizing every dip and swell with an elegance that bordered on the sensual.

Had Mr. Hayes noticed? But of course, he must have. There was nothing his eyes didn't see, even if he *was* only regarding her for artistic purposes.

She took another bite of her sandwich, washing it down with a drink of her tea. The Darjeeling was lighter and more delicate than her usual blend of Assam. Floral and crisp, and wholly unique. It felt decadent to be drinking it.

"I haven't a father any longer," she said as she blotted her mouth with her napkin. "I suppose my brother might commission a portrait of me in theory, but he never would in fact. And even if he did for some crack-brained reason, he'd never hire a handsome young painter for the job. Certainly not one with revolutionary ideas about the purpose of art."

Mr. Hayes's teacup froze halfway to his mouth. He arched a brow. "*Handsome?*"

Stella blinked. Good heavens! Had she said that part aloud?

But she wouldn't be sorry for it. She'd spoken the truth. There was no shame in that.

She lowered her napkin to her lap, carefully smoothing it back into place. "Has no one ever said so before?"

"No one whose opinion mattered." His smile held a glint of masculine amusement. The expression was at odds with the one in his eyes. His blue-gray gaze was unusually grave. "Thank you for that."

She shrugged one shoulder in a casual dismissal that she didn't really feel as she resumed eating.

So, she was the first lady to describe him as handsome. It seemed rather poetic, considering that he was the first gentleman who had ever called her beautiful. Indeed, the first who'd ever professed to notice anything about her at all, other than her one glaring flaw.

Unlike her friends, Stella had never before been the object of masculine interest. She'd garnered no offers during her seasons in

London. No attention—at least, none of the positive kind. Her sole moment of notoriety had arisen, not from her beauty, her wit, or even her riding skills, but from the anonymous rude verse a gentleman had penned about her hair.

> *Behold the Gray Lady as she enters the room;*
> *A husband-seeking specter who'll lead you to your doom.*
> *Pallid face, pallid charms, and your grandmother's hair;*
> *Neither suitable for marriage or a fleeting affair.*
> *What man will she catch in her silvery net?*
> *No chap exists who is that desperate yet!*

It had gone on from there, with increasing ribaldry.

A mortifying recollection. Stella had laughed at it at the time, recognizing that there were many in society who mistook cruelty for cleverness. What else could one do but laugh? She wasn't the sort to weep, or to hide, or to indulge in excessive episodes of self-pity. But by God, it had *hurt*. She'd been humiliated. Disappointed. Heartbroken, in truth, for that thoughtless verse had destroyed all hopes of romance during her first season. It had confirmed what she'd always feared—that no gentleman was capable of seeing past the alarming prospect of her hair.

Not until now.

And Mr. Hayes wasn't just any gentleman. He was well traveled. He was clever. And he was talented. Alarmingly talented, if his current painting was to judge.

Her curiosity about him grew by the minute.

How was it that he found himself confined to a chair at his age? Had he taken a fall from his horse? Suffered a carriage accident? Or had he always been in this chair? Was it as much a part of him as the clothes he wore?

It didn't matter.

It *shouldn't* matter.

Nevertheless . . .

She helped herself to a slice of cake. "May I ask how you—"

"Scarlet fever," he said brusquely.

She inwardly winced. "I'm sorry. I wasn't going to—"

"You weren't going to ask me how I ended up in this chair?" His smile remained, but it was no longer edged with amusement. "It's no matter. I've nothing to hide." He sat down his teacup. "I took a fever four and a half years ago. In the aftermath, my spine was affected, and then, ultimately, the muscles in my legs. They weakened considerably, so much so that they're all but useless to me now."

Stella felt like an absolute monster for having broached the subject. Drat her curiosity! "I'm sorry," she said again, chastened. "It's none of my business."

It was his turn to shrug. The movement was as unpersuasive in its dismissal as her own shrug had been. "I told you," he said. "I have nothing to hide. My condition is plain for anyone to see."

There was nothing plain about it. Even his explanation was, Stella suspected, a vast understatement of the events that had left him reliant on a wheeled chair. Only the severest of fevers could affect the use of one's limbs. She had seen that firsthand during her many years of accompanying her brother as he ministered to the sick.

"Yes, of course," she said. "I only asked because I feared . . ."

Mr. Hayes's jaw tensed almost imperceptibly. There was an expression in his eyes that was hard to read. "What?"

"I feared it had been caused by a horse," she blurted out. "Which would have been dreadful indeed."

A bewildered look crossed his face. "Worse than scarlet fever?"

"Yes." She briefly closed her eyes on a silent groan. "I mean, no. Obviously."

"What *do* you mean?"

"I'm a horsewoman," she said.

He stared at her from across the table. "Another puzzling non sequitur. Am I to conclude that you're fond of horses? Therefore, an injury caused by a horse would be—"

"Dreadful indeed," she repeated lamely. She moved to set aside her napkin, leaving her cake and tea unfinished. The best thing she could do now would be to go. She'd already offended him beyond bearing.

But Mr. Hayes's sharp eyes kept her pinned to her seat. The wry amusement in his face gradually returned. "A horsewoman," he said. "A real one? Or merely the sort that's led about on an aged pony by her long-suffering groom?"

Stella relaxed a fraction. She recognized when she was being teased. "I don't ride an aged pony. I have a mare. A spirited one. Her name is Locket. She's by Stockwell. You may have heard of him."

Mr. Hayes regarded her intently. "I haven't."

"He was a famous racing stallion. Gray, like Locket. Quite spirited, too. Locket inherited the worst of his temperament, I fear. She can't be ridden by just anyone."

"But you can ride her?"

"Oh yes. Some have called her dangerous, but for me, she goes like a dream. The slightest pressure of my leg and she's off, fast as quicksilver, as though she has the same wings I used to draw on my horses as a girl. I've never felt anything like it on this earth. The untrammeled power! The sheer freedom! It makes me want to gallop forever. And Locket never tires. She'd run her heart out if—"

"Do you always sparkle so brilliantly when you talk about your horse?" he interrupted.

Stella broke off, belatedly recalling where she was—and with whom she was speaking. Her cheeks heated. "I don't know," she said, abashed. "Probably. Was I rambling?"

"You were glowing."

"Was I?" She smiled, a little self-conscious. "I daresay I get as exercised about horses as you do about art."

Mr. Hayes didn't seem to hear her. His attention was wholly focused on her face, as though he'd been entranced by something he found there. "This is how I would paint you," he said gruffly.

A rush of heat flooded through her. That a man should look at her so! "Mr. Hayes—"

"Teddy."

"Teddy, then," she said. "I've already told you it's impossible. My brother would have an apoplexy. There's nothing more to say on the subject."

"Then . . . may I sketch you, at least?"

She opened her mouth.

He forged ahead before she could offer another objection. "I would use pencil, not paint. And you may keep the sketch afterward. You could tear it up if you like. Burn it. Whatever you will. There'd be no possible danger of it harming your reputation."

Stella lapsed into uncertain silence. A sketch? Something that would be hers and hers alone?

She was tempted. Dangerously tempted. She longed to see herself as he did. As some brilliant, glowing star that could dazzle a person at first sight.

And it *was* only a pencil sketch he was proposing. Surely that could do no harm? Not if she burned it after he was finished?

She came to an abrupt decision. "Very well," she said. "I'll allow it."

Teddy's handsome, clever face spread into a grin. There was relief in his eyes. It was coupled with an unmistakable flash of triumph.

She at once understood why. It wasn't only a pencil sketch, was it? Indeed, it wasn't a sketch at all. It was an apple in the proverbial garden. He'd finally coaxed her into taking the first bite. All that remained was for her to devour the rest of it.

And Stella was ravenous.

Nine

❦

Stella was late to her rendezvous with Teddy the following day. It wasn't because she'd had a change of heart. Despite the doubts that had plagued her through the night, and continued to follow her into the morning, she was keenly aware of the honor he'd bestowed on her by asking her to sit for him.

Altogether *too* aware.

As a consequence, on returning to her room after a chilly morning ride with Anne and Mr. Hartford, Stella had lingered far too long at her toilette. She'd washed with lilac-scented soap, chosen her gown with care, and spent long minutes in front of her dressing table, carefully concealing her gray hair beneath her borrowed black crepe-and-lace morning cap. It wasn't every day one posed for a portrait, after all, even if it was only a sketch.

But when Stella at last entered the private parlor, nearly ten minutes past the appointed time of their meeting, Teddy didn't seem to register the extra effort she'd put into her appearance. Busy assembling his art supplies, he spared her only a fleeting glance. "Take a seat in the chair by the window, if you please."

A dainty shield-back chair, made of sinuously carved elm, had been positioned there at an angle. It would give him a view of her face in three-quarter profile.

Stella went to it and sat down. She arranged the full skirts of her gown about her legs. It was one of the most flattering day dresses she'd commissioned from Mr. Malik. Made of mazarine blue silk, it was trimmed with black passementerie and boasted a high neckline, wide cord-edged sleeves worn over crisp, white muslin undersleeves, and a dainty cord-and-silk belt that buckled neatly at her waist. It had taken Stella ages to close the tiny row of black cord-covered buttons that ran down the bodice's snug front—a task she'd never have managed if her corset hadn't been cinched so dashed tightly.

"I'm sorry I'm late," she said.

"You're here, that's what's important." Teddy continued lining up his supplies on an inlaid table beside his easel. Unlike Stella, he didn't appear to have put any effort into his appearance. Quite the opposite. He was rather underdressed.

His coat had been discarded over the back of the settee, leaving him in his shirtsleeves. His cuffs were partially rolled up—a practical action, given his occupation, but one that revealed a scandalous expanse of leanly muscled forearm.

Stella made an effort not to stare. "I was out riding with Lady Anne and Mr. Hartford," she told him.

She'd borrowed a placid little gelding from the earl's stable. It had been nothing to riding Locket, but it was still riding. The exercise had done her a wealth of good.

"As I observed," he said.

"You saw me?"

"I saw all of you setting out this morning. I've a perfect view of the stable yard from the window of my room."

Stella frowned. His tone was unusually opaque. She couldn't tell if he was irritated or indifferent or . . . something else.

Did it bother him to see others engaging in an activity that he could no longer engage in himself? Surely not. If that was the case, he wouldn't have attended the opening night ball, would he?

"We'll be going out again later," she said. "Lady Anne and Mr.

Hartford have got a smallish party together to visit the ruins at Odiham Castle. You might join us if you like."

He flicked her a dry glance. "On horseback?"

"No, of course not. We're taking carriages. It isn't terribly far, I believe."

"When is this thrilling expedition meant to take place?"

"At half past eleven. Will that give you enough time to complete your sketch?"

"No."

"Oh." Stella hadn't expected him to be so definite. Talented as he was, this was only a rough sketch he was making, not a masterwork. How long could it truly take? Her own sketches rarely required more than an hour. "I suppose I could—"

"We'll have to meet again," he said brusquely.

An unexpected rush of girlish giddiness rose in her breast. She realized, in that moment, just how much she wanted to meet him again.

And again, and again.

Never mind that it was ill-advised. That it may be, potentially, hazardous to her reputation. It was wonderful to have a gentleman's undivided attention. She was parched for the lack of it.

And not just any gentleman.

Teddy Hayes's attention meant something. He wasn't some insensitive society coxcomb or some boorish country squire. He was thoughtful. Discerning. He'd studied art in Paris, for heaven's sake.

Stella managed to keep her countenance. "Very well. When do you propose?"

"Tomorrow morning," he said.

Her spirits sank a little. Much as she'd like to meet him in the morning, her remaining two days at the house party weren't wholly her own. She was here as Anne's guest, not as a guest in her own right. It was to Anne that Stella owed the bulk of her time. Especially now.

Knowing that Stella was limited to activities where she wouldn't draw attention to herself in covering her hair, Anne had planned for a surfeit of outdoor amusements. Not only riding and visiting nearby places of historic interest, but sledding and sleighing, too.

Stella couldn't absent herself from the very activities that had been arranged with her in mind. "The afternoon would be better," she said. "If that's convenient."

"The entire afternoon? Or only another hour?"

"I can't promise the whole afternoon. Lady Anne may have need of me."

"May she, indeed. In that case, we'd better begin." Opening his sketchbook, he selected a pencil from the row of supplies beside him as solemnly as a Roman gladiator choosing a weapon for the arena. "If you would be so good as to look in the direction of the clock," he said. "And lift your chin a fraction."

Stella obeyed his directions. She could no longer easily see what he was doing, except for a glimpse out of the corner of her eye. The whisper of his pencil grazing softly over the paper tickled her ears. "Must I be silent?"

"On the contrary. You must tell me about your horse."

She smiled. "You wish me to glow again, I perceive."

"That's the idea."

It was easier said than done. She was unused to making meaningful conversation on command. It was one thing to engage in mindless small talk. *That* she could do in her sleep. But to expound on the subject she loved best, wholly to produce some ephemeral change in her countenance, was quite another matter.

"Well?" he prompted. The question was punctuated by another scrape of his pencil.

"I'm deciding what to say," she answered. "I confess, I feel a bit foolish. Is there anything particular you wish to know about Locket?"

"Where do you keep her?"

"In London, when I'm there."

"And the remainder of the time?"

"At home in Derbyshire. My brother and I have a cottage near his church. There's an old barn and paddock attached to it. Locket is there now, waiting for me to return. My groom's old gelding, Crab, keeps her company. They're the only horses at present."

"You keep no carriage horses?"

"We keep no carriage. My brother feels it would be unseemly for a clergyman in his position."

"Yet he escorts you to London for two consecutive seasons?"

"He hasn't a choice." Stella stared fixedly at the clock. She was already prone to speaking too freely when in company with Teddy Hayes. The steady scraping of his pencil loosened her tongue still further. "My father left a small portion for me in his will. Part of it is mine absolutely. The remainder was held in reserve, designated specifically for my launch into society. My brother could either carry out the duty of chaperoning me himself or hire a companion to do so, with funds from his own pocket."

"So, it's a matter of economy," Teddy observed.

"Something like that," Stella said.

Exactly that, in fact.

Daniel was an excessively frugal man. If it were up to him, Stella would have voluntarily relinquished her portion long ago. Even now, more than ten years after the unfortunate loss of their father, he still made occasional remarks about how her meager funds would be better spent in helping the poor.

Or in helping to support Daniel's own hobby.

Though her brother would never admit to it being such. It was a calling, he said. A long-winded treatise he was writing on the modern manifestations of original sin. He'd been working on it for more than seven years. Stella had often played secretary for him during his endeavors, transcribing his notes and assisting with his research.

"Is it economical to keep two horses?" Teddy asked as he worked.

"It would be cruel not to. Horses are herd animals. They do best with other horses nearby. Anyway, it's nothing to do with my brother."

Teddy flashed her an interested glance.

Stella felt the inquiring look as much as saw it. "I subsidize her stabling expenses myself," she explained. "The income from my inheritance isn't very large, but it's enough to keep Locket in relative comfort, and to afford the expenses of her groom and his mount. That's all I require."

"She means that much to you?"

"She means everything to me."

"More than your own independence?"

"Locket gives me independence. More than I'd have in any other circumstances."

"I can think of a few circumstances where you might have more," he said as he resumed his sketching.

Stella was aware of them. She'd thought of them often enough. "Only marriage and widowhood. And, unfortunately, the latter state can only be arrived at by the former. As far as anything else . . ." Her brows knit. "An unmarried young lady can't keep a house for herself. Not without a chaperone of some sort. Even then, it would be considered wildly peculiar."

"Your chaperone needn't be a chaperone in fact," Teddy replied. "Before my sister's marriage to Mr. Archer, she and I lived under the care of our old aunt Charlotte. But it was my sister who ran the household. Aunt Charlotte was merely there to lend us countenance."

"I don't have an aunt Charlotte, regrettably. There's only my brother. And now that my second season is at an end . . ." She couldn't finish the thought. Not out loud.

The scratch of Teddy's pencil went quiet on the page. There was an uncomfortable silence.

Stella chanced a look in his direction. But she didn't find him looking back at her with concern. He was glaring down at his sketch-book, scowling at the page as though vexed by something he saw there.

As she watched, he retrieved a piece of Indian rubber from his row of supplies and used it to erase part of the sketch. It wasn't a very promising development, if his expression was to judge.

"What will you do?" he asked distractedly.

Stella stared back at the clock. She had no desire to discuss her lack of options. Not with Teddy or anyone. Certainly not when he wasn't wholly attending to what she was saying.

She didn't want to think about the bleakness of her future. The house party was meant to be a respite from all that, if not an outright solution. One last chance for pleasure and merriment before it must all come to an end.

And it must.

The provision in her father's will didn't stretch to a third season.

"I will return to Derbyshire," she said.

"After which . . . ?"

Stella set her shoulders. "There is no 'after which.'"

Teddy once again raised his head. He was troubled by what Stella had been telling him. By the prospect that, in a very short while, she'd be retiring to Derbyshire, permanently out of his reach. But, at the moment, something else troubled him far more.

He held his sketch pad an arm's length away from him, hoping that a bit of perspective might improve his opinion of his progress.

It didn't.

A building irritation rapidly soured his mood. Something wasn't right. Here she was at last, his luminous star, seated in front of him, a willing subject—for today and tomorrow, at least. And he couldn't capture her. Not the way he wanted.

This time, it wasn't the light that was at issue. It wasn't even the information she'd been imparting, grim as it was. It was something else. Something he couldn't quite put his finger on.

Seeming to sense his growing displeasure, Stella again turned her head. A guarded expression came over her. She'd plainly realized that she'd said too much—confided too much. Unmarried ladies weren't meant to converse so freely with unmarried gentlemen. "What is it?" she asked. "What's the matter?"

He chewed the inside of his cheek. "I'm not sure."

"Is it something I've said?"

"No."

"What, then?"

"It's . . ." He studied her face, his frown deepening. She had on the same black crepe cap she'd been wearing yesterday, and like yesterday, it masked the entirety of her hair. Teddy wasn't one to comment on the vagaries of ladies' fashion. Even so . . . "Why have you taken to wearing that dreadful cap?"

Some of the color drained from her face. She touched a self-conscious hand to the dull black ribbons that trimmed the offending article. "It's not dreadful."

"It is," he assured her.

"Many ladies wear caps indoors."

"Only matrons and aged spinsters. Neither of which you are."

"I *am* a spinster," she said. "Technically. And I like the way it looks. I think it's rather stylish."

"It's rather hideous, is what it is," he replied frankly. "I trust you didn't pay overmuch for it."

"I didn't pay anything for it. I-I borrowed it from Lady Arundell."

That explained the dour color and the old-fashioned style, but it didn't explain Stella's reason for wearing it. The Countess of Arundell was a stately older lady who existed in a perpetual air of mourning. Stella was practically a child by comparison, and not one who had any reason to mourn, not so far as Teddy was aware.

"You'll have to remove it," he said. "It's covering all of your hair."

She recoiled at the suggestion. "What difference does *that* make? You don't approve of my new hair color anyway."

"No, I don't. But I'd rather see your hair as not."

"I'd prefer you didn't. Unless . . ." She went paler still. "Must you?"

"If I'm to get this sketch right, yes. There's a lack of balance and proportion because of it. I couldn't discern what the issue was until now. I need the whole of you, unaltered by"—he pointed his pencil at her head—"whatever that is."

Stella bit her lip. Her eyes flicked anxiously to the open door of the parlor. The hall outside was silent. There was no one about. No servants, and certainly no guests. Not in this part of the house. Not unless summoned specifically.

She slowly untied the ribbons of her cap. "Very well," she said. "But you mustn't say anything."

"What else is there to say? I've already seen your hair. It isn't as though—" Teddy broke off as she slipped the crepe-layered atrocity from her head. His jaw threatened to drop.

Bound up in a neatly plaited roll at her nape, her hair was once again the color of fine sterling: beautiful, lustrous, and uniformly gray.

He gaped at her. "When did *that*—?"

"The night of the dance," she said shortly. "The auburn dye washed out unexpectedly. That's why I've taken to wearing a cap indoors. It's the only way to disguise it."

His mouth went dry. "I see."

"And if you make a single unkind remark—"

"I wouldn't," he said. "I haven't."

"No, but I can tell what you're thinking. You're thinking—"

"It's lovely," he interrupted hoarsely. "Just as it was the first day I saw you."

She huffed. "Yes, I daresay."

"I'm not quizzing you, Stella."

She met his eyes. Whatever she saw there seemed to reassure her.

The color gradually returned to her face. "Well . . ." She folded the cap in her lap with restless fingers. "You're odd, as we've established."

His mouth pulled into a brief smile. "Would you . . . ?" He motioned to the clock.

She was still visibly flustered. She nevertheless dutifully resumed her pose.

He turned the page of his sketchbook to a blank sheet and started his outline anew. His pulse was racing. This was the shining star he'd seen in the King's Gallery. The vision that had plagued his every waking hour, and his dreaming hours, too. He felt a decided sense of urgency, afraid the moment would once again slip through his fingers before he'd committed her image to paper.

By God, a sketch wasn't enough. A single oil portrait wouldn't be enough. Here was a lady who could inspire a dozen canvases. The Pleiades. The moonlight. The stars over a raging seascape that would put Turner to shame. Teddy wanted to paint her in every light. In every mood.

But *want* was too weak a word.

He *had* to paint her.

"This is, I take it, the reason you haven't been at table these past several days?" he said. "Or at the dance?"

"It is," she admitted. "There wasn't time to have a fashionable morning cap made in the village. And I couldn't borrow one from any of the other guests without raising suspicion. Lady Arundell's cap was the best I could manage. I'm fully aware it does me no favors."

"You still might have come to dinner or—"

"On no account. I may be reduced to roaming the remote corridors of Sutton Park with my hair covered in a borrowed matron's cap, but I'd as soon not expose myself to the other guests at a meal, or a ball, or over a hand of cards. They'd find it as strange as you did. I'd be thought an absolute eccentric."

"There are worse things in life."

"Any number of things, I'm sure. That doesn't make this any less problematic. An unmarried young lady can't afford to be thought peculiar. She can't afford to be obtrusive at all."

"You'd rather be ordinary?"

"What I'd rather be," she said, "is inconspicuous."

He gave her a sharp glance.

How often had he felt the same? That the very fact of being different had put him under a painful variety of scrutiny? He didn't aspire to ordinariness. Far from it. But conspicuousness was a loathsome alternative. If Teddy was to be recognized at all, he'd rather it be for his skill with a brush and pencils than for the fact that he was a young man, in the very prime of life, stuck in a wheeled chair. His injury wasn't the whole of him. It wasn't even the most interesting part. It irked him to no end that, to some people, it was the only thing worthy of noticing.

Is that how Stella felt about her hair? Is that why she desired to be ordinary?

"Were you so inconspicuous before?" he asked. "Unless . . . You weren't born with this hair color, were you?"

"No, indeed. When I was a girl, my hair was a plain, nondescript mouse brown. The color didn't begin to change until I was fifteen. By sixteen, I was completely gray."

"And you've no idea why it happened?"

"The village doctor offered suggestions. So did my brother. But they neither of them understood the why of it any better than I did. All I know is that it's come to define me. It's the first thing people notice. Often the only thing."

"Do you care so much what people think of you?" Teddy asked. It was the very question he'd frequently posed to himself.

"I wish I didn't," she said. "But I must."

"Because you're in search of a husband." He was unable to disguise his disdain.

Stella responded to his tone with a faint smile of amusement.

"You refer to my efforts with contempt. And yet, you must eventually marry."

"Must I?"

"Every gentleman does eventually."

"I won't," Teddy said bluntly. "I have no wish for a wife."

She flashed him a surprised look. "What? Never?"

"I'm not the marrying sort."

She returned to staring at the clock. He could tell what she was thinking. She assumed it had something to do with his chair.

And perhaps it did. To be sure, it was a large part of the reason he'd vowed to remain a bachelor. But it wasn't the entirety of it.

"I'm too fastidious and particular," he said, answering the question she'd been too polite to ask. "A wife would only get in the way of my painting. Either that or she'd bore me. And I despise being bored, almost as much as I despise having my work interrupted."

"A wife's purpose isn't to entertain a husband. She's meant to be a helpmeet."

"A helpmeet," he repeated. "Just what I've always desired—said no man ever."

"My brother has said so."

"Your brother is a clergyman."

"A clergyman can't be so different from other men."

"I can't speak to the inclinations of all men," Teddy said, "only for my own."

"What about love?" she asked.

"Ah. Love. That old fairy tale." He chuckled to himself, recalling the ridiculous infatuation he'd suffered in his youth. "I can personally confirm that it isn't all it's cracked up to be."

She flashed him an odd look. "You've been in love before?"

"I thought so at the time. I was but a lad. And she—"

"A French girl?"

"English to her core. Her name was Henrietta Talbot. She had golden ringlets, a dimpled smile, and all the charm of a provincial petty tyrant." He paused. "She was our near neighbor in Surrey. Most of the gentlemen thereabouts fell in love with her at one time or another. It was practically a rite of passage."

"What happened?"

"I grew up," he said. "End of story."

"That isn't the end. You could still meet someone else one day. Someone you liked better."

"No, thank you. I'm looking to decrease the amount of interfering people in my life, not augment their numbers. By this time next year, I shall be wholly independent—no family, no overbearing friends, and certainly no wife."

"Independence is a state greatly to be desired," Stella replied solemnly. "Alas, a lady in my circumstances must be realistic."

"Which means—?"

"Which means that self-delusion serves no purpose on the marriage mart. A young lady must acknowledge her weaknesses, however discomfiting they are. She must understand how she rates in the scheme of London society and formulate her plans accordingly."

Teddy couldn't hide his disappointment at her pronouncements. She hadn't struck him as a wallflower, cringing about at the edges of society. Not on any of the occasions he'd observed her. She'd seemed singular. Remarkable. "In other words," he said, "a young lady must know her place."

His disapproving tone brought the smile back to Stella's lips.

She briefly turned to meet his eyes. The cold light from the window sparkled in the thick plaits of her silver hair, making her appear, for an instant, every inch the starry goddess he'd imagined her. "Know it, yes," she said. "That doesn't mean she must accept it."

Ten

❧—❧

I suppose the announcement of Mr. Neale's parentage could have gone worse," Anne said the next morning as she and Stella tramped up the snow-covered hill that rose alongside the woods bordering Sutton Park.

It was the same hill that Stella had found Teddy painting on Christmas, topped by the same aged oak tree. A perfect hill for sledding.

The other guests marched ahead through the snow, sleds in hand, all of them snugly wrapped up in heavy coats, scarves, and fur-trimmed cloaks. Mr. Hartford walked along with them, carrying Anne's and Stella's sleds. He was courteous enough to give the two friends a semblance of privacy as they talked.

"I wish I could have been there to lend my support," Stella said.

She'd excused herself from dinner again last night, in favor of a tray in her room. It had meant missing the announcement about Mr. Neale. Stella had been excoriating herself over it all morning. She'd never in her life abdicated a duty to one of her friends. And to have done so solely on account of her hair! It was unforgivable.

"My dear," Anne replied. "Don't distress yourself. There was nothing you could have done."

"Of course there was. I could have stood in solidarity with you and Mr. Hartford. And I could have glared down anyone foolish enough to engage in malicious whispering. You've said yourself that there's no greater defense against gossip than a united front of friends and family."

"I appreciate your willingness, but safeguarding your reputation is far more important at this stage. We've come this far without anyone realizing your hair has changed color. We've only another day to get through."

"Yes, but still—"

"But nothing. I'll not have you raking yourself over the coals on account of this." Anne linked her arm through Stella's. "The announcement was all very perfunctory, in any case. The earl rolled it in as a matter of course when he stood to thank various far-flung guests for having made the journey to Hampshire. *'Thank you to the Bedlows for traveling from Cardiff, and to the Archers for coming all the way from Grasse. And many thanks to my natural grandson, Mr. Neale, for having joined us on the eve of his departure to Inverness.'"*

"His *natural* grandson?"

"That's how he phrased it. A perfect description, to my mind. Not at all tawdry."

Stella wasn't so sure. Calling someone a natural child was just a polite way of stating that the child was a bastard. No one at dinner would have mistaken the meaning. "How did everyone react?"

"Lord Brookdale and his wife were pinch faced but resigned. The earl was pale but determined. And Mama was perfectly marvelous. She raised her glass to Mr. Neale, the dear. As for the rest of the guests . . . they were fit to burst with excitement at the news. I suspect the earl will find himself short of ink and paper by tomorrow's end, with all of them writing to their friends in London to spread the news. People love a good scandal."

Stella's lips compressed with disapproval. "How dreadful of them.

Especially after enjoying the earl's hospitality. You'd think they'd exhibit more loyalty."

"Their letters will do naught but aid the situation," Anne said. "This sort of scandal can only be blunted by sunlight, and the more of it, the better. Once everybody knows, it will fade into memory. Another scandal will soon come to take its place."

Stella cast a concerned glance at Mr. Hartford. Snowflakes swirled about his tall frame, landing lightly on his dark wool overcoat, as he climbed up the path ahead of them. "How is he?"

"Cheerful in the face of adversity, as ever."

"And how are you? You're not upset or—"

"No, indeed. It would take more than a familial scandal to put me out of countenance." Anne gave Stella's arm an affectionate squeeze. "It's *I* who should be asking after *you*, not the other way around. I hate leaving you on your own so much. It wasn't at all part of the plan in inviting you here. You were meant to be enjoying yourself."

"I was meant to be thwarting my brother's matrimonial campaign for Miss Trent," Stella said.

"In that, at least, you will have been successful."

"A fleeting success, I fear. Daniel is bound to marry someone eventually, if not Miss Trent, then another young lady. Now he's thirty, he says that he must, or else risk the displeasure of his parishioners."

Anne's sturdy boots crunched over the snow. "What have they to do with it?"

"Many of them believe that to be unmarried is to be unnatural. It's why Daniel would rather I wed Squire Smalljoy than remain his spinster sister. The villagers don't like spinsters. I daresay they suspect us of being up to no good."

"Another reason you shouldn't remain in Fostonbury."

"Small-minded people aren't limited to remote Derbyshire

villages," Stella pointed out. "They reside in every corner of the realm."

"And they're all of them frightened of women with power," Anne stated unequivocally.

"By that measure, they've no need to be frightened of me at all. I haven't any power to speak of."

"Nonsense. You still have the power of choice."

Stella cast her friend a half-smiling look. Anne was descended from a long line of formidable aristocrats. She'd never yet met a problem she couldn't conquer through sheer, blue-blooded strength of will. It was unfathomable to her that anyone could find themselves a true victim of circumstances.

"If only I could choose without consequence," Stella said. "And without regard to the limitations of my pocketbook." She gazed out at the snow for a moment in frowning contemplation. "I tried to befriend her, you know."

Anne drew Stella closer against the morning chill. "Who? Miss Trent?"

"When we met in Exeter. Her bearing seemed sweet enough on first acquaintance, and she's of a similar age to us. But she didn't want to be friends. All she wanted was my brother, and to be rid of me in the bargain. We'd not been alone together ten minutes before she was advising me on altering my behavior—*and* urging me to give up Locket."

"No!"

Stella's mouth twisted in a bitter smile. "Miss Trent takes my riding as a personal affront."

Anne was incredulous. "She objects to horses?"

"She objects to the expense."

"An expense you subsidize out of your own inheritance," Anne retorted indignantly.

"Exactly. She'd rather I let my brother have my income for good works than waste it on my own selfish pleasures."

Anne snorted. "Good works, my eye. What she really means is that if your brother had your money, he might keep a carriage and hire more servants. She could then swan about the village like the lady of the manor."

Stella suspected Anne was right. "One can't blame her for looking out for her own interests."

"She could at least be honest about it," Anne said. "Instead, she cloaks her self-interest in a shroud of piety and virtue, which she then uses as an excuse to lecture you on your behavior. *You!* The dearest and sweetest among us! As far as I'm concerned, your brother is well shot of her."

Stella pressed Anne's arm in wordless acknowledgment of her praise. "I'm just relieved I no longer have to worry over having her as my sister-in-law. She'll have returned to Exeter by now. With luck, my brother's affections will cool in her absence, and he'll never mention her more."

"One can hope," Anne said. They passed beneath the snow-laden branches of a tree. "I only wish you could have had a better time while you were here. It seems to have been one catastrophe after another, hasn't it?"

"It hasn't been all bad. I've had great fun riding and visiting the ruins. And today's sledding is sure to be one of the highlights of my stay."

"There will be sleighing tonight, too, if the snow is deep enough for it."

Stella brightened. There were few things more enjoyable than flying across the snow in a horse-drawn sleigh, the moon shining bright above. "How wonderful!"

"It is. Still . . . It's not a romance." Anne exchanged a meaningful look with Stella. "You'd hoped to meet someone during your stay."

"As to that—"

"Though, I don't suppose there was anyone here to spark your interest," Anne went on. "Not unless you count Mr. Hayes."

Stella tensed. "What about Mr. Hayes?"

"He's an interesting fellow."

"Yes, but . . . not in a romantic way." Not unless Stella thought about his hands. Or the intensity in his eyes. Or the broadness in his shoulders. Not unless she recalled the compliments he'd lavished on her.

"I only meant that he's rather amusing," Anne said. "Charming, in fact, if one can dismiss his youth and chronic insolence."

Stella laughed. Teddy *was* insolent. And young. And arrogant. He was also clever, and talented, and entirely self-assured.

He knew how to be quiet, too. Something Stella appreciated, as much in a friend as she did in a gentleman. Much of the time Teddy had spent sketching her had been in silence. A silence punctuated by the sound of his pencil scraping, and the steadiness of his breath. She'd been still, too. Never mind that the regular weight of his gaze on her had raised her temperature by several degrees.

If Teddy had experienced a similar disruption in body heat, he hadn't betrayed it. They'd parted yesterday with no more compliments on his part, nor even any particular sense of warmth. No. His warmth had been reserved for his sketch. He was still toiling over it with that same fever-bright intensity when she left him. He'd looked up just once as she'd walked out the door of the parlor, and only to remind her of her promise to return the following day.

Stella had reminded herself, then, just as she reminded herself now, that he wasn't the marrying kind. He'd made that fact abundantly plain during their session yesterday. Almost too plain. It was as though he'd wanted to put her on her guard.

Did he fear that, in her desperation to make a match, she'd set her cap for him? He was, after all, a gentleman of means. A handsome one, too. He must have had many admirers during his years on the continent.

"He was invited to come with us today," Anne said. "He's been invited on all our outings, and has consistently refused."

"Has he?"

"Mr. Hayes prefers to paint. It's why he accompanied the Archers in the first place, apparently, for Sutton Park's artistic inspiration. Lord March has given him use of a private parlor to serve as his studio for the remainder of his visit."

Stella briefly averted her gaze. Anne didn't need to know that Stella was intimately familiar with that private parlor, or that she—not Sutton Park—was currently serving as Mr. Hayes's inspiration.

"I expect he's one of those artistic people who prefer living in their own head to living in the greater world around them," Anne said. "Though it hasn't prevented him from joining us for every other entertainment. He's been in the drawing room each evening, and attended both dances in the ballroom." She gave Stella a regretful look. "I wish *you* could have danced during your stay, instead of having to hide yourself away upstairs."

"So do I," Stella said feelingly. "I'd have loved waltzing, even if it *was* only with an altruistic neighbor gentleman that Mr. Hartford had conscripted as my partner."

"It's not your last chance for romance. You shall be in London again in the spring."

Stella's smile turned quizzical. "Shall I?"

Anne's eyes twinkled back at her. "I expect you at my wedding in March."

Stella's brows swept up in astonishment. "So soon?"

"Hartford and I are set on marrying on the first day of spring. We've waited seven years to be together. We neither of us wish to wait any longer."

"But I thought it was to be a grand society affair?"

Most aristocratic weddings took months and months of planning, not to mention all the travel arrangements that must be sorted out for extended family.

"It will be," Anne said. "The earl and my mother are sparing no expense. Mama will be planning most of it. All I've insisted upon is the date, and that I must have three bridesmaids—you, Evie, and Julia."

"Oh, Anne." Stella's heart swelled. She desperately wanted to be there. And not only for her friends, but for herself.

London suited her far better than Derbyshire. Far better, indeed, than any of the rambling, remote places in the country. She and Locket were made for town living. Not the fashionable parties or the fast-paced social whirl, but for the energy and the industry. For the museums, the galleries, and the shops; and for the wild—and completely improper—gallops in the park.

"I won't take no for an answer," Anne said. She caught Mr. Hartford's eyes as they met up with the others. "Hart! Come and persuade Miss Hobhouse."

Mr. Hartford was immediately obedient to Anne's summons. He joined them on the path, his mouth tipped in a smile. "On what subject?"

"You must convince her to return to London for our wedding," Anne said.

Mr. Hartford looked at Stella, a bit surprised. "Will it take convincing?"

"No, indeed," Stella said quickly. "I want to come. It's my brother that's at issue. He won't be eager to escort me back to London so soon after we've left it. He means us to remain in Derbyshire through the summer."

Through the end of time, more like it. But Stella wasn't inclined to be specific.

"If he won't bring you," Anne said, "I'll come fetch you myself."

"You will not," Stella said. "I won't have you disrupting your wedding planning on my account."

"I mean it." Anne's face held a gleam of unchecked determination. "The instant you need me, I shall be there, come what may."

Stella felt a fierce rush of love for her friends. For Anne and for each of their sister Furies—all of whom, Stella understood, would do anything for her. "I know you will," she said.

But when the worst happened, as it was bound to eventually, Stella had no intention of summoning her friends to save her. She loved them too well to burden them.

"I shall find a way to be at your wedding," she promised Anne. "You may depend on me."

Teddy was wheeling himself to the library later that morning, hoping to have a word with his sister, when he encountered Felix Hartford in the corridor. It was the first Teddy had seen of anyone, except Jennings and Alex, since breakfast. Most of the others had gone sledding, with Stella having no doubt been among them.

Alex and Laura were among the few who had stayed behind, owing to Laura having awakened with an uneasy stomach. It was somewhat concerning. Teddy's sister was rarely in ill health. Even the enduring effects of the scarlet fever were no match for her physical determination. A keen swimmer, Laura was forever pushing herself to her limits in an effort to strengthen her lungs and improve her general well-being.

It wasn't like her to linger in bed. She didn't have the patience for it. When he'd gone to check on her earlier, Teddy hadn't been surprised to learn that she was already up and dressed, and had nipped down to the library in search of a book to relieve her boredom.

Jennings had helped Teddy down the stairs and into his chair so that Teddy might find her. The manservant remained several paces behind Teddy as Mr. Hartford approached.

"Mr. Hayes," Hartford said. "Just the man I was looking for. Are you going to the library?"

"I am," Teddy said.

Hartford held the door open for him. "Can you spare me a moment?"

"Of course." Teddy wheeled into the room. On entering, Jennings dutifully withdrew to the corner, mutely awaiting the moment Teddy would have need of him again.

The library at Sutton Park was as vast as a cathedral, with a ceiling that rose two stories high. Leather-bound books lined the walls, and groups of overstuffed chairs and sofas were arranged in quiet nooks, both on the richly carpeted lower level and in the iron-railed gallery that surrounded the library's second floor.

Some of the older guests were availing themselves of the chairs in front of the library's cavernous fireplace. To Teddy's disappointment, Laura wasn't among them.

"Sledding was enjoyable, I trust?" Teddy inquired absently as he came to a halt by the library's terrestrial globe. Cradled in a blackened mahogany stand, it was set in an alcove, far enough away from the fireplace to ensure a modicum of privacy.

"It was great fun," Hartford said. "Though most of us were woefully out of practice. We spent more time headfirst in the snow than flying over it in our sleds."

Teddy managed a smile. He used to go sledding with Laura when he was a boy. He used to do a lot of things. "I can imagine."

"I was speaking to Mr. Archer before we set out," Hartford said. "The subject of your chair came up."

Teddy stilled. He fixed Hartford with the whole of his attention. "Oh?"

"Something about the inhospitableness of the outdoor terrain—and the indoor terrain. He said it was one of the reasons you haven't joined us for any of our excursions out of doors."

"He was making excuses for me," Teddy said. "He needn't have done. I already told Lord March that I would be working through most of my stay."

"Yes, quite. Nevertheless . . ." Reaching into the inner pocket of his coat, Hartford withdrew a folded sheet of paper. "It's what put the idea into my head."

Teddy's brows lifted. It took an effort to remain polite. He didn't like people talking about his disability behind his back. Not even his family members, and not even to help him. "What idea?"

Hartford lowered his voice. "It's not widely known, and I'd prefer to keep it that way, but I invest in the odd patent. New technologies mostly, with a practical bent." He paused before elaborating. "A re-engineered independent feed pump for a locomotive engine. An improved wringing-and-mangling machine for doing the washing. Even a patent for a steam-powered horseless road vehicle."

"Fascinating," Teddy said stiffly. "What has any of that to do with me?" *Or with my chair*, he nearly added.

Hartford handed him the folded paper. "This came across my desk several months ago. Or rather, something very like this. I've attempted to draw it from memory. Forgive me. Unlike you, I'm no artist."

Teddy took the paper from him. He stared down at the image.

"It's a wheeled chair," Hartford explained. "One not unlike your own, but possessing a distinct advantage. The wheels of this chair are made of iron, not wood, and they're covered in a hollow tube of vulcanized India rubber that's filled with pressurized air."

Teddy glanced up sharply from the drawing. *"Air?"*

"Odd, I know. But the purported benefits are significant."

"What benefits?"

"A more comfortable ride, greater speed with less effort, and easier movement over troublesome surfaces. Apparently, the rubber doesn't sink into loose gravel or soft ground as readily as traditional wheels."

Teddy couldn't help but be intrigued by the possibilities. "Is that true?"

"I believe so. These wheels were inspired by an aerial carriage wheel patented some years ago. There was a demonstration of it in Regent's Park when I was a lad. A promising invention, but it never caught on. The rubber wheels were too expensive for the average carriage owner to purchase and maintain, not to mention the cost of manufacturing them. But this inventor has adapted them to a smaller scale. I imagine he hopes his idea will appeal to wealthy invalids in search of greater mobility."

Teddy's interest piqued. He wasn't wealthy by any means, but neither was he poor. The income he drew from the perfumery was a comfortable one, certainly enough to stretch to purchasing a patented wheeled chair. "Have you invested in it?" he asked.

"No. Not yet. I dismissed it, initially. It seemed too niche an invention. One ill-suited to the masses. The cost of production is exorbitant—and the proposed price even higher. Still, given the possibilities, I begin to think I was too hasty." Hartford leaned down, examining the drawing along with Teddy. "Is it something you could use?"

"Very possibly, yes."

"Would you be game to try a prototype?"

"I would." Teddy gave a short laugh. "Hell, if it does everything it claims to, I'd buy one myself."

Hartford smiled broadly. "That's all I wanted to know." He straightened. "The inventor chap is in London. He's seeking an initial investment of capital to build his first half dozen chairs. I expect, with enough funds at his disposal, he'll have them ready by the spring. Will you be in town?"

Teddy nodded. "I'm staying in Half Moon Street until the end of March. After that . . . I have no fixed address."

"But you'll still be in London?"

"I will," Teddy said categorically.

"Splendid. I'll see that you get the first prototype. Your opinions will be invaluable." Hartford took a breath. "Can I assist you with anything before I go? Fetch you a book or a—"

"I didn't come for a book," Teddy said. "I'm looking for my sister."

"Here I am." Laura's voice rang out, a trifle breathlessly. She hurried to join them from across the library, carrying a thick leather book in her hand. The full skirts of her wool day dress floated behind her as she approached. "I was in the gallery. I saw you both come in."

Mr. Hartford bowed to her. "Mrs. Archer. Mr. Hayes. If you'll excuse me."

Teddy and Laura bid him good morning.

"Nothing's wrong, is it?" Laura asked the instant she and Teddy were alone.

"Nothing at all," Teddy said. "I went to your room to check on you, and Alex told me you'd gone to fetch a book. I thought you'd be in bed."

"I've been in bed too long already this morning," she said. "Was Alex still at his letters?"

"He was." Teddy's brother-in-law had been toiling over perfumery correspondence when Teddy had left him. He'd seemed more distracted than usual, with a restless air in the scratch of his pen and a deep groove of disquiet set in his brow. "How are you feeling?"

"Better." Laura smoothed a stray lock from her temple, tucking it back beneath her lacy matron's cap. "It's strange. I was quite nauseated when I woke, but now I'm wholly myself again. It must have been something I ate."

Teddy's mouth dipped in a thoughtful frown. "Yes, I suppose it could have been."

She smiled at his seriousness. "Is that why you're here? Checking up on me? You needn't have worried, you know. Alex has been as attentive as any nurse."

"Of course I worry. But that isn't why I was looking for you." Teddy wheeled his chair beside his sister as the two of them departed the library, with Jennings following behind.

As ever, Teddy was loath to ask his family for help. He didn't like them being involved in his private business. They were too involved already. But in this case, there was no other alternative. Unless he was mistaken, Laura possessed exactly what he needed.

"I wondered," Teddy asked his sister, "if you might be inclined to do me a particular favor?"

Eleven

＊

Teddy peered over the top of his sketch pad as Stella entered the room. She was wearing another of her fashionable dresses. The same lush-textured, tight-bodiced variety of garment that had, during their last session, done inexplicable things to his pulse. The dangerous effect of it was tempered somewhat by her appalling black crepe matron's cap. Just as yesterday, it covered all of her hair, its dull black ribbons trailing about the slender column of her neck.

"Good afternoon," she said. "I hope you haven't been waiting for me?"

All my life, he was tempted to say.

It was true, wasn't it? He'd dreamed of being inspired in this way. And here she was, for but one night longer. Tomorrow she would be gone. Back to Derbyshire and out of his world forever.

He cleared his throat. "No, indeed. I'm early, as usual." He motioned to the shield-back chair. "If you would?"

"May I see it yet?" she asked, coming closer. It was the same question she'd asked yesterday.

Teddy gave her his same answer. "It isn't finished."

"I know that," she said. "I'd still like to see it. I could offer my opinions on your progress."

"This isn't a collaborative process."

"Naturally, it is. What is posing if not collaborating?"

"You sit in that chair, and you stare at that clock. That's where your part of the collaboration ends." He again motioned for her to take a seat. "If you wouldn't mind?"

"Very well," Stella said with a disgruntled scrunch of her nose. "If you will insist on being a stickler."

She crossed the room, the fabric of her skirts rustling softly about her legs. She smelled of lilacs, just as she had on every occasion they'd met. It was a sweet, ephemeral fragrance, too subtle to be perfume. Her soap, very likely, or the scented oil from her bath water.

Whatever it was, it was doing Teddy's powers of concentration no favors.

She sank down on the chair, fluffing her velvet-ribbon trimmed skirts about her legs.

"Your cap," he reminded her.

"Oh yes. I'd nearly forgotten." She swiftly removed the black monstrosity, revealing her neatly coiffed silver hair. It was arranged in a large roll at her neck, secured with a heavy plait. A fashionable style, but not an ostentatious one. Not a seductive one, certainly.

A simmering heat nevertheless pooled low in Teddy's belly. He ignored it. Picking up his pencil, he returned to his sketch.

Intense artistic inspiration could often be mistaken for another kind of attraction. It wasn't unusual to feel it. As a consequence, many artists became involved with their female subjects. Emotionally. Physically.

It didn't necessarily detract from their work. On the contrary, the intimacy of the connection often added additional depth to a portrait. If an artist knew his subject—truly *knew* her—he could depict her with a sensitivity that was otherwise lacking.

Joanna Hiffernan was currently Whistler's mistress. Rossetti had wed his primary model, Elizabeth Siddal, after a long and passionate affair. And there was Millais, of course, who had famously married his muse, the former Mrs. Ruskin.

But Stella wasn't Teddy's wife. She wasn't his mistress. She was an unmarried young lady who should be treated with respect. A clergyman's sister, by God. And one who hadn't even agreed to let him paint her portrait.

This sketch was merely a consolation prize. It wasn't the beginning of anything. It was the ending.

Furrowing his brow, he focused his attention on shading in the delicate shell of her ear with his pencil. It was all light and shadow. An impression of her, not an exact duplicate. A sketch that would, when it was finished, evoke the same feelings that Teddy had whenever he looked at her.

He was nearly done with it. A few finishing touches were all that remained. And then this brief, blissful interlude would be over. In the morning, they would go their separate ways—her with his sketch, and he with nothing of her at all.

It wouldn't do.

He needed to paint her in oils. To depict her standing over a shimmering, twilight sea, her hair unbound, with a glittering gauze shift skimming the curves of her body. The human embodiment of the Pleiades.

But it was never going to happen. Not if she wouldn't allow it. And not if she was permanently retiring to some remote bloody village in Derbyshire.

"Will you never return to London?" he asked abruptly.

She turned her head, briefly meeting his eyes. "It's odd you should ask."

"Why odd?"

"I learned this morning that Lady Anne and Mr. Hartford's wedding will be in March. They plan to marry in London, at St. George's Hanover Square, on the first day of spring. I'll be expected to attend." She paused. "I *want* to attend."

Teddy's pulse quickened. March was a long way away yet. Still . . . it was a vast improvement from never. "What's stopping you?"

"Nothing yet. I've only to persuade my brother to bring me." She resumed her pose. "Where will *you* go after the house party? The night of the ball, you mentioned us crossing paths again in London. Will you be stopping there before returning to France?"

Teddy's fingers tightened reflexively on his pencil. He had to force them to loosen. "I'm not returning to France. I mean to find lodgings in town."

"With your sister and brother-in-law?"

His pencil stopped on his sketch pad, frozen on the shadows he was creating along the length of Stella's neck. A troubled frown creased his brow.

She again turned to look at him. Her silver-blue gaze was steady and grave. "Forgive me, I seem to have misspoken."

"Not at all." He used a stump to blur out his shading, still frowning. "My sister and brother-in-law will be returning to Grasse in the spring. I'll remain in London."

"Alone?"

His muscles tensed. Was his independence so outlandish of a proposition? "I'll naturally have Jennings to assist me."

"The large man I've seen following you about?"

"The very one." Teddy scowled at his sketch pad, muttering, "For the time being."

She continued gazing at him, her face possessed of the same tender gravity. It was the exact expression she'd worn when studying the van Dyck drawing in the King's Gallery so many months ago. The very expression Teddy longed to paint.

Putting aside the stump, he again picked up his pencil.

"London surely can't be as pleasant a place to live as Paris," she said. "Not for an artist."

"Funnily enough, you're not the first to say so."

"But it's true, isn't it? Why remain in England if you can return to France?"

"Turner painted in England."

A smile crept into Stella's voice. "Ah yes. Turner. Your idol."

"I'm not ashamed to say so."

"Why should you be? Though . . ." Her brows notched. "His paintings of the sea *are* rather volatile. The sky and the clouds are all storming color and light, and the water is a frightening tumult."

"Exactly," Teddy said. "It's why I take inspiration from him. So do many painters of the new age. Turner's seascapes are unparalleled. Had I a fraction of his talent, I would count myself a lucky man." He finished shading the curve of her throat, warming to the subject. "He was born in London, you know. He lived above his father's barber-shop in Maiden Lane."

"I didn't know that."

"It's true."

"That doesn't make the subject matter in England any more compelling."

Teddy glanced up from his work to find her still looking at him. It did odd things to him, that look. Some of the tension in his expression softened. A smile edged his mouth, even as his heart skipped a beat. "The subject matter satisfies me very well at present."

Stella's soft, voluptuous mouth ticked up at one corner in reluctant reply. "You're absurd."

"What I am is pressed for time." He pointed his pencil at the mantel clock in an unspoken command for her to return to her pose. "If you would be so good?"

Stella suppressed a smile as she resumed staring at the clock. He meant her, of course, the rogue. She was, for the moment, more appealing to him than all the beauties of France.

It was utter rubbish. Shameless, self-serving flattery to persuade her to continue posing for him. The sentiment nevertheless provoked a delicious warmth in her veins.

"Who inspires *your* sketches?" he inquired as he resumed his work. "Any particular artists?"

"I'm fond of Mr. Landseer's paintings," she answered. "He portrays horses so beautifully."

It was a simple answer. Edwin Henry Landseer was one of England's foremost animal painters and sculptors. Anyone drawing horses would naturally look to him for inspiration. Either that or to the paintings of the late Mr. Stubbs.

"Do you use his work as a guide for proportions?" Teddy asked.

"But rarely. My sketches are from life. And since I have a horse with me at most times, I have no need to look elsewhere to find the harmony of equine proportion. The breadth of Locket's wither and the length of her hock are written on my soul."

"A fine way of putting it."

"It's what I feel."

"I'd be honored to see your work sometime," he said. "Unless, that is, you still consider me too much a stranger."

She recalled her words to him in the drawing room on the second night of the house party. Then, she'd dismissed his desire to see her sketches as a pedantic masculine impulse. She knew now that she'd been wrong. Teddy's interest in her work didn't stem from a need to put her in her place. He was genuinely interested in her talent.

"Must I?" she quizzed him. "I thought you disapproved of collaboration?"

"For works in progress, yes. Have you no finished sketches you could share?"

"A few," she said.

Her portfolio at home was filled with sketches of Locket, and of Anne's golden stallion, Saffron; Julia's black gelding, Cossack; and Evie's blood bay Andalusian, Hephaestus. Stella had drawn them in every gait and every mood, to the very best of her ability. Indeed, she sketched the way other ladies of her acquaintance practiced the piano or labored over their needlework. It was her only true accomplishment outside of riding.

"Regrettably, I don't have them with me. I have only the half dozen or so sketches I've made of the earl's horses since I've been here in Hampshire."

"A half dozen? My pieces take rather longer."

"As I perceive. Are you nearly done yet?"

"Just a bit more shading," he said.

She sighed. "So much effort. It seems a waste if I'm only to burn it."

Her statement was met with several seconds of profound silence. It was long enough for her to regret speaking so glibly. She was just opening her mouth to apologize when she heard him set down his pencil.

"It would be a shame if you did." He tore the page from his sketchbook. "There. It's finished. It's yours."

She turned fully in her chair to find him extending the sketch to her. She eagerly reached for it. Their bare fingers brushed. It was only for an instant. The space of a breath, a heartbeat. But it was long enough.

A jolt of unmistakable heat shot through Stella. Her eyes jerked to Teddy's. Their gazes locked and held for a moment—hers questioning and his dark with a sudden intensity.

It was the first time they'd touched—ungloved skin to skin. A second's contact, merely. Yet, Stella had the uneasy sense that it had changed something between them. Indeed, the very air around them crackled with a palpable tension.

She could think of nothing else to do but take the sketch and resume her seat. She focused her full attention on it, doing her best to ignore the quickening of her pulse.

Had she not just experienced a cataclysmic physical response to the touch of a gentleman's hand, she might have experienced one from viewing the way that gentleman saw her.

He'd reproduced her image in subtle pencil lines and artful shading that softened the contours of her face and lent an otherworldly luminosity to her countenance. He'd made her beautiful. Serene. A grave-eyed creature of stillness and shadow, gazing at the mysteries of some distant horizon.

A lump formed in Stella's throat. This wasn't what she saw when she looked in the glass of her dressing table. This youthful, dignified, alluring creature who was somehow equal parts Athena, Artemis, and Aphrodite herself.

She lifted her eyes to Teddy's in cautious wonder. "Is *this* how you see me?"

"I see you as you are," he said. "It's what I've tried to convey, limited by the abilities of my pencil."

"It's . . ." She swallowed hard. "Goodness."

His brows lowered. "You don't approve?"

"I do," she assured him. "Oh, but I do. It's only that . . . you've managed to surprise me."

"You presumed I'd present you with something amateurish?"

She shook her head. "No. I knew it would be good. What I didn't know was that it would be—"

"What?"

"Extraordinary."

His mouth curved slowly. "I'm glad you like it." He paused. His voice deepened. "Please don't burn it."

Stella held the sketch to her bosom. She couldn't believe she'd ever considered destroying it. Not even to guard her reputation. "I shan't burn it," she promised him. "I shall treasure it always."

His smile turned wry. He closed his sketchbook. "Well, I suppose that's something."

Stella knew he was disappointed that he couldn't do a formal portrait of her. Given the quality of his sketch, she was disappointed, too. "I'm astonished you're not tempted to keep it yourself," she said.

He flashed her an unreadable glance as he put away his pencils.

Stella belatedly realized how vain she must sound. "Not because it's of my face, obviously," she added, "but because it's such a fine example of your work."

"Your face is the only reason I'd consider keeping it," he said frankly. "But I don't need to." He tapped his forefinger to his temple. "You're etched up here, more indelibly than a pencil drawing. I won't easily forget you."

Her heart beat hard. She couldn't think how to respond.

Teddy saved her the trouble. "I have something for you, by the way." Reaching into his supply case, he withdrew a small, tissue-wrapped bundle. He extended it to her.

Stella took it with an uncertain frown. An unmarried young lady wasn't supposed to accept gifts from a gentleman. Not unless that gentleman was courting her. And then, the gifts could be only something small and transitory, such as flowers or candy. Anything more would be unseemly.

"What—?"

"It's not a gift," Teddy said, seeming to read her mind. "It's only something I borrowed from my sister."

Stella cautiously opened the rose-colored, tissue-paper wrappings. A scrap of finely wrought blonde lace lay within. It was, she realized in some surprise, an elegantly crafted matron's cap. Possibly the most fashionable one she'd ever beheld.

She lifted her gaze to Teddy's. "I don't understand."

He resumed putting away his supplies. "You've been absent from dinner nearly every night this week because of your hair. I thought, if you had something better to wear than that dreadful black cap, you might come down this evening. It seems a shame for you to spend the last night of the house party alone."

A sudden prickle of moisture stung at Stella's eyes. "How thoughtful of you."

"It wasn't thoughtfulness. It was artistic revulsion. I've taken an aversion to that cap of Lady Arundell's. My sister's cap will be a marked improvement."

"It's beautiful." Stella fingered the delicate lace. It was entirely opaque, and in combination with the elaborate ribbon ties, might very well succeed in covering her hair as thoroughly as Lady Arundell's black crepe monstrosity. "Surely your sister will mind my borrowing it?"

"She won't," he said. "Laura has dozens of the things, all of them made in Paris. My brother-in-law keeps her outfitted in splendid style. She was happy to spare it for you."

Stella's stomach sank. "Do you mean that she knows about—"

"She knows that your hair is gray. I told her about you after you and I met at the British Museum. But no. She doesn't realize it's gone gray again. I wouldn't betray your confidence." He glanced at her. "Can you use it this evening?"

"I believe so," Stella said. "Thank you. You're . . . That was excessively kind." She gathered her courage. "Teddy . . ."

He stilled.

It was the first time she'd used his given name unprompted. He must have registered it in the same moment that she did. Must have known that it preceded a new level of intimacy between them. An intimacy that had nothing to do with art.

A dull red flush appeared high on his neck, just above the line of his collar. It was the only thing that betrayed the imperviousness of his manner. That, and the unexpected scrape of gruffness in his voice. "Yes, Stella?"

"We're all going sleighing tonight, if the snow will support it."

It was plainly not what Teddy had been expecting her to say.

He returned to putting away his supplies. "Oh?"

"Will you come with us?"

"No, thank you."

"Because you don't like the out of doors?" she asked. "Or because you'd rather paint?"

He didn't reply.

She pressed on, despite the tickle of warning in her brain that told her to hold her tongue. "Or is it because you don't want people making a fuss over your chair?"

His lips compressed in a hard line as he put the last pencil back into his case. "All of the above."

"I think you should come."

"Do you." It wasn't a question.

She answered it anyway. "Yes. I know why you're reluctant. I understand better than anyone. But—"

"You don't understand."

"I do. My hair has often caused undue awkwardness for me. It's why I resorted to that dye. I—"

"It isn't at all the same."

"I know *that*. All I meant was that I can comprehend how—"

"You altered your hair to make yourself ordinary. While I—"

"Not ordinary. I wanted to be beautiful, if only for a—"

"You *are* beautiful. If people discount it because of your hair, that's their problem." He thrust his remaining supplies into his art case. "Whatever their issue, it can't compare with the bother my chair creates for everyone when I go out of doors. It's trying even among friends. Among strangers, it's something else. And with the weather, and the amount of effort—"

"What does a little commotion matter in the grand scheme of things? It's a winter wonderland outside—all frosty and white. And there's a full moon tonight. You could see the beauties of Sutton Park firsthand, instead of from the window. Not to mention . . ."

"What?"

Warmth crept into her cheeks. "It's our last night here. Wouldn't it be jolly to spend it having a sleigh ride under the stars?"

He gave her another of his unreadable glances. "With you?"

Stella's heart beat heavily in her chest. "With me."

His jaw tightened. For a moment, it seemed he would refuse. And then: "Very well," he said brusquely, snapping shut his case. "I'll come."

Twelve

❖

Teddy gripped hard to Jennings's shoulder as Jennings slowly conveyed him down the curving marble staircase, step by laborious step. It was the usual method by which they managed stairs, with Jennings's arms firmly around Teddy's midsection, hoisting Teddy up so that his legs fell straight beneath him, and his booted feet just brushed the floor.

It would, perhaps, have been easier if Jennings had simply carried Teddy. That's how Teddy had been moved from one place to another in the early days of his injury. How he'd abhorred that mode of assistance! The sense of helplessness—of somehow being less than a man—had been insupportable.

He far preferred the feeling of leaning on Jennings to that of being cradled by the man like a babe. It made it no less awkward with so many people watching.

Ladies and gentlemen trotted past them down the staircase on their way to the entry hall below, all of them bundled up in their warmest coats and cloaks in readiness for an evening of sleigh rides through snow. They threw countless pitying glances Teddy's way as they descended. Alex and Laura, who were following close behind Teddy, no doubt registered every one of them.

Teddy marked them, too, but unlike his sister and brother-in-law, he did his level best to ignore the looks and the whispers. Over the past two years, he'd had a great deal of practice in ignoring such things.

That didn't mean he was blind to the obstacles awaiting him this evening. He'd been contemplating the difficulties that a sleigh ride would entail all afternoon. It wasn't just climbing into the vehicle that was at issue. It was the ordeal of descending to the hall, and then of making his way down the icy front steps to the sleigh below, all amid a flurry of goggle-eyed guests who hadn't the sense not to gape at him like simpletons.

But Teddy had given his word to Stella. And really, this wasn't so different from the tedious logistical maneuvering he dealt with every day. It was only that tonight there was a larger audience to it.

"I don't object to you going sleighing," Laura said as Jennings settled Teddy into his chair at the bottom of the stairs. "I only question your going alone."

Teddy straightened himself in his seat. Gripping his wheels with his gloved hands, he rolled his chair toward the closed doors of the hall. "Who said I was going alone?"

Alex's face was impassive as he kept pace with him. "You'll be joining a young lady, I presume."

Laura took her husband's proffered arm, walking along with him. "Why would you presume that?"

"What else could have persuaded him to participate in an outdoor activity?"

Teddy shot a narrow glance at his sister and brother-in-law. "If you must know, I've agreed to join Miss Hobhouse." He didn't wait for them to respond. "Jennings? The door."

Jennings darted ahead. Snowflakes swirled into the hall on an icy gust of air as he opened the door. Outside, a slim, velvet-cloaked lady waited at the top of the snow-covered stone steps in company with one of the footmen. It was Stella.

Steeling himself, Teddy wheeled his chair outside. "Miss Hobhouse."

She turned sharply, a leatherbound book tucked under one arm and a fur-trimmed muff dangling from her hand. Her eyes brightened with something like relief. "Mr. Hayes."

He realized then that she'd been uncertain of him. That she'd thought he wasn't coming.

"My apologies," he said. "It took rather longer than I expected to fetch my coat."

"Not at all," she replied. "Your timing is perfect. Lady Anne and Mr. Hartford have just driven off. I've been standing here only a moment."

A small sleigh awaited them at the bottom of the steps. Adorned with red ribbons and greenery, it was hitched to a restless bay horse. He danced in his traces, sending the bells on his harness jingling. A groom with a heavy scarf wound round his neck stood at the horse's head, holding its bridle.

"Is that your sketchbook?" Teddy tossed a pointed look at the book under her arm. He had recognized the nature of it immediately. He'd had similar ones of his own over the years.

"It is," Stella said.

"With your sketches of winged horses?"

"Just horses. I ceased drawing wings when I was fourteen."

"Pity," he said. "I should have liked to see them."

"You don't wish to see these? I thought you might like to before I leave tomorrow."

"There won't be much light for it during our drive."

"Lord March has had torches placed on the path." She moved toward the sleigh. "Shall we climb in before another couple beats us to it?"

Teddy sensed his sister and brother-in-law hanging back in the hall like two doting parents. He felt an irritating flush of embarrassment. He wished they'd go away. He wished *everyone* would go away. Bolstering his acquaintance with Stella would be so much easier if he could board the sleigh under his own power and then drive off with her into the moonlight, away from the eyes of prying strangers and concerned relations.

"A capital idea," he said tightly. "Jennings?"

Jennings materialized at his side. "When you're ready, sir."

Teddy gave the manservant a terse nod. There was no avoiding the indignity of what followed. Putting an arm around Jennings's shoulders, Teddy gritted his teeth as Jennings took hold of his midsection and hauled him up out of his seat. It was a well-choreographed movement. One practiced hundreds of times over the years.

Teddy's heart pumped hard with equal parts effort and anxiety as Jennings conveyed him to the sleigh. He was always at his most vulnerable during those moments when he was out of his chair. It was then he felt the full brunt of his disability. It was why he so rarely indulged in outdoor excursions—outings during which he'd have to be lifted in and out of his chair any number of times, and all of them in the presence of a group of other people. It simply wasn't worth the trouble.

But Stella was.

She waited patiently as Jennings helped Teddy into the seat of the sleigh, and then, with the footman's assistance, she climbed in to join him. Her full skirts bunched against Teddy's leg. He couldn't feel them, but he heard the rustle of her petticoats and crinoline—of starched linen underthings and soft velvet outer things whispering with a sensual friction. Her arm brushed his as she drew her cloak more firmly about herself, sending a surge of heat through his veins.

They'd never been this close before. Perhaps it was too close. She was all laundry soap and lilacs. An intoxicating combination of practicality and femininity.

"It's me who should be handing you up," he grumbled.

"According to whom?"

"Good manners."

She wedged her sketchbook next to her before settling her oversized muff on her lap in lieu of a lap blanket. Her cheeks were rosy from the cold, her gray hair hidden by a close-woven net and a stylish plum velvet bonnet. She'd arranged the amethyst satin bonnet ribbons in an oversized bow on the left side of her face. It gave her a rakish air.

"Do good manners also dictate that you drive?" she inquired. "Or shall I take the ribbons?" Her silver-blue eyes sparkled with good humor. "Though I warn you, I'm nowhere near as good a driver as I am a rider."

"In that case"—Teddy gathered the reins—"I'll do the honors." He signaled to the groom to stand away, and then, with a slap of the leather, gave the horse the office to start.

The rangy bay leapt forward at a bouncing trot down the torch-lined path that led away from the house. He had a powerful gait, as well as an inclination to take the bit in his teeth. Teddy was thankful he'd spent so much time in strengthening his upper body. If he hadn't, he'd have found himself in for a devil of a fight.

"He's a spirited one," Stella said appreciatively.

Teddy steered the horse through the snow. "Like your mare?"

She was surprised into a laugh. "Not by half. Locket is too temperamental to pull a vehicle of any kind. I doubt I could control her if I wasn't on her back."

"She sounds more and more like a horse unsuited for a lady."

"She is," Stella agreed with an unmistakable twinkle of pride. "Entirely unsuited." She slipped her hands into her velvet muff. "While this fellow is merely feeling his oats. He's not truly dangerous, I suspect."

"No," Teddy said. "He's only testing me. Trying to see how much he can get away with."

"Perhaps you should give him his head?"

"And let him bolt? No, thank you."

"A good gallop always puts Locket in a more convivial mood."

"A good gallop would see us both pitched into a snowbank," Teddy said. "Not ideal, given the circumstances."

"I suppose you're right."

It took most of Teddy's attention to keep the horse from breaking into a canter. "How was dinner?" he asked. "I couldn't see you from the bottom of the table."

He'd caught sight of her only once, as the ladies had risen to withdraw from the dining room. She'd been wearing the fashionable lace cap he'd loaned her. It had effectively concealed her hair, without making her look like too much of an oddity.

"I couldn't see you, either," she said. "The earl does insist on that long row of epergnes to display his flowers."

He cast her a glance. "Who were you seated between? Anyone interesting?"

"Lord Gaines and Mr. Moncrief. They're friends of Lord March, and both old enough to be my grandfather."

Teddy felt an inexplicable flicker of relief. "Not matrimonial prospects, then."

"By no means. It was a fortunate thing, really. They were far too stuffy to ask why I've been absent from dinner most of the week. I suspect they were too embarrassed. Lady Anne has apparently put it about that I've been suffering from a mysterious stomach complaint."

Teddy's lips twitched with amusement. "So I've heard."

She gave an eloquent grimace. "Is there anything more indecorous? A stomach complaint could be anything, from indigestion to—"

"Quite."

"I told Anne as much, but she said that it must be my stomach. She claims there could be no other believable reason for me to absent myself at meals while still appearing for all the outdoor activities."

"She's not wrong," Teddy said.

Stella heaved a sigh. "I'm not persuaded that anyone truly cares anymore. Between Lady Anne's engagement and the revelations about Mr. Neale's parentage, my participation—or lack of it—must be the least interesting thing at this house party."

"I wouldn't let your guard down just yet," Teddy advised. "At any moment some well-meaning busybody could importune you about your illness—or, more likely, about your cap. I trust you have a convincing story at the ready for why you wore it at dinner?"

"I intend to credit the French."

"Ah yes. The French. Let the gossips try to argue with that logic."

"They can't. We none of us can. Not when it comes to fashion." Her expression became serious. "Thank you again for lending it to me. Both you and your sister have been exceedingly generous."

"It was all to the good. You could hardly have justified going sleighing if you'd missed dinner."

"I'd have found a way," she said stoutly. "But I take your point."

He skillfully guided the horse around the curve of the road, turning toward the path that ran alongside the woods. A row of torches blazed ahead. He stopped the sleigh beneath them. "Will this do?"

Stella stared at him blankly for an instant before comprehending his meaning. She gave an eloquent grimace. "My sketches! Of course." She hurriedly extracted her sketchbook from the seat beside her. "Amid all the excitement, I'd nearly forgotten."

She offered the book to him, a little self-conscious. He gave her the reins to hold in return.

The horse stamped its hooves restlessly in the snow as Teddy examined Stella's drawings in the torchlight. It was a new sketchbook. Most of the pages were still empty, save a half dozen at the back. Those were covered with detailed pencil sketches of horses. Teddy recognized the subjects. They were the retired horses who resided in the pastures at the back of the earl's estate.

One sketch stood out among the others. It depicted an aged cart horse, stocky legged and thick fetlocked, with a pronounced sway in its back. It was standing in a snowy paddock next to a smaller companion—an old hack, boasting a thin mane and a wild tuft of forelock. The two retirees rested, bodies listing toward each other. The larger horse's muzzle was turned toward the smaller one, though not close enough to touch him.

It was an excellent rendering. True to life in its proportion, and commendable for its use of light and shadow. But that wasn't where its strength lay. It was in the composition of the scene itself.

The whole of it gave an impression of kinship. Of solidarity against an unkind world. And more than that. There was a shelter nearby, but neither horse was beneath it. They chose instead to gain warmth from each other, despite the promise of protection nearby.

Teddy swallowed hard. "You taught yourself? Is that right?"

"For the most part." Stella looked at the drawing with him. "Do you think it very amateurish?"

"You know it isn't."

"Well, I do feel it's rather good," she said. "But I'm not the expert."

He looked up at her. "You have a rare talent for inspiring emotion. You should engage a drawing master to help you perfect it."

Stella's eyes shone. "Truly?"

"I wouldn't lie to you."

"No, I don't expect you would." She accepted her sketchbook back from him, handing him the leather driving reins in return. "I shall see if I can find a tutor when I return to Derbyshire. There must be someone thereabouts who is qualified to teach me."

Teddy's stomach clenched on a bewildering twinge of longing. He had the sudden, stupid wish that it might be him.

A ridiculous notion. He wasn't a drawing master. Nevertheless . . .

The fragments of a picture formed in his mind. A vision of the two of them sketching together in a studio somewhere. Just he and Stella, in companiable silence. Rather like those two horses.

Shaking off the vexing mirage, Teddy gathered the reins and urged the horse forward. The restless bay walked on through the snow with a bounce in his step, taking them deeper along the edge of the wood. The torches were spaced further apart there, giving a sense of privacy in the moonlit gaps between them.

Stella tucked her sketchbook beside her. She watched him handle the ribbons. "You're an excellent driver."

"I don't know about excellent, but I can manage well enough."

"Do you drive out often when you're on your own?"

"Not often, no," he said. "Not alone. Jennings must accompany me. But I used to drive a good deal."

"Used to?"

"I wasn't always in that chair. When I was a lad in Surrey, I drove our little gig all over the village."

"I'd rather ride than drive," she said.

Teddy shot her a wry look. "Regrettably, I haven't that option any longer."

Her eyes turned thoughtful. "Did you ride? Before?"

"I did." His brows pulled into a reflective frown. "The truth is, I preferred walking. I was a great walker. I could stroll for hours in the woods, examining the bluebells and the forget-me-nots, hoping to spark a flash of inspiration."

"For your paintings?"

"Always. Nature provides any number of subjects. All a man must do is keep his eyes open."

"A bit more difficult now that you paint portraits. You can't simply walk into the woods any longer. Not if you're trying to find a lady to pose for you."

"Nor for any other reason."

She flinched. "I didn't mean—"

"I know you didn't. It's merely the reality of things." Teddy saw no point in skirting around the issue. His walking days were over. It wasn't as if he could conceal the fact. "My sources of inspiration haven't diminished just because I'm in a chair. There are avenues in Paris with as many interesting faces as there were flowers in that wood."

"Interesting faces?" she repeated. "Not beautiful ones?"

He smiled to himself. "Are you angling for a compliment, Miss Hobhouse?"

"Not at all. I only wonder how fleeting your interest might be in my face, with so many other flowers to divert your attention."

"You've kept my attention for three full months. I expect you'll still command it three months from now, when we meet again in London."

Her bosom rose and fell on a weary exhalation of breath. "Not that again. I've already told you—"

"So you have. And yet . . . you'll be in London in March, as will I. What harm is there in meeting again?"

"I can't imagine the circumstances where we would."

"Then you lack imagination."

"Really—"

"A museum. A gallery. The theatre. A shop in Bond Street. We could cross paths in any of those places, or wherever else it is you go for amusement."

"Rotten Row," she informed him without hesitation.

"Riding, of course. But surely that can't take all your time?"

"Most of it. I must take Locket out at least twice a day. She needs exercise to blunt the edge of her temper. I ride her once at dawn, and then again during the fashionable hour. Sometimes I ride at midday as well, when the weather is fine."

"In Rotten Row, then," he said. "That's where we'll see each other."

"You would visit the row in your wheeled chair?"

"If you were there, I would. If"—he added—"there was the smallest chance I could persuade you to sit for me."

"I wish I *could* sit for you," she said frankly. "I wish I could take the risk."

He gave her an alert look. "Nothing is stopping you but your outdated ideas of propriety."

"Not outdated. Not for a young lady in my position. Besides, I already push the bounds of propriety far more than I should."

"In what respect?"

Removing a hand from her muff, she enumerated the ways on her leather-gloved fingers. "I gallop when I should walk. I dance with my friends when we haven't any gentlemen partners. I color my hair. I—"

"And here I thought you didn't aspire to be thought an eccentric."

"I don't. That doesn't mean I must embroider pillows all the day long."

He grinned. "How do you plan to spend your days, then, now that your final season is over?"

"Aside from riding and sketching? I don't yet know. My future is too uncertain to make firm plans. If my brother decides to get married—"

"To the tyrant."

She winced. "I shouldn't have called her that. It was uncharitable of me. Miss Trent was doing nothing more than any other determined young lady might do to secure her own happiness."

"Alienating potential in-laws?"

"Attempting to consolidate her power."

Teddy flicked her an amused glance. "You speak of young ladies like military generals at war."

Stella half smiled. "I don't expect it's vastly different. Not if you consider it properly. After all, what is the London season if not a campaign?"

"By that measure, your brother's future wife sounds like Wellington."

"Which would have made me Napoleon, on the verge of being exiled to Elba."

"He didn't stay on Elba long."

"Saint Helena, I meant," she amended. "Luckily, with me out of the way, my brother won't have proposed. My final defeat will have been averted. Or, at least, postponed for a time."

Teddy's brows notched with concern. "Is it that bad?"

Her smile dimmed. "Not entirely. Not yet, anyway. I still have my friends to sustain me, even if only through the post. And I haven't yet lost my reputation. I needn't retire from the field in complete disgrace."

He frowned. Was that why she was so reluctant to risk her good name? Because she felt her reputation was all she had left? "Small comfort."

"I take what I can find." She gazed out at the dark, snow-covered landscape in silence for a moment. "Where will you live in London?"

"Somewhere that I can be entirely on my own. Away from family and well-meaning friends. Someplace I can be free to make my own decisions, even if they're the wrong ones."

"You desire to live alone?"

"As alone as I can be with a manservant to assist me and a cook-housekeeper to ensure my clothes are clean and my meals fit to eat."

"Won't you be lonely?"

"I shall be content," he said. "More importantly, I'll be productive. My work suffers from too much interruption. All this traveling to and from France, and the people stopping in to visit or to conduct business at the perfumery. I'd prefer to remain in London. To stay in one place long enough to form a circle of artistic friends. Perhaps submit a piece to the Royal Academy—if I can produce something worthy enough."

"It sounds as though you have your future entirely planned out."

"All that remains is to put that plan into action."

"You're a man," she said. "There's nothing preventing you."

"Only duty and obligation." He adjusted the reins, guiding the horse along the edge of the darkened woods. "I must first spend a few more months with my family. We're traveling to Devon tomorrow. My brother-in-law's childhood friend, Captain Thornhill, has a cliff-side estate on the coast. Thornhill is married to Lady Helena, the sister of the Earl of Castleton. She and her husband expect us to stay for at least a month."

Stella looked at him with interest. "Your brother-in-law has a varied acquaintance for a tradesman."

"Because he's friendly with the sister of an earl? Not really. Lord Castleton is something of a tradesman himself. He owns a tea plantation in Darjeeling where he spends the bulk of his time. The tea they produce there is almost as good as the blend we shared together that afternoon in the small parlor."

She smiled again, remembering. "First flush Darjeeling. It was special, wasn't it? Unquestionably the finest tea I've ever had the privilege to drink."

"Darjeeling is often called the champagne of teas," he said. "Indeed, some people might say that our first meal together consisted of cake and champagne."

She cast him a speaking glance. "Some people might be foolish beyond permission."

Teddy smiled at her as he slowed the horse to a walk. Her perfect oval face was aglow—pink cheeked and bright eyed—set in its frame of plum velvet and amethyst satin. It was likely only the cold that made her so radiant. Nevertheless . . .

A peculiar ache settled in his chest. His smile dimmed as he returned his attention to the road. How was it that every time he saw her, she became more beautiful? It was a bewildering sort of magic. One that was conjured by their growing friendship. The more he knew her, the lovelier she became. It was, he supposed, because she was a lovely person. He was only just beginning to realize how lovely.

And now it was too late. Tomorrow she would be gone.

A part of him was tempted to keep her out in the sleigh even longer in a feeble attempt to make up for it. To drive for another mile or more. But he'd already taken her too far. She had the remainder of the evening's merriment still to get through. All the mulled wine and carols, and party games with her friends.

Teddy wouldn't curtail her pleasure to bolster his own. She'd already missed too much of the party on account of her hair.

He turned the sleigh back toward the house. The horse had calmed significantly after its exercise. He was now content to walk, albeit with a spring in his step to be returning to the warmth of his stable. The bells on his harness jingled.

"I'd better return you to the party," Teddy said. "With luck, you'll have time to steal a final kiss under the mistletoe before everyone retires."

Stella tipped her head back to look up at the stars. A smile sounded in her voice. "Foolish beyond permission, just as I said."

"Why foolish?"

"I won't be kissing anyone under the mistletoe this evening."

Teddy didn't believe it. He'd seen the way some of the gentlemen had looked at her that night in the drawing room as she'd passed them, silk clad and auburn haired. She could have had her pick of any of them.

He mustered a weak chuckle. "Had your fill already, have you?"

"Don't be absurd," she said. "I've spent most of this week in hiding, and the rest of it either with Lady Anne or with you. Who exactly am I meant to be kissing? There's been no mistletoe for me, and no willing partners. Disappointing, really, given the season. Even the grimmest frump garners a dry peck on the cheek at this time of year." She exhaled a visible puff of breath. "I suppose I shall have to chalk it up alongside every other failed effort—"

"Do you require mistletoe?" he asked abruptly.

She turned her head. "I'm sorry?"

"For a kiss," he said. "Must there be mistletoe hanging about?"

She considered the proposition. "No," she replied. "Not in theory."

Before he could counsel himself against it, for the second time that evening, Teddy brought the horse to a halt in the snow. He tied off the reins and turned to face her, his heart thumping heavily. By some miracle he managed to keep his nerve. "It's unlucky anyway, in my opinion. Who wants to share a kiss under a poisonous parasite? Wouldn't it be better out here, in the moonlight, under a shimmer of stars?"

Stella had gone unnaturally still. There was a glimmer of alarm in the blue-gray depths of her eyes. That, and something else. Something Teddy couldn't precisely identify. Whatever it was, it made his pulse pound with a frightening power.

"Yes," she answered slowly. "I rather suppose it would be."

"Well, then?"

"Are you asking if you can kiss me?"

"May I?"

She nodded, only the subtle tremble in her breath betraying that the prospect of a kiss was anything other than the veriest commonplace.

He brought his hand to cradle her cheek. His eyes looked steadily into hers. "I expect I should make a humorous remark now. Either that, or say something romantic."

Stella's throat bobbed on a delicate swallow. She appeared to be at a loss for words.

"Very well." His leather-gloved thumb moved over the curve of her cheek in a lingering caress. "Romantic it is."

Thirteen

◆◆

Stella couldn't move. Couldn't breathe. She was frozen in the sleigh, her eyes riveted to Teddy's.

Though frozen wasn't wholly accurate. Indeed, despite the snow swirling all around them, she wasn't cold at all. Quite the reverse. She was as warm as a furnace beneath the layers of her cloak and gown. Warm in her limbs, and in her blood, and in the deep core of her stomach where butterflies wafted their wings in tremulous anticipation. It was a heat that had been ignited by the touch of Teddy's gloved hand, and by the look in his eyes, so unwavering in its intensity.

He brought his face closer to hers. His nose brushed her cheek. She felt him inhale. "Lilacs," he said.

"I beg your pardon?" Her voice was a trembling squeak.

"The scent you're wearing. Your soap, I presume?"

It was too personal a remark not to inspire a blush. "Yes, if you must know. But why—"

"I'm the son of a perfumer. My family paints their life in terms of fragrance. Lavender, roses, jasmine, and orange blossom. A single scent can conjure the past as vividly as any painting. But I had no memories to associate with lilacs. Not until you." He stroked her cheek. "It's your fragrance now, absolutely," he said. "I'll never again encounter it without thinking of how luminous you are in this moment."

Stella's heart beat swiftly. "That is, indeed, very romantic," she managed. "If only I could believe you meant it."

"I mean it," he assured her in a husky undertone. And then, bending his head, his lips found hers.

Her own lips parted on a flustered breath. He'd said he was going to kiss her. It was why he'd stopped the sleigh. Why he'd complimented her, for heaven's sake. But now the moment was upon her, she felt herself completely unprepared for it.

She realized in that instant that she'd never been kissed before. Not truly. Daring as she was—willing as she might have been—there had only ever been fleeting pecks on the cheek. Chaste, meaningless nothings—more avuncular than romantic.

But this was something different.

Teddy had a sensual mouth. She'd marked it that night in the anteroom. But little had she anticipated how that mouth would feel pressed to hers. It was the only soft part of him, unhindered by the sharpness of his intellect and the dryness of his wit. Lips that were gentle but firm, shaping effortlessly to hers with a warm, seeking pressure.

Stella tentatively pressed back, kissing him in return.

It was likely the most virginal, inexperienced kiss he'd ever received. But there was nothing dry about it. Nothing chaste. Their lips lingered against each other, warm and half-parted, clinging sweetly for an instant. Her breath mingled with his—an extraordinary intimacy.

He tasted of peppermint and mulled wine. He smelled of it, too—that and faint traces of lavender and spice. It was his shaving oil, very possibly. Something produced at the perfumery owned by his family. It stirred Stella's senses, along with the brush of his lips, the touch of his hand, and the furnace-warm heat of his body so perilously close to hers.

She felt a bit dizzy as they separated.

Good gracious.

This was why ladies swooned. Why chaperones were invented. Why there was a booming industry in vinaigrettes. Kisses like these had the power to alter a lady's entire constitution.

And, perhaps, a gentleman's, too.

Twin flags of color blazed high on Teddy's cheekbones. "May I write to you in Derbyshire?" he asked suddenly. His voice had a peculiar rasp in it.

Stella drew back from the curve of his hand, still alarmingly off-balance. She had no doubt but that if she'd stood in that moment, her legs would have given way beneath her. "On no account," she said. "A gentleman can't write to an unmarried lady."

"Another tedious rule."

"One I'm in no position to break. It's my brother who oversees the post when we're at home. Were he to see a letter arrive for me from a man, he'd consign it straight to the fire—after reading it himself, of course."

Teddy caught up the reins. "*You* wouldn't burn it, would you?" He grimaced before she could answer. "Good Lord. It seems I'm constantly imploring you not to burn things."

She smiled in spite of herself. "No. Indeed, I'd likely write back to you. But, as I say—"

"Rules are rules."

"Yes, rules are rules," she agreed bleakly.

A chill wind whispered over her face as the horse pulled the sleigh back to Sutton Park. The warm glow she'd felt when he'd touched her and kissed her was rapidly dissipating.

Tomorrow she was returning home. There was every chance she'd never see him again. The prospect was suddenly too dire to contemplate.

"Perhaps we *might* meet again in London," she volunteered as the lights of the house came into view. "To be sure, I hope we will."

Teddy's handsome face set with resolve. "We will," he vowed. "You may depend on it."

Fourteen

❖

Stella departed Sutton Park at daybreak the following morning. Lady Arundell and Anne drove her as far as the station, where they saw her safely onto the train.

Lady Arundell sent a manservant to accompany Stella on the journey. An unmarried young lady couldn't travel alone, certainly not as great a distance as from Hampshire to Derbyshire, and not with having to change trains not once but twice. Anne had suggested that she and her mother go themselves, but Stella had declined the offer. It was miles out of their way, and she was tired of putting everyone to inconvenience on her behalf.

"A manservant is quite generous enough, thank you," she'd said. "Besides, no one is likely to meddle with a gray-haired lady."

"You must take care all the same," Anne had replied, giving her one last hug and kiss goodbye. "You never know what desperate characters you might meet in a railway car."

Desperate, indeed.

Stella's sense of impending doom swelled greater as the train bore her ever closer to home. This, at last, was the end of her adventures. There would be no more seasons. No more chances for romance.

No more Teddy.

Her thoughts drifted to him with increasing frequency as the train rattled down the track, carrying her further and further away from their brief week's idyll in Hampshire. It began to seem so much a dream.

Good heavens, but she'd kissed him!

Or rather, he'd kissed her.

The sweet, pulse-fluttering memory of it was sufficient to occupy her thoughts for the first hundred miles of her journey. She wondered whether it was better to have been kissed like that just once, or to have never been kissed at all. The latter, she decided morosely. At least then, she'd be ignorant of what she was missing.

But not now.

Now she would have to live on the memory of that kiss until she expired as a dried-up, dependent spinster, buried in Fostonbury churchyard, her headstone proclaiming her "Daughter of" and "Sister of," but nothing much else at all.

It was wholly unacceptable.

She expended the next twenty miles composing alternative epitaphs for herself. "Daughter, Sister, Horsewoman, and Friend," or "Horsewoman, Friend, and Beloved Wife of—"

Of someone.

The final miles home were spent calculating the expense of purchasing her own headstone, to have engraved in advance exactly as she chose. Was it morbid to invest in one so soon? Would she stir even more gossip among the villagers?

"I *am* the desperate character," she murmured to herself as she stared out the window, lost in her own gloomy thoughts.

She arrived at Fairhook Station later that evening, cold and tired, as the sun was sinking beneath the snow-covered Derbyshire peaks. It was the nearest stop to Fostonbury. Stella's village was too small and insignificant to have a platform halt of its own. Normally, on returning from town, she and her brother hired a cab to take them home. Tonight, however, on descending the platform, she found Squire Smalljoy's carriage waiting for her.

Stella stared at it in the light of the gas lamps that flanked the station. Never before had the squire offered the courtesy of his conveyance—not to Stella or to her brother—as far as she was aware. The significance of the gesture was unmistakable.

As death knells for her future went, it was as resounding as the clang of steel in a locomotive collision.

"The squire sent us to collect you," the footman said, taking Stella's bags from Lady Arundell's manservant. "With your brother's permission."

"I see," Stella said.

Drat Daniel and his matchmaking!

Under other circumstances, she would have mustered the fortitude to refuse the offer. But it was freezing out, and the chance of finding a cart to drive her to Fostonbury seemed unlikely at this hour.

She looked to Lady Arundell's manservant. Her ladyship had instructed him to see Stella all the way to her door. "If you'll join us?" Stella said. "You may like something to eat at the vicarage, and perhaps a bed for the night, before you resume your journey."

"I shan't need a bed, miss," he said. "But a cup of tea wouldn't be amiss."

"You can ride outside with me, sir," Squire Smalljoy's footman said as he carried Stella's bags to the carriage.

Stella grudgingly followed. She permitted the footman to hand her up into the coach.

The coachman called out to the team of chestnuts, sending the coach surging forward with a shudder. Given the snowfall on the roads, it took a good half hour to arrive at the gates of the vicarage. A swirl of smoke coiled from the modest dwelling's crooked stone chimney, alerting her to Daniel's presence. He was doubtless awaiting her in his book room, armed with a stern lecture regarding the dangers of women indulging in pleasure jaunts instead of adhering to familial duty.

Stella wasn't eager to hear it. Her heart was yearning for Locket. Disembarking from the carriage, she paused only long enough to direct Lady Arundell's manservant to the vicarage before making her way to the stable.

It was a humble structure made of green-painted wood. Locket stood inside, safe within the confines of her loose-box, bedded down for the night on a thick layer of straw. The flighty mare shifted anxiously on her hooves, uttering a shrill whinny of greeting as Stella approached.

"There's my wild girl," Stella murmured. Stripping off her gloves, she caught the mare's elegant head in her hands, holding it gently as she pressed a kiss to her velvety, dark gray nose. "Have you missed me dreadfully?"

Locket snuffled in reply, emitting warm, hay-sweet puffs of breath against Stella's cheek.

Stella inhaled deeply. Her world tipped back into place, righting itself on its axis. Everything else fell away, leaving her calm and composed, and once again her familiar, capable self. Good heavens, had she really been composing her own epitaph earlier? This was what came of being separated from Locket for any length of time.

"I've missed you, too," she said. "But I'm back now. I shan't leave you again for a long while. Not if I can help it."

Turvey emerged from the feed room with a bucket of mash. An unflappable older man with a shock of white hair, he'd been Locket's groom since Stella had purchased her, and could be relied on to remain steady when the temperamental mare was at her worst.

"Welcome home, miss," he said.

"I'm happy to be home, Turvey. How has she been keeping? Not giving you too much trouble, I hope."

"She's much herself." Turvey let himself into the loosebox. He set down the bucket in the corner. Locket wasted no time in abandoning Stella in favor of the hot mash.

"She looks in fine trim."

"Aye. She's eating well enough, though there's been less sugar in her diet with you away."

Stella smiled. "I shall soon remedy that."

Locket loved lumps of sugar. Stella kept them in the pocket of her habit so she could give them to the mare while she was on her back as a reward for good behavior. Locket was adept at bending her neck to retrieve them from Stella's outstretched hand.

"She was off a hair on her left front Christmas morning," Turvey said, exiting the loosebox.

"Was she?" Stella eyed her mare with concern. Locket sometimes strained her legs after indiscriminate running and jumping in her paddock. Stella was accustomed to treating such strains herself, massaging the mare's legs and rubbing them down with liniment. "Did you—?"

"Aye," Turvey said, answering the question before she'd asked it. "I rubbed her legs down morning and evening. She was well recovered by the next day."

"I'll rub them down again before I retire," Stella said. "Just as a precaution."

With one last fond glance at her mare, and a few final words with Turvey, Stella took her leave.

Their housekeeper, Mrs. Waltham, awaited her at the front door of the vicarage. "Your brother has been asking after you every five minutes. I told him you'd have gone to the stable first."

Stella divested herself of her bonnet and cloak. She handed them to the housekeeper along with her gloves. "Is he in his book room?"

"Yes, miss."

"And Lady Arundell's manservant? I trust he found his way to the kitchen."

"Cook has given him tea and biscuits, and the squire's coachman has promised to run him back to Fairhook directly after he's refreshed himself." Mrs. Waltham followed Stella down the hall. "Shall I bring a pot of tea in for you, miss? And some bread and butter?"

"That would be lovely," Stella said. She smoothed her wool traveling dress before going to her brother.

The book room was Daniel's private domain. He spent hours inside alone, working on his treatise. Stella had often assisted him there, head bent over the small secretary desk in the corner, silently transcribing his dour words on the subject of original sin as he pontificated from in front of the fire.

He was there now, seated in his favorite armchair, in the half circle of dwindling firelight. A threadbare banyan worn over his plain shirt and trousers was his only concession to comfort.

Stella quietly entered, shutting the door softly behind her.

Daniel glanced up from his book with a perturbed frown. With his prematurely balding pate and his severe expression, he bore no resemblance to Stella, except for a slight similarity about the eyes. In every other respect, they differed. Where her hair was gray, Daniel's was brown. Where her lips were soft, his were thin. And where her figure was robust from exercise, his was hollow from self-imposed deprivation.

He looked far older than his thirty years. Stella blamed herself. He'd had the charge of her from too young an age. It was a burden he hadn't wanted. One that had served to alter both his appearance and his disposition.

"I expected you this afternoon," he said, rising.

"I sent you a wire." She crossed the room to press a swift kiss to his cheek in greeting. "You must have received it, else Squire Smalljoy's carriage wouldn't have been waiting for me at the station."

"The squire was generous enough to offer it."

"You shouldn't have accepted. I don't wish to be under an obligation to the man."

"Why shouldn't I accept? Squire Smalljoy is a decent, God-fearing gentleman. If he professes an interest in you, I won't discourage him."

"Rather the opposite, it seems." Stella's words held an unmistakable note of reproach.

The squire's estate, Castaway Green, was fewer than five miles from the vicarage. He'd lived there for as long as Stella could remember, both while married to his late wife and during his subsequent years as a widower. But it had been only recently that Daniel had begun inviting the man to dine with them—an occurrence that had directly coincided with Stella's return from her first failed season in London. It promised to be worse now that she had another failed season to her name. She was dreading the prospect.

"May I remind you that the man is nearly sixty?" she said. "He has three grown daughters older than me."

Daniel's lips flattened with displeasure. "You've no business being so particular. After all the time and money that's been wasted these two years in your efforts to obtain a husband, the least you can do is show a pleasing face to the one remaining man who'll have you."

Stella's chest tightened with anger and—she loathed to admit to herself—no little hurt. She wasn't an antidote, for goodness' sake. Teddy had called her beautiful. A shining star. And Stella had the sketch that proved the truth of his words. She wouldn't allow her brother, or anyone, to diminish her.

"That's unfair," she said. "As well as being unkind."

"Is it unkind to encourage you to face your future? The sooner you—"

"I'm exhausted, Daniel. Let's not quarrel." She sank down in the worn chintz chair across from his. "All I desire is a cup of tea and my bed."

Daniel resumed his seat. "Of course, all this tiresomeness could have been avoided if you'd only had the sense to remain in London with me for Christmas. Instead, you must traverse the country, putting coachmen and servants to as great an inconvenience as you put myself and Miss Trent."

At last, Stella thought. The estimable Miss Trent. The true reason for her brother's uncommon irritation.

"If you'd had the generosity of spirit to remain in town, Miss Trent and her mother might have stayed with us," he said. "We could have shared all our meals together, and spent companionable hours discussing my treatise."

In short, they would have spent all their time together—morning, noon, and evening. It would have been a sure recipe for romance between Daniel and Miss Trent.

Stella didn't regret her role in preventing such intimacy. Better that Miss Trent and her mother had returned to Exeter for Christmas than that they'd remained in town to engineer an engagement.

"A great pity, yes," Stella said. "But I promised Lady Anne I would attend Lord March's house party. And thank heaven I was there. Lady Anne and Mr. Hartford became engaged on the first night. It was a great cause for celebration."

Daniel's brows elevated with evident skepticism. He didn't approve of Stella's friends. "Lady Anne is engaged to be married?"

"She and Mr. Hartford plan to wed at St. George's in the spring. I've said I'll attend."

"You were foolish to tell her so. We've only just returned from town. I'll not be traveling back again for any reason."

"But the circumstances are exceptional, you must agree. I'm to be a bridesmaid."

He shook his head. "Impossible. I've already overburdened my curate once too often. He's a capable fellow, but he didn't come to Fostonbury to take over the entirety of my parish duties. He's depending on me to resume my work with no more interruptions. I can't be escorting you to town at your every whim."

"I shall go alone, then," Stella said. "I shall take the train."

It was a bluff. She'd never traveled alone in her life.

Daniel snorted. "And make yourself infamous in the process? You'll do nothing of the sort. Miss Trent has already remarked unfavorably on your propensity for flitting about the country with your questionable female friends. I'll not have her sensibilities outraged any further. You bring both your name and mine into disrepute."

Stella stifled a caustic reply. Would the specter of Miss Trent never cease plaguing her? "Even if that was true, I don't see what it has to do with Miss Trent. She isn't any relation of mine. She is nothing to me."

Daniel's face darkened. "She is the most estimable young lady of my acquaintance! You will show her the respect she deserves."

A sinking suspicion took root in Stella's heart. "Did you see her in London while I was gone?"

"I did."

"I thought she and her mother were returning home?"

"They had planned it so, but when it came to the point, Mrs. Trent found herself unequal to the journey. She took rooms for herself and her daughter at the Bell and Crown. Less convivial surroundings at Christmas cannot be imagined."

Stella began to anticipate the worst. "You called on them there?"

"Daily," he said. "And dined with them. Indeed, we were blessed to share Christmas dinner in one of the inn's private parlors. It was there I made the discovery that your absence wasn't as much a detriment as I'd anticipated. On the contrary, according to Miss Trent, your presence has so far constrained her."

Stella stared at her brother with a mixture of incredulity and indignation. She'd never once said anything to quell the sanctimonious Miss Trent's unending stream of humble boasts and helpful advice. Stella doubted she could have silenced the woman if she'd tried. "Whatever is *that* meant to mean?"

"Miss Trent spoke more warmly, and more freely, than she had during our previous meetings," Daniel said. "It was owing to your absence. She told me so herself."

Did she, by heaven. The sly creature!

Stella understood at once that she'd made a grievous error in judgment. In all her scheming to thwart her brother's matrimonial plans, she'd never considered that Miss Trent might use Stella's absence to her advantage.

"I confess, the minds of women are a mystery to me," Daniel went on. "One would think she would be at greater liberty with you present to assure her virtue. But I'm in no position to complain." His mouth curved in a complacent smile. "Taking into account Miss Trent's encouragement, and my own feelings on the state of matrimony, not to mention that of the villagers and my congregation, I felt the moment ripe to make Miss Trent an offer of marriage."

Given the turn of the conversation, Stella had half expected the news. She still felt a chill in her veins to hear it confirmed.

"You proposed to her," she said flatly. "I assume she said yes?"

Daniel's chest puffed with pride. "She did me the very great honor of accepting me, yes."

The hourglass of Stella's fate turned over with a resounding thump.

So much for thwarting his matrimonial plans. It seemed that, for all her efforts, all she'd done was accelerate her brother's speed to the altar.

She began to wish that, on returning from the stable, she'd gone straight to bed. She would require a good night's sleep, and a good gallop on Locket, before she'd be in any frame of mind to sort out what she was going to do next. For she'd have to do something. That much was clear.

The door to the book room creaked open. Mrs. Waltham entered with a small tray bearing Stella's tea and toast. "Here you are, miss." She placed the tray on the low table between Stella and Daniel. "I've had Polly turn down your bed, and put a hot water bottle in. It will be nice and warm for you when you retire."

"Thank you, Mrs. Waltham," Stella said. "You're too good."

"Will you be requiring anything else, miss?" Mrs. Waltham looked to Daniel. "Sir?"

"That will be all, Mrs. Waltham," Daniel said.

The housekeeper withdrew, closing the door behind her.

"We will have many things to address in the coming months," Daniel said as Stella poured her tea. "There's the calling of the banns, and the question of what's to be done about our living arrangements."

"Miss Trent aspires to somewhere grander than the vicarage?"

"Don't be flippant. We will live here, naturally. Miss Trent assures me that a small village is exactly to her taste. She does, however, desire to gain some familiarity with Fostonbury—and with the running of the household—before the ceremony. She suggested a visit."

"Did she." Stella took a sip of tea. It was plain, sturdy English tea. Nothing to compare with the Darjeeling she and Teddy had shared in Hampshire.

She wondered if he'd reached Devon already. If he was there now, firmly ensconced in Captain Thornhill's cliffside estate, sitting at the window and sketching the sea, all thoughts of painting Stella forgotten.

The prospect left a sour taste in her mouth.

Daniel helped himself to Stella's toast. He bit into it with a dry crunch, scattering a spray of crumbs over his banyan. "Rather than her and her mother lodging somewhere in the village, I thought it prudent to invite them to join us as honored guests at the vicarage."

Stella's teacup froze halfway to her mouth. Surely, she'd misheard. "Miss Trent and her mother are to stay *here*?"

Daniel withdrew his handkerchief from his pocket and used it to dust the crumbs from his chest. "There's nothing objectionable in it. They might be guests of yours for all anyone knows. Friends you've invited to stay the month."

"*A month!*" Stella was aghast.

"I expect her and her mother to arrive in a fortnight, with plans to stay through Valentine's Day at the very least."

"That's *more* than a month, Daniel."

"The length of her visit isn't at issue. If we can contrive it, I expect Miss Trent and I will marry during her stay, and then she will remain here permanently."

Stella's already plummeting spirits sunk still further. The situation was rapidly spinning out of her control. She sensed there was precious little she could do to stop it. "She can't marry you while staying in the same house," she pointed out in a last feeble attempt at preventing this debacle. "Think of the talk it would generate."

"If necessary, I will take a room in the village while the banns are called." Daniel brushed the remaining crumbs from his hands. "By the by, Mrs. Waltham's words about the hot water bottle have reminded me. Perhaps you might give Miss Trent and her mother your room while they're here? It's less prone to dampness at this time of year."

"The very reason I chose it," Stella said tightly.

"Quite," he agreed. "And you have the better view of the church. Miss Trent will appreciate it more than you do."

With an effort, Stella resumed drinking her tea. "Where am I to sleep while she's here? The airing cupboard?"

"You can have the box room," he said.

The box room was no bedroom at all. More of a storage closet, its narrow bed with its sagging mattress was presently covered in old linens, dusty clothing, and other donated items waiting to be sorted for distribution to the poor. It was a room that baked hot as Hades in the summer and froze as cold as an arctic glacier in the winter. A place in which it was impossible to be comfortable for more than ten minutes at a time.

But Stella knew better than to argue. The house was Daniel's. It was he who had the living. He who employed the servants and paid for the food, the coal, and the candles. She could never afford any of those things herself, not with Locket to provide for and Turvey's wages to pay.

"Very well," she said. "Far be it from me to be thought ungracious."

It was only for six weeks. After that, Miss Trent would be Mrs. Hobhouse and could safely remove herself to Daniel's bedchamber. Unless, of course, she was one of those married ladies who demanded a separate room from her husband. In which case, Stella presumed she would be relegated to the box room indefinitely.

Daniel tucked his handkerchief back into his pocket. "We must take care to present the vicarage in a favorable light," he said. "We shall have a formal dinner to welcome her and her mother. You must arrange it. And you must invite Squire Smalljoy."

The devil she would.

"Is it wise to offer him so much encouragement?" Stella asked. "We both know I've no desire to wed the man."

"He's not proposed to you yet."

"No, thank goodness. But you've planted the ridiculous notion in his head, and now he seems to think himself as good as my suitor. Never mind that he's already a grandfather ten times over."

Daniel's face settled into its familiar lines of priggish superiority. "The age disparity between the two of you has much to recommend it. To be sure, an older gentleman will suit your impetuous nature better than a young one. You require someone to take you in hand. I've often said so."

"I've often heard you." Setting aside her cup with a clatter, Stella rose from her chair. She had no more stomach for tea, or for her brother's conversation. "Forgive me, I'm tired."

Daniel stood, following her to the door of the book room. "I'm aware you don't find the squire a romantic enough figure for your tastes, but I ask you to give the man a fair hearing. You may yet discover that being his wife is preferable to remaining as you are."

A burden, he meant. An unruly charge on her friends and relations.

Was marriage to an old, overbearing squire preferable to that? Despite her misgivings about her future, Stella didn't think so.

"I shall be civil to him," she said.

But nothing more than civil, she added privately.

Her brother may be disposed to encourage the squire's attention, but when the man next came to dine, Stella had every intention of doing the opposite.

Fifteen

DERBYSHIRE, ENGLAND
JANUARY 1863

The day of Miss Trent's visit arrived with unsettling swiftness. Stella spent the morning just as she'd spent every morning and afternoon since returning from Hampshire—on Locket, galloping through the woods that abutted the vicarage. Riding had been Stella's only respite from the endless chores she'd been tasked with in preparation for their guests.

A fresh snowfall covered the ground. Locket's hooves flew over it with ease as she and Stella charged along their favorite route—a meandering trail that ran through a stand of silver birch trees, alongside a frozen stream, and then up a hill to join with the main road to the village.

Locket loved the familiarity of the flats and the challenge of the ascents. She was a creature who gained confidence through the terrain. The firmer the footing, the greater the length of her stride.

Stella leaned forward over Locket's silvery neck as the mare surged beneath her through the snow, the earthly incarnation of a star streaking across the sky. Icy wind tore at the net veil of Stella's high-crowned riding hat and whipped at the heavy skirts of her habit, sending them flapping behind her in a stream of mazarine-dyed wool.

A coach rolling down the road in the direction of the vicarage slowed as she and Locket flew by. Stella paid it no mind. She wasn't thinking of scandal or spectacle. She was only thinking of speed.

Anne had once said that if given her head, Locket could bolt all the way to Bridgehampton. Stella wished it were true. Wished she could loosen the reins and let Locket carry her far away from Fostonbury, all the way to London.

Or to Devon.

Not for the first time, her thoughts turned toward Teddy in his cliffside estate. To that scorching kiss they'd shared in the sleigh. Who knew when Stella would see him again? Or *if* she would see him again.

Daniel was still set against accompanying her to Anne's wedding. Never mind that Stella had exerted a herculean effort to soften his resolve. She'd spent the past two weeks diligently copying and organizing his notes, accompanying him on parish visits to the sick and elderly, and overseeing a thorough cleaning of the vicarage. She'd made the box room fit for occupancy, inventoried the linens, and prepared a month's worth of menus. She'd even penned an invitation to Squire Smalljoy in her own hand, personally inviting him to join them at tonight's dinner to welcome Miss Trent and her mother.

All to no avail.

Daniel was no more inclined to take Stella to London than he'd been on the first night she'd asked him.

Stella said as much in the letters she wrote to Julia and Evie. But not to Anne. Stella told her nothing of the troubles she was presently enduring. The last thing she wanted was Anne making good on her threat to come and collect Stella personally. And Anne would, too.

It wouldn't do. Stella would simply have to find another way to get to London this spring.

Turning Locket back toward the vicarage, Stella trotted the mare, then walked her to cool her out. By the time they reached the rear entrance of the stable, Locket was calm and steady, and ready for a bucket of mash.

"She'll be quiet until this afternoon, I reckon," Turvey said, taking Locket's reins as Stella dismounted. "Doesn't take her but a few hours to get restless again."

"She and I both," Stella murmured. She gave her mare an affectionate scratch on the neck. "We're of a similar temperament, aren't we?"

Turvey respectfully refrained from answering as he led Locket away to untack her.

Stella walked back to the vicarage, shaking the gray horsehair from the skirts of her habit as she went. There was still much to be done before this afternoon. Miss Trent and her mother were due to arrive at Fairhook Station at half past two. Daniel would be going to fetch them in a hired gig.

But as Stella crossed the grounds to the front of the house, she saw—much to her alarm—the same coach she'd passed on the road now parked in front of the vicarage door. Two petite ladies in sturdy cloaks and bonnets had descended from the vehicle, one young and one old.

It was Amanda Trent and her mother.

The portly, brassy-haired Mrs. Trent was overseeing the removal of a number of trunks and leather traveling cases from the coach, with Daniel's help. Mrs. Waltham stood at the open door of the vicarage, looking rather harried, as she showed the footmen where to put them.

Stella briefly considered slipping away to her room to hurriedly wash and change, but it was too late. Miss Trent had already spotted her.

"Miss Hobhouse!" Miss Trent exclaimed. "I *thought* it was you we saw on the road." She swept across the drive to meet Stella. Not much more than five feet in height, she possessed all the steely purpose of a conqueror come to finalize her battle plans—an effect completely unmarred by her flaxen ringlets and her tiny pink rosebud of a mouth.

"I told your brother that you would be back directly," she said, "as wild a pace as you were keeping."

"Miss Trent." Stella exchanged curtsies with the young woman. "This is a surprise. We weren't expecting you to arrive until this afternoon."

"You must call me Amanda," Miss Trent insisted. "And I shall address you as Stella. We shall be family soon, shan't we?"

"Yes. It seems we shall."

"The very reason I suggested we take an earlier train. Why delay the start of our lives together? I assured Mama that you and dear Mr. Hobhouse wouldn't mind. *'Miss Hobhouse will have all in readiness,'* I told her. *'She is an excellent housekeeper to her brother. Unmarried sisters always are.'*"

Stella pasted on a smile, ignoring Amanda's barbs. This is how it always began with her. The subtly cutting comments and treacle-covered darts. Amanda Trent was an underhanded opponent. It was impossible to war with her openly, but it was war all the same, and they both knew it.

"You are welcome at any hour, of course." Stella gestured to the front door, conscious of her soiled riding habit and the wild strands of her gray hair sticking to her perspiration-damp brow.

No doubt she looked a fright, especially to someone as notoriously fastidious as Amanda. The young lady had just traveled all the way from London, but still appeared as fresh as a nosegay.

Daniel shot a severe glance in Stella's direction as she passed. He'd warned her not to embarrass him in front of their guests, and here she was, offending everyone's sensibilities in the very first moment.

"I beg you would excuse my sister's unfortunate appearance," he said. "Stella? Hadn't you better change before joining us in the parlor?"

"Indeed," Stella replied. As if she hadn't been intending to do that very thing!

"It appeared an exciting ride." Amanda linked her arm with Stella's as they walked to the door, affecting an intimacy the two of them didn't share. "Though, if you'll permit a word of advice, not perhaps an excessively wise one. A lady should never gallop her horse. Mama was quite shocked to see you doing so. She mentioned it to your brother straightaway."

Stella's spine went rigid at the reprimand. It was one thing for Amanda to meddle in every other aspect of Stella's life, but to dare to interfere with her riding?

"I don't believe in absolutes," Stella said with a creditable degree of composure. "Words like *always* and *never* leave no room for extenuating circumstances."

"Are there any such circumstances when it comes to riding so recklessly?"

Stella could think of half a dozen or more. But there were only two that applied to her wild rides on Locket. "My horse requires a good gallop to keep her civil," she said. "As do I."

"*Requires*," Amanda repeated with a titter of indulgent amusement. "Such an interesting choice of words. One requires so little in life, really. And do consider, if you would but exercise self-restraint in your habits, you would find yourself amply rewarded by your brother's esteem. Pray, let me be your example."

"You are too kind," Stella said tightly.

"I might offer guidance in other respects as well," Amanda continued. "Your brother tells me that you're eager to engage a drawing master?"

"I've made inquiries, yes," Stella admitted. She hadn't had much luck in her search. All the gentlemen drawing masters recommended to her had either been too far away, or too expensive.

"A costly indulgence," Amanda said. "And an unnecessary one now I am here. My watercolors have often been praised in Exeter. I shall be pleased to offer you the benefit of my humble expertise."

"How generous of you," Stella said.

Behind them, Amanda's mother entered the hall on Daniel's arm. She acknowledged Stella's presence with a cool nod. Mrs. Trent rarely paid Stella any attention, unless she was making herself infamous in some way. The remainder of the time Mrs. Trent treated her future son-in-law's sister as someone possessing no more importance than an unattractive piece of furniture in an otherwise pleasant room. A shabby chair or a garish ottoman, jarring in its appearance, but easily dispensed with at the first opportunity.

"Careful with that!" she snapped at the footman who was trailing behind them, struggling with the larger of her trunks. "It contains more than your position is worth!"

"Beg pardon, ma'am." The footman readjusted the heavy trunk on his shoulder.

"Good servants are impossible to come by," Mrs. Trent said to Daniel. "It stems from laziness. A great affliction among the poor, and one of the chief reasons for their sad state. You've referenced it yourself in your scholarly writings."

"Quite true, madam," he said. "Laziness is a terrible vice."

Stella shot a look of apology to both the footman and Mrs. Waltham, the latter of whom had received Mrs. Trent's words with an expression of barely concealed outrage. "Laziness isn't at issue among the people of Fostonbury," Stella said. "We're all hard workers hereabouts. Isn't that so, Mrs. Waltham?"

"Yes, miss," the housekeeper answered with offended dignity.

"Would you be so good as to bring the tea tray in?" Stella asked her. "Miss Trent and her mother will be in need of refreshment after their journey." Extricating herself from Amanda's steely grasp, Stella moved to ascend the stairs. "Please allow my brother to entertain you while I change out of my riding things. I shall be back promptly."

◆─✕─◆

The remainder of the day devolved at a rapid rate. By the time Squire Smalljoy arrived for dinner, Stella's nerves were rubbed raw, and

Daniel, who had already been growing weary of her at the best of times, had since—under the barrage of helpful criticism from Amanda and her mother—begun to look on Stella as the greatest burden of his life.

Add to that the old-fashioned masculine condescension that the squire spewed forth with every breath, and the evening possessed all the necessary ingredients for absolute disaster.

Stella had only to hold her tongue until the final course was served to avert catastrophe. It shouldn't have been difficult. Neither Daniel, Squire Smalljoy, nor the Trents required conversation from her. She had only to answer yes or no, to smile dumbly, and to bob her head in agreement with every insipid remark.

Naturally, she did none of those things.

"You can't honestly consider Lord Palmerston to be a moral authority," she said in response to a comment the squire had made about the prime minister. "The reports of his sordid affairs are too many to number. I've heard that some in Westminster have taken to calling him Lord Cupid."

Her words were met by four shocked faces at the round, lace-covered mahogany table.

Squire Smalljoy was the first to break the appalled silence. "A politician's personal indiscretions don't matter a jot when his policies are in good order," he said as he chewed an oversized bite of fatty mutton. He was a hearty man with a hearty appetite, in every respect. White-haired and full-whiskered, he ate and drank with gusto, rode hard to the hounds, and—at eight-and-fifty—had already sired a passel of children.

The clinking of cutlery resumed as the guests continued their meal. Mrs. Waltham had laid the table with care this evening, putting out their finest silver and the set of blue-and-white china bowls and plates that had belonged to Stella's parents. Coupled with the lace tablecloth, sparkling glass goblets, and extra branches of costly beeswax candles, the effect was one of genteel elegance.

"His policies are no better," Stella said. "Had Lord Palmerston not authorized soldiers to invade Peking three years ago, the Summer Palace would still be standing. Instead, it was burned to the ground. And what about his views on women's suffrage?"

Mrs. Trent coughed loudly into her white linen napkin. Seated at Daniel's left, she was clad in a plain dinner dress with an untrimmed matron's cap over her hair. Amanda sat on Daniel's right, garbed in a similarly modest fashion. She gave Daniel a speaking look.

Obedient to the unspoken plea from his betrothed, Daniel leveled a warning glare at his sister.

Stella ignored it. The only way to extinguish the squire's interest in her was to illustrate how ill-suited they were. And she could hardly do that while remaining silent. "Palmerston says that it's enough for fathers, husbands, and brothers to have the vote," she continued, undeterred. "He claims they'll act for the benefit of the ladies in their care. What he fails to consider—"

"You do have opinions, missy," the squire interrupted. "I blame you, Hobhouse. Shouldn't let females develop such notions."

"I've tried to educate her," Daniel said apologetically.

"There's your error." The squire washed down his mutton with another mouthful of wine. "Education is wasted on the female brain."

"Rubbish," Stella said under her breath as she cut into her boiled potato.

Daniel flashed her another stern look across the table. Mrs. Trent and her daughter marked it, just as they'd marked all the others. It seemed to Stella that they exchanged a smug glance every time Daniel sent a scolding frown Stella's way.

But though the Trents triumphed in her brother's worsening opinion of her, they had no interest in seeing Stella brought low in Squire Smalljoy's eyes. It was to both their benefit that the man think well of her. Once Stella was married, she would be out of her brother's house and permanently out of Amanda's way.

"I would agree with you, squire," Mrs. Trent said, daintily dabbing at her mouth with her napkin, "if your reference is to those subjects better suited to young men. But I can't believe you object to a young lady being schooled in the feminine arts."

"Not to those subjects, no," Squire Smalljoy said. "Singing, sewing, a bit of the piano, and a dabbling in French. Whatever course of study improves the prettiness of a girl and makes her a charming companion for her husband has my full endorsement."

"My daughter is well versed in all of those subjects," Mrs. Trent informed him proudly. "Along with a thorough course of spiritual education, which I've undertaken myself."

Daniel looked at Amanda with glowing approval. "Miss Trent is a testament to your wisdom, ma'am."

Amanda bowed her blonde head in meek acceptance of his praise. Her fair cheeks turned a delicate shade of pink.

Stella wondered if some ladies found it possible to blush on command. A useful talent, unquestionably, if one was trying to impress a pious country vicar with one's modesty and virtue.

"I have done my best, sir," Mrs. Trent said. "As have you, Mr. Hobhouse, in the absence of your dear departed parents. You are to be commended for your efforts. Miss Hobhouse will make some fortunate fellow a conformable wife."

Stella choked on her potato. She reached for her wine, hastily draining the glass.

Daniel glared at her. "I did stress the importance of adherence to a traditional course of study to my sister's governesses. But Stella has a mind of her own. She reads widely, and forms her own opinions."

"You must guide those opinions, Hobhouse," the squire said. "As must every man who has the responsibility of ladies under his care. No need for a woman to be troubling her head with politics or philosophy. Ladies should be small and quiet. It's ever been thus in a happy home."

"Perhaps in the past," Stella said. She ignored her brother's attempts to catch her eyes. "Modern minds take a different view. They understand that women are capable of making valuable contributions, both to scholarship and to conversation. Why, consider the Queen—"

"Small and quiet," Squire Smalljoy interrupted, addressing Daniel, not Stella. "That's a woman's place. My daughters learned it in the nursery. Best to focus on being good little wives and mothers. On cheering a fellow's spirits, not deadening his eardrums with all this newfangled nonsense."

"Ah, motherhood." Mrs. Trent beamed like a saint in a Renaissance painting. "The most sacred of institutions. A lady cannot wish for a more exalted state. Is that not right, squire?"

"Quite so," he grumbled. "Quite so. A fine daughter you've raised there, too, madam."

Amanda smiled, but said not a word. She didn't talk overmuch in company. The bulk of her speech was saved for private asides. That was where her power lay: in pitting brothers against sisters and mothers against future in-laws.

"Motherhood is a role Miss Hobhouse is eminently suited for," Mrs. Trent said. "Do you not agree, Mr. Hobhouse?"

"Oh yes," Daniel concurred. "My sister is very fond of children."

Stella refilled her wineglass. Her rising temper had been under questionable control all evening, but now, in the face of these blatantly obvious ploys to see her married off to a man she didn't like, it threatened to bubble over completely. "On the contrary," she said. "I find the company of children rather trying."

It wasn't true, of course. Stella *was* fond of children. Indeed, she'd always imagined she would have a family of her own someday. But to admit such a thing in the hearing of a gentleman like Squire Smalljoy would be tantamount to waving a white flag of surrender.

Too late, she realized that all she'd done instead was wave a red flag in front of a bull.

"What's this?" The squire turned to her at last. "Don't care for children?"

"It's not uncommon," Stella said.

"It's unnatural, is what it is. Hobhouse! Did you know of this?"

Daniel gave a hollow laugh. "My sister's poor idea of a jest. Pay it no mind."

"A dashed poor jest," Squire Smalljoy muttered as he resumed eating. "The finest quality in a female, mothering and bearing children. My late wife was a saint. Gave her life to my sons and daughters. Lost her life in the end, bearing my youngest. A noble sacrifice, I say."

"The noblest," Daniel said. "Very well put."

The views expressed weren't any different from those Stella had heard articulated hundreds of times, both by her brother and by the antiquated scholars in his old-fashioned set. She was weary of listening to them.

"Yes, well"—she raised her glass to her lips—"I'm not eager to sacrifice my life just yet. Not for children or anyone. There are things I still wish to do for myself."

The squire's brows snapped together. "*Things?* What things?"

"I don't know yet," she admitted. "But I do know that motherhood isn't conducive to riding, and I won't submit to anything—or any*one*—that prevents me from galloping my mare."

Amanda's eyes found Stella's in the guttering light of the beeswax candles. Anger glimmered in her face. "My advice was kindly meant."

"She prefers riding to motherhood?" Squire Smalljoy questioned Stella's brother. "What manner of girl—"

"Another jest," Daniel said with a weak laugh. "My sister is aware you're fond of horses. She's teasing you on the subject."

Mrs. Trent tittered. "What a sense of humor our Miss Hobhouse has. Her husband and children will never want for merriment, I vow."

The squire relaxed a fraction, only partially reassured. "Jolly company is nothing to disparage. A good jest, in its place, is always welcome."

"I never jest about riding," Stella said gravely.

"You've one of Stockwell's get, do you not?" Squire Smalljoy asked. "That gray mare with the dappled legs? I've seen you riding her about on occasion."

"Locket," Stella said. "That's her name."

"No idea who the dam is?"

"A half-blood Arabian, I've been told."

He harrumphed. "Could do better in terms of lineage. Still . . . with Stockwell as her sire, there might be possibilities. A cross with my Irish stallion could produce something worthwhile."

"I've no plans to turn Locket into a broodmare," Stella said.

The squire helped himself to the last serving of mutton. "Of course, she'll be a broodmare. What else is she for?"

"What indeed?" Stella murmured. It appeared the squire took the same view of mares that he took of women.

"I'll have a look at her after dinner," he said. "If she's fit for it, you can send her to Castaway Green when the weather clears. She can put up for the spring in my stables until she's caught."

Stella's fingers tightened on her fork. "I've already said no, sir. I won't change my mind."

The squire turned to Daniel. "Hobhouse. You're damnably silent. Have you no authority in these matters?"

"It will naturally be as you wish," Daniel said. "My sister and I would count it an honor for the mare to be sent to you."

This time, Stella set down her fork entirely. She couldn't guarantee she wouldn't use the utensil as a weapon. "Locket belongs to me. The authority over her is, therefore, mine and mine alone."

Daniel briefly closed his eyes, as if praying for divine patience. "Forgive my sister, sir. She forgets herself. She's been too long in London."

"Town ways," the squire said disparagingly. "Too many years there leaves a taint. Impossible to rub off. A girl forgets her place."

"Unmarried women do have rights, Squire Smalljoy," Stella said. "Even if most of the laws are set against us, we are still something, I believe, above mere chattel. We can own property, including horses. We can even string two thoughts together in conversation if we've a mind to."

"Enough, Stella," Daniel said. "You go too far."

Squire Smalljoy resumed eating. "Your sister has a sharp tongue, sir."

"For which I sincerely apologize," Daniel said. "I blame her health. She's still overtired from her journey."

"Frail health as well." The squire clucked. "Might have guessed it given"—he glanced at Stella's hair—"all that."

"Yes," Stella agreed, offended by his remark to the point of blatant incivility. "I *am* a questionable specimen. No better a breeding prospect than my mare, I daresay."

Mrs. Trent gasped in horror.

Amanda lost all color. She sagged in her chair as though she would swoon.

Daniel went as red as a beetroot. "*Stella!*"

Clamping her mouth shut, Stella returned to her meal. A pit formed in her stomach, making it nearly impossible to swallow down the remainder of her potatoes. She knew that she'd gone too far. She'd been not only uncivil but dangerously indecorous.

Squire Smalljoy took his leave soon after, not even bothering to remain long enough to share a glass of port with Daniel in his book room. Daniel followed the squire from the dining room, apologizing profusely.

Stella remained in her seat, under the molten glare of Mrs. Trent, the possible repercussions of her too-candid words sinking in with a sickening clarity.

How many times these last several months had she had cause to regret her behavior? And yet some small, mutinous part of her soul persisted in pushing her to do too much, to say too much, to take risks she shouldn't. It had become a habit with her. One that had no more place in Derbyshire than it had in London or Hampshire.

In the past, her lapses had fleeting consequences. But not this time. Whatever happened when her brother returned, Stella had the sickening premonition that, henceforward, her life would never be the same.

Sixteen

❖

The following morning, Stella entered Daniel's book room, hands clasped in front of her in what she hoped was a suitably penitent posture. Her brother awaited her within, seated behind his heavy, carved oak desk.

He had ordered her to meet him here at half past nine to discuss her future. There had been no discussing anything last night. On returning to the dining room, Daniel had been too angry to even look at Stella. Instead, he'd sent her to her room while he remained to deal with the chaos Stella had wrought among the Trents. Amanda had required sal volatile to revive her, and Mrs. Trent had been up in arms.

"My daughter's tender sensibilities have been thoroughly outraged, sir!" she'd declared. "I little thought such vulgarity would be present in a clergyman's home!"

Stella had been relieved to make her escape. But the humiliation had still stung her to her soul. She couldn't recall when she'd last been ordered to bed like a disobedient child. Nor when she'd last been summoned to stand in front of Daniel's desk like a prisoner awaiting sentence.

"Well, brother?" she prompted after a prolonged period of taut silence. "You wished to speak with me?"

Daniel's anger didn't appear to have lessened overnight. He regarded her from behind his desk with barely controlled fury. There were shadows under his eyes from lack of sleep. "Your behavior last night was inexcusable," he said. "To speak as you did, addressing a gentleman of Squire Smalljoy's station in such an indecent manner. And in front of my betrothed! Had you taken leave of your senses?"

Stella remained standing in front of him. He hadn't offered for her to sit. She didn't particularly want to. With luck, their interview would be brief. She didn't think she could bear a lengthy scolding. "It *was* badly done of me," she acknowledged. "But you must own that I had ample provocation."

"What right had you to consider yourself provoked? Squire Smalljoy is a pillar of the community. He might have made you a capable husband. But no longer. After how you comported yourself last evening, the man wouldn't touch you with a barge pole."

"A state of affairs which suits me very well."

"You're two-and-twenty, Stella. Soon to be three-and-twenty. Have you no appreciation for the perilousness of your situation?"

"My situation is more than tolerable," she said. "I'm in good health. I'm possessed of wonderful friends, and an excellent mare. And I—"

"None of which fulfills your duty on this earth. A woman's purpose is to marry and produce children. It's all that matters in God's eyes."

Stella had heard this assertion before, too many times to count. It never failed to grate. "On that fact, brother, we must agree to differ."

"What then, pray? Do you propose to remain a burden on me for the rest of your life? To continue to live here at the vicarage, inspiring the village gossips with your rebellious ways, and stirring talk with the way you look?"

She flinched inwardly. "I can't help the way I look."

"You could be small and quiet as the squire said. You could be an asset to me instead of a liability. Had you given the sum Father left you to the church instead of parading yourself in London—"

"Not *this* old argument again."

"It would have been a start," he said. "Had you remained in Fostonbury, nursing the sick and tending to the poor, you'd have done more to merit my regard than—"

"I already nurse the sick and tend to the poor. The only difference is that I have a bit of money of my own. If I'd given it to you for your charitable causes, then I truly would have been a burden. You'd have resented me for having no means to support myself as surely as you resent me now."

He uttered a scornful huff. "What do you expect to happen when I marry Miss Trent? That you'll carry on in this parasitic existence? Doing as you please whenever you please, without any consequences?"

Parasitic?

Stella's chest constricted as though recoiling from the sharp point of a knife. "I've always done more than my share. Always. I ask hardly anything for myself, except to ride Locket and to occasionally visit my friends."

Her brother was too angry to listen, let alone acknowledge the truth of her words. "You won't be visiting your friends anytime soon. Not under my chaperonage. I've discharged my duty to our father, escorting you to town so you might find a husband. But no more. This is *my* time now. If you insist on remaining here to live on my charity, by God, you will learn to behave yourself! Do you hear me?"

Stella was certain the whole house had heard him. She held herself rigid with the remaining threads of her dignity. "Is that all, Daniel?"

"That is *not* all." He made a visible effort to regain his composure. "You will apologize to Miss Trent and her mother."

"Very well." Stella had planned to do that anyway. She might have already done so if either Amanda or her mother had deigned to appear at breakfast. Instead, they'd remained in their room—Stella's room—as though Stella's conduct had caused them a physical injury from which they still must recover.

"And you will write a note of apology to Squire Smalljoy," Daniel said.

Stella stiffened at the prospect. "I will not."

"It is *not* negotiable!" His fist came down with a crash onto the surface of his desk, making the scattered papers jump. "I want the note written and delivered before nightfall. You can send it to Castaway Green with your groom. It's too late for the morning post. The wretched postboy came early today."

Stella's stomach sank. She'd thought, at the very least, she had dispensed with the threat of Squire Smalljoy. That threat would only be revived if she was obliged to write to him. He would doubtless take any apology as encouragement. And then where would she be?

But her brother could not be reasoned with.

"It will be as you wish." Stella turned to leave.

"Take your post with you," Daniel said.

She immediately went back for it. It wasn't unusual for her to receive bundles of letters, newspapers, and ladies' journals. There was little else to break the monotony in Fostonbury.

But there was only one letter today.

Her brother handed it to her—a thick envelope that had been sealed with a pale blue wafer. "Who is Mrs. Archer?" he asked.

Mrs. Archer!

Stella's guttering sense of hope sprang into a brilliant flame. Taking the letter, she pored over the return address in a rush of excitement. It was sent from Devon—a house called Greyfriar's Abbey in a place called King's Abbot.

"She's a lady I met in Hampshire," she said distractedly. "The wife of a well-to-do tradesman the earl invited to view his roses."

Daniel grunted. "Singular."

"Not at all. There were many tradesmen in attendance. The earl has a wide and varied acquaintance." Stella caught up the skirts of her morning dress, moving to the door. "If you'll excuse me?"

Exiting the book room, she crossed the empty hall and bounded up the steps to the box room. There, the door shut firmly behind her, she sank down on the edge of the sagging mattress and broke the seal of Mrs. Archer's letter. It was a lengthy one, if the thickness of the envelope was to judge.

But on unfolding the letter, it was revealed to consist of only a single outer page, with another, longer letter folded small inside of it.

Stella's pulse quickened as she read the outer letter. It was merely a polite missive—cordial and frank in its offer of friendship, but quite clearly a tissue-thin formality to shield the possibility of scandal from the smaller letter within.

It was *that* letter Stella hastened to unfold, knowing full well who it was from.

My dear Miss Hobhouse (it began),

Forgive my sister's complicity. I assured her that you would welcome a letter from me. I trust I'm right, and that I've not presumed too much upon our short acquaintance in Hampshire.

How are you faring in Fostonbury? How is that famous mare of yours? Have you been riding this past week—or should I say galloping?

I am presently in Devon, at Greyfriar's Abbey, not lacking for company. The Abbey's owner, Captain Thornhill, and his wife, Lady Helena, are in residence, along with their little daughter, Honoria. So, too, is Tom Finchley, a capital attorney, and his wife, Jenny; and Neville Cross, a farmer; his wife, Clara; and their newborn baby, George. These men are something like brothers to my brother-in-law, all of them raised in an orphanage together many years ago. It's a bleak history that has made for a strong bond between them, and puts me in the position of having a rather larger family about me than I can creditably tolerate.

I spend most of my time in the drawing room. It has an enormous window that looks out toward the sea. Seascapes are, as ever, my occupation in Devon. I can't get enough of painting them. Jennings has been obliged to procure additional canvases for me from the village, when the cliff road isn't washed out from the storms. And it does wash out with alarming regularity, leaving the abbey all but isolated.

The sea is a beguiling subject. Of course, if I had my way, I'd be painting quite another prospect, the inspiration of which still haunts me day and night.

Has my humble sketch at all managed to change your mind? I endeavor to hope that, on reflection, you may see some merit in my committing your likeness to canvas. I do believe it would be the making of me. And who knows but that it might not have a favorable effect on your life as well? There are worse ways to end one's days than to be made immortal.

Write back to me if you're so inclined. I seem to recall that you said you would. But perhaps I only dreamt it. There were stars at the time, and a brief moment in a sleigh that rather muddled my senses.

Your friend,
Teddy Hayes

Seventeen

*T*eddy cast another distracted glance out the drawing room window at the rain-flooded cliff path below. During foul weather, the road to Greyfriar's Abbey was impassible. No one from the village would dare risk it with horse or carriage, and only the bravest of men would hazard it on foot.

Fortunately, Alex and their host, Justin Thornhill, were two such men. As boys, they'd clambered over the North Devon cliffs indiscriminately, in company with fellow orphans Tom Finchley and Neville Cross. A walk down to the village didn't intimidate them, not now the rain had stopped and the sun was shining.

They had left over an hour ago to fetch the post, the daily papers, and a few supplies from the market for the ladies. Teddy awaited their return with uncharacteristic restlessness.

Perhaps he'd been too bold in writing to Stella?

Then again, what had ever been achieved through faintheartedness?

"You're n-not painting today?" Neville joined Teddy at the window. He was a large man, well over six feet in height, with short cropped blond hair and a noble countenance more suited to an Arthurian knight than a stammering Devonshire farmer.

Teddy closed his sketchbook. He'd spent most of the morning idly penciling ideas for his portrait of Stella. A frustrating exercise. He'd left Hampshire no closer to her agreeing to sit for him than when he'd first asked.

All he'd achieved during the house party was to form a strange sort of friendship with her.

And to kiss her.

The memory of that moment in the sleigh had lately been plaguing his dreams.

Good Lord, what had possessed him? He might have at least restricted the intimacy to a brief peck on the cheek or an even briefer one on the lips. Instead, he'd taken his time, making a thorough romantic business out of what might have otherwise been a perfectly ordinary holiday custom.

"Teddy is in a world of his own," Laura said. She sat a distance away by the drawing room fire, in company with Lady Helena Thornhill, Clara Cross, and Jenny Finchley.

The four ladies laughed softly together at Laura's remark. Garbed in warm wool dresses and swathed in fashionable cashmere shawls, they were of a similar age, and since marrying their respective husbands, had become as close as sisters.

Jenny held little Honoria Thornhill on her lap. The raven-locked child was two years old. Small and plump cheeked, she was generally possessed of her father's air of quiet reserve. But not at this time of day. Now, she was red faced and on the verge of tears, desperately in need of one of her twice-daily naps.

"If you'd give me more than five seconds to formulate an answer," Teddy said to his sister, "I may yet make one."

Neville sank down in a chair next to him. "Take as long as you n-need."

Teddy's mouth quirked. If anyone understood lengthy pauses it was Neville Cross.

Neville had suffered a brain injury when he'd fallen from the cliffs as a boy. Though he'd recovered admirably over the years, he still found it difficult to formulate speech with any degree of ease. He paused often, sometimes appearing to drift off in his own head as though he'd fallen into a daydream.

Teddy didn't mind it. On the contrary, he shared a strong sense of fellow feeling with Neville. Before his marriage to Clara, Neville had lived at the Abbey under Justin's protection. Neville knew firsthand what it was like to have to fight for autonomy over his own life.

"I'm expecting something in the post," Teddy told him. "A letter from someone who might be important to me. It's made me too restless to settle to anything this morning."

"A young lady?" Jenny asked, smiling. "Do tell."

"It's forward of her to write to you directly, is it not?" Lady Helena wondered aloud. "When I was a girl, young ladies weren't allowed to correspond with unmarried gentlemen."

"She's not corresponding with my brother," Laura said. "She's corresponding with me."

"Ah." Jenny nodded her approval at the subterfuge. "An excellent compromise."

Teddy ignored them. Their teasing grated, but he had no right to privacy, not when he'd willingly invited his sister into his plan to contact Stella. Laura had agreed, albeit reluctantly.

"If Miss Hobhouse doesn't want to hear from you, we're both going to look like dreadful people," she'd warned him. "You for imposing yourself, and me for participating in such a devious trick."

"She wants to hear from me," Teddy had assured his sister.

But as the weeks wore on, he was no longer certain.

What if Stella had taken offense at his letter? Or what if—

Good God. What if she'd never received it at all?

Teddy hadn't known the name of her village. He'd had to enlist Tom Finchley to discover it for him. Another violation of Teddy's privacy. It went against the grain, asking his friends and family for help. He hadn't liked to do it, but faced with the prospect of never hearing from Stella again, he'd been obliged to swallow his pride.

Tom was currently ensconced in the library reviewing some legal documents for Justin. Teddy briefly considered going to him to ask if he was perfectly sure he'd given Teddy the right address.

Honoria fretted loudly on Jenny's lap, giving every indication she was about to cry.

"She's due her nap," Lady Helena said. "Shall I take her?"

"Oh, let me," Jenny said.

"I wouldn't mind singing her to sleep," Clara offered. "She's such a sweet little thing."

Clara and Neville's own baby, George, was already napping in the nursery. He had his parents' placid disposition, and unlike Honoria, slept easily and often. Teddy had seen the golden-locked little chap only twice since he'd arrived.

"What about you, Laura?" Lady Helena asked. "You're not going to argue for a chance to put my darling girl to bed?"

Laura stroked Honoria's plump little cheek with the back of one finger. A strange, soft look came over her face. There was something almost wistful about it.

Catching sight of his sister's expression, Teddy frowned.

"You go," Laura said to the others. "It will give me a moment to speak with my brother."

"Join us when you're done," Lady Helena said as the ladies stood. "Honoria is a stubborn soul, just like her father. It sometimes takes a long while to convince her that sleeping is a good idea."

"Not her." Clara smoothed a hand over the baby's curly head as they departed the room. "I won't believe she has a difficult bone in her body."

"What's wrong with being difficult?" Jenny asked.

The ladies laughed in reply, Jenny along with them. The sound trailed away as they departed, punctuated by the wails of the baby, leaving Laura behind.

Neville rose. "I've the horses to see to d-down at the stables."

Laura walked to the window, wrapping her shawl more firmly about her. "Don't let me drive you off."

"I want to go. I'll meet Alex and Justin on . . . on the path. They'll be b-back soon."

"Very well," Laura said. "But do be careful, Neville."

Teddy exchanged a commiserating glance with Neville before he left. Neville liked to be fussed over no more than Teddy did.

Laura took the chair that Neville had just vacated. "I'm sure you'll hear from her today."

"I'm not concerned," Teddy lied. The subject of Stella wasn't open for discussion. He'd already shared too much of her with his family. He didn't plan on sharing anything more. "What is it you'd like to talk to me about?"

Laura smiled. "Nothing to worry you, I promise. Indeed, it's happy news."

Teddy tucked his sketchbook beside him in his wheeled chair. "You're expecting a baby, I suppose."

Laura appeared startled for an instant. But only for an instant. She exhaled an exasperated breath. "Must you spoil every surprise?"

"It's no surprise to me. I've suspected it ever since that day you were ill at the house party."

"Why didn't you say anything?"

"Because," he replied frankly, "I'd hoped I was wrong."

Laura's face fell.

Teddy hastened to reassure her. "It isn't that I don't wish you and Alex every happiness," he said. "And it isn't that I wouldn't like a little niece or nephew."

"Then what?" she prompted softly.

"It's because . . . I'm selfish."

"In what way selfish?"

"If you're expecting a baby, I shall have to do my utmost not to upset you."

She half smiled. "You were anticipating upsetting me?"

"I was," he said, with the same brutal candor. "Imminently."

Laura's brief smile faded. A sad understanding entered her gaze. "You don't want to return to France."

"Alex told you." Teddy wasn't entirely surprised.

"He's been laying breadcrumbs," she said. "I gathered you were considering the possibility of not coming home."

"It's not my home, Laura."

"It is. It's all our home now. You, me, and Alex. And don't forget Magpie."

A fleeting smile edged Teddy's lips at the mention of his family's temperamental piebald cat. Magpie had lived with Teddy and Laura in Surrey for years before Laura had married Alex and they'd all removed to France. Magpie was now settled contentedly at their farmhouse in Grasse, where he spent his days patrolling the lavender fields and dozing beneath the bitter orange trees.

"You and Alex have made a home there," Teddy said. "Magpie, too. Now you're having a baby, your family will be complete. You don't need me anymore."

She took his hand, pressing it hard. "Don't be stupid."

"I don't mean it in a self-pitying way," he said. "I *want* to stay in England. I have my own life to make. I want it to be in London. That's where Turner began his career."

"Not Turner again."

"If I had a small studio of my own, and if I'm able to complete the painting I envision, I know I shall make a success of it there."

"I've no doubt of your talent. It's everyone else that gives me pause. London isn't a welcoming place to someone in a wheeled chair."

"No place is. What's that to do with it?"

"You might be robbed or taken advantage of. Not to mention the accidents that could befall you. What if Jennings were to forget his duty and leave you to—"

"That's a risk anywhere." Teddy pressed her hand with a

reassuring grip before releasing it. "I survived in Paris, didn't I? And yes, I realize you stayed there for a time. You needn't have, you know."

"There was *every* need. I've seen what people are like to those they deem vulnerable. I feared you would be entirely at the mercy of those around you."

"When have I ever been at the mercy of anyone?" Teddy asked. "I'm not a child anymore, Laura. I'm a grown man, perfectly capable of looking after myself." He paused, adding, "So long as I have enough coin to engage the right people."

"But what if—"

"What if, what if," Teddy echoed impatiently. "Had you and the others half as much concern when Neville left Greyfriar's Abbey to strike out on his own? And look how he's thrived on his farm."

"Neville isn't my brother. And he isn't in a wheeled chair. Besides, he wasn't alone with only hired servants to depend upon. He is married to Clara."

"Is *that* what it would take to set your mind at ease? Me marrying some selfless young lady?"

"I daresay it would do," she said. "If I knew she would look after you and protect you as fiercely as Clara does Neville. But Clara does that because she loves him. And love matches aren't easy to come by at the best of times."

An image of Stella came, unbidden, into Teddy's mind.

It was that kiss again. That warm, tender, soul-quaking kiss. He'd thought, in the moment, that it was some manner of goodbye. His last chance to touch her—to taste her—before she slipped from his grasp forever. It was that which had prompted him to take such a liberty.

But he'd been wrong.

The kiss they'd shared that night under the Hampshire stars hadn't been a goodbye. It had been the start of something, not the ending of it.

I can't stop thinking about you, he'd almost written to her in his letter. *It isn't only because I want to paint you. It's because—*

But he didn't know the why of it. All he knew was that he must see her again.

"I'm not interested in love matches," he said brusquely. "Only in art. A canvas, pencils, and paints—that's all I need."

Laura shook her head. "Teddy . . ."

Before she could offer another objection, their conversation was blessedly interrupted by Alex's return. He entered the drawing room still in his overcoat, a stack of letters in his gloved hand.

Laura was instantly on her feet. "Thank goodness," she said, crossing the room to meet him. "I feared you might have done yourself an injury."

Alex circled her waist with his arm as she embraced him. "I'm only muddy, love." He kissed her. "Now you are, too."

Drawing back, Laura flicked a rueful glance at her bodice. "What a nuisance. We shall both have to have a bath."

"A splendid idea," he murmured.

She rubbed a smudge of dirt from his cheek. "Where's Justin? You didn't lose him along the way, I hope."

"He went straight up to change. He's muddier than I am."

Teddy rolled toward them in his chair. "Is that the post?" he interrupted.

"It is," Alex said. "There's nothing for you specifically. It's all perfumery business from France. That, and"—he withdrew a small envelope from the stack—"a letter for Laura from Derbyshire."

Teddy sat up straight in his chair. He exchanged a sharp look with his sister.

Laura took the letter from her husband. "Don't tease. You know it's meant for him." She passed the letter to Teddy. "Or rather, I assume it is. Unless Miss Hobhouse is writing to reprimand me for aiding and abetting your crime."

Teddy took the small envelope. The direction was written in black ink, penned (he suspected) in Stella's own delicate hand. He ran his thumb over the soft indentations left by the nib of her quill. "There's no crime in wanting to paint her."

"Is that all there is to it?" Alex asked. "A desire to commit her to canvas?"

"That's all," Teddy said.

"I don't recall you engaging in correspondence with any other of your models."

"I doubt that most of them could read or write."

"A fair point," Alex said. "One you'd do well to mark."

Teddy glanced up sharply from examining the envelope. "Meaning?"

"Miss Hobhouse isn't from the usual ranks. She's a young lady, not a Parisienne prostitute."

"As I'm aware."

"Take care," Alex said. "You may well be playing with fire."

Teddy barely registered the warning. The instant his sister and brother-in-law left the room, he tore open Stella's letter. She'd arranged it in a similar fashion to the one he'd sent her, with a small letter folded within the single sheet of an outer letter. The outer letter was addressed to Laura—a few brief and exceedingly polite lines. Teddy gave it the barest glance before turning his attention to the smaller letter within. Addressed to him, it was written in an entirely different tone.

24 January 1863

Dear Mr. Hayes,

Thank you for your letter. What a surprise it was to receive it. How did you discover the name of my village? I don't recall having mentioned it to you.

   Your stay at Greyfriar's Abbey sounds to be a pleasant one with so many others in residence. I envy you the largeness of your extended family, even as I sympathize with your need for the solitude necessary to your work.

You mentioned Mr. Finchley. His name is not unknown to me. I met him, and his wife, briefly in London last year at the wedding of my dear friend Evelyn Maltravers to Mr. Ahmad Malik. Are you acquainted with Mr. Malik? Do you perchance know Evelyn? I scarcely imagined when we met that you and I would have London friends in common.

Here in Fostonbury, the vibrancy of town is a fond but distant memory. I have had no success in finding a suitable drawing master within fifteen miles, and my friends are too far away to easily visit. Locket is my only comfort. I <u>have</u> been galloping her every day, and fervently wish I might gallop away from this place. My brother has become engaged, you see. His intended joined us recently, along with her mother, and is staying indefinitely. I have had to give up my room for them. It is <u>not</u> a comfortable state of affairs.

It begins to seem impossible that I shall contrive to get away to London for Lady Anne's wedding in the spring. I have threatened to travel there myself on the train, but my brother's resolve is firm. He is rather unhappy with me at the moment, owing to a small scandal I have created with his betrothed, his future mother-in-law, and with one of my prospective suitors. I say "one of." What I mean is, my only prospective suitor. You may draw your own conclusions as to the fellow's desirability.

Suffice to say, I am in everyone's black books at present. I have been on my best behavior, to no avail. My brother despairs of me, and his new family wishes me to perdition. Were convents still in use for burdensome female relatives, I have no doubt that I would be sent to one posthaste.

Aside from Locket, your sketch is the only thing that has lately given me any pleasure. I look at it a good deal more than I ought. My original impression of your abilities has only grown with time. I do believe that you will be famous one day. Selfishly, I hope that day will be sooner rather than later. I could then sell your sketch for a tidy sum and use the proceeds to secure my independence. Though, I confess, the idea of parting with it does not sit easily with me.

I wish I could see myself as you saw me those days in the small parlor, or that evening in the sleigh beneath the stars. It has vexed me greatly trying to remember what I said to you afterward. Something inane, I suspect. Your Parisienne muses are doubtless more articulate in such circumstances.

Enclosed is a letter for your sister. Please thank her for interceding so that you might write to me. It would be my honor to hear from her again.

In friendship,
Stella Hobhouse

Eighteen

Miss Stella Hobhouse
The Vicarage
Fostonbury, Derbyshire

2 February 1863

My dear Miss Hobhouse,

I am grieved to hear of your difficulties. Who is this mysterious suitor? A local man? A man of property? I will not waste ink on telling you what you already know. A lady like you should be admired and celebrated, in London or Paris, or some other vibrant place. You are not meant for a backwoods existence, the wife of a villager or farmer in the middle of nowhere. (No offense to Fostonbury.)

How did I discover the name of it, you ask? It was simple enough. I merely mentioned it to Tom Finchley. He is a man of infinite resources. I had only to state the names of Derbyshire and Hobhouse and he was able to do the rest within the space of a week.

That is the reason my first letter didn't reach you sooner. Not for lack of interest, or because of any unwillingness on my part to nurture the connection we forged in Hampshire, but because, when I had you *before me, I was too caught up in the turn of your countenance to think about asking for postal directions.*

Regarding the Finchleys, the answer is yes—I have met Ahmad Malik, on several occasions. I have even met his wife, who I little knew had the honor of being one of your close friends. I do not believe in fate or spiritualism or all that other metaphysical claptrap, but more and more I see the threads of our lives intertwining and connecting us. Can it be more than mere coincidence? I begin to wonder.

In all seriousness, you mentioned selling my portrait. I beg you would hold on to it. If worse comes to worst, I shall buy it back from you myself. In the meanwhile, do consider that I would not expect you to pose for my oil painting for nothing. Artists' models are compensated for their work. When you come to London, and when you agree to my painting you, I promise that you will be well taken care of.

As for my experiences with Parisienne muses . . .

I will not say I have not had them. But the frozen starlit evening you are referring to cannot be counted among their number. To me it was a pleasure of a far more precious sort.

Your friend,
Teddy

❈

Mr. Edward Hayes
Greyfriar's Abbey
King's Abbott, Devonshire

7 February 1863

Dear Mr. Hayes,

It had not occurred to me that models received compensation. Is it enough for them to live on? And I don't mean a rented room above a rookery gin shop and a crust of bread for their supper. I mean live—truly live.

A lady in my position has little opportunity to make her own way. Not unless she has a fortune of her own. But to work, to <u>really</u> work, for a living and to be free to do as one wishes does indeed hold a profound allure.

Until now, my brother has had the management of my small inheritance. I do not dare approach him with questions about funding an independent existence. For that, I was obliged to meet with our village solicitor, Mr. Underhill. For a fee, he informed me of what I already know: that in order to afford food, lodgings, and the wages of a companion, I would have to give up the expense of Locket and her groom. It is something I would never do. Which puts me right back where I was when I returned home after Christmas—squarely at my brother's mercy.

It is not so terrible, not so long as I refrain from speaking and not so long as I submit to accepting Miss Trent and her mother's instruction and advice. They have so far refashioned all the arrangements of the household to their taste. Miss Trent has even put herself forward as my drawing master. (Her artistic style bears a striking similarity to that of my old governess, Miss Callis.)

My brother is in full accord with the Trents. He must be so. He and Miss Trent are set to marry in March. While they wait, I remain in the box room, which has begun to bear a striking resemblance to the Island of Elba.

You write of <u>when</u> I come to London and <u>when</u> I pose for you. How can you be sure that either will happen? Does your confidence know no bounds? As for me, I know full well that I cannot travel without a chaperone. And I will not leave my horse again. My only hope is that, once married himself, my brother will relent on the subject of taking me—and Locket—to London. We need not remain a week, only long enough to attend the ceremony. Lady Anne and Mr.

Hartford have already sent invitations. *Their wedding is set for the first day of spring.*

If I attend, perhaps I shall see you in town?

11 February 1863

Dear Stella (if I may presume to address you so),

Of course, you will come to town next month, and of course, you will see me there. I shall be in Rotten Row the second day of spring, sitting along the rail, in full anticipation of encountering you on your mare. What do you require to make it happen? A servant to accompany you? Money for railway fare? A groom to escort your horse? Perhaps you ought to sell back my sketch to me after all.

As for your own sketches—never mind a drawing master. Your skill surpasses most I have seen. It will not be hindered by lack of instruction until you can find someone worthy to guide you.

15 February 1863

Dear Teddy (as I shall presume since you so presumed),

I could not take money from you, not even for the return of your portrait. What kind of lady would do so?

19 February 1863

Dearest Stella,

An enterprising lady. A determined lady. In short, you.

26 February 1863

Dear Teddy,

I do not feel very enterprising. Indeed, since your last letter, a certain sense of finality has settled over me. My brother's wedding is scheduled for the tenth of next month. He has taken rooms in the village in the meanwhile. It would not do for him to stay in the same house as his betrothed while the banns are being called. I wish I might remove to the village as well, but I have been commanded to remain at the vicarage with Miss Trent and her mother, a mere figurehead of a hostess with no actual power over the household any longer.

The Trents are so keen to be rid of me that they have, on two separate occasions, invited my erstwhile suitor, Squire Smalljoy, back to the vicarage for tea. Under their persuasion, he has become convinced that my unfortunate outburst at dinner was due to a temporary bout of ill health brought on by too long a stay in London. He suggests that he might forgive me, given minimal encouragement. Did I mention that he's the variety of gentleman who takes breathing as encouragement?

4 March 1863

Dearest Stella,

Squire Smalljoy? Are you making that up? Your time in Fostonbury sounds more and more abysmal. Meanwhile, my holiday in Devon continues apace. I have completed two (two!) more seascapes, and am as unsatisfied with the results of them as I was when I started. I require a model for my portraits, and only you will do.

How is the view from Elba?

Please tell me that your miseries have weighed in my favor.

9 March 1863

Dear Teddy,

Is it a misery? There are people in the world who have it far worse than I, certainly. Here on Elba, I at least have food to eat and a roof over my head. Perspective is all. Or so I keep reminding myself.

As I do so, I am practicing being small and quiet. It is not as difficult as you might imagine. I was already quite a good listener to begin with. All that has changed is that, now, all I do is listen.

Two more seascapes? What will you do with them? Are they for keeping or for selling? I should like to see them one day, even if you are dissatisfied with them.

Would you really prefer painting portraits? How could a lady— any lady—ever compete with the sea?

13 March 1863

My dear Stella,

You may as well ask how the stars can compete. The answer is, there is no competition at all.

How was your brother's wedding? And how are you, now that he and his bride have settled into the vicarage? Are you still practicing being small and quiet? What a deplorable state!

I trust that you have made progress on your plans to come to town next week. We are preparing to travel there ourselves on the sixteenth. You may write to me care of Mrs. Jenny Finchley in Half

Moon Street. I shall be staying with her and her husband until I can find rooms of my own.

The search for suitable lodgings will be an interesting one. My needs are quite specific, as you can imagine. The perfect place will be both home and studio, and must be accessible for my chair. You shall see the premises yourself when you come to pose for me.

I expect you there, if not at my studio, then certainly in London. Do not forget—the second day of spring in Rotten Row. Look out for me on the rail.

Stella slowly refolded Teddy's latest letter. Tucking it back into its envelope, she placed it safely inside the brass inlaid walnut box where she kept the rest of her treasures. The velvet-lined interior held her parents' yellowed wedding lines, a lock of her mother's hair (brown in color), a few brief, affectionate notes her father had penned to Stella when she was a little girl, and now . . . a whole, ribbon-tied stack of Teddy Hayes's letters. His sketch was folded inside, too, a bittersweet reminder of her unmet potential.

Those distant days in December, Teddy had drawn her as something like a goddess. But Stella hadn't felt very deity-like in the weeks that followed as she'd dutifully trudged through her days in Fostonbury, every hour becoming smaller and smaller under the oppressive weight of Daniel's disapproval and Amanda's unending criticism and advice. There was little joy in sketching any longer. Even Stella's rides on Locket had begun to feel lackluster. It was beyond worrying. If riding didn't raise her spirits, what on earth ever could?

It was a terrible thing to be an unwanted third. Daniel and Amanda had each other. They were forming a life together. Refashioning a home. There was no room in it for Stella. Day by day she became more invisible. Soon, she feared, she would disappear altogether.

Closing her box of treasures, she slid it back into its hiding place under her sagging mattress. The box room was cold and damp as ever. She had no fire in the hearth to warm her, only an extra pair of socks and a thickly woven shawl. Twisting the latter more firmly around her nightgown-clad figure, she climbed into her narrow bed.

A single taper burned on her bedside table, its flame flickering valiantly in the draft from the unlit fireplace. Stella blew it out. Darkness consumed her.

This was why women gave in. Why they ended up married to men who didn't suit them. Didn't love them. Men who wanted only the raw materials of some untried young lady to fashion into their idea of a conformable wife.

But weary as she was, Stella wasn't yet ready to cede the fight. She was still one of the Four Horsewomen. Still one of the Furies. And Furies didn't give up *or* give in. They *fought*.

It was exactly what she intended to do.

This afternoon, she'd taken the first step. During the second of her daily gallops on Locket, she'd ridden to Fairhook Station and purchased a railway ticket to London.

She *would* be attending Anne's wedding on Friday. And nothing and no one was going to stand in her way.

◆◆

The next morning, at breakfast, Stella informed her brother of her plan.

Daniel dropped his fork to his plate with a clatter, leaving the remainder of his eggs and toast untouched. His narrow face tightened with weary anger. "Are you trying to ruin yourself?" he asked. "Or is it *my* reputation you seek to blacken with your wild antics?"

"I'm trying to support my friend," Stella said. "She expects me at her wedding, and I've promised to be there. Since you refuse to accompany me, I have no choice but to—"

"I'm a newly married man! I can't be boarding a train to London at the snap of your fingers!"

Amanda sat across from him at the table, a frilly matron's cap pinned over her flaxen curls. She paused in the act of pouring his tea. "Pray, don't let her behavior draw you into anger, husband."

"How else to react, my dear? We were wed less than a fortnight ago and already my sister demands to be taken to town. How is such selfish behavior to be borne? As if I would abandon my bride for—"

"It's a day's journey each way, that's all," Stella said. "Hardly akin to abandonment. It isn't as though I intend to remain for another season." On the contrary, she'd be returning directly. She'd have to, or else risk Locket pining for her again.

"Can you afford it, sister?" Amanda asked with deceptive sweetness. "I should have thought, with the expense of your horses and your groom, you would be at pains to economize."

"Naturally she can afford it," Daniel said. "She isn't obligated to expend her capital in a more responsible fashion. Not with me subsidizing all the necessities of her life."

"Obligated, no," Amanda said. "But one would hope that Christian duty might compel her to spend her resources on other than her own pleasure."

"I am sitting right here," Stella said. "You needn't speak over me as though I were invisible."

"I wish that you were," Daniel retorted uncharitably. "Instead, every day brings a new misery. Arguments over ordering the coal, instructing the servants, and the manner in which I receive guests in my own home. My wife is daily at pains to placate your whims, and Squire Smalljoy himself has said—"

"Not Squire Smalljoy again," Stella objected.

"A man who would provide a happy solution to our current troubles if you would but rid yourself of the ludicrous notion that remaining unmarried is a choice."

"It certainly is a choice," Stella said. "Though what it has to do with my being a bridesmaid in Lady Anne's wedding—"

"Had you a husband, *he* could take you to London," Daniel said.

"Or not," Amanda murmured. "Indeed, sister, the wisest scholars teach that true contentment begins at home. It is to her own household a lady should direct her attention, not to the dubious pleasures of the outside world."

Spoken like a person who had never galloped in Rotten Row, danced among the colorful lights of the Chinese pagoda at Cremorne Gardens, or thrilled in the giddy company of a group of like-minded friends.

Stella opened her mouth to say as much, let the consequences come as they may, only to have her tart reply forestalled by the unmistakable sound of carriage wheels on the gravel drive outside the window.

Daniel shot an accusing look at her. "Did you summon a cab to take you to the station?"

"Don't be absurd," Stella said. "I'm not leaving until tomorrow."

He turned to his wife. "Are you expecting someone, my dear?"

Amanda's mouth curved in a smugly satisfied smile. "Perhaps it's the squire?" she suggested, all innocence. "He mentioned something about coming to look at that gray mare of yours."

"That gray mare of *mine*," Stella corrected automatically as she rose from her chair. "And if he did, you had no business encouraging him. I've already given him my answer on the subject."

"You were in a temper," Amanda said. "I knew that, when your ardor had cooled, you would see the sense of his proposition. One wouldn't wish to cause a rift with an esteemed neighbor. Not over something so trifling as his interest in a horse."

"It's no trifling matter to me." Stella moved to the window. She drew back the curtain to peek out at the drive. The carriage that had rolled to a stop at the front of the house bore no crest on its door. On the contrary, it appeared to be a hired cab, of the sort one could find at the railway station in Fairhook.

"It's not the squire," Stella said. "It's . . ."

Her voice trailed off as the door to the carriage opened and an imposing gentleman in a black overcoat leapt out. He was tall, dark, and broad of shoulder, with a sinister scar traversing the right side of his face.

Good Lord, it was Julia's husband, the notorious Captain Blunt!

And he hadn't come alone. He turned to gently assist Julia out of the cab. She was garbed in a dark blue traveling dress and matching cloak. As she paused to fluff her flounced skirts, she caught Stella's stunned gaze in the dining room window. Julia's face spread into a mischievous grin.

Stella's mouth pulled into a swift smile in return.

Daniel stood from his chair. "Who is it?" he demanded.

Stella let the curtain fall. "It's Mrs. Blunt and her husband."

"Captain Blunt?" Daniel's face turned ashen. He was aware of the captain's black reputation—a reputation inspired as much by rumors of Blunt's brutal conduct in the Crimea as it was by the fact that he brazenly housed three of his bastard children under his roof at Goldfinch Hall in Yorkshire.

If that wasn't enough to shock, the circumstances of his scandalous elopement with Julia would surely have done so. Last summer, while Stella and her brother were in Exeter, Captain Blunt had carried an ailing Julia away from her parents' house in Belgrave Square, stoking rumors that he'd abducted the vulnerable young heiress in order to compromise her and force her into matrimony.

It wasn't strictly true, not according to Julia. But Stella's brother and sister-in-law didn't know that.

Amanda was at once on her feet, the very picture of offended modesty. As a pious young lady, newly wed to a vicar, the very idea of a man of Captain Blunt's ilk visiting her home was enough to spark her outrage. "What have *they* come here for?"

Stella strode out of the room to greet her friends, tossing an answer at her disgruntled sister-in-law as she went. "I believe," she said, "that they've come for me."

Julia retained both Stella's hands in hers as she drew back from kissing her cheek in greeting. "You didn't truly believe I'd let you miss Anne's wedding, did you?"

"I scarcely imagined you would come to fetch me yourself," Stella said.

"Who else but me? You wouldn't permit Anne to know of your difficulties. And Evie and Mr. Malik could hardly travel all the way to Derbyshire from London, not with his court dressmaking commissions to think of. Besides," Julia added in a portentous whisper, "it's *my* husband who's needed here."

Captain Blunt stood in the entry hall, looking so fearsome that Stella might have swooned herself if Julia hadn't confided how loving and tender the man was to her. "I shall take full responsibility for Miss Hobhouse's welfare while we're in town," he informed Daniel after the introductions had been dispensed with. "You need have no fear for her reputation."

Amanda uttered a strangled laugh. "No fear for her reputation, sir? When she's traveling in company with *you*?"

Captain Blunt ignored the insult. "I've reserved a suite of rooms at Brown's Hotel," he said to Daniel. "We'll be staying a fortnight."

Julia's eyes shone. "What a merry time we shall have! Anne will shortly be leaving on her honeymoon, but Evie will be in town. The three of us can ride every day."

"I can't ride without Locket," Stella said. "And I couldn't leave her for an entire fortnight. Not after—"

Julia silenced Stella with another reassuring squeeze of her hands. "My husband will see she's brought to London. He has our groom riding Cossack there as we speak. Perhaps if your groom did the same?"

"Turvey can't ride Locket," Stella said. "She's too dangerous for him. He'll have to lead her by stages. It will take some doing."

"Jasper?" Julia gave her husband a hopeful look.

"Leave it with me," Captain Blunt said.

"There, you see?" Julia beamed at Stella. "My husband can solve any problem in our path. All that's left is for you to pack your things, and then we'll be off."

"Not with my sister, you won't." Daniel moved in front of the door, barring the way. "I won't allow it."

Stella felt a rush of mortification. Must her brother be such a confounded stick in the mud? It was bad enough that he refused to take Stella to London himself, but to insult Julia and Captain Blunt when they were attempting to do so exceeded all limits. "You're not being very gracious, Daniel," she said. "Our guests will think you rude."

As if they didn't already! Neither Daniel nor his new bride had invited Julia and her husband to sit down or offered them any refreshment. The message was clear. The Blunts weren't welcome.

"They may think what they like." Daniel looked to the captain, only a faint flinch betraying that he was in any way intimidated by the man. "I won't permit my sister to return to London in your company, sir. The scandals surrounding your life, and your recent union, are such that the mere association with you would be enough to taint—"

"Daniel," Stella interrupted in a mortified whisper. "How *can* you?"

He shushed her with a violent wave of his hand, his attention still directed on an increasingly stone-faced Captain Blunt. "I don't seek to give offense, but my sister's good name is in my keeping. I won't allow her to go with you under any circumstance."

Stella stiffened with unexpected anger. It wasn't just about the inconvenience of accompanying her, was it? It was about control. About forcibly shaping her to be something she wasn't. Small and quiet. An obedient spinster sister with no thoughts or opinions of her own.

"I *am* going," she informed him. "I don't require your permission."

"You do," Daniel returned. "So long as you live under my roof, you will abide by my rules. If you insist on defying me, you needn't come back."

A spark of satisfaction glittered in Amanda's eyes. This was her doing. All the weeks of syrupy comments and helpfully expressed concern, every one of them designed to pit Daniel against his sister. And here at last was the result of it. The culmination of her malicious campaign.

Julia drew Stella closer, as though she might protect her. "I'm sure you don't mean that, Mr. Hobhouse."

"Oh, but I do," Daniel replied acidly. "I have reached the limits of my patience."

"Be reasonable, Daniel," Stella said, making one last attempt to appeal to her brother's better nature. "It's only a fortnight. And you couldn't wish for a better chaperone for me."

Amanda snorted.

Julia glared at her with ill-disguised indignation before returning her attention to Stella's brother. "The two of us are to be in Lady Anne's wedding," she explained to him as though he was a petulant child. "Our bridesmaids dresses have already been made. The whole of fashionable London will be in attendance."

"What care I for fashion when my duty and honor as a clergyman are at stake? No." Daniel shook his head. "My mind is made up, Stella. If you defy me to go with your friends now, you must go your own way entirely. My house isn't a stopping ground between your revelries. This is a home—a sober, quiet home—and going forward the ladies in it will behave accordingly."

Julia flashed her husband a look of dismay. Stern and silent, he, in turn, looked to Stella, waiting for her to render her judgment on the situation.

The final grains of sand in the hourglass of Stella's fate fell to the bottom. She understood that this moment, standing here in the vicarage hall, was to decide the course of the rest of her life.

She gathered her courage. Her future loomed ahead of her, empty as one of the blank pages in her sketchbook, both frightening and exciting by turns. She didn't know what it held. Perhaps she would impose on her friends for a time. Perhaps she would seek genteel employment.

Perhaps—just perhaps—she might pose for a portrait or two.

"Very well, Daniel," she said at last. "If that is what you wish, then so be it. Henceforward, I shall go my own way."

Nineteen

*T*he first step in Teddy's journey toward independence was one of mobility. For that, he didn't just require his wheeled chair. He required a suitable conveyance.

It was Tom Finchley who helped him to procure one. Deceptively innocuous in appearance, with a slim build and a bookish demeanor, Tom was, as Teddy had written to Stella, a solicitor of infinite resources. He was acquainted with people in every corner of London, including the odd horse trader, wheelwright, and carriage maker. Many of them owed him favors for having helped them out of a spot of legal bother. Others were in his debt for more sinister reasons.

"I haven't always been the decent, upright citizen you see before you now," Tom said wryly as they exited the Finchleys' elegantly appointed house in Half Moon Street.

Teddy had been staying there for the past two days, along with his sister and brother-in-law. It was their regular stopping place when visiting London. The Finchleys would have it no other way.

"Are any solicitors decent and upright?" Teddy asked, wheeling his chair through the door.

Tom's eyes twinkled behind his silver-framed spectacles. "You may well wonder."

Outside, three stone steps led to the street below. With Tom's help, Jennings eased Teddy's chair down them without first removing Teddy. The wooden wheels clattered with bone-jarring sharpness, prompting Teddy to grit his teeth. It was rough going. He nevertheless preferred it to being carried down separately. It was less bother for only a few steps, and far less spectacle.

Half Moon Street was moderately busy this afternoon. Fashionable carriages passed with regularity, and several people were out walking, taking advantage of the fine weather. It was the first day of spring, a day that had dawned rather inauspiciously with a heavy downpour. Fortunately, the foul weather hadn't lasted. By breakfast, the dark clouds had dissipated, burned away by a brilliant blaze of sunshine.

It boded well for Teddy's meeting with Stella tomorrow in Rotten Row.

Assuming she'd be there.

He didn't yet know if she'd managed to find her way to London. He fervently hoped she had. Stella's arrival was as much a part of his plan as his search for lodgings and his purchase of a carriage.

The Finchleys' groom awaited them in the street. He stood at the head of a sturdy, liver chestnut gelding. Samuel, as the placid horse was called, was hitched up to a gleaming black and vermillion lacquered wagonette.

Teddy had bought the smart-looking vehicle only yesterday. Larger than a tilbury, it had four wheels instead of two, with a front-facing bench for the driver, and two rear benches arranged so that passengers could sit facing each other. It wasn't as dashing as a sporting gig, but the back area was large enough to accommodate Teddy's wheeled chair while he was driving.

"I don't expect you'll need to worry about your horse bolting," Tom remarked. "He appears a quiet sort."

"'Unflappable' is what the seller said," Teddy replied. "And easy to keep, whatever that means."

"It means that wherever you end up, you'll require a coach house and a stable. Either that or a livery stable nearby. Keeping a horse in London is no small expense."

"Two horses," Teddy said, recalling Stella's advice. "Horses are herd animals. I have it on good authority that it's cruel to keep one alone."

"Another expense to keep in mind as you look at properties."

"I'm keeping a thorough mental accounting."

Jennings assisted Teddy out of his chair. Hoisting him by the waist, he lifted him up onto the leather padded driver's seat of the wagonette.

"All right, sir?" Jennings asked.

"Right enough," Teddy said. He straightened himself on the seat, carefully positioning his legs in front of him, before taking the reins from the groom.

He'd driven the wagonette around the park when he'd tested it before buying it, but driving down the busy streets of London's commercial district was quite another proposition. A flicker of apprehension made his fingers curl tighter on the leathers. He had no desire to find himself pitched out, helpless, onto the paving stones.

Jennings placed Teddy's wheeled chair in the back of the wagonette before climbing into the back himself.

"Alex and your sister will be returning from Harley Street at any moment," Tom said. "Are you sure you won't wait for one of them to accompany you? I know they'd like to view any potential lodgings."

Teddy was certain they would. He was equally certain that none of the premises he had in mind would meet with their approval. Especially not now that Laura was beginning to feel the effects of her delicate condition.

Approaching the third month of her pregnancy, her bouts of morning sickness had only increased. Alex had insisted they consult with a physician while they were in town. One of those highbrow society accoucheurs who would insist on wrapping Laura in cotton-wool. The very sort of man whose restrictions would further serve to impinge on? Teddy's grasp for independence.

"No, thank you," he said. "I've an appointment with Mr. Chakrabarty in Newman Street. I'm already cutting it rather fine."

"Very well." Tom backed away from the wagonette. "But take care, Teddy. London isn't Grasse. It isn't even Paris. I should know. I've traversed the worst of these streets. You don't want to find yourself at the end of the wrong alleyway."

"Jennings can handle himself." Teddy urged the dozing Samuel into a walk. The wagonette gave a rattle before lurching forward into the street.

"Give Chakrabarty my regards," Tom called after him.

"I shall!" Teddy replied.

It was Tom who had provided Teddy with the introduction. Mr. Chakrabarty was himself a solicitor, with premises in Regent Street. He dealt primarily with estate matters, acting in the role of agent for various properties in London, and was reputed to have more than a passing familiarity with the art community.

Teddy navigated his new wagonette through the midday traffic, steering Samuel in the direction of the British Museum. The house in Newman Street was the first property he would be visiting today, and, if the solicitor had taken Teddy's list of requirements into account, hopefully the last.

On arriving in front of the house's imposing redbrick façade, he found Mr. Chakrabarty waiting. He was a short, stocky gentleman, with an air of impatient efficiency.

"Mr. Hayes, I presume," he said as Teddy brought his wagonette to a halt. He stepped up to the driver's bench to meet him. "How do you do, sir?"

"Mr. Chakrabarty." Teddy shook the man's hand. "Sorry for the delay. The traffic around Oxford Street was rather worse than I anticipated."

Mr. Chakrabarty nodded in sympathy. "A perpetual challenge, the congestion in London. One must accustom oneself."

Jennings hopped out of the back of the wagonette. He lifted Teddy's chair down to the street and wheeled it up alongside the driver's bench.

"You have your manservant, I see," Mr. Chakrabarty said. "Could Mr. Finchley not accompany you?"

"He isn't involved in my letting a place," Teddy said. "But he does send his regards."

"An excellent fellow, Mr. Finchley. You take care to tell him that I've done right by you."

"I shall." Teddy looked up at the towering building. "Is this the house?"

"It is, sir," Mr. Chakrabarty said. "Are you able to come inside? Perhaps if your man would help you?"

"Quite." Setting the brake and tying off the reins, Teddy motioned to Jennings.

Jennings helped Teddy into his chair. Mr. Chakrabarty stood back, politely averting his eyes until Teddy was settled. He then enlisted a neighbor boy to stand with Samuel while he and Teddy entered the house. Jennings followed close behind.

"It was built in fifty-nine," Mr. Chakrabarty said as he escorted Teddy through the lower reception rooms. "A good house, and a good street for an artist. Mr. Rossetti had his studio here for a time, and there are still many others hereabouts who draw and paint."

Teddy was familiar with the works of Rossetti and the rest of the Pre-Raphaelite Brotherhood. There was no question they were talented. Groundbreaking even, for their time. But their lush, vivid paintings, which had found fame in the previous decade, were nothing like the new school of art embraced by the painters Teddy had studied with in Paris. He found no inspiration in the Pre-Raphaelite's religious themes and medievalism. It was light Teddy was after.

"It won't do, I'm afraid." He turned his wheeled chair toward the exit before Mr. Chakrabarty could persuade him to venture upstairs.

Mr. Chakrabarty was crestfallen. "But it is a very good house, Mr. Hayes," he said, trailing after Teddy. "The best on offer, and only slightly more than the top of your budget."

"The extra cost would be nothing if the light was right. Not to mention all these stairs."

"Stairs are unavoidable, sir."

"Yes, but I'd rather there not be so many of them. The floors above would be all but useless to me."

"Your servants could make use of some of the rooms," Mr. Chakrabarty suggested. "The others you might rent out for a fee."

"To people who would disrupt my work with their incessant comings and goings? No, thank you. I've no interest in being a landlord." Teddy cast one last look about him, frowning. It was a pity the house didn't suit. It was in a prime location. "I trust you have other properties to show me?"

"One or two in your budget," Mr. Chakrabarty said. "The neighborhoods, however . . . They are not so genteel as this."

Teddy wheeled himself out the door. "Show me."

Nearly two hours and three houses later, Teddy was beginning to feel discouraged. None of the residences the estate agent had shown him were what he had in mind.

As they exited the final property, Mr. Chakrabarty paused to think. "Is your budget fixed, sir? I have another house coming available soon, but you might find the cost of refurbishing it excessive."

"I have some flexibility," Teddy said. He wheeled his chair to the edge of the street where his wagonette was parked. "Where is this property?"

"In Covent Garden," Mr. Chakrabarty said.

Teddy gave him an alert look. "Where in Covent Garden?"

"In Maiden Lane, sir."

Teddy's pulse leapt. Good God. Was it possible? Could there truly be a suitable place on the very street where Turner had his famous beginnings?

"It's in a poor state of repair," Mr. Chakrabarty said, "but it has a good deal of potential. If you're willing to look past its deficiencies—"

"I'd like to see it," Teddy said abruptly. "Do you have time to show it to me today?"

Mr. Chakrabarty withdrew his pocket watch from his vest to check the time. He nodded slowly. "Yes, yes, if we make haste."

"To Maiden Lane, then," Teddy said. "With alacrity."

Stella joined Evie and Julia in an upstairs bedroom of the Earl of March's stately town house in Arlington Street to assist Anne out of her wedding dress and into her traveling clothes. Anne and Mr. Hartford would be departing for their honeymoon within the hour. Their destination was so far a secret. It was considered bad luck for the guests to know where the bride and groom were headed. But judging by the steamer trunks the servants had been carrying down earlier, with instructions to convey the luggage to St. Katharine's Docks, Stella suspected that a honeymoon in Paris was in her friend's near future.

It would certainly fit with the romantic theme of the day. And it *had* been a romantic day, from start to finish, from the moment Lord March walked Anne down the aisle to the moment when Anne and Mr. Hartford had bounded, beaming, to the vestry to sign the registrar.

After departing the church, they and their guests had repaired to Arlington Street for a sumptuous champagne breakfast. It, too, was hosted by Lord March. Better him acting as patriarch, Anne had stated before the wedding, than her odious distant cousin Joshua

Deveril, the new Earl of Arundell. Anne loathed the man, and neither he nor his equally odious mother had been invited to the ceremony.

"I don't regret excluding them," Anne said as her maid helped her to step out of the lace-trimmed, white satin skirts of the exquisitely tailored wedding gown that Mr. Malik had designed for her. "And I don't give a toss that some of the Deveril relations are saying that Joshua should have given my reception in Grosvenor Square."

It hadn't been the only source of gossip at the wedding. The presence of Mr. Hartford's half-siblings, sitting unashamedly in a pew at the back, had prompted its own share of outraged whispers.

"Ignore the gossips," Evie said. "Don't let them ruin your day."

"And what a beautiful day it's been!" Julia proclaimed, flouncing the double skirts of her apricot silk bridesmaid dress as she took a seat on the edge of the bed. Her cheeks were flushed as much from the romance of the occasion as from the two glasses of champagne she'd imbibed at the wedding breakfast. "Did anyone else see the rainbow that fell across Anne's gown inside the church?"

Evie and Stella wore matching apricot silk dresses, each of them short sleeved and double skirted. Wreaths of roses and lilies adorned their hair, made to match the stunning bouquet that Anne had carried down the aisle.

Stella helped unfasten the tiny, satin-covered buttons on Anne's bodice. She was grateful for something to do. Anything to take her mind off her own troubles.

The initial exultation she'd felt at leaving the vicarage forever—that potent fizz of possibility that had propelled her into Captain Blunt's hired carriage—had gone flat within hours of departing Derbyshire. Now, Stella felt only a building apprehension at the reality of her situation. She had no home any longer. No family. It was a terrible thing. Even when one's family was terrible themselves.

But she still had her friends. They were more precious to her than ever. She refused to let any of her cares spoil Anne's special day.

"It was the sun shining through the stained glass in the Venetian window," Stella said. "I believe it came out today just for you."

Anne smiled. "I can't take credit for the sunlight. We must chalk that up to the season. But I won't argue with the sentiment. It was a magical day, wasn't it?"

Stella smiled warmly at her friend in return. "Completely enchanting."

Although the day had begun with showers, by the time Anne arrived at the church, the skies had cleared, culminating in a bright and wholly perfect spring day.

The first day of spring.

It was a fact that had been lingering at the back of Stella's mind since she'd awakened to the sound of raindrops against the windowpanes in her elegantly appointed room at Brown's Hotel. She had sent up a silent prayer for sunshine as she'd washed and dressed, knowing only too well that a downpour would put paid to any hope she had of meeting Teddy tomorrow.

He'd said he would be in Rotten Row waiting to meet her. There, on the rail, during the fashionable hour. The prospect of seeing him again had been one of the only things that had kept Stella from falling into despair after breaking with her brother. Teddy believed in her. Believed she was destined for great things.

Perchance it was only flattery designed to persuade her to sit for him. But Stella didn't think so.

"It was the most beautiful ceremony I've ever witnessed," Julia said. "Equally as moving as Evie's wedding and my own."

"High praise," Anne said.

"And so passionate, too! Did you see the look on Lady Brookdale's face when Mr. Hartford kissed you in the vestry?" Julia laughed merrily to recall it. "I thought I would need to lend her my smelling salts."

Anne carefully stripped off her lace-covered bodice, with Evie's help. She handed it to her maid, who promptly placed the delicate garment inside a shroud of tissue paper. "Hartford's aunt is one of those ladies who believe embraces should be confined to the bed-chamber," she said. "And sometimes not even then."

"How sad for her," Julia said.

"Or for any lady who finds acts of affection unseemly," Evie added. "If you love someone, there's no part of marriage that need be a chore." She smiled, adding wryly, "Except perhaps tending to the account books."

Julia paused in folding the dainty, cerulean blue wedding hand-kerchief that Anne had kept tucked into her corset during the ceremony. "You tend to the household ledgers yourself?" she asked, curious.

"For both my husband's shop and for our home," Evie said. "I've a good head for numbers. I used to keep the accounts at home in Sussex, too, much as I disliked it."

"You don't like reconciling numbers?" Julia asked. "Even though you're good at it?"

"Being good at something doesn't mean you enjoy doing it," Stella said. "I'm good at organizing my brother's notes, but I despise playing secretary."

"You needn't do so any longer," Julia said. "Not now that—"

Stella silenced her friend with a stern look. Both Julia and Evie had agreed not to tell Anne about Stella's troubles until after her honeymoon. It was the only way to ensure Anne's happiness. Stella knew that the moment Anne learned of her difficulties, she would be incapable of focusing on anything else. Anne had never yet met a problem she didn't rush to solve—even to her own detriment.

"We're all good at riding, however," Evie interjected, coming to Stella's rescue. "And that we *do* love, thank heaven."

Anne affected a scolding air. "Don't mention riding." She removed her corset cover. "I'm furious with the three of you. To think, you've brought Hephaestus, Cossack, and Locket to town and shall be enjoying gallops in the park without me."

"Furious, ha." Julia helped fold away Anne's garments as Anne discarded them. "You'll be too busy enjoying your honeymoon in Venice to think about riding."

"Or is it Rome?" Evie teased.

"Paris, I'd have thought," Stella said, smiling. "Complete with romantic strolls along the Seine."

Anne's brown eyes glimmered with laughter. "I'll never tell. But I *shall* write to you when I arrive there."

With the assistance of her maid and her friends, Anne changed into a heavy silk cord traveling dress. Stella, Evie, and Julia—still in their fluffy bridesmaids' gowns—followed her downstairs to the hall where Mr. Hartford awaited her. Like Anne, he'd changed into traveling clothes—an eyebrow-raising pair of blue-and-green-plaid trousers and a matching plaid coat.

Anne took his arm, her face aglow with unfiltered love for him. Hartford gazed down at her in return, a foolish, lopsided smile at his lips, as though there was no one else in the entry hall but the two of them.

The majority of the guests had already gone. Only Lady Arundell, Lord March, Mr. Fielding (Evelyn's uncle), and Evelyn's and Julia's husbands remained.

Mr. Malik stood back against one of the silk-paneled walls, looking striking in an exquisitely cut, black three-piece suit. He'd no doubt tailored the dashing ensemble himself. Straightening to his full height, he extended his hand to Evie. She took it, allowing him to draw her close.

At the same time, the soberly clad Captain Blunt slid a protective arm around Julia's midsection. He seemed to be aware that she'd had a trifle too much to drink. Julia leaned back against him gratefully, covering his arm with her own.

Stella lingered at the bottom of the stairs, wistfully observing her friends as they returned to their husbands. A hollow ache filled her chest. She felt, all at once, how utterly alone she was. Not friendless, no, but forever standing on the outskirts, with no partner to beckon her close—to shield her and protect her.

To love her.

Seeing Anne, Julia, and Evie so happy and fulfilled—so thoroughly accepted and looked after—Stella's own romantic future appeared bleak in comparison.

She'd told herself that love didn't matter. That it would be enough to find a husband who could support her. Respect her. But perhaps it wasn't true. Perhaps she'd always be alone, even in marriage, so long as that union was lacking in love.

Lady Arundell came to join the newlyweds. Her expensive silk dress was black in color, but softened with ruffles and lace, it bore no similarity to her typical mourning garb. A dazzling diamond necklace and matching drop earrings illuminated her face. "Do you have everything you require, my dear?" she asked her daughter. "An extra handkerchief for the journey? And your shawl?"

"I have everything I need, Mama." Anne briefly stepped away from Mr. Hartford to enfold her mother in an embrace.

Lady Arundell hugged her daughter fiercely. She had tears in her eyes. "Enjoy yourself," she commanded, releasing Anne. "And don't dare waste a thought for me. Fielding and I have a full diary of spiritualist business slated for the weeks ahead. I shall be well entertained."

"I leave my mother in your hands, sir," Anne said to Mr. Fielding.

Mr. Fielding was an older gentleman. Rather an eccentric, with a perpetual air of preoccupation about him. He and Lady Arundell had a longstanding friendship. "They are good hands, my lady," he replied. "You may rest assured."

There were more embraces, interspersed with handshakes and well wishes. Calls of "Good luck!" and "Bon voyage!" filled the air as Anne and Mr. Hartford exited the house.

Along with the others, Stella followed the happy couple outside to their waiting carriage. She waved them off, ignoring her feelings about her own desperate situation. This was Anne's day, not hers.

She was still smiling, a bit painfully, eyes clouding with tears, when she felt a slim arm circle her shoulders.

It was Evie, bless her. She drew Stella close. "Tomorrow morning, we ride," she said bracingly. "A good gallop will clear your head."

Stella wrapped an arm around her friend's waist, wordlessly conveying her gratitude for her support. Evie was right, of course. A gallop always put things in perspective.

Today may be bleak, but tomorrow Stella would be back in her sidesaddle. She'd have the wind in her face and the unstoppable power of Locket beneath her.

Yes. Galloping was something to look forward to.

And not only galloping.

Teddy would be there in the afternoon when Stella embarked on her second ride of the day. There, during the fashionable hour, waiting to see her.

It may not be a romance, but it was something.

Twenty

※

Teddy had lied to Stella. He wasn't waiting along the rail at five o'clock in the afternoon on the second day of spring, watching the fashionable equestrian throng trot by. It would have been impossible to do so.

For one thing, he'd underestimated the difficulty in getting there in his chair. The ground was still saturated from yesterday morning's rain, with patches of ankle-deep mud that would have played havoc with his wheels. For another, the crowds were such that navigating through them would have taken more time and effort than he had to spare.

Instead, he'd arrived in his new wagonette, with both his wheeled chair and Jennings disposed in the back of the vehicle, at the ready should Teddy require them.

He gripped the reins hard as he entered the South Carriage Drive of Rotten Row, ably steering the placid Samuel through the growing traffic. He was no amateur when it came to handling the ribbons. It nevertheless took the whole of his attention. He was acutely conscious of his limitations—the fact that all of his control derived from the strength of his upper body. He was equally conscious of the obtrusiveness of his chair, strapped down in the back of the wagonette. It was a glaring announcement of Teddy's condition to everyone he passed.

He wasn't ashamed of it—neither his chair nor his disability. But the fact that he must give over his sense of privacy in his own body never failed to rub him on the raw. His health was no one's business but his own. And yet, the presence of his chair made it everyone's business. Strangers felt at complete liberty to gawk at him. Or worse. Over the past several years, some had the audacity to interrogate him about his condition or to offer their unsolicited advice.

"Have you tried an electricity machine?" a matron lady had once asked him at a shop. *"It did my invalid mother's withered leg a world of good."*

"See Dr. Fairbank in Blackheath," a gentleman stranger had recommended. *"He'll have you out of that chair in no time."*

"Simple exercises, performed daily, are the thing," another man had declared when encountering Teddy at a gallery. *"Have you ever tried stretching?"*

As though Teddy hadn't been to every doctor and performed every exercise. *Had he ever tried stretching?* Had he, hell.

Regrettably, there was no avoiding the stares and the remarks. Not unless Teddy became a complete recluse. And that wasn't an option anymore. Not now he had his artistic future to contemplate and his muse to secure.

But nearly twenty minutes later, there was still no sign of Stella Hobhouse and her famous gray mare.

A leaden weight settled in Teddy's gut. She'd told him, in her last letter, that she hadn't yet persuaded her brother to bring her to town. He'd nonetheless expected her to be here. Lady Anne had been married yesterday. Teddy had seen mention of it in the papers this morning.

Had Stella missed the ceremony? Was she, even now, in Fostonbury, still practicing being small and quiet?

He brought Samuel around a bend. The gelding jogged gamely forward as Teddy scanned the crush of riders for any sign of his muse. He'd almost given up hope when he saw her.

Stella emerged from the crowd, trotting forward on a striking, pale gray mare. The horse's coat shimmered like silvery vapor in the sunlight. So, too, had Stella's hair shimmered in the parlor at Sutton Park as Teddy had sketched her, shining pearly bright in the cold winter light that had poured through the windows.

But Stella's hair color wasn't visible now. Her tresses were covered in a close-woven net and topped by a jaunty plum riding hat. Her habit was made in a similar hue—that deep shade of purple that appeared almost magical when fitted to her figure. Its skirts draped gracefully over her legs, rippling provocatively against her mount's side as Stella picked up speed.

Teddy saw her before she saw him. She was gazing out toward the rail as she breezed by, looking for him, perhaps, or for someone else of interest. Her groom followed close behind on a stocky chestnut gelding.

She'd almost passed Teddy when he finally brought himself to speak.

"I thought you'd be galloping for certain," he said loud enough for her to hear over the drumbeat of hooves.

Her head jerked in his direction. A smile spread over her face. "Mr. Hayes!" She slowed her mare. "I didn't know you'd be driving."

"Nor did I." Teddy shortened his reins, easing Samuel out of the way of traffic, as Stella turned her horse to ride up alongside his wagonette. "I only bought it a few days ago. What do you think?"

"It's very smart." She glanced at the back, taking in the presence of both Jennings and Teddy's wheeled chair. "Practical, too, I see."

"Naturally," he said. "I'm the soul of practicality."

Her eyes twinkled with laughter.

His mouth pulled into a foolish grin in return. By God, but it was good to see her again.

During their months apart, he'd begun to wonder if he'd imagined how beautiful she was—how very perfect she was for his painting. But he hadn't imagined anything, had he? Indeed, it was possible that his memory had blunted the effect of her.

He felt that effect now at full force. It seemed to be magnified on her mare—the two silver figures amplifying each other with the brilliance of twin stars.

"Your mare is excessively energetic," he said.

"You should have seen her this morning, when I was galloping with Mrs. Malik and Mrs. Blunt. Locket had far more energy then. Now, she's actually quite manageable."

Teddy arched a brow at the mare's dancing legs and trembling nostrils. If this was manageable, he couldn't imagine what the horse was like when she was *un*manageable. "I thought she would be darker for some reason," he remarked.

"She was when she was a filly." Stella patted her mare's shoulder with a slim, gloved hand. "Gray horses fade as they get older, but her mane is still silver and she has dappling on her legs, as you see."

"She's nearly white everywhere else."

"A white horse. How appropriate." She let the mare prance alongside the wagonette for a few steps as they drifted further from afternoon traffic. "My friends and I have often been called the Four Horsewomen. Either that or the Furies."

"There were only three Furies."

"We *were* three to begin with. Then, when Mrs. Malik arrived last season, we were four. Now, regrettably, there's only one of us left. Just me, a gray lady on my white horse. An ominous figure, I daresay, if one countenances the biblical symbolism."

"I'm no Pre-Raphaelite," Teddy said. "Biblical symbolism is lost on me." He drove on alongside her in the direction of the Serpentine. "I can tell you, however, that in terms of light, you and your mare are magnificent."

Stella briefly turned her head away from him, embarrassed by the compliment. "In terms of light," she repeated as though examining the phrase. "What manner of light? Is it the sun? The shadow?"

He caught her eyes. "Starlight, of course," he said solemnly. "For you, it will always be starlight."

Her cheeks took on a faint hint of color. "You're incorrigible. I haven't even asked how you are yet, and you're already plying me with your beastly artistic compliments."

They weren't purely artistic anymore. Not after that kiss. Teddy wasn't too proud to acknowledge it, even if it was only to himself.

"You can still ask me," he said. "If you must insist on preserving the proprieties."

"How was your journey from Devonshire?" she inquired.

Teddy's smile broadened at her air of formality. "Long," he replied frankly. "The Finchleys accompanied us. We're staying with them in Half Moon Street for the remainder of the month."

"And your other friends? Did you leave them in good health?"

"They were hale and hearty enough when we departed Devon. The only person suffering any ill effects is my sister. Though it's to be expected, given her condition. She and my brother-in-law have lately learned that they are to be parents."

"Oh!" Stella's eyes lit. "What happy news! You shall be an uncle."

"Indeed."

"You don't sound very enthused. Don't you like babies?"

"They're very loud, in my experience. And perpetually sticky, with I don't know what. Other than that—"

Her mouth quirked with amusement. "Spoken like a confirmed bachelor."

"But true, nonetheless," he said.

They continued over the rolling green that led away from Rotten Row. Hyde Park was a vast expanse, with more in common with a rambling country woodland than an isolated patch of grass in a bustling city. The further they drifted from the daily promenade, the fewer horses and carriages there were to distract them.

Stella allowed her mare to stretch into an extended walk. If she'd given a cue, Teddy hadn't seen it. He at once comprehended why.

She had extraordinarily quiet hands, and an equally quiet seat. It was all of a piece with the mask she often wore. That beguiling expression of tender gravity that had left him riveted the first time he'd set eyes on her. It was beguiling precisely because of the fathomless depths beneath.

Indeed, she appeared to ride as she lived. Under her luminous stillness, she was subtly at work, managing her high-spirited mare with invisible aids—slight shifts in her weight, unseen pressure from her leg, and delicate crooks of her fingers.

"Is Mrs. Archer very ill?" she asked.

"A minor indisposition," Teddy said. "It's not uncommon in her condition, but it makes crossing the Channel at the end of the month an uneasy prospect for her. She isn't much looking forward to it."

"Sea sickness, of course. It must be doubly trying if one is expecting a baby."

"Undoubtedly," he said. "Though, Laura claims that the happiness of her condition outweighs any discomfort."

"I'm sure it does," Stella said. "She and Mr. Archer must be overjoyed. Please convey my best wishes to them."

"I shall." Teddy again caught her gaze. He hadn't come to the park today to talk about his sister and brother-in-law. "Enough about my family," he said. "How are *you*? That's more to the point."

"I'm very well. I am here, as you see."

"I never doubted you would be. But how did you manage your escape from Elba? I trust you didn't travel alone, as you threatened to do."

"I would have done," she said. "I'd even purchased a rail ticket to London, to my brother's dismay. But before I could use it, the imperial guard arrived to rescue me."

"The imperial guard?" He laughed.

"In the form of my friend Mrs. Blunt. She and her husband, Captain Blunt, came to Fostonbury to fetch me. It was on their way from Yorkshire, so not too much of an imposition, I endeavor to hope."

"Mrs. Blunt is one of the Four Horsewomen, I take it."

Stella nodded, another smile springing to her lips. "I'm staying with her and her husband at Brown's Hotel until the end of the month. They're only remaining in London a fortnight, and then they shall return to Yorkshire."

"I see I must act quickly then."

"What to do?" she asked.

"To lure you to my new studio," he said.

Stella's cheeks flushed with color again. She cast another guarded glance at Jennings.

In his eagerness to speak with his muse, Teddy had temporarily forgotten that his manservant was but a few feet away, witnessing every look and every word. The abrupt reminder caused his chest to tighten on an unexpected surge of bitterness.

It wasn't uncommon for a fellow to drive out with a groom or tiger in attendance. Were Jennings one of their number, his presence would be ignored. But Jennings was no ordinary servant. His function was more personal and therefore more intrusive.

So, too, might an elderly invalid travel with their nurse—an attendant empowered to convey them here or there, and to tend to them when their condition became too onerous to manage alone.

Teddy had long ago resolved not to be self-conscious about the fact that he needed such care. As Alex had said when he'd first hired the man, Jennings's presence was the very opposite of a burden. He was there to help Teddy gain a measure of independence.

But this was different.

For the first time in a very long while, Teddy yearned to be, once again, that athletic young man who had strode through Talbot's Wood five years ago in search of inspiration for his paintings. A man who could meet a young lady on terms of equality, unencumbered by attendants and appliances.

Stella resumed looking straight ahead as she rode. Her own groom followed several lengths behind, too far away to hinder them. "You've secured a studio?" she asked in a tone of polite but disinterested inquiry.

Teddy tried not to take it to heart. He told himself that she was merely conscious of Jennings and, therefore, anxious to preserve the proprieties.

At least, Teddy hoped that's all it was.

Serpentine Bridge lay ahead, and with it a smattering of riders and drivers who had, like them, drifted away from the Row. The moment was no longer suited for private conversation. Not when Stella was riding, and he was driving.

"I'd like to show it to you," he said. "If you'd be willing."

She hesitated before answering. "When?"

"May I call on you Monday afternoon at Brown's? We could drive out to see it, if you're not otherwise engaged. It's only but two or three miles from here."

Another lengthy pause. And then: "I am not engaged," she said, softly meeting his eyes.

Teddy's pulse gave an unsteady leap. "Splendid."

He could talk to her at the studio. There, they could be alone, just the two of them, while Jennings remained on the street with the wagonette. She would be leaving London in less than a fortnight. It would be Teddy's last and best chance to convince Stella to pose for him before she returned to Derbyshire. He was resolved to do whatever it took.

"Monday, then," he said. "You may expect me at two o'clock."

Twenty-One

◆✦◆

*Y*ou don't mean to tell me that you've already signed the lease?"
Alex gave Teddy an incredulous look across the Finchley's pol-
ished mahogany dining table before turning an accusing glare on
Tom. "Did you know about this?"

"I did," Tom said. "It was I who provided the introduction to the
estate agent."

The four of them were seated in the Finchleys' dining room in
Half Moon Street after having just finished their dinner. Two
branches of half-melted candles flickered valiantly between them,
illuminating the remains of their meal.

Alex crumpled his napkin and tossed it onto the table. "Good
God, Tom. I wouldn't have thought you'd be so careless."

Jenny carefully folded her own linen napkin before laying it, very
precisely, alongside her plate. "Tom is never careless. He always does
the exact right thing."

Tom met Alex's glare with a wryly cocked brow. "I defer to my
wife."

Alex was in no mood for brotherly banter. His manner had been
strained since the four of them had sat down to dine. He was brood-
ing and preoccupied, and far from his usual devil-may-care self.

Laura had been similarly out of sorts. She sat beside Alex, the round neckline of her silk dinner dress adorned with a heart-shaped opal brooch her husband had bought her in Paris. Her eyes were unusually grave. "It isn't right this time, Jenny," she said. "Not with the news we had from Dr. Jepson this afternoon."

Teddy's eyes jolted to his sister. He was aware that she and Alex had visited Harley Street again today. Their carriage had been returning to Half Moon Street at the same time Teddy had been returning from seeing Stella in the park. At the time, he'd thought their second appointment the veriest commonplace. "What news?"

His sister gave him an apologetic look. "We were going to tell you all over coffee this evening. We didn't want to spoil everyone's dinner."

Jenny regarded Laura with frank concern from her place across the table. Jenny's plaited auburn hair gleamed like fine copper in the light of the candles. "Oh dear. Is it bad? You're not—"

"No, no," Laura said hastily. "There's no imminent danger. Not if we do as Dr. Jepson tells us to."

Alex ran a protective hand up and down his wife's silk-clad back. "He's advised us to return home without delay."

Alarm bells instantly went off in Teddy's head. He searched his sister's face. "Why? What's wrong?"

"He's merely being cautious," Laura said. "Considering the lingering effects of the scarlet fever on my lungs, and given my recent bouts of illness and how faint I've been feeling, he thinks it's best I don't travel in my condition. He says that, if I must return home, I should do it sooner rather than later to minimize the risk."

"I've already booked passage," Alex said.

"You *what*?" Teddy stared at them both in astonishment. His wheeled chair was rolled up to the opposite side of the table from his sister and brother-in-law. The candles crackled and snapped, casting shadows over their faces. "For when?"

Alex's normally roguish expression was grim with resolve. "Wednesday."

Wednesday? They were meant to stay another two weeks!

Laura hurried to explain. "It was either that or remain in London until after the baby is born in August."

"You could if you'd like," Jenny offered. "We've plenty of room here."

"I agree," Tom said. "We'd be delighted to have you."

The door of the dining room opened. The Finchleys' dour house-keeper, Mrs. Jarrow, bustled in, a starched apron over her plain stuff gown. "Shall I serve the coffee in the parlor, Mrs. Finchley?"

"Not yet." Jenny looked briefly at the old retainer. "Give us a moment, if you please, Mrs. Jarrow."

The housekeeper cast a glance at the taut faces around the table and then, brows lifted and lips pursed, took her leave, swinging the door shut behind her.

"The business would never withstand it," Laura said after the servant had withdrawn. "Alex is needed in Grasse, as am I. We've already left things too long with our foreman."

Teddy scanned his sister for any signs of illness. She was absent the stark paleness she sometimes exhibited in the morning—that trembling, pallid demeanor that telegraphed the reality of her condition to the world. After having eaten most of her dinner, she seemed her usual healthy self.

"I thought your symptoms were normal," he said. "That's what you told me."

"For the most part, I believe they are," Laura replied.

"Then perhaps that Jepson fellow is overreacting?"

"Teddy has a point," Tom said. "Some of the fashionable doctors in town don't believe in women being active during their confinement. His advice might be a needless precaution."

"Would you take a chance with your own wife?" Alex shot back.

Laura set a hand on her husband's arm. "There's no point us arguing about it. The fact is, we've already decided to go. All that remains—"

"Did you purchase a ticket for me?" Teddy asked.

Laura fell quiet.

Teddy turned on Alex, the muscles in his shoulders gone tense with anticipatory outrage. "*Did* you?"

"We did," Alex said. "For your sister's sake."

A cold fury roared through Teddy's veins. "Don't even begin to frame it that way," he warned him. "You *knew* I'd decided to stay. Both of you did."

"That was before," Alex said. "Surely you must see that Laura needs you."

Teddy opened his mouth, on the verge of pointing out the obvious. His sister had a husband. She had servants. She didn't need Teddy in Grasse to look after her. She didn't need Teddy full stop.

"It isn't that," Laura cut in before Teddy could give voice to his thoughts. "It's just that I worry so about you staying here on your own. Alex is afraid it will affect my health."

"What about *my* health?" Teddy retorted.

Laura gave a guilty flinch. "It's not forever."

Teddy's fingers curled on the arms of his chair so tightly he felt an ache in his knuckles. If the wood had splintered into his hands he wouldn't have been surprised. "You have no idea what leaving would mean for me. What I'd lose if I went now. My plans for my career— my whole life—"

"You're four-and-twenty, Teddy," Alex said. "You'll have plenty of time to strike out on your own in the years ahead."

"It's not about my age! Though why that should weigh against me, I haven't the vaguest idea. Prince Albert was younger than me when he married the Queen. By my age he'd already sired three children."

Alex was unmoved by the argument. "As that may be, unlike the late Prince Consort, you have no entanglements that would necessitate you remaining in town. You're at perfect liberty to return with us on Wednesday."

"On the contrary," Teddy said. "I have a house. A studio. And I'm an inch away from securing my model."

"Miss Hobhouse is here?" Laura asked, briefly diverted. "You didn't say."

"She hasn't agreed to sit for me yet," Teddy replied. "But she's going to. I can feel it. If you drag me away now—"

Alex scoffed. "No one is dragging anyone anywhere. I'm asking you to come, for your sister's sake."

"What about a compromise?" Tom asked.

Jenny smiled at him. She had absolute faith in her husband and had plainly been waiting for him to solve this dilemma so they might all retire to the parlor for coffee.

Alex's brows lowered with suspicion. "What kind of compromise?"

"Teddy could stay with us," Tom said. "If Jenny agrees?"

Jenny exchanged a warm look with her husband. "Yes, of course. That's exactly what he must do." She turned to Laura. "Would that put your mind at ease, dear?"

Laura's face suffused with relief. "It would," she admitted. "I know he'd be well looked after here."

"*Looked after,*" Teddy repeated under his breath. He glared, first at Alex and then at Tom. "Are you serious?"

"Just as a compromise," Tom said. "It needn't be permanent."

Teddy rolled himself back from the table in a burst of frustration. "Well, what am I to say to that? I can't stop you from pushing me here or pulling me there. I'm in a wheeled chair, after all. I have no ability to walk out of here and wish you all heartily to the devil."

Jenny moved to rise. "This is a family matter. We should leave the three of you to discuss it."

Tom stood to pull out his wife's chair. "An excellent idea. We'll withdraw to the—"

"Why bother?" Teddy interrupted. "My freedom of movement is already up for debate. If that's not an assault on my privacy—"

"I'm afraid for you!" Laura cried. She leaned toward him from across the table, her eyes shimmering with emotion. "Can't you comprehend that? I love you and don't want anyone to hurt you!"

The room went silent. It wasn't like Laura to lose her composure. She was usually the most steady and rational of creatures. She'd had to be during their years in Surrey, stretching every shilling to meet their needs as she'd struggled to look after Teddy and their aged, dotty Aunt Charlotte.

Jenny slowly sat back down, and Tom resumed his seat. Their faces were vivid with concern.

Alex put his arm around his wife. He murmured something to her. Laura leaned into him, murmuring back. "It's all right, love," Alex said. "Teddy understands."

Teddy felt a deep spasm of remorse. He knew he shouldn't be upsetting his sister in her condition. Indeed, he didn't *want* to upset her. At the same time . . .

He recognized all at once the full powerlessness of his position. There was only this thread—this thin, shining filament of independence—for the first time dangling within his reach. He had the sinking sense that, if he didn't grasp it now, it would be lost to him forever.

"I do understand," he said tightly. "You want me close. Either that, or living with someone who'll keep me safe."

Laura wiped a stray tear from her eye. "Yes."

"And yet, I'm not an invalid. Despite all this"—Teddy motioned to his legs and his chair—"and despite the fact that Jennings must trudge after me everywhere like the dratted angel of death. There are gouty old gentlemen more infirm than I am, and they maintain entire estates, not to mention houses in town."

Alex leveled a warning look at him. "Your sister and I have made our wishes plain. They're not unreasonable. You can return to France with us on Wednesday, or you can remain in town with Tom and Jenny. I think their offer is more than generous."

The whole of Teddy's spirit revolted against the ultimatum. And the fact that Alex was the one issuing it! Alex, the very man who had encouraged Teddy to regain his independence, to find a French art teacher, and to live for a time in Paris studying with Gleyre, for God's sake.

From the beginning, Alex had supported and encouraged Teddy in all his efforts.

But this wasn't Alex now, Teddy realized. This was a husband and, soon to be, first-time father. A man who was, himself, scared and uncertain of what the future might hold. That's why he was behaving so bloody irrationally, tossing out warning glares and infernal ultimatums. Because he'd do anything, sacrifice anything, to safeguard the well-being of his wife and his unborn child.

Deep down, Teddy understood that. It made the ultimatum no easier a pill to swallow.

Jenny smiled at Teddy encouragingly. "If you stayed with us, we could have our coachman convey you to your studio each day. It wouldn't be too terrible, would it?"

"An existence by your leave?" Teddy asked. "By all of your leaves?"

"It's either that or return to Grasse with your sister," Tom said. "That seems to be the consensus."

A consensus? Since when did a man's freedom of movement require a consensus? It didn't. It shouldn't, regardless of his physical condition. Not if that man had reached his majority.

Teddy's mouth twisted with bitterness. He rolled back his chair from the table. "Two whole options, and neither of them of my own devising." He angled his wheels to leave. "I'm spoiled for choice."

"I leave it to you to make it," Alex said as Teddy rolled to the door. "The steamer departs on Wednesday morning. Unless you've come to a prior arrangement with the Finchleys, I expect you to be on it."

Twenty-Two

> ❖

"Mr. Hayes?" Evie said in surprise. She brought her blood bay Spanish stallion, Hephaestus, back down to a trot. "The gentleman who uses a wheeled chair?"

Stella reined in Locket. The mare shook her silvery white head in protest, preferring to continue the spirited gallop that Stella and her two friends had just been enjoying down the length of a secluded avenue on the north side of Hyde Park, far from the intrusion of the less-experienced riders in Rotten Row.

"He mentioned that you'd met before," Stella said.

"We have." Evie brushed back one of the curling black feathers of her stylish green felt riding hat. It was made to match the green of her habit—a masterpiece of tailoring that hugged her voluptuous figure in all the best ways. It had been the first riding costume her husband had made for her. "Mr. Hayes was staying with Mr. and Mrs. Finchley in the autumn, at their house in Half Moon Street. I was introduced to him on one of the evenings Mr. Malik and I went to dine."

Julia slowed her ebony gelding, Cossack. Like Evie and Stella, she wore an immaculately fitted habit of Mr. Malik's design. Rich black in color, with a stylish velvet collar, it complemented the sheen of Cossack's coat. "Who is Mr. Hayes?" she asked.

"A gentleman artist," Evie replied.

"One of considerable talent," Stella said. "Though perhaps not in the fashionable sense."

"I meant who is he to *you*," Julia amended.

Stella straightened her skirts over her legs. Her own habit was a dark plummy purple, every dart and seam placed with expert intention. It was the same one she'd worn yesterday afternoon when meeting Teddy in Rotten Row. "He's a friend," she said.

"Is that all?" Evie inquired.

"As to that . . ." Stella wavered before confessing. "He may have asked me to model for one of his paintings."

Julia's brows flew up. "Did he, by heaven? What extraordinary cheek!" She reduced Cossack to a walk, giving Stella her undivided attention.

Evie did the same with Hephaestus, her hazel eyes alert.

Stella turned Locket in a half circle to quiet her before resuming her place among her friends. "He didn't mean it as an insult. If you saw his work, you'd recognize it as a singular honor."

"Still," Evie said sensibly, "modeling for a painting isn't advisable, is it? Not when you have your reputation to consider."

"Artists' models have a reputation all their own," Julia added. "And not one any young lady would aspire to."

"Yes, I realize. Which is precisely why I told him no." Stella paused. "Initially."

Julia and Evie both burst into conversation at the same time.

"You haven't agreed to pose for him!" Julia exclaimed.

"If this is about earning enough money to support yourself—" Evie began.

"It isn't wholly about money," Stella cut in. "Though, he did offer to pay me."

Julia's mouth fell open. "Good heavens, Stella. How is that not an insult?"

"I doubt he intended it to be," Evie said. "On the few occasions we met, Mr. Hayes impressed me with his single-minded attention to art. Other concerns didn't seem to enter his mind."

"They don't," Stella said. "He's rather plainspoken, in fact. I initially thought it impertinence, but I believe it's owing to his passion for his work—and to his condition."

"He had a fever as a boy that paralyzed his legs," Evie explained to Julia. "That's what Mr. Malik told me."

"Not as a young boy," Stella said. "Indeed, Mr. Hayes hasn't been in his chair above five years."

"How old is he?" Julia asked.

"Four-and-twenty," Stella answered promptly.

Evie and Julia exchanged a glance.

Stella knew what they must be thinking. "We found ourselves in each other's company a good deal at Sutton Park," she explained. "And Mr. Hayes is remarkably candid."

A cool wind rustled the branches of the trees lining the path ahead of them. More riders were approaching, and one of them coming at a quick clip. It was an older man on a dun gelding, posting at an extended trot. He touched his crop to the brim of his tall hat in a silent salute as he rode by.

The three of them inclined their heads in distracted acknowledgment.

"Is that all that inspired such confidences?" Evie asked after the rider had passed. "Mr. Hayes's propensity for candor?"

"That and his desire to paint me," Stella said. "He's invited me to visit his studio on Monday afternoon. I've said that I will. He'll be coming to collect me at the hotel."

"Goodness," Julia breathed.

"This begins to sound more and more like a courtship," Evie said.

"It's not a courtship, I promise you," Stella informed them before they could get too carried away. "It's about art, that's all. Mr. Hayes is at great pains to convince me to sit for him. There's nothing else to it."

"So . . ." Julia's brow puckered. "He only sees you in terms of how you might appear on his canvas?"

Stella hesitated before answering. The truth was, she didn't know how Teddy saw her. All the compliments he'd lavished on her had been in relation to her charms as a potential model.

Except for what he'd written to her about their kiss.

He'd said it was a pleasure of a precious sort. More precious than the pleasures he'd shared with his Parisienne muses.

For whatever that was worth.

"How else should he see me?" she asked at last. "As Evie said, he's single-minded when it comes to his work."

"It *is* about money, then," Julia pronounced grimly.

"In part, yes." Stella wasn't ashamed to own it. "I must find ways of supporting myself. I can't very well go back to Fostonbury, can I?" She doubted whether Daniel would have her. And if he did permit her to return to the vicarage, he was sure to make her grovel first.

Evelyn frowned in thought. "A modeling fee won't be enough to keep you. Not unless Mr. Hayes pays you an exorbitant sum."

"And even if you did accept money from him," Julia said, "that wouldn't equate to a career. You would have to be hired again and again by all manner of painters—some of whom aren't gentlemen, I fear."

Stella guided Locket to the opposite side of Julia, keeping Julia's gelding firmly between Locket and Evie's stallion. Hephaestus rarely made overtures, but when in each other's presence, the mare and stallion always had an added spring in their steps and a certain quiver at their nostrils. It made each of them even more difficult to control.

"I don't anticipate making a profession of it," Stella said. "I intend to find other employment."

Julia flashed her an exasperated look. "I don't know why you won't permit us to help you."

"Perhaps because our help would make her as dependent on us as she once was on her brother," Evie suggested.

"Nonsense," Julia said to Stella. "We're nothing like your brother. We're your friends."

"And I'd like you to remain my friends," Stella replied. "Which is why I won't come and live with either of you. Not permanently, anyway."

"Impermanently, then," Evie said. "You can lodge with me for a time. You'll need somewhere to stay once Julia and Captain Blunt return to Yorkshire. Just until you find your footing."

"Her footing as an artist's model?" Julia made no effort to hide her misgivings. "I'd far rather you return to Yorkshire with me. Captain Blunt and I would be glad to have you at Goldfinch Hall. You and Locket could stay as long as you like. There's plenty of room."

"And I'd be, what?" Stella asked. "Your lady's companion?"

"You'd be my friend," Julia said.

"No. Once I moved in with you, I'd be a houseguest. And houseguests aren't tolerable for any length of time. Not even the ones you like." Stella gave Julia a faint smile. "I appreciate the invitation all the same."

Julia huffed. "You're too proud. That's the trouble."

"I'm practical." Stella set her shoulders. "I shall find a position in London."

"Doing what?" Julia asked.

Therein lay the question that Stella had been racking her brain to answer ever since she'd left Derbyshire.

"I don't know," she admitted. "I'm not qualified to be a governess or a teacher. Indeed, aside from riding and sketching, I'm not skilled at anything at all."

Her friends both protested at once.

"I am good at listening, however," Stella continued, undeterred.

"And I know something about how to comport myself in society. More importantly, I excel at being invisible. All qualities which would make me the perfect lady's companion."

"I thought you didn't want to be a companion!" Julia objected.

"Not to one of my friends." Stella looked out between Locket's elegantly curved gray ears in solemn contemplation. "But I believe I could stomach it if it earned me a wage and provided me with room and board."

"Most of the wage would *be* your room and board," Evie pointed out.

"It would be worth it if I could remain in town," Stella said. "I could house Locket, Crab, and Turvey at a nearby stable out of the income from my inheritance. The rest could be subsidized from what I earned in my new position. My needs wouldn't be many."

"To have them met, you'd have to live with a stranger, and be subject to their megrims." Julia rode up closer to Stella. "Wouldn't you rather live with one of us? We wouldn't order you about or make you sleep in a drafty attic room."

Stella gave her friend another brief smile. Julia's heart was, as ever, bigger than her head when it came to rational matters. "The difference is, if I was employed, my duties would be firmly delineated. I would know where I stood from one day to the next. I would never have to feel as though I was a burden, or . . ." Her smile dimmed. "A parasite."

Again, both her friends spoke in unison.

"You could never be a burden!" Julia cried.

"Did your brother say that to you?" Evie demanded.

"He did," Stella admitted. Daniel's unkind remark lingered in her heart, a pernicious bruise that refused to heal. It didn't just sadden her. It made her doubt her worth.

That was the power of words. Especially harsh words from someone you'd once loved.

All Stella could do was ignore the pain. Ignore the doubt.

She lifted her chin. "It doesn't matter anymore. That part of my life is over. I must make my own way now, and I'm resolved to do it. It only remains for me to find a suitable employer." She gave Evie a hopeful look. "Might Mr. Malik know of someone?"

Evie's brows knit. "He does have rather a lot of wealthy old widows patronizing his shop at present. I could certainly ask him if any of them might require a companion."

"And I suppose I could ask my parents," Julia said, rising to the occasion. "They know every medical man in the city, and have countless invalids among their acquaintance. There must be one among their number who's searching for a companion."

Stella was both grateful and humbled by her friends' efforts to rally around her. "Thank you," she said. "Both of you. You're splendid, truly."

Julia brought Cossack up closer to Stella. "Are you sure it's what you want?"

"It is," Stella said, more confidently than she felt. Locket pranced beneath her, blowing out air from her trembling nostrils. She sensed Stella's secret anxiety. There was no way of hiding it. Stella stroked the mare's neck to soothe her. But only a gallop would suffice.

Hephaestus tossed his head in a wordless expression of agreement. Cossack seconded the sentiment with a swish of his tail.

"Shall we let them have their heads again before it gets too crowded?" Stella asked.

She didn't wait for her friends to answer. Leaning forward in her leather sidesaddle, she set her left heel lightly against Locket's side. The mare responded to the cue like a lightning strike from the sky. Any thought that Evie and Julia had about interrogating Stella further about her uncertain future was drowned out by the thundering of hooves as their horses, too, sprang into action.

Teddy arrived at Brown's Hotel on Albemarle Street on Monday afternoon at two o'clock precisely. He wore a loose-fitting melton wool driving coat over his dark waistcoat and trousers. He'd driven straight there from Half Moon Street and, on arriving, had left his wagonette in the charge of one of the hotel footmen.

Brown's was a luxurious establishment—rather like a richly understated country house—all dark paneled walls and elegantly carpeted floors, with fashionable people drifting through the halls. Jennings held the door open for Teddy as Teddy wheeled his chair into the hotel's public drawing room.

Stella awaited him there, perched on the edge of a lavishly upholstered hotel chair. She wasn't alone. A lady and gentleman waited with her, seated beside each other on the settee across from her. Stella's hosts, presumably—Captain and Mrs. Blunt.

Mrs. Blunt was a young woman—blue eyed, raven haired, and petite. Her husband towered over her, dark and forbidding. He had a jagged scar across his face.

Catching sight of Teddy, Stella's face betrayed a flicker of relief. She stood as he came to join them, smoothing a self-conscious hand over her carriage dress. It was made of plain, tobacco-colored silk, trimmed in a modest flashing of black velvet.

Captain and Mrs. Blunt rose from the settee to stand alongside her.

"Miss Hobhouse," Teddy said, with an inclination of his head.

"Mr. Hayes." Stella dropped a brief curtsy. "May I present my friends, Mrs. Blunt and her husband, Captain Blunt?"

"Mr. Hayes." Captain Blunt bowed.

"Mr. Hayes." Mrs. Blunt regarded Teddy with frank curiosity. "How do you do?"

"Captain. Ma'am." Teddy gave an approximation of a bow. "A pleasure."

Mrs. Blunt stepped closer. "You're an artist, is that correct? And have come all the way from Paris."

"By way of Devon," Teddy replied. "I was lately on the coast visiting friends."

Captain Blunt frowned. "You're staying with Mr. Finchley in Half Moon Street?"

"I am, sir," Teddy said. "I often do when I'm in town. My sister's husband is something like a brother to Mr. Finchley."

The answer appeared to satisfy Captain Blunt in some small way that Teddy wasn't a dangerous fiend preparing to drive Stella straight to ruin. "Mr. Finchley is an excellent fellow," he said. "My wife and I are both acquainted with him."

"He's a first-rate gentleman, I agree." Teddy looked to Stella. His mouth tugged into a smile. "I trust you're ready for our drive?"

"Indeed." Stella turned to Mrs. Blunt and her husband. "If you don't object?"

"What manner of gig are you driving, Mr. Hayes?" Captain Blunt asked brusquely. "A curricle?"

"A wagonette," Teddy said. "It's an open carriage."

"And your horse? Not too wild, I trust."

"Quite the opposite. Samuel would rather doze than take the bit between his teeth."

"Where are you bound for? Hyde Park?"

"Covent Garden. We'll be back within the hour."

Stella flashed Mrs. Blunt a meaningful look.

Mrs. Blunt slipped her hand through her husband's arm. "I'm sure she'll be fine, my love."

"I'll take care of her, sir," Teddy promised them both. "You may rest assured."

Captain Blunt withdrew his pocket watch. He made a point of checking the time. "I'll expect Miss Hobhouse back by three o'clock."

"Of a certainty," Teddy said. "Miss Hobhouse? Shall we?"

"Yes, indeed," Stella said.

Moments later, she and Teddy were seated in the front of his wagonette, with Jennings and Teddy's wheeled chair firmly ensconced in the back.

Teddy gave Stella an interested glance as he started his horse. "Captain Blunt is rather protective of you."

Stella rested a hand on the seat between them. Her skirts were bunched against the outside of Teddy's leg, just as they'd been during their sleigh ride. "Only because he promised my brother he'd look after me," she said. "And only because I'm a close friend of his wife. I do believe he'd pave the moon if Julia asked him to. Theirs was a love match, you see."

Teddy had gathered as much from the way Captain Blunt and his wife had looked at each other.

"They were married last summer," Stella said. "Indeed, all of my friends have recently married. Anne's wedding was only last week."

"I saw mention of it in the papers. It sounded like a grand affair."

"The grandest. The Countess of Arundell does nothing by halves." Stella gazed out at the afternoon traffic. Carriages and omnibuses passed in a clatter of wooden wheels and steel-shod hooves.

Teddy moved easily among them, Samuel completely unfazed by the encroaching traffic. Teddy himself was somewhat less sanguine. He was still thinking of the row he'd had with his sister and Alex. Of that dratted ultimatum Alex had given him and what it would mean for Teddy's plans to paint Stella.

Granted, it wasn't as if Alex would put Teddy onto the steamer against his will. Things hadn't yet stooped to that level. All Alex had done was give Teddy a choice. A false choice, to be sure, but a choice all the same. Teddy could either accompany them back to France, thereby keeping the peace, or he could remain in London, both breaking Laura's heart and imperiling her health—and the health of her child—in the process.

What was a devoted brother to do? A brother who desperately wanted his freedom?

The only gentlemanly solution was to temporarily acquiesce to the Finchleys' guardianship. Teddy would stay with them for the next several months. They wouldn't interfere with his work, he knew. They were sensible people, and sensitive as well.

That didn't make the prospect of their chaperonage any less irksome. Teddy recoiled from it on principle.

"Tell me about your studio," Stella said. "It's in Covent Garden, you said?"

"In Maiden Lane."

She furrowed her brow. "Maiden Lane? I can't recall—"

"It's where Turner was born."

Her mouth tilted with humor. "Ah yes. I remember. But you don't mean you've really managed to let a place there?"

Teddy's spirits perked, recalling how he'd felt as Mr. Chakrabarty had led him through the house's lower rooms. He'd known immediately that it was the place for him. "I have. The property just came available. It's been rather neglected. The solicitor nearly didn't show it to me."

"It's not Mr. Turner's actual house?"

"Lord no. That was torn down ages ago." He guided Samuel around a hackney cab blocking the road. "No, this place is a distance away. But it's not the house itself that's important, it's the location of the street. It's near the river."

"Why is that important?"

"The water. The fog. The atmosphere."

"The light?"

"And the light." Teddy smiled briefly. "It's not as I'd like in the house itself, but outside . . . yes. It suits me perfectly."

The bustling streets of Covent Garden, with its theatres, fruit stalls, and flower market, lay but a mile from the luxury of Brown's Hotel in Mayfair. Teddy continued driving north of the Strand, turning down one street and then another until, finally, arriving at a narrow lane that was flanked on either side by shops, pottery works, and close-set blocks of private dwellings.

He slowed the wagonette in front of a slightly sagging, three-story redbrick house with a splintering white wooden arch over its entrance. A single, shallow front step led up to the door.

Stella gazed up at the place with doubtful curiosity. "This one is yours?"

"As of two days ago, yes." Teddy cast a thoughtful eye over the half-boarded windows and the peeling paint on the door arch and window frames. The house was old, and crooked on its foundation, but, with its inviting front entrance and the effect of the sunlight reflecting off the leaded windowpanes, it had character in abundance. "It won't look like this long. I'll have stonemasons, painters, and paper hangers in presently. With some minor refurbishment, it will be good as new."

Getting the place up to snuff would take the lion's share of Teddy's income from the perfumery, but he reasoned to himself that it would be worth it. Inspiration was a large part of art. And this house, with its inherent charm and storied location, was inspiration personified.

Stella surveyed the shabby property from her seat in the wagonette, looking from the disintegrating roof tiles to the cracked stonework below. Her expression brightened at the sight of a black-and-white tomcat wandering boldly past the step.

"Does he come with the house?" she asked.

Teddy had seen the cat before when he'd visited the property with Mr. Chakrabarty. The fluffy feline reminded him a little of Magpie. "As far as I'm aware, he has no fixed abode."

"Poor thing," Stella said. "Now you've taken the place, you must take care to feed him."

"He looks well fed enough to me," Teddy said. "No doubt he's already getting free meals from every tenderhearted shopkeeper on the street."

"You make him sound rather mercenary."

"Most cats are. I say that with affection. My family keeps a cat, not unlike this one. Magpie is his name. He's as mercenary as they come."

She gave him a curious look. "You never mentioned you had a cat."

"Should I have done?"

"You might have," she said. "It occurs to me that, outside of art, and the fact that you once loved a young lady named Miss Talbot, I don't know very much about you."

"Love is stretching the word where Miss Talbot was concerned. As for not knowing anything about me—you know my family makes lavender water. And you know I studied with Charles Gleyre in Paris."

"Art again," she pointed out.

"Very well. How about this—I don't only like cats. I like dogs, too. And birds. I enjoy visiting the seaside. I prefer the city to the country, Beethoven to Brahms, and my favorite dessert is charlotte russe."

Her chin dipped, concealing a smile.

"Shall we go in?" he asked abruptly.

Stella blinked. She clearly hadn't expected they'd be getting out. "Is that—" She stumbled over her words, briefly flustered. "It wouldn't be too inconvenient for you, or difficult—"

"Not at all." Teddy called to his manservant. "Jennings? If you'll assist Miss Hobhouse down?"

Stella uttered no further objections as Jennings handed her down from the wagonette. She then waited, quietly, while the manservant attended to Teddy.

It was a painstaking process that first required Jennings to remove Teddy's wheeled chair from the back of the wagonette and place it on the house's doorstep. The manservant next lifted Teddy down from the driver's bench and—leaving the placid Samuel dozing in his traces—bodily conveyed him up the house's shallow front step to his waiting seat.

Teddy didn't look at Stella as it happened. He was fully focused on doing his part—his jaw tense and the muscles in his neck corded with effort as he gripped Jennings's shoulders. It was only when Teddy was firmly established in his wheeled chair that he turned his attention back to her. His face was heated from the exertion.

Or perhaps it was embarrassment.

She'd witnessed him at his weakest, both when he'd boarded the wagonette and now when disembarking from it. She'd seen him vulnerable and reliant, just as he'd been when he'd joined her in the sleigh in Hampshire.

He didn't want her to view him that way—as a man who must rely on the strength of others. He'd rather she recognized that he was strong himself.

Jennings used the key Teddy gave him to unlock the door of the house. He opened it wide before backing away from the threshold to make room for Teddy and his chair.

The piebald cat watched them from a safe distance, eyes squinted and tail swishing.

Stella glanced back at the horse. A gust of wind down the lane stirred the hem of her skirts and ruffled the wide silk ribbons of her spoon bonnet. "Who will stay with Samuel?"

"Jennings will," Teddy said. "I don't need him for the next part." He paused on the threshold. "After you."

Twenty-Three

—❖—

Stella could have refused. Indeed, she should have done. A young lady shouldn't be going into an empty house, or anywhere so private in nature, with a gentleman unaccompanied. But she *knew* Teddy. She trusted him. And she was too dratted curious to deny herself the opportunity to see his future studio firsthand.

Entering the small, shadowy hall, with its steep, narrow staircase, she waited as Teddy rolled in after her. He left the front door open behind him in a minor concession to propriety.

"This is nothing impressive," he said. "But beyond it are four good-sized reception rooms."

He wheeled himself down the hall to a doorway on the left. It led to an expansive drawing room flanked by several windows. One of them was the same half-boarded front window Stella had observed from the street. Rays of light shone in through the grease and the grit, casting dancing shimmers over the dusty, slatted wood floor.

"The previous tenant had this as a parlor," Teddy said, "and the others as a study, library, and music room. But I have another idea for how to use them."

Stella wandered at his side as the two of them surveyed the large room. There was some abandoned furniture scattered about—a sagging settee with the stuffing coming out of it, and a tall chair propped in the corner with a torn damask cushion. A broad wooden seat, built for the purpose, had been fitted low in front of the window. Its lacquered finish bore several deep scratches.

"Will this be your studio?" she asked, looking about her.

"It will. Not only because of the light, but because it's at the front of the house. It will be less tiresome if people come in to look at my paintings."

"And the back rooms will be your private residence?"

Teddy nodded. "A parlor, and bedrooms for myself and Jennings."

She followed him to look at the other reception rooms. They were as grimy as the large reception room had been, but Stella could nevertheless see the appeal. "All of your needs will be met on the ground floor. You'll have no cause to go upstairs."

"That's the idea," Teddy said.

"But there must be several rooms above."

"Not too many, actually. Just enough for a housekeeper-cook, and the occasional houseguest. You can go up and look at them if you like."

"You wouldn't mind?"

"Not at all."

Stella briefly considered demurring out of politeness. But only briefly. Once again, her curiosity got the better of her. "I shan't be a minute," she said.

"I'll be here." Teddy stopped his wheeled chair by the large window in his future studio. "Find me when you're done."

She retreated back to the staircase in the hall. The banister was a good solid oak, with only minor damage to one of the posts. She examined it briefly as she ascended, just as she examined the snug bedrooms located above. There was no draft. No damp. With a little paint and paper, and a few colorful furnishings, the house wouldn't just be habitable. It would be cozy. Charming. To be sure, it would be a home.

Returning downstairs, she found Teddy waiting in the same

spot beside the window where she'd left him. His expression was pensive.

His mouth curved faintly when he saw her. "Well? What's the verdict?"

"I like it immensely." Stella sank down on the window seat, bringing their eyes level. She preferred talking to him this way to standing over him. It was more companionable. More intimate. "I expect you'll be very happy here."

"Yes, well . . ." He ran a hand over his hair. "That was the plan."

She inhaled a deep breath, sighing a bit dreamily as she once again took in the light through the windows. It wasn't the most brilliant of rooms. Not as bright, certainly, as the small parlor at Sutton Park. But there was something otherworldly to it. Almost magical.

Perhaps it was the gleam of the grease on the windowpanes. Or perhaps it was the fact that the two of them were alone—wholly alone.

"Is this where you would have painted me?" she asked.

"Yes."

"And paid me, according to your letters."

His clever blue-gray eyes were suddenly intent. "You've been considering it."

"I confess, I have."

"And?"

Stella's pulse skipped. She understood what she was doing. She was taking a risk with her reputation. With her entire future. But she was seeking employment, wasn't she? By that measure, the decision was practical, not reckless. Any payment she received from Teddy would be used to offset her living expenses.

"I've decided to do it," she said.

Teddy's eyes blazed. But he didn't say anything. He only looked at her steadily.

Stella feared she hadn't made herself plain. "I'll pose for your painting," she clarified. "If you still want me—"

"I want you," he said. "Make no mistake. I only—" He broke off. "Things have become a bit complicated of late. But . . . regardless . . . I'll still be using the house as my studio. Providing the repairs can be done expeditiously, and providing you're at liberty to come each day until the portrait is finished. It could be months. And with you returning to Derbyshire next week—"

"I am not returning to Derbyshire."

His gaze bore into hers, making her pulse skip its rhythm. "*What?*"

"I'm not ever returning." Stella gave Teddy an abridged explanation of the events that had transpired at the vicarage—of Daniel's ultimatum and her dire response to it. "So, you see, I'm completely on my own now, and fully at liberty to do as I please."

Rather than being encouraged by the news, Teddy appeared to be vexed by it. His face darkened with evident concern. "But . . . where will you live?"

"After Mrs. Blunt and her husband return to Yorkshire, I shall stay with Mrs. Malik for a time. But only temporarily. I intend to seek employment."

"Doing what?"

"The only thing I'm qualified for. I shall find work as a lady's companion. I'm already adept at being inconspicuous. The only difference is now I shall hopefully be compensated for it."

Teddy's ebony brows sank ominously. He didn't look at all enthused by her plan. Rather the reverse.

"It will suit perfectly," Stella said, attempting to make him understand. "I'll pay Locket's expenses with the income from my inheritance, and take care of my other needs with the wages from my new position. For anything else, I shall use the money I earn from posing for you." She gave him a quizzing look. "So, you mustn't attempt to stint me."

He didn't laugh at her teasing. He didn't even smile.

Stella's own smile faded. A knot of building indignation formed in her chest. "You don't approve."

"No," he said bluntly. "I don't."

"May I ask why?"

He rolled a half turn away from her. His handsome face was hard and humorless. "You've just articulated to me your master plan to make yourself invisible for the remainder of your life. A lady's companion? A drudge, more like. Even if you spend twice a day in the saddle, galloping your heart out, the remainder of your hours will be spent doing the bidding of some high-handed lady who'll expect you to blend into the woodwork."

"What do you think I've been doing for the last two-and-twenty years?" Stella asked, affronted. "Just because I ride with abandon, and just because you once observed me foolishly color my hair, doesn't mean I'm not acquainted with the drudgery of the day to day."

"I know you are. I've seen how you strive for it. Even when we met in the park."

She inwardly flinched. And here she'd thought she looked rather fetching in her habit! "What about the park?"

"You covered your hair."

"I always do when I ride."

"Because you want to be inconspicuous?" He wheeled away, turning his back on her. "How I begin to despise that word."

Stella refrained from pointing out that it was her hair she wanted to be inconspicuous, not the rest of her person. It wasn't Teddy's business. He had no right to judge her. "This from the gentleman who refused every single outing at Sutton Park merely because he didn't wish people to observe him being moved in and out of his chair."

Teddy's shoulders tensed visibly at her words.

Stella feared she'd gone too far. She rose to follow him. "But I don't judge you for it," she went on quickly. "Because I understand the impulse." She stopped several feet away from him in frustration. "In any case, I don't know what all that has to do with my posing for you. Considering how you kept after me, I thought you'd be over the moon!"

Teddy grumbled something under his breath.

Stella stepped closer to him. "I'm sorry. What did you say?"

"I said," he ground out, "you deserve more than a life in the background."

A surge of emotion took her unaware. She ruthlessly suppressed it. "Yes, well . . . People seldom get what they deserve. One must be sensible. Which is why I've fixed on being a companion. My friends are inquiring after opportunities on my behalf. I hope to be settled somewhere within a month. So, unless you can suggest a more favorable alternative for—"

"Perhaps there is one," he interrupted. "Something better suited to the both of us."

Stella didn't know what *he* had to do with it. She asked him nevertheless. "What do you propose?"

"Just that." At last, Teddy rolled his chair around to face her. "A proposal."

Stella looked at him blankly. "I *beg* your pardon?"

Teddy faced her, his jaw gone hard. The muscles in his arms, shoulders, and abdomen contracted as though preparing to receive a blow. But he didn't think about the consequences to his pride. He only thought about what Stella needed in that moment.

And what *he* needed.

"I'm asking you to marry me," he said.

She stilled. Her face went pale.

"I see the idea shocks you."

"No," she protested. "That is—"

"Before you refuse out of hand, allow me to make an argument for the case." Teddy cleared his throat. His cravat felt damnably tight all of a sudden. "Firstly, you require a home of your own. I have a home now. A large enough one, with ample room for both you and your mare. There's a coach house at the back. Did I mention it?"

"No." Her voice was a mere thread of sound.

He doggedly continued. "Secondly, you require your independence. I can give you that, too. What woman has more independence than a married lady? You could go where you choose—with whom you choose. There would be nothing to stop you any longer."

She opened her mouth to speak.

Teddy forestalled her. "Thirdly, you require a drawing master. Who better than me? I could teach you here. It would be my pleasure to do so." He plowed on before he could lose his nerve. "As to the other impediments—the fact that we would be married, and that we would, by necessity, be obliged to live together, I say again: the house is a large one. You could have the upstairs to yourself, and I the downstairs. We need only meet when I paint you, or when I'm helping you with your sketching."

An expression of reluctant understanding came over her. "You're proposing a marriage of convenience."

"Something of the sort, yes." Teddy honestly didn't know why he hadn't thought of it before. It would easily solve both their problems. From his desire to set up his own establishment, to her need to have a home of her own. He had no doubt they could make it work. They were neither of them fools.

Folding her arms, Stella paced to the window, the hem of her velvet-trimmed skirts brushing softly over the slatted floor, stirring up dust motes. Her back was very straight. "But you don't want to marry me."

"Don't I?"

"You don't want to marry anyone. You've said so before. You don't want anyone to bother you."

"And you would?"

"I daresay I might." She glanced at him over her shoulder with a fleeting, bitter smile. "I may be quiet and unassuming in most of my life, but make no mistake, I have a wildness in me. It bursts out on occasion in the most alarming ways."

Some of the tension in Teddy's muscles eased. He comprehended her meaning. He'd seen that very wildness, shimmering beneath the surface of her ladylike façade. It was that which had first called to him so many months ago. Not her stillness or her gravity, but the untamed spirit beneath, as strong and unpredictable as the raging seas in a Turner painting.

"You couldn't alarm me if you tried," he said.

"Don't be so sure." Stella tugged restlessly at the fingers of one of her gloves. "I like to go fast. To take risks on occasion. To feel as though I'm a pulsebeat away from peril."

"Galloping your mare, I know."

"Not only galloping, but in other ways. Try as I might to behave myself, I inevitably do something rash. It might subject you to scandal."

"What care I for scandal? I'm an artist, not a country vicar."

"An artist with your reputation to consider. What if my conduct gave rise to malicious talk? What if . . . What if someone in society made me a figure of fun?"

"Remote possibilities, surely."

She gave a hollow laugh. "Not so remote. I've had a poem written about me once already. It was a powerful thing. A few words, carelessly composed. Enough to ruin me, practically."

"*A poem?*" Teddy arched a brow. This was the first he'd heard of it. "What did it say?"

"That I was a gray wraith searching out a husband like some manner of grandmotherly succubus."

He was surprised into a crack of laughter.

But Stella wasn't laughing. "It was hard enough to bear it myself. But you won't appreciate being made a joke, not when you're just starting out. And not when I'll be the model of your first major piece."

He rolled a half turn closer to her, his expression sobering. "Who wrote it?"

"The poem? I don't know. It was anonymous."

"You must have your suspicions."

"None. There were any number of snickering young lords hanging about during my debut. Any one of them could have been the culprit—or more than one. The point is, I can only be small and quiet for so long, and then—"

"Forget being small and quiet," Teddy said in a burst of passionate impatience. "I'm asking you to be conspicuous with me! To marry me and live here with me in Maiden Lane. We can do what we want, when we want. There will be nothing and no one to rein us in, save the limits of our own inclinations."

Stella turned to him. There was a storm of conflict in her eyes. He'd confused her. Overwhelmed her. "I don't know what I want," she admitted. "I've never had the freedom to properly discover it."

Teddy felt a fierce rush of tenderness for her. He wheeled his chair the rest of the way across the room, joining her by the window. "If we marry, you'll have all the freedom you require," he said. "I can't promise you a conventional life, but I can promise you that."

Stella slowly lowered back down onto the window seat, bringing them eye to eye. "As much freedom as a husband is willing to give a wife?"

"More," he said. "We wouldn't be marrying to satisfy some antiquated social convention. We'd be marrying to please ourselves."

"Would it please you?"

"Would it you?"

She briefly looked away. "I suppose that, deep down . . . I'd always hoped I might marry for love, as my friends have."

A sense of impending rejection tightened his throat. Good God. After all that—the risk to his pride, to his very heart—was she truly going to refuse him? His voice went hoarse. "Have you someone in mind? Another gentleman?"

"No. I've never met anyone I liked enough." Her eyes returned to his. There was an endless pause. "Not until you."

Teddy swallowed hard. "There you are, then. You have your answer. It may not be love or romance or some high-brow courtship struck up during the season, but we like each other well enough. It's more than most couples can boast."

"What about children?" she asked.

His stomach tightened. "What about them?"

"Do you want children?"

"Do *you*?" he countered.

Her cheeks darkened with a rising blush. "What if I did?"

An answering heat crept up Teddy's neck at the unspoken question. He might have known she would be bold enough to broach the subject. "I'm capable," he said, "if that's what you're asking."

It was the truth as far as he knew, though he'd never yet fully tested the proposition. Despite the many prostitutes who had come to pose at the atelier, most of whom had engaged in regular affairs with the other artists, Teddy hadn't yet experienced the ultimate intimacy.

Not because he was unnecessarily prudish, or on account of some high-blown romantic ideal. It was a question of vulnerability. He'd have to trust a woman—really trust her. And perhaps something more. Not love, no. But a certain sense of mutual affection and care. There would have to be that, at least, to offset the chance of any difficulty.

And there might very well be difficulty.

What if things didn't work as he'd hoped? What if he lost control? Made a fool of himself?

A prostitute would have undoubtedly managed his deficiencies with an air of jaded professionalism. But Teddy had never wanted that experience. Not with a stranger who cared only for his coin.

"Then, would you want . . ." Stella struggled for words. "Would you expect . . ."

"I have no expectations in that regard," he said. "But I daresay we could come to some arrangement. If that's what you really wanted."

Her blush deepened from petal pink to crimson. "I don't . . . I only wondered—if we *did* marry—"

He gently took her hand, silencing her embarrassed stammering. "All I ask," he said, "is that you give me three months to complete this painting. After that, your time will be your own."

She went quiet, considering the proposition. Having done so, she appeared to collect herself. "As tempting as the arrangement sounds . . . I don't want a marriage of convenience."

The rejection struck Teddy as powerfully as a blow. He nearly released her hand. And then—

"If we marry," she said, "I intend to fall in love with you."

Teddy struggled to keep his countenance.

He'd been wrong. She wasn't rejecting him. She was raising the stakes. *Love*, she'd said. Not *like* any longer. Not *convenience*. But *love*.

He looked at her steadily. "I should be honored if you did."

The response seemed to settle her doubts. She took a deep breath. Her expression turned serious. "We would need some sort of legal agreement to protect Locket. I'm not so ignorant of the world that I'd let her fall within a husband's power. Not even an unconventional husband like you."

His mouth ticked up at one corner. "I know an excellent solicitor."

"And I must have my inheritance protected." Stella's businesslike tone was belied by the brilliance of color in her cheeks. "I refuse to be left destitute should things fall apart."

"You shall have everything you require," he vowed.

"What do *you* require?"

"Only you."

"Only me, acting as your model, you mean."

"I mean *you*," Teddy said. He pressed her hand. "And if anyone ever again has the temerity to insult you, through their rubbish poetry or by any other method, I promise you that henceforward they shall answer to me."

Stella's face fractured. She tugged her hand from his, eyes filling with tears.

Teddy moved toward her in swift dismay. "What have I said? I meant to reassure you, not upset you."

She swiped at her cheeks. "I'm being excessively stupid. It's only that . . . no one has ever defended me before, except for my friends. My brother was forever intimating that any insults were my own fault for inspiring them. He said I was too loud and opinionated—"

Teddy was learning to despise Stella's sanctimonious brother. That anyone should try to dim her brilliance!

He brought his hands to frame her face, halting her speech. She broke off, meeting his gaze with quivering uncertainty. He heard her inhale an uneven breath.

"Be loud," he told her. "Be opinionated. Be as much yourself as you wish—and then some. Once we're wed, you and I will answer to no one but each other."

Stella's mouth trembled.

His head was already bent to hers. There were but a few inches left between them, taut with mingled breath and heat and the stirring fragrance of lilacs. The temptation was too great to resist. Heart thundering madly, Teddy closed the distance and pressed his lips to hers.

Her eyes fell shut as he captured her mouth. A soft murmur of assent throbbed in her throat.

The sound sent a wild rush of heat through his veins. But he wasn't precipitate. This was too important. He kissed her again, with passionate deliberation.

She curled her fingers around his wrists as he cradled her face. It wasn't a restraint. She was holding him to her, not pushing him away. Her lips softened beneath his, warm and sweet, and she was kissing him back, just as she had in Hampshire.

The grubbiness of the house fell away. The grime, the dust, and the grease-streaked, half-boarded windows. There was no one else—not Jennings, nor Teddy's family, nor any of Stella's friends. It was only the two of them.

I intend to fall in love with you, she'd said.

But Teddy had already fallen, with no intention whatsoever. He knew that now, beyond all doubt.

At length, he drew back from her. His thumbs moved over the blushing curves of her cheeks—tender, reassuring, distinctly proprietary. She was made to be his. He'd recognized it the first time he saw her.

"So, what say you, my beautiful shining star?" he asked huskily. "Is it a yes?"

Stella gazed back at him. Her lips were swollen, her breath unsteady. Her tear-damp eyes took on a gleam of determination. "Yes," she said. "Yes, Teddy, I'll marry you."

Twenty-Four

The upstairs parlor in the Finchleys' house in Half Moon Street was a cozy sanctuary, filled with overstuffed chintz sofas and chairs, tassel-trimmed ottomans, and dark wood tables that held towering stacks of leather-bound books and assorted trinkets from the Finchleys' travels to India and beyond. A small pianoforte sat in the corner, heaped with sheets of music—the works of Chopin and Brahms mixing freely with the latest popular music-hall tunes.

A fire had been lit for the evening. The coals glowed merrily in the grate, casting off more heat than a wood fire.

It had begun to rain again late in the afternoon, not long after Teddy had returned Stella to Brown's Hotel, the two of them largely at a loss for words after the kiss they'd shared and the agreement they'd come to.

"Shall I write to your brother?" Teddy had asked at last before bidding her goodbye.

She had met his suggestion with a look of alarm. "What on earth for?"

Jennings had cocked his ear from his place in the back of the wagonette, hanging on every word.

Teddy had shot the manservant a quelling look before replying to his newly minted fiancée. "I had the antiquated notion that I should ask his permission."

"You needn't," she had said. "He's made it very clear that he's no longer part of my life."

"But if you wanted me to—"

"I don't," she'd stated firmly.

As Teddy sat in his wheeled chair beside the fire in the Finchleys' parlor, he vaguely wished he might enjoy the same option. He didn't want to upset his sister again, and he had no great desire to enter into another quarrel with Alex.

But needs must.

"Your maid and valet already have you packed, I see," Jenny said, sipping her after-dinner cup of tea. "I'm impressed. It takes Tom and I weeks to get ourselves sorted before a journey."

The Finchleys sat next to each other on the sofa, close enough that the skirts of Jenny's silk dinner dress spilled partially over one of Tom's legs. The tea tray was arrayed on a low table in front of them.

"They've had ample practice," Alex replied from his place on the sofa opposite. Like Tom, Alex was seated beside his wife with what many in society would deem an unseemly level of closeness.

Fashionable married couples were meant to keep a polite distance from each other in company, whatever they might feel for each other in private. It wasn't the thing to display affection for one's spouse, even among family. Indeed, it was considered common.

Not that either of the couples in the parlor ever cared. Since Laura had married, Teddy had witnessed endless displays of mutual affection between her and Alex.

Was it any wonder that Stella didn't want a marriage of convenience? That she wanted love? Tenderness?

"I'd always hoped I might marry for love," she'd told him.

But it was no longer a hope. It was an intent. She'd told him that, too.

A small private part of him, deep beneath his cynical armor, thrilled to recall it.

"We've been the veriest vagabonds these last months," Laura said. "From France to London, then to Hampshire, and from there to Devon and back to London again. The servants have had to pack and unpack our things I don't know how many times. I daresay they can do it with their eyes closed."

Alex took his wife's hand. Raising it to his lips, he pressed a kiss to her knuckles. "Had I known we might be in anticipation of a happy event, I'd have insisted we forgo our travels this year."

Laura briefly stroked his cheek with the edge of her finger. "I'm not at all sorry we came. I'm only sorry we must leave early. And without Teddy, too. That is . . . if he's decided to stay." She turned to Teddy with a look of guarded expectation.

Returning his teacup to its saucer, Teddy balanced the painted porcelain dish on his knee. "I have," he said. "If Tom and Jenny won't mind my inconveniencing them for a time."

An expression of relief came over the Finchleys. There was relief in Laura's eyes, too, albeit mingled with a distinct shimmer of regret that he wouldn't be accompanying her back to France.

Teddy wasn't unsympathetic. For years after the scarlet fever had come, it had been just the two of them, with Laura bearing the full weight of responsibility for his health and welfare. It was a hard habit to break.

Tom returned his own teacup to the tea tray. "It's no inconvenience. We're happy to have you. I hope that goes without saying."

"Indeed," Jenny agreed. "And Maiden Lane isn't so far that you can't travel there and back each day to work on your paintings."

Laura gave Teddy a wobbly smile. "I won't claim I'm not heartbroken to leave you, but you staying with Tom and Jenny does help to set my mind at ease."

Only Alex remained silent. A former sharper, he knew when an opponent wasn't laying all their cards on the table. He watched Teddy from across the room, a frown in his eyes.

Teddy had no intention of bluffing his brother-in-law. What would be the point? "Yes, well, the fact is," he said, "I won't be staying here for long. I intend to remove to my new house as soon as the renovations are completed."

Tom, Jenny, and Laura went still.

But Alex didn't appear at all surprised by Teddy's plans. The frown in his eyes took on a dangerous edge. "We're not arguing about this again. I've already explained our position."

"Yes, I know," Teddy said. "You don't want to risk me living alone. You want me to be properly looked after."

"Exactly," Laura said. "I thought you understood."

Teddy looked at his sister. He loved her dearly, and he owed her more than he was worth. But he didn't owe her his life. He refused to feel guilty about claiming it for himself. "What if I was married?" he asked abruptly.

This time, four stunned faces fixed on him in unison. Even Alex was temporarily struck speechless.

But only temporarily.

"But you're not married," he said in a voice of perilous calm.

"You're only four-and-twenty," Laura added lamely.

Teddy didn't know why she must continue to harp on his age. He may not be as old as Alex or Tom, but he was no lad just out of the schoolroom. "Prince Albert was but twenty when he married the Queen."

A muscle flexed in Alex's jaw. "If I hear one more word about the late, lamented Prince Albert, I vow I shall not be responsible for my actions."

Teddy ignored him. Laura was the one Teddy had to convince. It was her well-being that was making Alex behave unreasonably. "You said that you never worried about Neville leaving the Abbey because he had Clara with him," he reminded her. "Do you remember?"

"Yes, but—"

"If I was married, you'd have no more reason to object to me setting up a household of my own, would you?"

Her brows pulled into an uncertain line. "I suppose I wouldn't."

"Not unless you tied yourself to some artist's model for hire who'd rob you the instant you fell asleep." Alex narrowed his eyes at Teddy. "That *is* what you're contemplating, I presume."

Teddy didn't answer.

For an instant, his brother-in-law appeared genuinely furious. "If I thought for a moment that you were going to do something that stupid, that bloody reckless and foolish, all so you could remain in London in that godforsaken house you've let—"

"Alex—" Laura's fingers curled around his hand. "He wouldn't."

"My sister's right," Teddy said. "I'd never marry a girl who'd be so vulgar as to rob me in my sleep." He raised his teacup back to his lips. "I've chosen someone wholly respectable. Indeed, you've both met her."

Laura gaped. "Not Miss Hobhouse!"

"Why the tone of shock?" Teddy's wry question was threaded with an unmistakable edge of challenge. Didn't they believe a respectable lady would have him? Didn't they think he had enough to offer?

"Are you serious?" Alex asked.

"I am," Teddy said. "I proposed to her this afternoon, and she did me the honor of accepting."

Saying the words, Teddy still couldn't quite believe it. Nor could he believe the romantic nonsense he'd murmured to Stella after kissing her. The way he'd held her face in his hands and gazed into her eyes, his breath coming quickly, and his voice sinking deep. *My beautiful shining star,* he'd called her.

Marriage of convenience? Like hell. He'd only offered such antiseptic terms to persuade Stella to accept him. But she hadn't wanted that. She wanted something real.

By God, so did he.

"Is Miss Hobhouse the young lady you were corresponding with while we were in Devon?" Jenny asked.

"She is," Teddy answered. "She's presently in London, staying with Captain and Mrs. Blunt at Brown's Hotel. They return home next week. After that, Miss Hobhouse will be stopping briefly with Ahmad and his wife."

"Ahmad!" Jenny exclaimed. "She's acquainted with he and Evelyn, too?"

"Miss Hobhouse is one of the Four Horsewomen," Tom explained quietly. "You'll have seen her in the park, riding with Evelyn, Mrs. Blunt, and Lady Anne Deveril."

"The gray-haired young lady?" Jenny's brows lifted. "Well, that's a turn up. I'd no idea Teddy even knew her."

"But this is too sudden," Laura objected. "Only a short time ago, she refused to even let you paint her. And now I'm to believe she's willing to marry you?"

"She's not only willing," Teddy said. "She's determined." He held his sister's gaze. "And so am I. Which reminds me—" He addressed Tom. "Miss Hobhouse will need to consult with you about legal mechanisms to protect her assets. She has her horse, and a small inheritance she'd like to shield in the event the marriage breaks down."

"What about *your* assets?" Laura asked, indignant. "Tom must surely act to secure your interests, not hers."

"No," Teddy said emphatically, leaving no room for debate. "Miss Hobhouse must have the best. I shall deal with another solicitor. Tom can recommend one to me."

"I shall do what I can for Miss Hobhouse, of course," Tom said. "And for you."

"Thank you," Teddy said. "I'll tell her."

Alex studied Teddy's face. His frown deepened, but no longer with anger or impatience. He was thoughtful. Amazed. "My God, you *are* serious."

Teddy had never been more so. "As soon as the property is habitable, and we've had time to publish the banns, Miss Hobhouse and I intend to marry. Depending on the length of the repairs, it could be as early as May. Then again, knowing how stonemasons and painters delay, it may not be until the summer."

Laura's face fell. "It would be impossible for us to attend the ceremony. The baby is due in August."

"It's no matter," Teddy said. "I don't expect it will be a grand affair. A registry office will suffice. It's the marriage that's the thing, not the ceremony."

"Is this what you really want?" Laura asked. "I know you liked her well enough as a prospective model, but . . . marriage?"

"All the better to paint her," Teddy answered, far more glibly than he felt. "Once we're residing under the same roof, she'll be completely at my disposal."

"If that's all that's behind this," Alex said, "that, and a desire to break free of us, I'd advise you to think twice."

"What if she has second thoughts?" Laura interjected. "What if she says something, or does something? Once you marry her—*if* you marry her—she'll be in a unique position to hurt you."

"What if she does?" Teddy countered. "I won't melt, will I?" He turned on his brother-in-law. "And that's *not* all it's about, obviously. Give me some credit."

"But what if—" Laura began.

Teddy cut his sister off with gentle finality. "Life is too short to waste time with what-ifs. I mean to be happy, that's all. Without that, what else is there?"

Julia's eyes flashed with triumph. "I *knew* it!" She sat across the cab from Stella, shoulder to shoulder with Evie as the carriage wheels clattered over the road.

The three of them were en route to Bond Street to have a look at a new milliner's shop that Evie had recommended. Captain Blunt had hired a carriage for them for the afternoon. Julia's lady's maid— a wide-eyed country lass from Yorkshire—rode on the outside with the coachman.

"You can't have known it before I did," Stella said. The wide skirts of her mulberry poplin day dress, worn over starched petticoats and a heavy crinoline, pressed against the billowing skirts of her friends, making the interior of the cab a veritable sea of fabric.

"Nonsense," Julia replied. "I recognized his attraction to you the moment I was introduced to him. The way he smiled at you! I told Captain Blunt directly—'*Mark my words*,' I said, '*the two of them will soon be sweethearts.*'"

Stella smoothed her dyed kid gloves, embarrassed by her friend's exultations. Though she'd expressed her intention to fall in love with Teddy (a shocking recollection! What had possessed her?), he'd said nothing about loving her in return.

But she knew what had possessed her.

Seated next to Teddy in his future studio, her hand settled firmly in his, she'd realized that she'd come too far since breaking from her brother to start compromising. She wanted love in a marriage. She'd recognized it at Anne's wedding. And if Stella must manifest that love herself, then so be it.

It wouldn't be difficult. She was already half in love with Teddy Hayes as it was. Yesterday's encounter had only confirmed it. As for Teddy's own feelings . . .

He'd said nothing about love. It was a marriage of convenience he'd offered, not a lifetime of romance and adoration.

But he'd kissed her.

Oh, how he'd kissed her!

"Mr. Hayes smiles that way at everyone," she informed Julia. "Tell her, Evie. You must have noticed it yourself."

"He *is* a good-humored gentleman," Evie allowed. "But in a droll sort of way, as though he were amused by a private joke of some kind."

"There was nothing droll in the way he looked at Stella." Julia plumped back in the seat of the cab, a self-satisfied look on her face. "Wait until Anne hears the news."

A flare of alarm took Stella unaware. "Oh no," she protested quickly. "Pray don't tell her."

"Why not?" Evie asked.

Stella struggled to articulate the reasons for her reluctance. "Because . . . Anne is on her honeymoon. And because I'd rather wait to tell her myself. Not in a letter, but in person."

Of all Stella's friends, Anne was the most likely to throw cold water on Stella's plans. Not out of mean-spiritedness, but out of an instinctive desire to shield Stella from being hurt.

Yes, he wants you now, Anne would say in her rational, lemon-tart voice. *He is in the throes of some sort of artistic mania, desperate to paint you. But what will happen afterward? What kind of life will you have with him when he's on to his next subject and the next, and you're still there, in his house, overlooked and perchance unwanted?*

Or possibly it wasn't Anne who would ask Stella those things. Perhaps they were the worrisome questions Stella was already asking herself.

Julia and Evie exchanged an opaque glance.

"It's not the same anyway." Stella attempted to explain what she didn't fully understand yet herself. "It's not a love match like you and Captain Blunt, or like you and Mr. Malik."

"What is it, then?" Julia asked. "A friendship? That's what you called it when first you mentioned him to us in Hyde Park."

"Friendship can often lead to more tender feelings," Evie said.

Stella recalled how Teddy had held her face in the cradle of his large, black-gloved hands. How he'd kissed her so warmly. So thoroughly.

Heat suffused her cheeks.

Yes, there were tender feelings in abundance. At least, on her part. And surely on Teddy's, too. Gentlemen didn't kiss just anyone, did they?

"It's not only a friendship," she said.

Julia was encouraged by the prospect. "Well, that's something, isn't it?"

"Something wonderful, to be sure," Evie said. "It must be. I vow you're positively glowing."

"You are," Julia agreed. "Indeed, you look rather different. More . . . more . . . something."

"It's your hair," Evie noticed. "You're not wearing a silk net."

Stella touched a self-conscious hand to the simple roll at her nape. She rarely ventured out without masking her hair in a close-woven net. But today she'd refrained. Her gray color was plain for everyone to see.

"Forget being small and quiet," Teddy had said yesterday. *"I'm asking you to be conspicuous with me!"*

The words had awakened something in Stella, as surely as a sorcerer's spell. They had summoned the boldness in her heart, too long stifled by her fear of society's censure. In the past, she'd been afraid to expose herself, lest she provoke the sort of malicious cruelty she'd endured during her first season.

But no more.

If she was going to live conspicuously, she must begin somewhere. Her hair had seemed the obvious place to start.

"That's it!" Julia's eyes sharpened. "But you always wear a net over your hair when you go out."

"Does it look dreadful without it?" Stella asked.

"Not at all," Evie replied. "You're radiant."

"Your connection with Mr. Hayes must agree with you," Julia said.

Stella looked between her two friends. "Then you both approve? You don't think I'm mad to have accepted him?"

"Would our opinions change your mind?" Julia asked.

"No," Stella admitted. "I don't expect they would."

"There's your answer, then," Evie said. "You've chosen correctly.

If you hadn't, you'd be looking for any excuse to retract your acceptance of his proposal."

"I don't want to retract it," Stella said.

On the contrary, having accepted Teddy's proposal, she felt more hopeful about the future than she had in ages. Perhaps that was why she was glowing, if indeed she was.

She hadn't been lying to him when she'd told him that he was the first gentleman she'd ever liked. And it wasn't just because of his kisses and compliments. It was because she enjoyed being with him. He was interesting. Amusing. Vexing at times, but never dull.

The fact that he used a wheeled chair hadn't even come into it. Not until it had occurred to her that his condition might impact her dreams for a family.

Good heavens. Had she really asked him about it outright?

And had he really answered her?

"I'm capable," he'd said.

Capable. Whatever that meant.

She had some idea, of course. She knew about horses, and about other animals. And she knew something about the marriages of her friends—though neither of them had ever given explicit details, except to share that it was exciting and intimate, and that it involved removing one's clothes (or sometimes not, as Julia had once confided).

Evie reached across the carriage to clasp Stella's hand. "I'm glad. I've longed to see you happily settled. And Mr. Hayes is an amusing gentleman. Whatever else happens, you'll never be bored."

"We must do something to celebrate." Julia brightened. "I know, I shall buy you an engagement gift! A new hat from the milliner? Or a beautiful new shawl? Anne recently mentioned a marvelous India shawl warehouse in Ludgate Hill."

The three of them chattered on, talking and laughing together as the carriage set them down in Bond Street. They visited the milliner, the draper's shop, and stopped to look at the bejeweled trinkets in the window of a goldsmith's establishment. It was as they were walking down a side street to stop in at a bookseller that Julia liked to frequent, that the door of a stationer's shop they were passing opened and Laura Archer emerged, stepping directly into their path.

"Miss Hobhouse!" Mrs. Archer came to an abrupt halt. She wore a loose-fitting caraco jacket with a plain skirt—a suitable ensemble for a fashionable lady in a delicate condition. A maid and a footman, arms filled with packages, stood behind her.

"Mrs. Archer!" Stella froze.

She wasn't prepared to face Teddy's family. Had he told them yet? And, if so, how had they taken it? Stella dreaded to think.

"Mrs. Malik," Mrs. Archer said, smiling at Evie. "How do you do?"

"Mrs. Archer." Evie acknowledged her with a smile in return. "Have you met, Mrs. Blunt?"

Julia and Mrs. Archer bobbed polite curtsies to each other as they were introduced.

Pleasantries dispensed with, Mrs. Archer turned her attention back to Stella. "I was just preparing to stop for tea at the confectioner's shop across the road. Would you care to join me?"

Evie and Julia fell quiet.

Stella's mouth went dry. Her friends stood silent behind her, both holding their breaths. It was at once clear that Mrs. Archer knew about Stella's engagement to Teddy. She likely wanted to warn Stella off. Either that or interrogate her about her intentions.

But there was no point in delaying the inevitable. In Stella's experience, it was always better to get difficult encounters over with before one's anxiety about them grew out of all proportion.

Besides, Mrs. Archer was no ogre, was she? She was a kind and sympathetic older sister, who had already been open-minded enough to help her brother in contacting Stella over the winter. If anyone would be supportive of Stella and Teddy's unexpected engagement, it would be Mrs. Archer, wouldn't it?

"I would be delighted," Stella said. She looked to Evie and Julia. "If you wouldn't mind sparing me?"

"Not at all," Julia said. "Shall we come back to fetch you in, say, an hour?"

"That won't be necessary," Mrs. Archer replied. "I have the Finchleys' carriage at my disposal today. I shall be happy to return Miss Hobhouse to Brown's Hotel when I've finished with her."

Finished with her?

Stella swallowed. Perchance Mrs. Archer wasn't as happy about her brother's engagement as Stella had hoped. Indeed, as she took Stella's arm and guided her across the road to the tea shop, Stella began to fear that her future sister-in-law's feelings were exactly the opposite.

Twenty-Five

❖

"Please allow me to congratulate you," Stella said, after she and Mrs. Archer had sat down at a small table inside the confectioner's shop and ordered their tea. "Mr. Hayes tells me that you and Mr. Archer are anticipating a child."

"Do call me Laura," Mrs. Archer said. "And may I call you Stella?" Her face bore no malice. She appeared calm and steady, a slight smile on her lips and a measuring look in her slate-blue eyes.

A building sense of apprehension nevertheless made Stella's stomach tense. "Yes. If you like."

"Mr. Archer and I *are* expecting," Laura said. "And happily so, thank you. But it's *your* happy news I'm interested in. I understand that congratulations are due to you, as well?"

Stella didn't answer. She felt, for an instant, at a complete loss for words. "I-I don't know what Mr. Hayes has told you, but—"

"He told me, and all of us last night after dinner, that he proposed to you and that you've accepted. He hasn't mischaracterized things, has he? I'd be surprised if he had. Teddy rarely lets even the smallest details escape him. And an engagement is rather more than a small detail, wouldn't you say?"

The bell on the front door of the tea shop tinkled, announcing the entry of another couple. A lady and gentleman passed within inches of Stella and Laura, choosing a table nearby.

Stella cast them a wary glance. She lowered her voice. "He did propose," she admitted, conscious of their lack of privacy. "And I did say yes."

"May I ask why?"

Why?

Stella had no great desire to share her reasons. Not in such a public setting. And not when she hadn't yet discerned Laura's intentions. "Why does any lady say yes to a proposal?" she answered vaguely.

"For security. For money. For love." Laura searched Stella's face. "*Do* you love my brother?"

Stella's mask of composure briefly slipped, thinking again of the kisses she and Teddy had shared. Of the way her pulse fizzed to see him. To talk with him. To share their mutual interest in art and drawing. "I don't know that I—"

"You needn't tell me," Laura said before Stella could stammer out another vague reply. "Not if you haven't yet told him. Nor are you obligated to confess it to me if you've accepted his proposal for more mercenary reasons. Marriages are complex arrangements, I realize. Even ones entered into for love are also entered into for other reasons. Most gentlemen understand that. They know there's more to marriage than a moment's passion." She paused. "But my brother isn't like most gentlemen."

Stella frowned, temporarily forgetting their lack of privacy. "Because of his condition, do you mean?"

"Yes, because of that, but also because he doesn't think the way other people do. His art is the whole world to him. When he has a passion for a certain piece he's working on, it consumes his every thought. During those times, he doesn't exercise the best judgment."

At last, Stella began to comprehend where Laura was headed. It wasn't a very flattering direction.

"I know he wants to paint you," Laura said. "I've so far encouraged his obsession, even helping him in writing to you this winter. I'm sorry if that strikes you as contradictory, given what I'm about to tell you."

Stella stiffened slightly in her chair. "You're going to say that he didn't mean it when he proposed to me. That it was only about art."

Laura smiled gently. "Not at all."

"What, then?" Stella asked. "You clearly don't approve of us getting married."

"It's not disapproval you hear in my voice. It's concern."

Their conversation was interrupted by the return of the shop's proprietor, a heavily whiskered older man in an apron. He brought them a pot of tea, two teacups, and a plate of freshly baked currant buns. A jug of milk and a bowl of sugar followed.

After he'd gone, Laura lifted the round china pot to fill each of their cups. Her expression was unusually grave.

"My brother wasn't always as vigorous as you see him now," she said. "When the fever came to our village, we lost my father to it. I contracted it as well, leaving me with an unfortunate affliction of the lungs. But Teddy had it worse than either of us. He was too strong to die, but too weakened to fully fight the fever. It took root in his spine, ultimately affecting his legs."

"He mentioned something of the sort," Stella said.

"Did he?" Laura set down the teapot. "Did he tell you how the loss of his legs affected him in the immediate years that followed?"

"Not specifically, no." Given Teddy's strength of will, Stella had assumed he'd promptly accepted his limitations and set himself to learning how to get about in his wheeled chair. He was extraordinarily adept at doing so.

"Teddy and I were already in a precarious position after my father died. Our perfumery had temporarily shuttered, and our inheritance was tied up for a time. We struggled to make ends meet as it was. But for a young man of Teddy's age to suddenly lose the ability to walk—to be sentenced to his bed, made dependent on his family and servants for the smallest thing—" Laura stared pensively into her tea. "My brother fell into a deep melancholy. He refused assistance from his room. He rarely ate. He only drew and painted—subjects he observed from his chamber window. By the time my husband entered our lives, Teddy had wasted away to a shadow."

Stella's teacup stilled halfway to her lips. Her brows notched in confusion. "But I'd thought—"

"That he's always been this energetic and determined? No, indeed. It was my husband who encouraged Teddy in that, initially. Mr. Archer has a way about him. He can generally manage people without putting their back up. And, of course, a young man always takes the advice of another gentleman better than he does from a mother or a sister."

"Why are you telling me this?" Stella asked.

"Because I want you to have no illusions about my brother. Just because he's confident in his work, and precocious in most other respects, don't imagine he's incapable of being hurt. All that life in him, the sensitivity in his art and his ability to see things in all their light and shadow, stems from his own vulnerability. He's not so far removed from those days of melancholy in his room. Indeed, there are times when he still struggles mightily with his condition."

Stella slowly returned her cup to the table, leaving her tea untouched. She recalled how Teddy had been at Sutton Park. His consistent refusals to join them out of doors. The way Jennings had to lift him from his chair, and the red flush of exertion—and possibly embarrassment—in Teddy's face as he'd gripped the manservant's shoulders.

It had struck Stella then, and again yesterday as Jennings had assisted Teddy in and out of the wagonette, how easy it was to forget that Teddy had anything to struggle with. The force of his personality so often overshadowed his physical limitations.

But Stella wasn't unaware of Teddy's challenges for all that. She was only ignorant of what she should do to address them. Teddy didn't want help. He didn't want pity or sympathy or any degree of fellow feeling. He wanted to be recognized for the things he could control, not for those things he couldn't. By that measure, wasn't it better to ignore his disability rather than to always be drawing attention to it with questions, concerns, and offers of assistance?

"I know he struggles," Stella said. "I have no illusions. But that had nothing to do with me accepting his proposal. I don't view him that way. To me, he's just . . . Teddy."

"That he is, isn't he?" Laura smiled again. She nudged Stella's teacup toward her. "Do drink something, please. You look rather pale."

"I've had a great many surprises in the last week."

"Change is always surprising. Frightening, too. But it can ultimately be wonderful, in my experience."

Stella took a reluctant sip of her tea. "Your brother told me that you and he had the benefit of an aged aunt looking after you when you lived in Surrey. But I have no one but myself. I must trust my own judgment."

"Do you trust it?"

"I do," Stella said, confessing it as much to herself as to Laura. "I daresay I feel things as deeply as your brother. And I feel that this is right. That he and I are right for each other. I can't explain it—"

"You don't need to. Not to me. It's enough that I can see you care for him. That's all I require to reassure me." Laura's smile turned rueful as she drank her tea. "I know you must think me ridiculously overprotective of him, and doubtless I am, but the thought of anything happening to him—"

"I wouldn't hurt him," Stella said. "I mean to make him happy." *And myself,* she added silently.

Laura's expression softened. "I wish I might be around to see it. Alas, my husband and I return to France in the morning. It's necessary for my health. But it means we won't be here to attend your wedding."

Her wedding.

The phrase took Stella off guard. "I confess, I hadn't thought that far ahead."

"Teddy has," Laura said. "He laid it all out for us last night, to our astonishment. He's even secured Mr. Finchley to act for you in protecting your assets." Her eyes twinkled with sudden humor. "That's when we knew it was serious. When he was willing to forgo having Finchley for himself so that you could have the very best. If that isn't love, I don't know what is."

A blush threatened. "I didn't ask him to do *that*," Stella said.

"No, indeed. Which made it doubly impressive." Laura helped herself to a currant bun. Tearing off a piece, she buttered it with her knife. "Will you join us for dinner this evening in Half Moon Street?" she asked. "It won't be as grand a party as I would have liked to give to celebrate your engagement, but I hope you'll come all the same. My husband and brother will be there. And the Finchleys, of course."

"Does Teddy know you're inviting me?"

"Teddy was off at daybreak this morning to meet with his estate agent about repairs to the property in Maiden Lane. So, no, I haven't yet broached the subject with him. But he won't object to it. He'll want to see you, surely."

Stella dearly hoped he would. "Very well. I would be happy to attend, if . . . if my hosts can spare me."

"I shall invite Captain and Mrs. Blunt, as well," Laura said. "And Mr. and Mrs. Malik, too, if that would help to ease your anxiety."

Stella's shoulders relaxed. She hadn't realized that she'd been bracing herself. "Yes, it would," she said gratefully. "Thank you."

Teddy refilled his champagne glass, only half listening to the loud buzz of conversation around him. There were so many people at dinner that Mrs. Jarrow had to add an extra leaf to the mahogany table and set out two additional branches of candles. In addition to Alex and Laura, and Tom and Jenny, Ahmad and Evelyn had come, along with Ahmad's cousin, Mira, and her fiancé, Tariq Jones. Mrs. Blunt and Captain Blunt were in attendance, too.

And Stella.

She sat across the table between Tom and Ahmad, talking to each of them in turn as the courses were served. First julienne soup, then braised beef à la flamande with dishes of tomatoes and green peas, followed by a decadent charlotte russe topped with strawberries, and accompanied by several bottles of celebratory French champagne.

Initially, Teddy had been angry to learn that Laura had invited Stella to dine. And it wasn't only because his sister had gone behind his back—which was aggravating in itself. It was because (he realized with a certain degree of masculine chagrin) he didn't want to share Stella with his family. Indeed, he didn't want to share her with anyone.

But share her he must.

For some infernal reason, Jenny had insisted on adhering to a seating plan this evening. The guests were arranged in a traditional male/female pattern, and none of the spouses or betrothed couples sat next to each other. It meant that Teddy had scarcely exchanged ten words with Stella all night.

As he ate and drank and engaged in tedious small talk with his seat partners, he could only look at her, seated across from him in a simple, long-sleeved silk dinner dress, the candlelight flickering over her face and throat, and shining in her neatly plaited silver hair.

The frustration he'd been feeling since leaving his last meeting with the workmen in Maiden Lane built to a fever pitch. Yes, Stella had agreed to let him paint her. And yes, she'd agreed to marry him. But the delay between that agreement and the manifestation of either event was beginning to seem insurmountable.

"How are things coming with your new house?" Julia Blunt asked from her chair on Teddy's right. "Mrs. Archer said you had been consulting with the estate agent today about renovations?"

The hum of conversation at the table went quiet as the rest of the dinner guests paused to listen to his answer.

"Oh yes," Jenny said. "You must give us a full report."

Stella met Teddy's eyes across the table. She lifted her brows.

He gave an eloquent grimace in response. "Poorly," he said. "There are more repairs required than I had anticipated."

"Major repairs?" Alex leveled a frowning look at him. "That doesn't bode well."

No, it didn't. But Teddy didn't like to admit it. Not when Alex and Laura had only just barely come to terms with Teddy setting up house on his own. "The landlord is taking responsibility for the exterior work," he said. "Mr. Chakrabarty saw to that. But the interior renovations will be left for me to arrange. I consulted with several workmen in the afternoon, to no success. They all equivocated on costs, and none of them would agree to a starting date."

Julia commiserated with him. "We have a dreadful time getting people to come to Goldfinch Hall. My husband has been obliged to take on some of the repairs himself."

"Surely it's easier to find workers in London?" Captain Blunt asked. Clothed in a severe black suit, he was seated between Jenny and Evelyn. The scar on his face pulled gruesomely as he spoke.

"Finding them isn't the issue," Ahmad replied from his place between Jenny and Stella. He'd come straight from his dress shop and was still wearing the plain but elegantly cut coat and trousers he wore when he worked. "It's persuading them to show up. All the best ones are already employed, and the ones who aren't are often unreliable. Either that or their craftmanship is shoddy."

"Worse and worse," Jenny remarked as she raised a forkful of cake to her mouth.

"Exactly," Teddy said.

"What does this mean for the house?" Stella asked. "Will it not be ready by summer?"

"The lower rooms will be habitable," Teddy said. "But as far as restoring the rest . . ." He shook his head.

He'd learned today that, in addition to painting, plastering, and minor repair to the stonework, there were countless other items in need of replacement. Some of the windows had cracked panes of glass, most of the latches on the doors and windows were broken, and there were no bell pulls or wires installed in any of the rooms. Add to that decaying roof tiles over the scullery, questionable drainage, and the very real possibility of rot in two of the upstairs bedrooms, and it seemed that Teddy and Stella would be lucky to take up residence any time before the new year.

Tom seemed to sense Teddy's frustration. "You can live in it while you restore it," he said. The candlelight glinted off the rims of his spectacles. "It's been done before."

Captain Blunt nodded. "That's what we're doing at Goldfinch Hall."

"Oh yes," Julia agreed as she finished her piece of charlotte russe. "And while we wait, we simply close off those parts of the house that are dangerous."

"Can you not do that in Maiden Lane?" Evelyn asked, sipping her champagne. "Close off the upstairs and live in the lower rooms until you can have the upper ones repaired?"

Teddy frowned. The rooms below were only sufficient for a studio, a parlor, and bedrooms for himself and Jennings. He'd promised Stella the upstairs would be hers. That she could live there, all but separately, if she chose.

A knot formed in his stomach. They'd been engaged fewer than eight-and-forty hours and he was already forced to break his word to her.

He chanced a look at her across the table.

She was raising her champagne glass to her lips. A line of worry etched her brow.

"I shall think of something," he said. "Have no fear."

Mr. Jones, Mira's fiancé, spoke up from his place beside Evelyn. "Must the workers you hire be master craftsmen?"

"Do you have another idea in mind?" Teddy asked.

"A bit of painting, plastering, and woodwork isn't beyond the skill of a sailor who is home on leave and short of coin." Mr. Jones was himself a sailor. A half-Bengali midshipman, recently home after a lengthy voyage. "There are plenty of men on the docks who would be grateful for the work. Not all of them Englishmen, though."

"I doubt Teddy minds it," Mira said. Dark haired and green eyed, she worked with her cousin, Ahmad, at the dress shop. She was a brilliant seamstress in her own right, as evidenced by the elegant embroidery on her maize-colored dinner dress.

"I don't," Teddy said. "Not so long as they know what they're about with a hammer and trowel."

Ahmad half smiled. "If you're lucky, one or more might have a background in masonry or carpentry already. Many of us had entire careers in our home countries before we set foot on English shores."

"Perhaps Mr. Jones can ask about for you?" Evelyn suggested. "You wouldn't mind that would you, Tariq?"

"It would be my pleasure," Mr. Jones replied. "I know several fellows who are eager for respectable employment. Women, too. There's a sailor's widow in our community—Mrs. Mukherjee—who would make someone an excellent housekeeper."

"We will be requiring a housekeeper-cook eventually," Stella said. "If that's something she, or anyone else you know, might be suited for."

Mr. Jones inclined his head to her. "I'm happy to make inquiries."

"Thank you," Teddy said. "We'd be grateful to you."

"The joys of staffing a new household!" Laura said, smiling at her husband. "How well I recall having to start from scratch when we moved to France. We were lucky to find so many good people."

"I was lucky in my wife," Alex said warmly, gazing back at her.

"To our wives." Tom raised his glass of champagne.

The rest of the gentlemen happily followed suit, each lifting their glasses high. "To our wives!"

"And to those who are soon to be so," Teddy added, raising his own glass in Stella's direction.

"Hear, hear," Mr. Jones cheered, lifting his glass to Mira.

"Handsomely done, as ever." Jenny smiled at Tom. "And an excellent reminder that it's time we ladies withdrew before you gentlemen get any more in your cups." She rose. "Ladies? If you'll follow me."

Later, after port and cigars in the dining room, Teddy and the other gentlemen joined the ladies in the parlor. Jenny played a rousing polka on the piano, and the guests laughed, danced, and talked amongst themselves. It was Alex and Laura's last night in London. The mood was both merry and a little sad, just as it always was at the close of their annual visits when the time had finally come for the friends to bid each other farewell.

Teddy and Stella sat beside each other near the window, he in his wheeled chair and she on an overstuffed chintz chair beside him. With so much music and merriment about them, they could converse in something like privacy.

"I could have happily strangled my sister when she told me how she'd commandeered you in Bond Street," he said, his words for Stella's ears alone. "What exactly did she say to you?"

"She was merely concerned."

"No doubt." He paused before asking again, "What did she say?"

Stella replied at length in a voice as low as Teddy's had been. "That you had been in poor health for a time after your illness."

Had she, by God.

A muscle tightened reflexively in Teddy's cheek. "I see."

"She was concerned that I might inadvertently hurt you."

Teddy could only imagine. "She's excessively overprotective. She's had to be in the past. I've had the devil of a time convincing her to give up the habit."

"It wasn't an exaggeration, then?" Stella asked softly. "About your being unwell?"

"Define unwell," he quipped.

"She said you'd fallen into a deep melancholy. That everyone feared—"

"Quite." He ran a hand over the back of his neck. "It's true," he admitted grudgingly. "Before—when I first realized I wasn't going to get better—" He broke off with a flinch of bitter memory.

It still stung him to recall the desperate hope he'd once cherished in those early years. The foolish dream that his paralysis was only temporary. That one day, as if by a miracle, he'd wake up and be himself again. Wholly himself.

"I had to withdraw for a time," he said. "I took refuge in my art, until . . ."

"Until when?"

"Until I was strong enough to deal with it all. I knew I must do so eventually. And I did. Though the delay in getting there has had rather a lasting effect on my family. They can't seem to let go of protecting me."

She smiled at him. "You're fortunate in your family."

"Am I?"

"Assuredly. You're not alone. You're surrounded by people who love you. All of these people, not only Alex and Laura but the friends they have who are as good as family to you. If they interfere, it's never to hurt you or diminish you. It's to shield you from other people doing so."

"I don't need to be shielded," Teddy said. "But point taken." His gaze drifted over Stella's face. "I'm sorry you feel so alone at the moment. You're not, you know."

"I don't feel alone."

"Absent family, I meant."

"Oh. That." Her smile faded. She straightened an unseen rumple in her skirts.

It was what Alex would call a *tell*. Teddy had gradually come to recognize it in her—this urge she had to smooth some nonexistent crease in her clothing whenever she was feeling vulnerable.

"You asked me yesterday if you should write to my brother about our engagement," she said.

Ah. So that was it.

"I still could," he said. "If you've changed your mind."

"I haven't. I don't require Daniel's approval. Not any longer. It's only that the habit remains. This dreadful anxious feeling of waiting for his permission—or, more often, for his censure. I suppose it's because he's the only family I've had since my father died. Now he's gone from my life . . . there's no one left."

Teddy extended his hand to her. "We shall soon remedy that," he said. "The minute these dratted repairs are completed, you and I will be married. I'll be your family, then."

She slid her hand into his. "My husband, yes." Her fingers curved around his. "It's rather more intimate than a meddling brother or sister."

"You'll have those as well," he assured her. "Alex and Laura will soon take you under their wing. In time, I vow, you'll prefer their company to mine."

"Don't be absurd." She looked at him again, with uncharacteristic shyness. "I love your company."

Love.

The word wasn't lost on him.

"And I love yours," he said. His mouth hitched in a smile. It was a convenient mask for the vulnerability beneath. "I love your face," he added.

She blushed. "Rubbish. It's my hair you love."

"That, too." He paused, frowning. "I wonder if we should recruit Ahmad to help us with fabric?"

She gave him a bewildered look. "What fabric?"

The chords of a merry jig sounded in the background as Jenny started another song on the piano. This time it was a popular tune from the London music halls. Alex swept Laura up in his arms to dance with him. She laughed and clung to his shoulder, her skirts flouncing as he turned her.

Teddy dropped his voice. "A drape of some sort. Have I not mentioned?"

Stella's expression turned wary. "A drape for what?"

"For you, of course. A star doesn't wear all these petticoats and crinolines."

Her eyes went round. She leaned toward him. "Do you mean, a drape for"—her voice sank to a shocked whisper—"my *unclothed* body?"

Teddy's smile held a hint of devilry. "Exactly."

"You never said anything about me posing in such a state."

He hadn't dared. It was difficult enough getting her to agree to sit for him without adding disrobing to the mix.

"I'm thinking it must be tulle or some kind of diaphanous net," he continued, enjoying her blushes. "Something with pearls sewn into it or colored glass, or another glittering type of stone that will catch the moonlight."

"Teddy, really—"

"We'll be married. Or soon to be so. There's no scandal in it. Anyway, it will just be the two of us to begin with. I'll lock the parlor door, and Jennings can take himself off for our sessions."

"What do you mean *to begin with*?"

"Part of the painting will necessarily have to be done out of doors. It's a twilight piece, with the sea at its back, and you in the foreground. One of the Pleiades come to earth."

"This begins to sound more and more out of the realm of comfort."

"Immortality is rarely comfortable, but we'll manage, I'm certain."

A glimmer of suppressed laughter danced behind her eyes. "I don't know whether you're teasing me again, or whether you're serious."

"Both, possibly," he said. And then, in distracted thought: "Tom has a point. We needn't wait to use the house while the repairs are being done. We needn't even wait until we're married. The drawing room only wants a good cleaning, and then I can set up my studio. I've already waited too long to start painting you. I can't wait any longer. The more I delay, the more chance the vision will slip away from me. If I don't commit it to canvas soon—" He stopped, belatedly realizing that he was talking *at* her rather than *to* her. He suppressed a grimace. "Unless you have an objection?"

"No," she said slowly. "Not so long as you don't expect me to undress right away. I shan't want to do *that* before we're married."

His heart thumped heavily. The implication was clear. "I won't ask you to," he promised. "*Yet.*"

Twenty-Six

※

*W*ithin a week, the front reception room in the house at Maiden Lane was put in order. The floors were swept, the old furnishings hauled away, and the boards removed from the windows.

True to his word, Mr. Jones had found several sailors who were willing to work on the house. They were capable men from Mr. Jones's own community. Lascars, most of them, either home on leave, or permanently set ashore because of age or infirmity. They spoke Bengali, with enough English mixed in to enable easy communication. For anything else, Teddy applied to Ahmad or Mr. Jones to translate, or to his new housekeeper, Mrs. Mukherjee.

Mr. Jones had brought Mrs. Mukherjee to Maiden Lane for an interview the morning after the Finchleys' dinner. A stout sailor's widow of late middle age, she had been struggling to make ends meet and was keen to take up regular employment. After consulting with Stella, Teddy had hired the woman to start immediately.

While Mrs. Mukherjee and the sailors righted the house, Teddy took himself off to Oxford Street to purchase what he'd need for Stella's portrait from Winfield and Sons—one of the many artists' colormen in the city.

Colormen provided all manner of services for painters, from

stretching and priming canvases to selling easels, pigments, and paints. At Winfield and Sons, Teddy bespoke a canvas that was fifty inches in height and forty inches wide. He then went to the shop of another colorman in Regent Street where he bought a selection of new hog-hair and sable brushes, and extra tubes of oil paint in French ultramarine, viridian green, cadmium yellow, lead white, and cobalt blue.

Like Whistler, Teddy intended to work with a limited palette. However, unlike *The Woman in White*, Teddy's portrait of Stella would be rich with color. Saturated with blues, greens, and yellows, used in various strengths, fading into each other in seamless harmony, rather than stark contrast.

On returning to Maiden Lane, Teddy spent the next several days—with the help of Jennings and Mrs. Mukherjee—laying out drop cloths, setting up his easel, and preparing his canvas. All was in readiness when the day at last arrived for Stella's first formal sitting.

Teddy was just mixing colors on his palette when he heard Mrs. Mukherjee greet Stella in the hall. There was a brief exchange—Mrs. Mukherjee offering to take Stella's bonnet and gloves, and Stella inquiring about how Mrs. Mukherjee was finding her work—before Stella was at last shown into Teddy's studio.

The preliminary sketches he'd made of her in Devon lay all about the room, along with new sketches he'd made during the last week— heavily shaded images of her staring into the distance, her eyes grave and her figure quietly seductive.

It was the first thing Stella looked at when she entered.

"When did you draw these?" she asked, walking toward them.

She was wearing the same dress she'd worn on the first day he'd sketched her in Hampshire—a deep blue silk trimmed in delicate black cording. The very dress that had begun to stir feelings in him that weren't entirely artistic. Her hair was neatly arranged in a plaited roll at her nape.

"Some of them in Devon," Teddy said. "The rest over the last week." He set down his palette. His coat had already been discarded and his sleeves rolled up. Streaks of green and blue oil paint stained his hands and fingers. "Did Mrs. Blunt come with you?"

Stella picked up one of the sketches to examine it. "She's busy at the hotel, overseeing the packing."

The Blunts were departing for Yorkshire tomorrow. In their absence, Stella would be removing to Ahmad and Evelyn's house. Her mare was already there, lodged in the Maliks' stable, along with Crab, the horse belonging to Stella's groom.

"If she didn't accompany you—" Teddy began.

"I took a cab," Stella said.

He frowned at her. "Alone?"

"Of course, alone."

His frown deepened to a scowl. They had been engaged fewer than two weeks, and already he didn't like the idea of her venturing out unaccompanied. A ridiculous masculine reaction. It was directly at odds with Teddy's principles. He'd never been one of those witless, overbearing men who thought women should be safeguarded and surveilled like pieces of valuable property rather than rational individuals.

Nevertheless . . .

She glanced up at him. "I can see what you're thinking," she said, setting down the sketch. "But I'm not a young lady having a season anymore. And I'm no longer the sister of a clergyman. I'm soon to be an artist's wife. The rules are different for us, I believe."

Teddy refrained from pointing out that she was still the sister of a clergyman. "You're not an artist's wife yet," he reminded her instead.

"I very nearly am. We've had an engagement dinner, I've met your family, and Mr. Finchley has only yesterday finished drafting the documents protecting my inheritance and my ownership of Locket."

In case things fell apart between them, she might have added.

But she didn't.

"The terms are very probably not enforceable, Mr. Finchley said," she went on. "Not by traditional legal means. But he's assured me that won't be an impediment with him as my solicitor."

Teddy imagined not. Tom had never yet met a legal objective he couldn't attain for one of his clients. It's what made him so dangerous. Teddy was glad Stella had him on her side, whatever the future might hold.

She crossed to his canvas, registering its size for the first time. "Goodness. Is all this for me?"

Teddy rolled his chair to join her. The wooden wheels caught briefly on a fold in the drop cloth. His biceps contracted as he forced his chair over it. "And for the sea. It's not a small piece by any means."

"How will you reach it all?"

"Different sized easels," he answered. On its own, the canvas was just an inch or two shorter than he was when seated in his chair. It would have to be raised higher at times, depending on which section he worked on.

"Do you already know exactly how you're going to paint it?" she asked.

"Not exactly, no." The vision wasn't set in stone. Far from it. It hovered ahead of him, just out of reach. A luminous, starry vapor, shifting and swirling, at times settling into the form of a woman. Of Stella.

He rubbed the side of his jaw, gazing at the blank canvas along with her. It had already been primed and prepared with a light background. He'd learned the technique from Gleyre in Paris, working alongside one of the atelier's French students, Mr. Monet, who was of a similar age to Teddy. A light background was better at reflecting the light than a dark one.

"Pity I couldn't have taken you to Devon with me," he said. "The cliffs overlooking the sea would have been perfect."

"Will that be an impediment? Beginning indoors as we are?"

"Not an insurmountable one. I've painted that sea so many times.

It's already here." He tapped his temple. "And here." He touched his chest. "Echoes of all the work I've done. I can conjure them whenever I like."

Her skirts brushed his leg as she drifted closer. He heard it, rather than felt it. That didn't stop his heart from losing its rhythm. Sometimes sound could be a physical sensation. Especially when it was the sound of her—her clothes, her voice, her breath.

"Am I there, too?" she asked softly. "In your heart and in your head?"

He met her eyes. There was the barest hint of uncertainty in her face. He recognized that look—that fear. It was the same fear he had about painting her. That vague but persistent feeling that, despite their engagement, despite the promises they'd made to each other, it might all slip away before he could truly grasp it.

Perhaps he'd continue to feel it until they were married. Until that moment when she was actually his.

"You're in both of those places," he said. "You have been since I first set eyes on you. But . . ." His brow creased. "I can't capture you in the same way as I can the sea. For that I need more than an echo. I need you here—in front of me."

She gestured to herself, half smiling. "I'm here, as you see."

"So you are," he said. The warmth of her nearness gave way to the overpowering urge to commit her to canvas. "Would you mind locking the door?"

Stella did as he asked her.

It was frankly a miracle that the door had a lock. It hadn't to begin with. Teddy had made a point of having the workmen install one first thing.

She returned, cheeks slightly pinker than they'd been before. "Should I stand, or—"

"Not yet," he said. "First . . . I need you to take down your hair."

An unreadable emotion flashed in her eyes. It may have been anxiety.

Or possibly excitement.

Whatever it was, it didn't prevent her from complying. She reached back to remove her hairpins. There appeared to be a great many of them.

"Mrs. Blunt lent me the services of her maid this morning," she said apologetically. "I fear the girl was a bit overzealous."

Teddy motioned to the window seat. The glass behind it was newly draped with sheer curtains, just thick enough to give them privacy without obscuring the light. "If I may?"

Stella bit the edge of her lower lip. After a moment's hesitation, she crossed to the window and sank down, her silk skirts billowing around her legs.

Teddy rolled his chair up next to her. She gave him her back, bending her head so he could help her. When seated, he was taller than she was. It subtly changed the dynamic between them. Made it that much more apparent that he was a man and she was a woman. *His* woman.

There was no other reason he'd be unpinning her hair. It was an intimate task. One that held a distinctly domestic connotation. That didn't stop his blood from heating and his chest from tightening with emotion.

He removed the first deeply anchored pin with a matter-of-fact efficiency that was only surface deep. He'd felt her hair before, touching it briefly as he'd kissed her.

But not like this.

As he loosened her coiffure, unraveling its rolls and plaits, the heavy strands sprang free, thick and lustrous, under his fingers. Her hair may have been gray, but it wasn't coarse. It wasn't brittle. It was as soft and glossy as spun silk.

His heart was hammering so, it took an effort to continue. By the time he'd finished, he could scarcely remember his own name.

Stella glanced back at him. "You have an excellent touch," she said. "Strong but sensitive. Mrs. Blunt's maid wasn't half so good."

"High praise." Teddy's voice had deepened to a rasp. "It's beautiful, you know."

"I would thank you for the compliment, but I have the distinct impression that you're biased when it comes to my hair."

"It's not bias. It's an empirical truth." He tipped his head to hers. His nose brushed the curve of her ear. "I could paint you a thousand times and still never manage to do you justice."

She inhaled an unsteady breath. "I've never heard you concede defeat before. Certainly not before you've begun."

"Even I know my limits."

"Limitations? You? What a strange conceit." She leaned into him as he nuzzled her cheek. He felt her smile again. "Apparently, I've come to the wrong house. This is Maiden Lane, isn't it?"

"The very place," he assured her. "Soon to be your permanent home."

If the repairs could be completed in a timely manner. If the house could be made fit for a lady, and the stable made comfortable for her beloved mare. A month, at most. If Stella hadn't changed her mind by then.

So many ifs. It served no purpose to dwell on them.

With an effort, Teddy drew back from her. It was either that or kiss her, and that wasn't why she'd come today. He returned to his canvas, resolved to focus on the task at hand.

"You'll be standing for this one," he said. "It won't be easy, holding the pose, but I shall give you rests as often as you require them."

Stella stood from the window seat. Her hair fell in loose waves down her back, reaching nearly to her waist. She no longer looked a proper, starchy young lady. She looked like a goddess inexplicably garbed in modern clothes.

Teddy could only imagine how she'd look when she was draped in glittering, diaphanous net.

She crossed to the opposite side of the room, instinctively finding the best light. "Where would you like me? Here?"

He rolled back, partially behind his canvas, so he could get a better view of the wall where she stood. The paint was chipped and peeling. There had been no time to repair it. But the backdrop didn't matter. It was the light, just as she'd intuited—the way it streamed from the newly curtained window to filter over the cracked moldings and the slatted floor.

"Just there," he said. "Three-quarter profile, facing the door. And if— Forgive me. If, ah, you wouldn't mind loosening your bodice?"

Her lashes lowered, veiling the expression in her eyes as she obediently unfastened the black cord buttons that closed the high neck of her dress. She opened her bodice slowly, inch by inch, first revealing the delicate hollow of her throat and then the elegant bones of her clavicle. Her corset cover was just visible—a delicate glimpse of lace-trimmed cambric—when she stopped.

"Is this enough?" she asked.

"That will do," Teddy said gruffly. He moved behind his canvas. His palette awaited him, his paints already mixed and ready.

"What now?" Stella asked.

Teddy picked up his brush. "Now the work begins."

Twenty-Seven

❖

S tella stood still as a marble statue in Teddy's studio in the house in Maiden Lane, her face turned to stare at an invisible point on the chipped wall to her right.

A large canvas was placed across the room, atop an easel. Teddy worked tirelessly behind it, absent his coat and waistcoat, his sleeves rolled up, and his sensual mouth set in a permanent frown of concentration.

He didn't talk or tease with her when he was working. Not like he had when he'd sketched her in Hampshire. To be sure, he rarely spoke at all, except to order her to "stop fidgeting," or to "be still."

Over the past month Stella had become adept at standing still. She'd spent all of April posing for Teddy, long stretches of motionlessness punctuated by rest periods seated on the new damask-covered settee, watching Teddy with interest as he mixed his colors, adjusted his shading, and—on some occasions—removed a portion of the work he'd just done and started over completely.

Julia and Captain Blunt had returned to Yorkshire last month. Since then, Stella had been staying with Ahmad and Evie at their farmhouse near Hampstead Heath. There was ample room there in the barn for Locket, and for Turvey's horse, Crab. And the heath provided plenty of space for Locket's twice-daily gallops.

Evie was a warm hostess, and Ahmad was a kind and welcoming host. They dined each night together at home, and breakfasted together in the mornings. The remainder of Stella's days were her own. She could do as she liked and go where she chose, and no one required her to have a maid or a chaperone any longer.

"Outside of fashionable society, things are done rather differently," Evie had confided. "We working people value our independence."

Stella had quickly come to relish hers. When she wasn't riding or helping Evie with various tasks related to the household or the dress shop, she was traveling to Covent Garden—either on horseback or by hired hack. There, she posed for Teddy for hours at a time, and then spent an additional hour seated with him as he instructed her in her sketching.

Thus far, he'd helped her perfect her perspective and composition, and had taught her new methods of capturing the changing effect of the light. Under his gentle guidance, she'd learned that art was less about exact replication and more about movement, color, and atmosphere.

Her portfolio had grown significantly. She was particularly proud of a portrait she'd drawn of Locket—a depiction of the mare galloping through the Fostonbury woods, hooves ablur and mane and tail flying. Teddy had guided Stella's hand for a portion of the sky— shading the clouds in gentle strokes—his callused fingers strong but gentle over hers, making her blood quicken and heat.

Yes, Teddy was a forgiving and patient drawing master.

He was markedly less so as a painter.

"Your riding habit is in the way," he remarked crossly from behind his canvas.

It was one of his regular complaints on the days that Stella rode Locket to Maiden Lane. She'd begun doing so often. Not only riding, but being conspicuous about it.

She no longer made any effort at concealment—not of her tresses and not of her destination. She boldly rode through fashionable traffic, Turvey trailing behind, past the theatres, the flower market, and the fruit stalls, until she reached Maiden Lane. The coach house at the back had been made habitable. Locket happily munched on fresh hay, along with Samuel and Crab, while Teddy and Stella toiled inside the house.

"There's no help for that, I'm afraid," she said.

Teddy emerged from behind his canvas. His hair was wildly disheveled, making him appear as unhinged as he was handsome. "You could take it off. Ahmad's sent over some fabric drapes we might try."

"No," she said. "Not until we're married."

"And we can't be married until the house is fit to live in," Teddy muttered, returning to his work. "The latest estimate is July."

July?

Stella's spirits sank. It didn't seem fair. Not when one considered that Teddy had already moved into the house a fortnight ago. He was working all hours on his painting now, with Jennings in residence to look after his personal needs, and Mrs. Mukherjee traveling in each day to do the cooking and cleaning.

Meanwhile, Stella was still waiting for her life to begin. A life where she wasn't an awkward third party on the fringes of some other couple's happily-ever-after, but one where she had a happily-ever-after of her own. She'd already been waiting so long.

And for what? Not love itself, but a chance at love. A chance to fall in love with him, and to make him love her in return.

Granted, the former required little effort. Her attraction to Teddy hadn't faded during the last month. Rather the reverse. It had only grown as a result of their frequent proximity. It made her notice his dwindling interest in her all the more.

Despite the long hours spent in each other's company, he gave no indication that he was pining for her, or longing for a repeat of the kisses they'd shared when he'd proposed. He was solely focused on his work.

She was his model, not his sweetheart.

But they were still engaged, she reminded herself. And a July wedding was surely better than no wedding at all.

"July isn't so far away," she said.

"It is for this piece. It's already too late to submit it to the Royal Academy for the Annual Exhibition. Had we not suffered these delays, I might have already done so." Teddy's brush slashed over the canvas. "Not that they would have accepted it. They rejected Whistler's piece readily enough. That's why he had to resort to a private showing."

And to a spate of poor reviews, Teddy might have added.

Stella was well aware that the new style he espoused wasn't yet widely accepted. It was a risk, posing for him. She might, in the end, be made notorious.

Or not.

She could scarcely tell. Just as when he'd sketched her in Hampshire, Teddy wouldn't permit her to see his unfinished work. He covered the canvas with a cloth drape when he wasn't working on it.

"Perhaps you could ask Mr. Whistler to render his opinion on your progress?" she suggested. She knew Teddy had written to the man before, and that he'd received a cordial reply. But the two hadn't yet met, not as far as she was aware. "You admire his work so. His thoughts might be of value."

"I don't show my work to anyone until I'm finished. Not even other artists, if I can help it." Teddy picked up more paint from his palette with the flat of his brush. "In any event, Whistler isn't in London. He's been in Amsterdam since April."

"You wrote to him again?"

"I did. There's to be an exhibition of works that have been rejected by the Paris Salon. I encouraged Whistler to submit *The White Girl*."

Stella's brows lifted. "Whistler's piece was rejected from the Salon as well?" This was the first she had heard of it.

The Royal Academy and the Salon des Beaux Arts represented

the two most significant art societies in existence. The fact that Whistler's painting had been rejected from both surely didn't bode well for the prospects of other newer artists who were painting in unconventional styles.

"It was," Teddy said. "Along with most of the other paintings submitted. The salon jury has lost all sense of proportion. There was such an uproar from the artists, that the emperor ordered the rejected works be exhibited alongside the accepted ones. They're calling it the Salon des Refusés." He translated for her. "The Exhibition of Rejects."

She gave an exaggerated wince at the name.

"It's better than the paintings getting no exposure at all," Teddy said. "And so I told him."

"Would you ever consider showing your own work at such an exhibition?"

"Would you not?"

"I don't aspire to display my work for the public's approbation."

"You should," he said. "It deserves recognition."

She felt a flush of pride. "Perhaps someday. Until then, it's your work that must be in a museum or a gallery somewhere."

"I'd prefer the Royal Academy," he replied frankly. "But I'd consider any showing, public or private—even an exhibition of rejects, if it came to it. Providing I can finish this piece before the month is out."

Stella refrained from pointing out that there was little hope for that. Not given their current circumstances. Unless . . .

"We could always do as Tom suggested," she remarked, feeling Teddy's frustration emanating from across the room.

"What's that?"

"We could marry while the renovations are being done."

"They've just ripped out half the walls in the upstairs bedrooms because of rot. Where do you propose to sleep?"

"I could stay downstairs," she said.

Teddy's brushstrokes went quiet on the canvas. There was a weighted silence.

Stella fidgeted where she stood, suddenly uncomfortable. One would think she'd just proposed they do something obscene.

"Downstairs," he repeated.

"Would that be so objectionable?"

"It isn't the arrangement we agreed to."

"I thought you offered that arrangement for my benefit," she said, breaking her pose. "You don't mean to tell me that it was for yours? That you'd prefer I stay away from you except when you're painting me?"

"It was for both our benefits." He resumed painting, his brush working on his canvas with unusual force. "You don't want to witness all the indignities I must put up with on account of being in this chair. And unless I roomed with Jennings and gave you Jennings's chamber in exchange, you'd be present for all of them."

"Don't be absurd. Of course I'm not going to stay in Mr. Jennings's room."

"I thought not," he said grimly.

"I'll sleep in your room with you."

Again, his brushstrokes stopped.

She exhaled an impatient breath. "You forget that I've spent most of my life in visiting the sick with my brother. There's little left that can shock me."

Her words were met with silence.

"That isn't to say that I equate you with the village sick," she added, in case he'd taken offense. "I only mean that I'm not apt to swoon at the sight of an injured limb."

"Two injured limbs," he said peevishly. "And no ability to move them."

"I'm well aware."

"Jennings must come and go at all hours to assist me. I won't have him barging in when you're in dishabille. I'd have to sack him for impertinence. And, much as I'd like to be rid of him, I rather rely on the insufferable fellow."

"You won't require Mr. Jennings to help you when I'm in the room with you. I'll help you myself, obviously. That's what married people do."

"I don't need a nurse, Stella."

"You're not getting a nurse. You're getting a wife." She felt the silence as well as heard it this time—an oppressive, throbbing thing. It was too much. She blurted out: "Unless you've changed your mind."

He stuck his head out from behind his canvas again to scowl at her. "Is that what you think?"

"I don't know." She was no longer teasing. "You have what you wanted—me as your model. Why bother with the rest of it?"

"I hope you're jesting."

"I'm not. From the beginning, you only ever wanted to paint me. It was I who wanted something more. Not you. Never you."

Teddy threw down his paintbrush. Before she realized what he was about, he'd wheeled his chair across the room. There was paint on his hands and on his shirt, and a smudge of French ultramarine across his brow. He reached for her arm.

Stella made no move to evade him.

He pulled her to him. *All* the way to him. Tripping over her skirts, she tumbled straight into his lap with a disgruntled laugh. "Teddy! This isn't funny." She moved to stand. "I don't want to hurt you."

He held her firmly against him. "Hurt me? Rubbish. I can't feel anything." His voice deepened. "Not in my legs, anyway."

She set her hands on his shoulders, her cheeks heating. "You're being ridiculous."

"*You're* being ridiculous," he retorted. And then, dipping her back in his arms, he captured her laughing mouth in a kiss.

She clung to his neck. Her laugh turned into a sigh. Her heart was racing. "Oh," she murmured.

"Quite," he growled. And he kissed her again.

Her lips softened and parted, yielding eagerly to his. She curved her fingers around the column of his neck. His skin was hot as a furnace. She was beginning to feel the same heat, simmering within her, a blazing fire roaring into flame.

They'd never been this close. They had kissed, yes. And held hands. But he'd never held *her*. Not like this. It was more thrilling than she could have imagined.

"Is this meant to reassure me?" she asked against his mouth.

"I'm not sure what it was meant to do when I began," he said, voice gone husky. "The moment you came into my arms, my brain turned to porridge."

"That's not very flattering."

"Do you want to be flattered?"

"What if I did?"

"I would tell you that I can't sleep for thinking of you. That I go mad waiting for you to arrive each day. That if you're a minute late—"

"Seriously," she objected.

"Seriously," he returned. "I do want to marry you. I never stopped. I just . . ."

"What?"

His lips quirked in a wry smile. "I don't want to repulse you before I've had a chance to enjoy you awhile. Rather selfishly, I'd prefer to have this—" another kiss, "and this—" and another, "before you must see me as an invalid in need of your nursing."

Her fingers twined in the hair at his nape. She gave a sharp tug.

"Ouch!" He winced, laughing. "What the devil was that for?"

"I am *not* your nurse," she said. "I shall never *be* your nurse." She gave another sharp tug of his hair, scolding him. "I want you to trust me. To trust that I won't think less of you for any reason."

"Not until you witness me—"

"Never," she swore to him. "Not so long as you continue to treat me kindly."

"Kindly?"

"Yes. It's that which I value. Your kindness."

"Hmm." He glowered at her. She suspected it was only partially in jest.

She stroked his hair to soothe his offended dignity. "I never knew I could sit on your lap."

"You never asked."

"As if it would occur to me!"

Again, he bent his head to hers. "As always, Miss Hobhouse, you exhibit a startling lack of imagination."

She smiled up at him, in imminent expectation of another kiss. He was a heartbeat away from claiming one when there was a harsh rap at the front door.

The two of them froze. They exchanged a startled look.

A giggle escaped from Stella. She slapped a hand over her mouth.

Teddy's cheeks dimpled in a boyish grin. "There's no one to answer it," he said. "Mrs. Mukherjee has gone to the market, and I sent Jennings out to purchase more tubes of paint."

Stella moved to stand. Teddy reluctantly released her. He tugged her skirt back into order for her as she slid out of his lap.

She batted his hands away. "You're not helping."

"You have a wrinkle, just here."

"It's a pleat, you ninny."

He caught her hand and kissed it, waiting until the last moment to release her, as she retreated to the hall. They were both grinning now like two naughty schoolchildren.

Stella gave her habit skirts another shake before opening the door.

A balding man in an ill-fitting suit stood on the threshold. He had an enormous wooden crate at his side. In the street behind him, a horse and cart were waiting, with two large men seated on the driver's bench. Whatever was in the crate, it appeared they'd had a hand in delivering it.

"Can I help you, sir?" Stella asked.

"Is this the residence of Mr. Edward Hayes?" the man inquired. He had a distinct cockney accent.

"It is." Stella surveyed the crate. It must have something to do with the renovations, but she couldn't think what. "Do you have an appointment?"

"No appointment, madam, but Mr. Hayes will be expecting me." He withdrew his card, handing it to Stella with a flourish.

She read it with interest.

Mr. Franklin Abbott, Gentleman Inventor

Her brows lifted. "May I ask what invention this might be in regard to, Mr. Abbott?"

"My patented pneumatic invalid's chair," the man announced proudly. "My chief investor, an esteemed gentleman who prefers to remain anonymous, did assure me that Mr. Hayes was eager to possess a prototype."

A pneumatic invalid's chair?

Stella stepped back. "I think you'd better come inside."

Teddy stared in wonder at the wheeled chair that emerged from the wooden crate. It was made of gleaming polished mahogany, finished with brass, and fitted with the exact rubber-covered wheels that Mr. Hartford had described to him in the library at Sutton Park.

Stella stood beside Teddy, both of them looking over the chair as Mr. Abbott extolled the many virtues of his invention.

"It's equipped with every comfort and convenience," Mr. Abbott boasted. "You'll never feel the lumps and bumps of the road. The ride is that smooth once the air is in the tires. The seat is covered in the finest leather, and the back and arms are adjustable, like so." He demonstrated, fiddling with a series of pins and hinges. "But this is a highlight, sir. This magic lever here. The invalid can press it himself, if he has the necessary strength. Observe." Mr. Abbott depressed the lever. Two matching brass brackets immediately descended to the wheels, locking them into place.

Teddy rolled forward in his own chair to examine the apparatus. "A hand brake," he said in amazement. "Is that what it is?"

"Exactly, sir."

"Is that important?" Stella asked, frowning.

"Why, it's essential, ma'am," Mr. Abbott said. "As Mr. Hayes can no doubt tell you. The invalid generally relies on an attendant to place him into his chair. With my invention, the invalid, with adequate strength, can now get in and out of the chair himself."

Teddy's pulse leapt at the possibilities. If it was true, it would mean no more Jennings in Teddy's bedroom, helping him in and out of his bed. No more Jennings lifting Teddy onto the settee or into a parlor chair. If the wheel brakes worked—if they were truly up to the task of holding the chair steady—Teddy could hoist himself in and out using only his upper body strength.

It would mean far greater independence, not to mention privacy.

"Would you like to try it, sir?" Mr. Abbott asked.

"My manservant is away on an errand," Teddy replied. "I shall have to wait until he returns."

"You don't need Mr. Jennings," Stella said. "I can help you."

Teddy inwardly recoiled at the offer. Only moments ago, he'd been holding her in his arms and kissing her. Laughing with her like any young man might do with his sweetheart. He'd felt giddy. Alive.

He wasn't going to ruin that by allowing her to help him out of one dratted chair and into another. An *invalid's chair*, by God! It was bad enough that she must be here to witness his enthusiasm over such a device.

"That won't be necessary," he said tersely. "Jennings will be back soon."

"Shall I assist you, sir?" Mr. Abbott offered. "It's best you become acquainted with the chair while I'm here. I can explain all its little ways to you."

Teddy's jaw hardened. "If you wouldn't mind waiting—"

Stella's hand came to rest on his shoulder. She gave it a wordless squeeze.

What it was meant to convey, Teddy didn't know. He glanced up at her. There was a streak of French ultramarine oil paint across her cheek. It was a stark reminder of the glorious embrace they had just shared.

The anxiety in his chest slowly began to ease, replaced with a growing weight of warmth.

He was still embarrassed. Still resentful in his vulnerability— afraid that she would view him as something less than a man. But he wasn't going to shut her out. Not anymore.

If she wanted to be part of his life, she could bloody well be part of it. And if it resulted in driving her away—

Well.

At least he wouldn't have driven her away first with his own surliness and bad temper.

"Very well," he said. "If you must."

Stella beamed. "What shall I do?"

"Will you hold my chair steady? As still as you can?"

She went behind him to grip the backrest. Teddy felt her there, as immovable as a pillar of steel. He had the vague thought that riding a difficult mare for so many years had given her an unseen reservoir of power. Luminous as she appeared, she was no will-o'-the-wisp. She was formidable. Strong.

"Mr. Abbott—" Teddy refocused his attention on the task at hand. "Would you bring the prototype right up next to me? Just there. Close enough for me to reach the seat. And if you could, please, lift the arm up on its hinges?"

Mr. Abbott did as he was told, at once appearing to understand what Teddy intended. "I'll set the brake, sir."

"Good man." One at a time, Teddy removed his booted feet from the footrests. He glanced back at Stella, feeling another flash of anxiety. "Don't let this chair move."

She gave him a bracing look. "No fear of that."

Inhaling a deep breath, Teddy placed his hands on the arms of his chair. Using all of his strength, he lifted his lower body up from the seat. It was nothing he hadn't done before when training his muscles. But this time, he didn't limit the movement to a straight up-and-down motion. He swung himself forward, bringing his hips right up to the edge of the seat.

Once there, he lowered himself again. His biceps were trembling, the muscles of his abdomen clenching with effort. Leaning forward, he placed a hand on the seat of the prototype. He gave it an experimental push. The prototype didn't budge.

"Are you going to—" Stella started to ask.

"Yes," Teddy said. "If I should fall in the process—"

"You won't," she told him. "Don't even imagine it."

He understood what she meant. Envisioning failure was as good as willing it into existence. One couldn't think that way. Not when one was risking their body. Their pride.

"Here goes," he said.

Using all his strength, he again lifted himself up from his seat, this time with one hand on the seat of his old chair and one on the seat of the new one. It was only a short distance. An angled swing of his hips, a split second of sheer panic, and then he landed with a thump onto the seat of the protoype.

His breath gusted out of him.

Stella was at once at his side. He felt her hands at his back, and then at his waist, attempting to assist him as he edged back into position. A lock of hair had fallen over his forehead. She brushed it back from his face.

"Good heavens!" she said. "That was perilous. Are you all right?"

"I did it," he said, a trifle stunned.

"Of course you did." She helped him lower the arm of his new chair. "That was never in question."

He met her eyes as she leaned over him. For the second time that day, the two of them grinned at each other like children.

And he realized that he wasn't just in love with Stella Hobhouse— his model, his muse, his shining star.

He loved her.

Twenty-Eight

LONDON, ENGLAND
JUNE 1863

Stella and Teddy had to wait three consecutive Sundays for the banns to be called. On the third Sunday, she finally worked up the nerve to write to Anne. The letter was posted but a week before Teddy and Stella's wedding.

It wasn't the only letter she wrote.

After much thought—and even more second-guessing herself—Stella penned a brief note to her brother in Derbyshire. It contained neither an invitation to her wedding, nor an invitation back into her life. To be sure, it was more in the manner of a goodbye.

Dear Daniel,

By the time you receive this, I shall be married. My husband is Mr. Edward Hayes, a respectable gentleman of good family, good fortune, and immense artistic talent. He sees something beautiful in me, and desires that I live my life without shame or apology. We will be settling in London, and plan to make each other very happy.

Your sister,
Stella

She had no expectation of a reply. Not from her brother. But she did suspect that Anne would have something to say to the news.

Sure enough, despite the lateness of Stella's letter and the very great distance from Somersetshire to London, when Stella arrived at the small church in Fleet Street for her wedding, she found Anne waiting in the vestry, along with Julia, who had journeyed back from Yorkshire for the ceremony.

"I should have known it would be him," Anne said, hugging Stella fiercely, as Julia stood by. "Indeed, I *would* have known had I not been so consumed with my own happiness."

"Which is exactly as it should have been," Stella said, pressing a kiss to her friend's cheek. "You've done enough looking after all of us."

"Rubbish. We look after each other." Anne stepped back. Some of the glacial hardness in her face—that frosty aristocratic look she'd had ever since Stella had met her—had gone. It was replaced by an expression of relaxed contentment. It appeared that life with Mr. Hartford was agreeing with her. "Why on earth did you delay in writing to me?"

"Because I knew you'd try to rescue me," Stella answered honestly. "And I didn't want to be rescued. I wanted to gallop ahead, come what may."

Anne laughed. "Nonsensical girl. Have you no respect for peril?"

"No, indeed." Stella smiled back at her. "I find I rather enjoy it."

"So says the young lady dressed like an angel," Julia said as she hugged Stella in turn. "You look beautiful, dearest."

Anne looked Stella up and down with approval. "Did Ahmad design your wedding dress?"

"He did," Stella said. "And Mira did the embroidery and trimmings."

The elegant gown was made of white tarlatan muslin, embellished with delicate whitework butterflies, and edged in Valenciennes lace. Ahmad and Mira had helped Stella into it at the Maliks' house before they'd departed for the church. It only remained for Stella to put on her veil. It had been too fragile for her to wear in the carriage.

Evie entered the vestry behind them, carrying the flowing piece of white netting draped over her arms. It was as finely wrought as a cobweb, and was, like the wedding dress, embroidered with butter-flies.

"I'm sensing a theme," Anne remarked, smiling as Evie affixed the gauzy veil to Stella's upswept silver hair.

"Mira says that the butterflies are a symbol of transformation," Evie told her. "Stella has begun the day as an innocent young maiden and shall be ending it as a respectably married lady."

"Transformed by love into a butterfly," Julia said. "How romantic."

"Indeed," Stella replied. "Though it seems to imply that I was a caterpillar before."

It also implied that Teddy loved her.

Which wasn't precisely true. They were friends, certainly. And doubtless he was fond of her. There was attraction there, too, as evidenced by the kisses and embraces they had shared. But was it love? Or was it still inextricably tied up in his passion for painting her? That was, after all, what had started it.

Try as she might, Stella couldn't rid herself of the niggling premonition that, when he was at last finished with his masterpiece, he would be finished with her as well.

And he was nearly done, she knew, though she still hadn't seen the portrait yet.

All that remained was for him to paint her *en plein air*—out of doors, along the Thames, the atmosphere of which, Teddy claimed, would stand in for the sea. He'd already chosen the drape Stella would wear. It was a soft, creamy pearl tulle, adorned with mother-of-pearl paillettes. Ahmad had sewn it over a flowing, sleeveless muslin shift that, when worn, would give the appearance that Stella was clad in nothing but the netting, while still preserving her modesty.

It was that which she was thinking of, even as she smiled with her friends, and readied herself for her walk down the aisle. Of the small but persistent fear that she and Teddy were reaching the end of things rather than embarking on a new beginning together.

"Who is giving you away?" Anne asked. "Not your brother, I presume."

Stella's smile dimmed to think of Daniel. She willed it back again. Today wasn't about regretting the family she'd lost. It was about celebrating the family she had. And friends were family, too. Often more than family, for friends were the family you chose.

"Ahmad is giving me away," she said. "It seemed right to ask him. After living with him and Evie for so many weeks, I've come to look on him as something like a brother."

"He was honored," Evie said. "Truly. He takes the responsibility very seriously."

Julia helped to adjust Stella's veil. "I had a peep into the church before I arrived. There were several strangers in the pews."

"I recognized the Finchleys," Anne said. "And Mira and Mr. Jones. But the other couples were unknown to me."

"It's Mr. and Mrs. Thornhill and Mr. and Mrs. Cross," Stella said. "They're friends of Mr. Hayes's family, and have come to stand in for Mr. and Mrs. Archer."

"His family couldn't come themselves?" Julia asked.

"His sister is entering her confinement and unable to travel from France," Stella explained. "And his aged Aunt Charlotte couldn't attend, either, on account of having a weak heart. They both wrote very kind letters, however. And Mr. and Mrs. Archer sent a lovely gift."

It was an exquisite ormolu clock. Stella had put it above the mantel in Teddy's studio. It wasn't the first bit of homeliness she'd added to the house in Maiden Lane. There was a new sofa and chairs for the parlor, a carved walnut dining set, and a large mahogany wardrobe for the bedroom.

Teddy had encouraged Stella to purchase whatever she needed, and told her to have the bills sent to him. He wasn't rich, but neither was he poor. And he was by no means tightfisted.

"They're here in spirit, I'm sure," Evie said.

Julia's gaze shimmered. She always grew emotional at weddings. "And Mr. Hayes has you now."

"And I have him," Stella said resolutely. She refused to let any more doubts steal her joy.

Ahmad entered the vestry. He wore a smart-looking morning coat with gray trousers. His thick black hair was combed into meticulous order. "It's time," he said.

Anne, Julia, and Evie bustled around Stella in a final rush, adjusting her skirts, straightening her veil, and putting her bouquet of lavender and roses into her hands.

"There," Anne said. "You're ready."

"You're perfect," Evie said.

"The prettiest bride ever," Julia agreed.

Ahmad offered Stella his arm. "Shall we?"

Stella felt a sudden resurgence of anxiety. "Is Mr. Hayes already at the alter?" she asked, taking Ahmad's arm.

What if Teddy hadn't come? What if he'd changed his mind? What if—

"He's there," Ahmad said, leading Stella from the vestry. "He's waiting for you."

And he was, of course. He was seated in his wheeled chair at the top of the aisle, looking unbearably handsome in his morning coat and gray-striped trousers.

Stella's gaze fixed on him the entirety of the way up the aisle, never mind their friends seated to the left and the right. There was no one but Teddy, filling her vision and filling her heart.

And suddenly, she knew. She just knew.

The realization struck her, less like a thunderbolt and more like a minor earthquake of the soul. It rolled through her, the culmination of something that had been building since the moment they'd met.

Half in love, she'd thought. That was all. Not wholly in love. But she'd been wrong. The full strength of the emotion had crept up on her as silent as a thief, stealing itself around her soul. She recognized it now beyond all doubt.

I love him.

Teddy hadn't cared about marrying in a church. He'd been more interested in speed than ceremony. But once a vicar's sister, he supposed, always a vicar's sister. And Teddy didn't intend to start things off on the wrong foot with his future wife merely because he found the trappings of a fashionable wedding tedious.

And they *had* been tedious, not to mention damnably inconvenient for his work.

Marrying in a church meant first finding a clergyman that could accommodate them. Tom had again worked his magic in the form of a small chapel in Fleet Street, not far from his law offices. Teddy and Stella had promptly booked the date, and even engaged the church's organist to play Mendelssohn for a fee.

After that, Teddy had suffered through multiple days without his model as the wedding preparations got under way. Rather than dutifully posing for his painting, Stella had been off for wedding dress fittings and shopping excursions, buying various things she would need before moving in with him in Maiden Lane.

Delivery men had been bringing furnishings, linens, and other domestic necessities for the last week, regularly breaking Teddy's concentration.

By the time the morning of his wedding day arrived, announced by an unseasonably heavy downpour of summer rain, he was fully ready to get the dratted thing over with. The sooner he and Stella were married, the sooner he could resume painting her.

But he hadn't reckoned for how he'd feel as he sat at the top of the aisle in the tiny stone chapel, with its single modest stained-glass window, surrounded by friends, and awaiting the arrival of his bride.

When she at last appeared on Ahmad's arm, clad in delicate white muslin and veiled in diaphanous embroidered net, Teddy could only stare at her, struck dumb by how beautiful she was and by the fact—the suddenly visceral, appreciable, soul-fracturing fact—that she was shortly going to be his.

All his.

The aged little white-haired clergyman who stood in front of them didn't waste any time. Rain beat against the high windows, nearly drowning out his creaky intonation as he began reading from the Book of Common Prayer.

Teddy gazed solemnly into Stella's eyes, and she into his.

He'd never thought to marry. Not since losing the use of his legs. He hadn't imagined trusting anyone. Loving anyone. Life to him, when he'd at last resumed it, had taken on another focus. Art had been the whole of his world.

But no longer.

"I will," Stella said, a faint tremor in her voice.

"I will," Teddy said, putting the ring on her finger. It was a fine band of gold, purchased from a jeweler in Bond Street. It didn't do what he felt for her justice. No mere piece of jewelry could.

Another few words from the reverend, and it was done.

Stella pushed back her veil herself. Teddy would have done so, but she was too tall in comparison to his chair, with no means of leveling them unless she stooped down in her dress. For a taut moment, it had appeared as though she might.

But no.

He was vaguely relieved. There would be time enough to kiss her, without engaging in spectacle. Instead, he took her hand. "Well, Mrs. Hayes?"

She didn't reply, only looked at him, the most inexplicable

emotion in her silver-blue eyes. She hung on to his hand, rather like a lifeline.

Teddy's chest tightened on a surge of tenderness. He could see she was overwhelmed. Was it by emotion? By the reality of what they'd just committed to? Both, possibly. "I just thought of another argument for our marriage," he said under his breath as they released hands, turning to face their guests. "No need to change the initials on your linens."

A shadow of a smile tipped her mouth. "I haven't embroidered the linens yet."

"Something to look forward to, then," he said. "Among other things."

They made their way back down the aisle together to the joyful strains of a Strauss march, he wheeling his new chair and she walking beside him, smiling now, though still a bit tremulously.

Behind them, their guests rose to follow. Mrs. Blunt was clinging to Captain Blunt's arm, dabbing her eyes with a lacy handkerchief, and Hartford was guiding Lady Anne from their pew, a hand at her waist as he pressed a discreet kiss to her temple.

Captain Thornhill and Lady Helena were smiling at each other, possibly remembering their own unconventional wedding, which had taken place not in a church but in a registrar's office after only a few days' acquaintance; Neville and Clara held hands, their faces aglow; and Tom and Jenny lingered, heads bent together in intimate conversation, exchanging soft words as they waited for Mira and Mr. Jones to join them.

Evelyn and Ahmad walked behind the guests, the de facto parents of the bride, reminding everyone about the wedding breakfast that Jenny Finchley was hosting for the newlyweds in Half Moon Street.

"Shall we go?" Teddy asked Stella, before their guests could overtake them. "Tom has engaged a carriage for us. The wagonette doesn't best suit the rain."

"I prefer a carriage today," she said.

So did he. In a closed carriage, there would be no Jennings looming over their shoulders.

Alas, Teddy couldn't dispense with the man completely. Not even on his wedding day.

Jennings waited at the church doors to assist Teddy down the steps and into the waiting carriage. The vehicle had been bedecked with garlands at the start of the day, but the rain had played havoc with the flowers. Scarcely a bloom retained its petals.

Teddy insisted that Stella precede him into the cab. Jennings obligingly trotted forward to hand her in while Teddy remained under the stone outcropping at the top of the church steps.

"Do take care not to get too wet, Mr. Jennings," Stella said to the manservant as she climbed inside the carriage. "You mustn't catch cold."

"I'm right enough, miss." Jennings reddened. "I mean, ma'am. I mean, er, Mrs. Hayes." He bowed awkwardly before bounding back up the steps to fetch Teddy.

Teddy's mouth quirked at the manservant's stammering. "My wife's civility must make a nice change from my infernal moods," he commented as Jennings hoisted him from his chair.

"I don't pay no mind, sir," Jennings replied, conveying Teddy to the carriage. "Mr. Archer said when he hired me as how I wasn't to take your bouts of temper to heart."

"Did he indeed?"

"He said none of it were personal. That it was all owing to frustration, on account of that chair of yours."

Teddy could easily imagine Alex saying just that. Making excuses for Teddy, even as he tried to smooth Teddy's path back into the land of the living. Teddy felt a distinct pang of gratitude for his brother-in-law, and for his sister, too. He hadn't always appreciated their interference—or anyone's, come to that—but he recognized when he'd benefited from it.

Despite his moods, his surliness, and his intermittent bouts of melancholy, his family had been there for him unreservedly. So, too, had his friends. Even new acquaintances like Felix Hartford had helped Teddy, often whether he liked it or not.

"The old chair, perhaps," Teddy said. "But not this one." He flashed a look at his mahogany and brass pneumatic marvel that had helped to further smooth his path in life. "This one has drastically improved my outlook."

"It won't be damaged in the rain, will it?" Stella asked as Teddy settled into the carriage seat beside her.

Teddy's hair was damp and his suit rumpled from Jennings's heavy-handed assistance. "The coachman brought a tarpaulin for it."

It took but a few moments longer to secure the chair to the carriage, and then Teddy and Stella were off, leaving their friends behind, waving them off on the steps of the church.

"You're not regretting it, are you?" Teddy asked her the instant they were alone.

Stella shook her head. "No," she said. "Are you?"

"No." He glanced out the window at the fog rolling over the street. "I'm just impatient to return to my work. The painting is nearly finished."

That same inexplicable look crossed her face. "Yes. I know."

"All it wants is the final touches. You in your gossamer net, and a bit of that fog over the water. I could paint it as it stands, providing it would cease raining long enough for me to set up my easel on the banks of the river."

"There's always tomorrow," she said.

"Yes," he agreed.

But before tomorrow, there was tonight.

Teddy returned his attention to Stella. His heart thumped hard, and not only from the effort it had taken to get into the carriage. After the wedding breakfast, and the ordeal of getting themselves back to Maiden Lane in what appeared to be worsening weather, there was still the wedding night to get through.

Is that why she was being so quiet? Why she'd appeared to have retreated behind her mask again? Brides were meant to be nervous on their wedding night. It was practically a tradition. It was a husband's responsibility to put his new wife at ease.

Teddy took her hand. His voice deepened with sincerity. "I'm so glad it's you," he said.

She turned to him. "It will be me a long while after your painting is finished."

"There will be other paintings," he assured her. "Haven't I told you so?"

"One thousand, you said once. You shall doubtless get bored after the hundredth."

"Bored of this?" He touched her cheek. "Never."

Her eyes softened. "Thank you."

"For what?" His hand curved around her neck. They were seated side by side like any other newly married couple—he in his wedding suit and she in her bridal gown. There was no Jennings. No wheeled chair.

"For proposing to me," she said. "For being so generous about furnishing the house, and making the stable fit for Locket." Her breath hitched as he drew closer, bending his head. "For letting us marry in a church. I know you'd rather have got it over with in an office somewhere or a—"

His mouth captured hers.

She closed her eyes, leaning into his kiss. Her arms slowly circled his neck. There was no doubt. No hesitation. She was soft, and warm, and welcoming, yielding to the pressure of his lips even as she claimed his lips for her own.

One kiss became two, and then another. Each dissolved into the next, punctuated by sweetly muffled words and sighs.

The Finchleys' carriage was more private than a sleigh. More dangerous than Teddy's studio. There inside the shadowy cab, with the curtains drawn, and the rain beating the windows, he felt closer to her than he'd ever felt before.

Was the carriage solely to blame? Or was it those vows? That ring?

"I'd do it all again, and more," Teddy said huskily. "Anything to have you."

"Was it purely selfish, then?" Stella asked, lips brushing over his. "Saving me from a life in the background?"

"It was you who saved me. I told you I'd run mad if I couldn't paint you. I would have done, you know."

"I cured you, did I?"

"Not completely. Not yet." He was still half-mad. Twisting his fingers in the thickness of her hair, he took her mouth again.

Raindrops fell in a continual drumbeat. It wasn't until the carriage turned onto Half Moon Street that the drops began to come further apart, eventually ceasing altogether. The carriage slowed to a rattling halt, giving Teddy and Stella ample time to collect themselves.

A footman opened the carriage door while Jennings fetched Teddy's wheeled chair. Fog blanketed the street. The sun had belatedly emerged behind it, streaking the landscape with brilliant color.

Teddy set a hand at Stella's back. "Look at that light," he said. "Pity I can't commit it to canvas."

She turned to him. Her lips were very pink, her face flushed from the passionate kisses they'd shared. "Who says you can't?"

"It's our wedding day. I wouldn't be so churlish."

"But we married to please ourselves. To do what we want, when we want."

"Today is about what *you* want," he said.

She looked steadily back at him. "I want you to finish your painting."

He searched her face, amazed by what he found there. Good

Lord, she was serious. He didn't know whether he should be disappointed or elated.

"I couldn't start until twilight," he said. "That's the hour I require, not the middle of the day. It might very well disrupt our evening."

Her blush deepened. "Twilight doesn't last forever."

Teddy's heart lost its rhythm. The meaning was plain. They would still have their wedding night, come what may. But first . . .

The artistic possibilities beckoned.

"In that case," he said, "if the weather holds and you don't change your mind—" His mouth tipped up in a sudden grin. "This evening, at sunset, I shall ask you very politely to change into your starry raiments and accompany me and my canvas to the banks of the Thames."

Twenty-Nine

⟶✖⟵

Stella had warned Teddy when he proposed that she enjoyed taking risks on occasion. And it wasn't only traveling to and from Maiden Lane without a chaperone, or galloping Locket in the park, absent the net Stella had long used to conceal the color of her hair.

It was now—boldly doing as Teddy had asked of her—standing on the banks of the river, wrapped in a dark cloth cloak with precious little underneath, as the fog rolled in from the water and the glow of twilight faded into evening.

There was no Locket beneath Stella to lend her strength. No Furies surrounding her to offer their support. Even Teddy was a distance away, seated behind his easel as he prepared his palette.

A shiver traced down Stella's spine. It wasn't from the cold. And it wasn't from fear or anxiety. She wasn't afraid. Far from it. She felt bold as a brass farthing. Confident, there in the mud, standing on her own two booted feet.

What a glorious day it had turned out to be! First married, then feted by their friends at the Finchleys', and now this—wild and unconventional and utterly conspicuous. The very opposite of the stultifying life she'd known before.

"I'm ready," she said, untying the fastening of her cloak at her neck.

Teddy's brows sank. He was having second thoughts. Third ones, too, by the looks of it. Never mind that it had been his idea. He wore the same expression he'd worn when he'd learned that Stella was traveling about the city unescorted. That visible conflict between the freedom he'd promised her and the masculine urge to protect her at all costs.

Stella registered his internal battle, but she didn't allow it to alter her course.

She slipped the cloak from her shoulders, revealing her bare arms, bare throat, and the shimmering, pearl-spangled net that made up her gown.

They weren't completely isolated on their tree-shrouded section of the river. Mr. Jennings stood with the wagonette at the top of the bank, respectfully giving them his back. Further on, beyond the tangle of ash, alder, and willow trees, lay meandering public walks and a curving, wood-lined roadway.

It would be scandalous to be observed. Reputation ruining, without doubt.

Once upon a time, Stella Hobhouse would have been concerned with such things. But she was no longer Stella Hobhouse. No longer, even, Stella Hayes, despite her and Teddy's marriage ceremony, and the lengthy wedding breakfast, and countless champagne toasts that had come after.

All that was gone the instant Stella shed her outer garments. She was one of the Pleiades now.

She tossed her cloak to Teddy. His hand reflexively shot out to catch it. But he wasn't looking at her cloak. He was staring at her, his jaw gone slack.

A thrill of feminine power went through her. "Don't you approve of Ahmad's design?"

Teddy's throat worked on a swallow. "It's, ah, a bit more revealing than I'd imagined it would be."

It wasn't, in truth. It was an illusion, merely.

Still . . .

"Isn't that rather the point?" She turned, giving him his preferred three-quarter profile. Her unbound hair fell back from her shoulders, the mother-of-pearl paillettes on her net gown tinkling in the breeze that drifted over the water.

He cleared his throat. "Stella—"

"I'm Electra now," she informed him. "Unless you've one of the other Pleiades in mind?"

He ran a hand over his hair. A scowl darkened his face. "Electra will do," he muttered.

She smiled briefly. "The sun is setting, mortal. Hadn't you better make the most of it?"

It was no easy thing to capture the changing light. An artist had to work quickly. For twilight, Teddy had no more than an hour. His brush moved rapidly, his head ducking repeatedly out from behind his canvas to glance at the river, the fog, the streaks of waning sunlight.

And at her.

He had to make an effort not to gape like a simpleton. He hadn't the time for it. But she lured him to her just the same, as surely as iron filings to a magnet. And not only because she was beautiful, and dynamic, and shining bright as a star. (Electra, by God!) But because she was fully herself, standing straight and proud, chin high and hair streaming, concealing nothing of her true, magnificent nature.

An ache of emotion infused his work. This was how he'd seen her from the first. How he'd known she would be if ever the ladylike mask was removed completely. This powerful, passionate, regal creature that had, by some miracle, become his wife.

His own insecurities lingered at the edge of his consciousness. Painting held them at bay. With a brush in his hand and his oils at the ready, he was powerful, too.

All too soon it was over. The sun set, and Stella once again donned her cloak, assuming the mantle of humble mortality. Jennings materialized with a lantern. Teddy's canvas was covered and loaded into the wagonette, and Jennings helped to push Teddy's chair up the bank, Teddy still in it, rolling the rubber-covered wheels through the mud.

At length, they were all of them in the wagonette. Teddy impulsively caught Stella's hand and kissed it. She beamed at him—face aglow with radiant happiness.

It was only as Teddy took up Samuel's reins to drive them home that he realized the damage he'd done, sitting out in the cold and the damp, so close to the river.

The first leg cramp materialized within ten minutes. The second soon after. By the time they'd reached Maiden Lane, he was gritting his teeth.

"What's wrong?" Stella asked as he brought the wagonette to a clumsy halt in front of their house. A lantern was lit in the front window, illuminating the stone steps that led to the door. Mrs. Mukherjee would have left it before departing for the evening.

"Nothing," Teddy said tightly.

Jennings jumped down from the wagonette to assist him.

"You look as though something is." Stella scanned Teddy's face. "You're not still cross because of my costume?"

"I was never cross."

"Is it the painting? Did you not get what you wanted?"

"It's not the painting," he gritted out. "It's . . . It's my legs."

Her brows knit with concern. "I don't understand. Did you hurt yourself coming up the bank? Or was it—"

"Nothing like that. It happens sometimes. The change in the weather. I can't—" He broke off as a cramp assailed him. He set a hand on his thigh, squeezing it hard. A groan escaped from between his clenched teeth.

Jennings hurried to lift him down.

"Not me," Teddy growled. "Help Mrs. Hayes."

"Don't be ridiculous," Stella said. "I can see to myself well enough." She suited action to word, leaping out of the wagonette with a recklessness that made Teddy's heart briefly jump in his throat.

"Good God," he snapped. "Do you want to break your neck?"

"There was no danger of that." She turned to Jennings. "What shall I do to help?"

"Do nothing," Teddy said. "It's Jennings I require. Not you."

A glimmer of hurt flickered briefly in her eyes. *But it's our wedding night*, she might have said.

As if Teddy didn't know that to his soul! As if he wasn't cursing himself for being brought this low. Cursing the scarlet fever. Cursing his dratted legs. Cursing Jennings, too, though the manservant was only attempting to help in his usual ham-fisted way.

"I'll carry you inside, sir," Jennings said.

"You bloody well won't," Teddy snarled. "Fetch my chair."

Stella waited, hands clasped in front of her, while Jennings readied Teddy's wheeled chair and then hoisted Teddy into it.

John Turvey, Stella's groom, emerged from the coach house to take charge of Samuel. "Anything I can do, ma'am?"

"Shall I send Turvey for the doctor?" Stella asked Teddy.

"No doctor," Teddy replied. "It's Jennings I require. Not anyone else."

The same stricken look appeared in Stella's gaze. It didn't last. She rallied herself in an instant, taking on an air of stern efficiency. "I'm not anyone else," she told him curtly. And then to Turvey, "Wait for my word. I may yet have need of you."

Turvey nodded gravely before leading Samuel away with the wagonette. Teddy's canvas, easel, and supplies were still covered in the back of it.

"I won't have my canvas left in the coach house all night," Teddy said to Jennings.

Jennings didn't stop to retrieve it. He rolled Teddy straight into the dimly lit house, with Stella following close beside them. "I'll fetch it inside later, sir. Soon as I've finished tending to you."

Tending to him.

As though Teddy was an invalid who must be nursed!

Teddy's fingers clenched on the arms of his chair. He stewed with anger, miserable to the point of incivility, his legs aching as though Satan himself were gnawing at the fraying sinew of Teddy's calf and thigh muscles.

Stella accompanied him into his bedroom, lighting the lamps as Jennings lifted Teddy onto the low, four-poster bed. Teddy had ordered it specially from a furniture warehouse in Ludgate Hill. Its height enabled him to move from bed to chair and back without assistance.

But not tonight.

Tonight, for as long as these blasted cramps lasted, Teddy was completely reliant on Jennings.

"Tell me what I can do," Stella said.

"You can go," Teddy replied. And then, the rasping words wrenched out of him on another brutal spasm: "I don't want you to see me like this."

Stella's taut expression softened with tender understanding. But she didn't leave. Instead, she sank down onto the edge of the mattress beside him, the paillettes on her net-covered gown tinkling like silver bells. "I'm your wife," she said simply.

And that was that.

Thirty

❖

Stella had never undressed a man before. Then again, she'd never had a husband.

How was a lady meant to behave in such circumstances? In Teddy's bedchamber for the first time—on their wedding night, by heaven. And here they were, on the bed together, while Jennings lumbered about the room, first kindling a fire in the hearth, and then tugging off Teddy's boots.

Stella ignored the trembling of her fingers as she unknotted Teddy's cravat and unbuttoned his jacket and waistcoat. She removed the garments from him one by one, tossing them onto the upholstered armchair that stood at the side of the unusually low mahogany bed.

This wasn't a romantic disrobing. Any idea of that had been dispelled before she'd begun. Teddy was as sullen as an injured bear, glowering at her as much as he glowered at Jennings.

"Leave my shirt," he said when she moved to lift it up. "It's my trousers that have to come off."

A blush threatened. Of course, his trousers must be removed. She felt a fool for not having thought of it straightaway.

Jennings was already at the end of the bed, having just dispensed with Teddy's boots. "Shall I help, ma'am?"

"Er, yes, thank you." Stella rose from the bed.

It wasn't virginal prudishness that made her withdraw. It was pure pragmatism. She hadn't ever touched Teddy's legs, let alone seen them. She didn't know what helped or hurt him. And she wasn't about to try to learn now at the cost of expediency. Not when he was so obviously in pain.

Teddy unfastened his trousers himself, shoving them down over his hips. Jennings took over then without being asked, stripping the trousers the rest of the way from Teddy's legs.

Stella was almost afraid to look. It felt like the rankest violation of Teddy's privacy. A violation to which it appeared he had already bitterly resigned himself. No longer snarling at them, he lay back against the pillows, silent and stoic. His brow was damp with perspiration, and a muscle worked rhythmically in his jaw. He stared straight ahead, his gaze fixed on nothing,

"You don't want to witness all the indignities I must put up with on account of being in this chair," he'd told her when she'd first broached the subject of their sharing a bedchamber.

And this is what he'd been afraid of. Moments like this one when he was vulnerable and exposed.

Stella didn't like to take advantage. But she was his wife, just as she'd told him. She was also his friend. She made herself look at him, steeling herself for a shock.

Fortunately for her blushes, Teddy wasn't wholly unclothed. He wore a pair of drawers beneath his trousers. Made of plain flannel, they came to the middle of his thighs, just a fraction longer than the length of his shirt hem. All the rest of him was exposed to her view. Lean, naked limbs, covered in a light dusting of black hair. Unmistakably male.

Heat rose in her cheeks.

Though the muscles in his legs hadn't completely wasted away, they were noticeably withered. It made her think of how he must have been before. Strong and athletic, striding through the woods in his village in Surrey. But she hadn't known him then. She only knew him now. And she didn't find him wanting.

Rather the reverse.

She felt the sudden restless urge to busy herself elsewhere. "Shall I fetch some hot water for a bath?" she asked. "If I'm ever sore after riding, a soak in the tub always helps."

"It's liniment he'll need, ma'am," Jennings said. "I've some in my room." He tramped out to fetch it.

Stella was left alone with Teddy, her husband of fewer than four-and-twenty hours. A man clad in nothing but his shirtsleeves and drawers. "Liniment?" she inquired in as casual a tone as she could muster. "Is he going to rub you down like a horse?"

"Something like that." Teddy gave a grimacing smile. "It's a paralytic liniment. More like a salve."

She drew closer, the paillettes of her net gown tinkling softly. "Does it help?"

"It calms the worst of it," he said. "The rest fades within an hour. Usually less, providing the damp doesn't aggravate it again."

Jennings promptly returned with a glass jar of salve. He opened it, releasing the faint fragrance of lavender and balsam into the room. "If you'll permit me?"

She again moved away from the bed, relinquishing her place.

The mattress sagged as Jennings sat down beside Teddy. Scooping out a measure of the salve, he rubbed it between his hands to warm it, and then, placing his hands on Teddy's right thigh, began harshly kneading the muscles.

Teddy groaned deep in his throat.

Stella winced in sympathy. "Must you be so rough?" she asked the manservant.

"Have to apply adequate pressure," Jennings grunted. "That's what the French doctor said as was to be done. Said I was to use all my strength."

Stella frowned. Jennings was a great big ox of a man, with hands the size of dinner plates. As for that French doctor, she didn't think much of any physician who prescribed cruelty as a cure. "I sometimes massage Locket's muscles," she said. "When she's stiff after a ride on a cold morning. There are ways of pressing deeply without brutality."

"A woman's touch," Jennings said, his tone edged with unmistakable disparagement. "Not much use for Mr. Hayes."

"Not just any woman," Stella informed him coolly. She returned to the bed, refusing to accept that she was useless to her husband. She met Teddy's eyes. "May I try?"

His shirt collar was open. A dull flush of red crept up his neck. For a moment it seemed he would refuse her request. And then, with a huff of resignation: "You can hardly do worse."

Stella's pulse quickened. She helped herself to a scoop of the salve. She waited for Jennings to move and then took his place. She rubbed the salve between her hands, softening it with her warmth. It appeared to be composed of beeswax and tallow, with a slight sting to it that might have been turpentine.

"Tell me if I hurt you," she said to Teddy.

"It's not hurting me that's the trouble," he said. "It's helping me."

"Oh, ye of little faith," she said, quoting Anne. "Don't give up on me just yet." With that, she pressed her hands gently into his thigh. His flesh was firm and warm. Her heart fluttered wildly. She did her best to ignore it. This was serious business.

His muscles were tightly contracted, solid as stone under her questing fingers. She applied additional pressure, pushing deep and pulling with her hands as she moved, her strokes fluid rather than jarring. She understood from working on Locket that the goal wasn't to bruise a muscle or to inflame it even worse. It was to soothe it. To convince the knots that it was safe to release.

Teddy inhaled a shaking breath.

"How's that?" she asked. "Any better? Any worse?"

"Better," he grunted.

"Should I move higher?"

Color crept into his face, burning across his cheekbones. He nodded tersely.

She moved her hands further up his thigh, working the spasmed muscle with single-minded attention. She went no higher than the top of his drawers. She wouldn't have dared. But she grew bolder as she continued her massage, helping herself to more salve, and switching to his other leg without asking permission.

Jennings stood back, arms crossed over his chest.

"Leave us," Teddy said.

"But, sir—"

"Close the door on your way out," Teddy added with a harsh rasp. Stella's hand was still on his thigh. "I'll call if I need you."

The manservant grudgingly withdrew, uttering one last grumble of complaint before shutting the door behind him. His boots pounded down the hall, echoing toward the back of the house as he went outside to retrieve Teddy's canvas and art supplies from the stable.

"You'd think he'd want the evening off," Stella remarked, continuing her massage.

"He fears you'll displace him entirely," Teddy said.

"That's hardly possible." Stella could never summon the strength to lift Teddy from his chair. As for the rest of Jennings's duties . . .

"How often is he obliged to do this?" she asked, running her slick hands over Teddy's leg.

"Not often. Only when the weather changes, and I've been too long exposed to the damp."

Her conscience twinged. "We shouldn't have gone to the river. Not if this was to be the result."

"A small price to pay for seeing you as you looked standing on the bank."

She smiled slightly at his attempt at levity. But glancing up at him, she saw that he didn't appear to be teasing her. He was looking back at her solemnly, his eyes unsettlingly heavy lidded, and his voice gone gruff at the edges.

"You're still in your starlight netting," he observed.

"There's been no time to change."

"Do it now," he said. "The worst is over. And even if it isn't . . . you can come back to me after."

Her heart thumped heavily. She sat back from him, hands still sticky with salve. "I shan't have any need to go in the first place. All of my things are here now."

An odd expression crossed his face. Had he already forgotten?

"What did you think the new wardrobe was doing here?" she asked, gesturing to the heavy piece of furniture across the room.

He scrubbed the side of his face, briefly at a loss. "These last weeks, I haven't noticed much outside of my painting, to be honest. Your portrait has occupied the whole of my thoughts."

Standing from the bed, Stella crossed to the basin. She washed the salve from her hands. "Just the portrait? Not me?"

"They're essentially the same thing."

Stella wasn't so sure. She went to the wardrobe and opened it. Her embroidered silk dressing gown was inside, along with her night clothes, underthings, and several of her day dresses. The remainder of her belongings were folded safely in two steamer trunks and a large leather portmanteau that had been sent over from the Maliks' house. Stella had yet to unpack them.

She withdrew her dressing gown, silently debating whether she would take the trouble to put on a nightgown or simply sleep in her chemise.

The latter, she decided. It would be less fuss.

She cast Teddy another glance over her shoulder. He was massaging his own legs now, kneading the muscles, first in his right thigh and then in his left one.

He caught her eyes. "Having second thoughts?"

"About what?"

"Undressing."

Her blush deepened. "No. I'm just— I'm wondering if I should—"

"It seems only fair that you should take some of your clothes off," he said. "For no other reason than to put us on equal footing."

She uttered an unsteady laugh. "Oh well, in that case . . ."

Sitting down in the chair by the bed, she swiftly removed her muddy half boots. Her stockings were damp. They would have to come off, too. She hesitated briefly before hoisting up her skirts to untie her garters.

It may have been only her imagination, but she thought she heard him suck in a sharp breath.

Some of the feminine power she'd felt standing on the banks of the Thames returned in a blood-fizzing rush.

She very deliberately untied her white satin garter and—extending her leg out in front of her—slowly rolled off her stocking.

The air in the room thickened with tension. She felt it as surely as she heard her pulse throbbing in her ears.

She removed her left garter and stocking in the same manner. Barefoot and bare legged, she stood and turned to face him.

Teddy was no longer focused on massaging his legs. He was watching her, his big body gone still, and his eyes darkened with a dangerous light.

Another flicker of hesitation went through her. Ladies didn't undress in front of gentlemen. Not even their husbands. Not as far as she knew.

But goddesses did.

And that was how Teddy saw her. She could see it in his face. He was enthralled. Enraptured. Hardly breathing for wanting her.

It gave her the courage to continue.

Her spangled shift was secured with only a simple clasp at her neck, and several other hook closures at her back and hips. She made quick work of them.

"Do you mean to send me to an early grave?" Teddy asked in a husky growl.

She smiled to herself. "No more than you meant to send me to one when you took off your trousers."

"I wasn't trying to bewitch you. I was in pain, lest you forget."

Holding his gaze, she shrugged her shift from her shoulders. It shimmied down over her bosom and hips, paillettes clinking softly as it fell to the floor. She wore nothing beneath it save a knee-length linen chemise. No petticoats or crinoline. Not even a corset.

"And how are you feeling now?" she asked.

"I'm aching like the devil," he said gruffly. "Come here."

She turned down the lamp. Crossing to the bed, she climbed in beside him. Her hair was loose about her shoulders, just as it was when she posed for him. But this time, the thick tresses fell on him, too, draping them both in a silvery veil as he enfolded her in a powerful embrace. She'd barely settled herself in his arms before he kissed her.

Her blood heated in a mighty surge. Her heart was beating so quickly. She could scarcely catch her breath. It didn't prevent her from kissing him back. She moved over him, her bosom pressed to his chest, and her hands first at his neck, then in his hair, then tugging impatiently at his shirt.

He helped her, pulling his shirt the rest of the way over his head and tossing it to the floor. His bare arms and chest were lean and hard with muscles. She ran her hands over him in raw appreciation, so bold that she shocked herself.

"Are you certain you're—" she began.

"Let me know if I'm—" he said at the same time.

Their words tumbled over each other, lips meeting again, as they both laughed breathlessly.

"Doubtless this isn't the way you imagined spending your wedding night," he said.

"*Our* wedding night," she corrected him. "And we've already proven that we do as we please. I don't see why we must resort to being conventional now."

"This evening promises to be nothing if not unconventional." He captured her mouth again.

She kissed him back with half-parted lips. He drew her closer, perilously closer, his hands curving at her waist and pressing at her hips, bringing her firmly against him. Any thought she'd had of their consummation being postponed evaporated into the ether.

"But, Teddy—" she broke off on a gasp, her earlier concerns emerging despite herself. "Are you really out of pain now? You're not just . . . being chivalrous?"

"Me? Chivalrous? Hardly. It's plain speaking I value, not artifice. As evidenced by the fact that I scared you off the first several times we met."

"You didn't scare me. I scared myself. I was too curious about you."

"Curious. Hmm. I'd rather it had been besotted, but—"

"Teddy, really."

"Really, sweetheart," he said. "The pain has eased. You have a magic touch. Jennings usually has to work on me for half an hour. With you, I felt relief within minutes. That's how the muscle spasms go—here one moment, seeming like the agony will never end, and gone twenty minutes later, a distant memory. It happened in Hampshire, too, when the weather changed."

"I didn't think you could feel anything in your legs anymore."

He held her close. His cheek brushed the top of her head as she cuddled against him. "It's not exactly a feeling. Not the way it was before my illness."

"What, then?"

"The muscles still move. They jump. Cramp. In the beginning I thought it meant my legs were waking up. But it doesn't mean anything except pain."

"I'm sorry." She smoothed her hand over his chest. "Have you—"

"Yes," he answered the question before she summoned the nerve to ask it. "We tried all manner of treatments when we moved to France. There were doctors in Paris touting electricity machines, surgical procedures, and tonics, salves, and tinctures. Needless to say, none of them had the desired effect."

Stella drew back to meet his eyes, indignant on his behalf. "Did your family make you endure such things?"

"No. They thought most of it claptrap. It was me. I was searching." His expression turned rueful. "When you're desperate, you'll believe anything, and there are countless swindlers whose business it is to promise you the world. I gave up soon after. I realized that nothing could be done. So . . . if you have any illusions that I'll be walking off with you into some glorious happily-ever-after . . ." A bleak vulnerability entered his gaze. "This is how it ends for me," he said. "Just me, in that chair, until the day I die."

Stella's throat closed with emotion. "Foolish beyond permission, as usual," she said. "It's not the end. And it's not just you, either. It's you and me. Forever."

Teddy bowed his head to hers. His throat worked on a swallow.

"Forever," she said again, touching his jaw. She forced him to look her in the eyes. "You can't be rid of me, Teddy Hayes. Not for any ridiculous reason like that. I'll still be here with you, even when you finish your masterpiece. I'll never leave you, not unless you tell me that you no longer want me—"

"I love you," he said gruffly.

Stella's heart stopped, uncertain if she'd heard him correctly. He'd spoken so deep. So low. She wondered briefly if it was possible to dream words into existence. She'd imagined him saying them so many times.

"I love you," he repeated. "I know you vowed to fall in love with me first, but it isn't necessary. You needn't make the effort. I love you just the same—I have since the day I asked you to marry me. And if all you can offer in return is friendship, I shall learn to be content."

Stella's eyes blurred with tears. "How can you speak of such things? Of mere contentment—of friendship!—when you've had the whole of my heart for months? I don't need to make an effort to fall in love with you. I *already* love you. I love you so much that I—"

Teddy seized her before she could finish. The rest was muffled by his lips. He kissed her. Held her. Expressed how desperately he loved her in words—

And without them, too.

A long while later, Stella lay, sated in Teddy's arms. They were both breathing heavily, still murmuring sweet nothings in the darkness and touching each other in lazy passes.

The sun had long set, the house all closed up and quiet. She was absent her chemise. He couldn't recall when he'd stripped it off of her.

He supposed, in hindsight, he'd behaved rather like a love-addled madman. But Stella hadn't seemed to mind his impatient enthusiasm. She'd been rather impatient herself. Bold and fearless, only the fleeting shyness she'd exhibited at the ultimate moment betraying her innocence and insecurity. He'd recognized it in her because he'd felt it, too.

"There were no Parisienne muses," he'd told her then, looking deep into her eyes. "Not like this. There's never been anyone but you."

It had, as it turned out, been the exact right thing to say.

Teddy's lips grazed her temple as she snuggled against him, loving her so much it still made his heart ache to touch her.

And she loved him in return. She'd said so.

No, what she'd said is that she'd loved him for months. *Months.* He still couldn't quite believe it.

But today had been a day of firsts. Their wedding, their painting session on the banks of the Thames, and now this. He'd revealed his deepest vulnerabilities to her, and she'd accepted him. Loved him.

He smoothed her hair from her brow. "Would you like to see something?"

Her cheek was resting on his chest. He felt her smile. "Haven't you already astonished me enough this evening?"

His mouth hitched in a lazy grin. "Something else, I mean," he said. "You'll have to put on your dressing gown."

She groaned in complaint, her soft, shapely body boneless on his. He nudged her gently. "I promise, it will be worth it."

"Very well." She slowly moved to rise.

His body went cold as she lifted away from him, depriving him of her warmth. He watched her walk to the lamp and light it. His blood ignited again. He had to suppress the urge to drag her back into his arms.

"Would you pass me my trousers?" he asked instead.

She slipped on her dressing gown, tying the silk sash around her waist, before fetching his discarded clothing for him.

He didn't require any help to dress. He could even get out of bed on his own, once Stella brought his wheeled chair up beside it and applied the brake. Hoisting himself up to a sitting position, he used his arms to swing himself into the seat. He adjusted his legs with his hands, setting his bare feet on the footrest.

Stella held the lantern aloft as she opened the door. "I hope we're going to the kitchen. I'm ravenous."

"My studio first," he said, wheeling through the doorway. "Kitchen second."

She padded along next to him through the darkness, their path illuminated in the small halo of light cast from the lantern.

Drop cloths still covered the floor of his studio. He rolled over them in his pneumatic chair, the rubber wheels overcoming the difficulty far easier than his wooden wheels had done.

"Shall I light the other lamps?" she asked.

"Please." He wheeled to his canvas. Jennings had returned it to the large easel, leaving it covered in the same cloth Teddy draped it in whenever he wasn't working.

Stella lit the lamps one by one. The studio was illuminated by degrees, first softly, then brighter and brighter until no corner of the room was hidden from view.

When she'd finished, Stella came to stand behind him. Her silver hair fell in waves all around her.

Teddy took hold of the corner of the drape that covered his painting.

"No, you mustn't," she objected, suddenly comprehending his intention. "You're not ready."

"I'm ready," he assured her.

"But it's not finished. You said that no one could see it until—"

"You're not no one. You're my wife." With that, he pulled the drape from his canvas, revealing his portrait to her for the first time.

Stella gasped. Her hand drifted up to cover her mouth. "Oh, Teddy. It's . . . It's . . ." She moved closer to examine it.

He'd depicted her in loose brushstrokes, a creature in motion, the glitter of her spangled dress and the shimmer of her hair emerging as one with the twilight. The sea behind her reflected the waning sun in a sensual tumult. So, too, did the paillettes of her dress, each of them aglow with a luminosity that drew itself from both water and sky. She appeared to have just alighted from the heavens—the moment of transition from star to woman captured a breath before the transformation had become complete.

Stella reached to touch the canvas, only to draw back her hand at the last moment. "It's extraordinary," she murmured. "The way you've brought the changing light into every facet."

"You approve, then?"

She continued to stare at the painting, visibly awestruck. "Everyone must do so. It's the most beautiful thing I've ever seen."

"It should be," he said. "It's a portrait of you."

Her gaze found his. Her eyes were glistening with emotion. She held out her hand to him and he took it. Their fingers threaded together in an intimate clasp. "I little knew what you intended when you first asked to paint me."

"I little knew, either." He drew her down onto his lap. She was a soft, womanly bundle in his arms, her curves unconstrained by corset or crinoline. "It's yours," he told her.

Her eyes widened. "But you can't give it to me. You're going to submit it to the Royal Academy. To sell it one day and—"

"Sell it? A portrait of *my* Stella? Never. Not for any amount—"

She threw her arms around his neck before he could finish, her mouth claiming his in a passionate kiss.

"You can still submit it to the Academy," she said, several scorching moments later. "Not because of me, but because of your talent. This piece is going to make the whole of the London art world stand up and take notice."

"Do you know," Teddy said, drawing her lips back to his, "in this moment, the art world is the last thing on my mind. The only good opinion I care about is yours."

"You have it." Stella kissed him again. "And my heart."

Teddy's own heart thudded heavily in answer—his love for her shining as brightly as she did. "And you have mine," he vowed huskily. "Always."

Epilogue

EIGHTEEN MONTHS LATER . . .

"They've displayed it beautifully, haven't they, my love?" Stella stood beside Teddy, admiring the placement of his portrait on the wall of the Berners Street Gallery. It had been hung at the sight line, a small plaque beneath it proclaiming its title: *Electra Descending*.

"A good thing, too," Teddy said. "It appears to be what most everyone is here for. A shame if they couldn't find it."

Ladies in elegant silk gowns and gentlemen in frock coats and top hats strolled past the portrait. Some stopped to stare in guarded appreciation. Others frowned with disapproval. Many more exchanged scandalized whispers.

This wasn't the painting's first public showing. In March, Teddy had submitted it to the Royal Academy, along with three of his best seascapes. The Academy had accepted the seascapes, to Teddy and Stella's joy, but the portrait of Stella as one of the Pleiades had been summarily—and somewhat disdainfully—rejected. One member of the Academy's selection committee had called it "too controversial in its style" and another had referred to it as "an incomplete effort."

Teddy and Stella's belief in the piece hadn't faltered. They had taken it to France in the spring, where it had predictably been rejected from the Paris Salon as well. From there, it made its way through various private galleries and independent exhibitions, first garnering mild praise ("*not without promise*") and then robust acclaim ("*a stunning achievement*").

Finally, back in England, the portrait still retained the glow of the modest fame it had garnered on the continent. Many had come to see it in Berners Street, both to admire and to ridicule.

"Scandalous," a lady murmured to her husband, as the pair of them wandered by.

"The use of light and color enthrall," a gentleman in a waggish neckcloth and velvet jacket remarked to an artistic companion. "But it's an impression rather than an expression. That is where it fails."

"Yet the piece holds raw power," the younger gentleman replied. "The brushwork is reminiscent of Turner."

Teddy and Stella exchanged a meaningful look. Turner was still Teddy's hero. To be compared to him was high praise indeed. It made any criticism pale by comparison.

A familiar gentleman, with unruly hair and a dark mustache, made his way through the crowd to join them.

Stella recognized him at once. "Oh look," she said to her husband. "Mr. Whistler has managed to come after all."

Teddy and James Whistler had struck up a warm acquaintance over the past year, first via correspondence and then through several dinners, both in Maiden Lane and at Whistler's home in Chelsea. Though their artistic styles differed—with Teddy focused on light and color, and Whistler committed to muted shades and precise brushwork—they nevertheless found cause to support each other.

"Jim!" Teddy smiled. "How do you do?"

"How do *you* do, more to the point?" Whistler shook Teddy's hand. "Mrs. Hayes." He bowed to Stella. "The portrait has been presented well."

"They've done it justice, certainly," Stella said.

"And they haven't changed its name," Teddy added. "That's something, at least."

"It's drawn a crowd," Mr. Whistler observed.

"Not entirely for good reason, I fear," Teddy said. "It's still rather controversial on this side of the Channel."

"Ignore the cretins," Whistler advised. "Your piece is one of the few things of value at this exhibition." He spotted another acquaintance across the room. "Forgive me. I must speak with Mr. Edwards before he departs. Do say you'll join me for dinner on Friday evening in Lindsey Row. Rossetti is coming."

"We should be delighted," Stella said.

"Give Edwards my regards," Teddy said before Mr. Whistler took his leave.

Stella's friends crossed paths with Mr. Whistler as they approached. All the Furies had come to show their support. Anne and Mr. Hartford had traveled up from Somersetshire. Julia and Captain Blunt had taken the train down from Yorkshire—a rare journey from home, with a new baby to look after. And Evie had arrived with Ahmad, who had left his dress shop early that afternoon to accompany his wife, despite the heavy demands his aristocratic customers were lately making on his time.

Laura and Alex had been unable to attend. They had welcomed a little boy last summer, and Laura was still unfit to travel. Stella and Teddy had gone to see them in Grasse in December. There, they'd spent a blissful three weeks coddling the baby, celebrating Christmas, and sketching the dormant flower fields. Stella had even met Magpie the cat, who did indeed bear a startling resemblance to the itinerant piebald tom who visited them daily in Maiden Lane to feast on Stella's offerings of diced chicken and cream.

"How do you find the public's response?" Julia asked. There was a gentle roundness to her features since delivering her daughter. It made her even more beautiful. "Is it any better than it was in Paris?"

Captain Blunt stood at her side, his hand resting on the small of her back.

"Not better than Paris, no," Stella said. "But better than when it was first submitted to the Royal Academy. Then, you'd have thought it was an aberration."

"The members of the Academy are old-fashioned," Teddy said. "They don't like anything new. Their first instinct is always to condemn."

"They'll change their views eventually," Stella said. "They must. And then one day—"

"Hopefully in our lifetime," Teddy interjected wryly.

"The good press must help," Mr. Hartford said. Anne was on his arm. She wore a black caraco jacket and a bright plaid skirt. The latter matched the suit that her husband was wearing.

"Oh yes," Stella acknowledged. "It just received a wonderful write-up from Mr. Stillwater in the *Gentleman Artist's Monthly*. He called it 'a masterpiece in the making.'"

Anne cast a glance at her husband, brows lifted. "Did he indeed."

"He sounds an astute fellow," Mr. Hartford replied to her soberly. "A genius, I suspect."

Ahmad and Evelyn stood next to them. Ahmad's face held an unmistakable note of approval as he examined Teddy's portrait. He was a good judge of color and harmony. "If Parisian taste influences art as much as it does fashion, you may soon be more famous than you ever desired," he said to Teddy.

"I don't desire fame at all," Teddy replied. "Only recognition."

"You have it now in abundance," Captain Blunt said. "You might find that you prefer the safety of anonymity."

"Not at all," Stella said. "We neither of us wish to live a life in the background."

"You can hardly do so now," Anne remarked to Stella. "First a Fury, then one of the Four Horsewomen, and now a star. What transformation is next, I wonder?"

"I'm eager to find out," Stella said.

Teddy flashed her a private smile. "The adventure awaits."

She smiled back at him in the same way, as much with her eyes as with the gentle curve of her mouth. Their gloved hands found each other, clasping in intimate understanding.

The day he'd proposed to her, he'd promised her the freedom to discover what it was she wanted of life. At the time, she'd had no way of knowing. She'd been made so small for so long, the words hadn't existed to articulate the wild yearnings within her.

But no longer.

She knew now what she wanted—what she'd *always* wanted. It was nothing more complicated than the very freedom Teddy had offered her. The freedom to want, to choose, to be. To live a colorful, conspicuous, unconventional life with the man she loved. A life that looked like no one else's but their own.

"Have you told them yet?" he asked her.

"Told us what?" Evie asked.

Stella's smile broadened with a hint of pride. "I've been working on my own sketches this summer, and hope to submit them to the Royal Academy next year."

"Oh, that's wonderful!" Evie exclaimed.

"I'm not at all surprised," Anne said. "I always knew your work would be on display somewhere in London one day."

"I shouldn't get too excited," Stella warned them. "Unless the tide of opinion changes in the traditional realm between now and then, I shall likely be pursuing the same course as my husband when it comes to exhibiting my work."

"The galleries of Europe!" Julia's face lit up at the possibilities. "Do you imagine your sketches of Cossack will be displayed there one day?"

"*And* your sketches of Hephaestus," Evie chimed in.

"And don't forget Saffron," Anne added.

"All of them will be included," Stella assured them. "I've sketched them more than any other subjects, both alone and together."

"You'll have no difficulty finding a title, I vow," Julia said.

"The Four Horses of the Four Horsewomen," Evie pronounced. "I can already see it."

Stella, Anne, Julia, and Evie laughed, and their husbands along with them.

Things hadn't gone exactly as any of them planned since they'd first met during their series of failed London seasons. There had been no dashing princes. No great wealth, or fashionable success. But together they had found friendship, acceptance, and the courage to follow their hearts. The result had been love matches for each and every one of them.

They had happy homes of their own now, deeply fulfilling lives, and wonderful husbands who unconditionally adored them.

And they had horses, too.

As happily-ever-afters went, it didn't get much better.

Author's Note

❖

The Muse of Maiden Lane was inspired by several real-life artists, inventions, and events from the Victorian era. For more about them, see my notes below.

The Rise of French Impressionism

French Impressionism can trace its roots to the romantic *en plein air* paintings of early nineteenth-century artists like Joseph Mallord; William Turner and his contemporary, John Constable. However, it wasn't until the 1860s, when young artists like Claude Monet and Pierre-Auguste Renoir attended the Paris atelier of artist Charles Gleyre that Impressionism first began to crystallize into something like a movement.

In *The Muse of Maiden Lane*, Teddy has recently returned to England after several years spent studying at Gleyre's studio. The style of painting he's embraced is similar to that of his fellow future Impressionists, with an emphasis on movement, color, and the changing effect of natural light.

This style wasn't widely appreciated at the time. Quite the reverse; Teddy's work is sometimes described as being "unfinished," or as "the barest impression" of a subject, rather than an exact expression of it.

Real-life Impressionist painters received similar criticism. Rejected by both London's Royal Academy and Paris's Salon des Beaux Arts (the twin bastions of traditional artistic excellence in the 1860s art world), the new school of painters was obliged to showcase their work elsewhere, in private galleries and, eventually, at the Salon des Refusés in Paris—also known as the Salon of Rejects.

Where does James McNeill Whistler fit in? Like Teddy, Whistler was a student of Charles Gleyre. Though not an Impressionist himself, Whistler's name is often mentioned among their number. He, too, was battering up against the artistic status quo. In writing *Muse*, I came to feel that his struggles, particularly the challenges he faced in relation to his controversial painting *The White Girl* (known today as *Symphony in White, No. 1: The White Girl*), best mirrored Teddy's own.

To that end, I was aided in my story by the wonderful archive of Whistler's correspondence at the University of Glasgow. Not only did these letters give me insight into the Victorian art world, they also inspired me to make Teddy's house in Maiden Lane a fixer-upper (based on Whistler's own account of the many repairs needed at a property he had taken).

Incidentally, there's a good reason I don't ever directly mention the French Impressionist movement in my story. The term didn't come into its current use until the next decade, in reference to Monet's 1872 painting *Impression, Sunrise*.

Victorian Wheelchairs

In the early 1860s, when *Muse* is set, wheelchairs were largely limited to bath chairs—chairs that were either pushed by an attendant or pulled by a horse or donkey. Chairs that could be operated independent of an attendant didn't appear until later in the century. In order to give Teddy a wheelchair that he could operate on his own, I had to merge (and accelerate) a bit of history.

The prototype of the pneumatic invalid's chair that Teddy receives in the story was partially inspired by an 1853 patent for a locomotive chair invented by Thomas Minniss. First displayed at the New York Crystal Palace Exhibition in 1853, the chair was subsequently reviewed in Horace Greeley's *Art and Industry as Represented in the Exhibition at the Crystal Palace, New York*, where it was described as "a model machine." The review went on to state that:

> *With a slight effort of one hand, the poor invalid can propel himself indoors and out, turning the shortest corners with ease, going back or forward, upon smooth surfaces, absolutely without labor.*

Teddy's chair was also inspired by various Victorian era advertisements I found for custom-made mahogany and brass invalid's chairs. Most wheelchairs of the time *were* custom made and could be configured to a user's particular requirements. The resulting expense was generally too great for the average Victorian to afford, which is why the pneumatic chair in the story is marketed to wealthy invalids.

For the wheels of Teddy's chair, I drew inspiration from Scottish inventor Robert William Thomson's 1845 patent for an aerial carriage wheel. This innovative wheel was, in fact, a pneumatic tire, made of a hollow tube of vulcanized rubber that was then filled with pressurized air. The wheels were demonstrated to the public in Regent's Park in 1847, just as Hart told Teddy, but they failed to catch on, partly owing to the high cost of the rubber.

Acknowledgments

❧

The Muse of Maiden Lane is a novel that has been tucked in my heart ever since I first introduced the character of Teddy Hayes in my Parish Orphans of Devon series way back in 2019. I wanted so much to give him his happily-ever-after! I felt the same way about Stella Hobhouse, the last of my Belles, my Furies, my beloved Four Horsewomen. I owe tremendous thanks to everyone who helped bring Teddy and Stella's love story to life.

To my tireless mom, thank you for reading early drafts, for babysitting my pets while I worked, and for the endless cups of Darjeeling. I couldn't do this without you!

Thanks are also due to my brilliant agent, Kevan Lyon; to my excellent (and very patient) editor, Sarah Blumenstock; and to Liz Sellers, Yazmine Hassan, Anika Bates, Jessica Plummer, Megha Jain, Caitlin Morgan, Jenni Surasky, Christine Legon, LeeAnn Pemberton, Rita Frangie, and the rest of the dedicated and hardworking team at Berkley/Penguin Random House, who do so much to get my Belles of London series in front of readers.

During the course of writing this series, it's been a true blessing to have the support and encouragement of so many authors I admire. I'm especially grateful to Kate Quinn, Jodi Picoult, Jennifer Robson, Meg Tilly, Evie Dunmore, Isabel Ibañez, Harper St. George, Kate

Pearce, Caroline Linden, Olivia Dade, Syrie James, Stephanie Barron, and Jane Porter, for their kindness and generosity. Additional thanks to art historian and friend Lucy Paquette, for assisting me with my nineteenth-century art research. To the wonderful Alissa Baxter and my irreplaceable assistant, Rel Mollet, for reading early drafts of this manuscript and providing such useful feedback. And to the amazing Lyonesses—always supportive and always available to help me put this crazy business into perspective.

Last but never least, many thanks and much love to my animal family—Stella, Jet, Tavi, Bijou, and Asteria—for variously acting as emotional support, stress relief, lap warmers, cowriters, cheering section, and as ever-present reminders that I don't have the luxury of giving up.

Ending a series is always hard, but I close this one with so much gratitude. Riding and writing are two of the great loves of my life. What a gift it's been to weave them together in book form. Thank you, thank you, thank you to everyone who came along for the ride. Horse girls forever!

The Muse
of Maiden
Lane

MIMI MATTHEWS

READERS GUIDE

Discussion Questions

—◆✕◆—

1. Stella Hobhouse's gray hair is her most distinctive feature. Was she foolish to dye it in order to fit in? What else might she have done to make herself more acceptable to fashionable society? Do you see any parallels to today's beauty standards?

2. Teddy Hayes has been in a wheelchair for the last five years after contracting a virulent strain of scarlet fever that weakened his legs. How was his mobility limited at the country house party in Hampshire? In what ways did his limitations make it more difficult for him to pursue Stella?

3. How does Daniel Hobhouse's courtship of Miss Trent impact Stella? How will Stella's role in her brother's household change once he marries? What alternatives could she have employed to maintain her position?

4. Teddy is determined to paint Stella's portrait. Taking into account that most Victorian models were considered little better than prostitutes, was it offensive of Teddy to ask her to sit for him? Under what circumstances might a young painter have respectably painted a young lady of Stella's class?

5. Teddy's disability inspires a range of reactions from the people around him. In what ways did Victorian society view people with disabilities? How have those views changed in modern times? How have they stayed the same?

6. Stella asks Teddy to join her for a sleigh ride even though she knows he is reluctant to draw attention to his disability. The result is a deeply romantic first kiss. What positive experiences have you had when venturing outside your comfort zone? Was it worth the risk?

7. Teddy's family can be overprotective at times. What reasons might they have for keeping him close to them? Are those reasons valid?

8. Stella uses the bulk of her inheritance to subsidize the cost of keeping her horse and groom. The expense drastically limits her prospects for independence. What benefits does she gain in exchange for her sacrifice? Are those benefits worth it?

9. Stella has a strong bond with her fellow horsewomen. How do her friends inspire and assist her in her quest for independence and love? How do they hinder her?

10. Teddy is supported by both his immediate and extended family. Who among them proves to be the most useful as he strikes out on his own? What could the others have done differently?

11. Teddy and Stella's life in Maiden Lane promises to be distinctly unconventional. In what ways have they already flouted mores of Victorian society? In what ways do they conform to it?

12. Stella's silver mare, Locket, is notorious for her high-spiritedness. In what ways might Locket's temperament symbolize Stella's own wild yearnings? How is the bond between them important to the story?

Don't miss

Rules for Ruin,

*the first book in the Crinoline Academy
series by Mimi Matthews.*

APRIL 1864

*E*uphemia Flite stood outside the iron gates that formed the fortress-like entrance to the bleak stone manor house beyond. The institution's name was wrought in heavy black filigree letters in the arch above: *Miss Corvus's Benevolent Academy for the Betterment of Young Ladies.*

Spring storm clouds drifted overhead, darkening an already gray sky. They lent an ominous air to the sprawling estate's barren gardens and high, weathered granite walls. To the public, it was nothing more than a charity school—the dignified remains of a once-grand property outside of London, where ragged orphans and street urchins were taught the skills necessary for honest employment.

It had been more than five years since Effie had last passed through its gates. Then, she'd been leaving—a headstrong girl of eighteen, cast out by the Academy's proprietress, Artemesia Corvus, herself. But it hadn't been an absolute expulsion. It had only ever been an exile. Effie had understood then, as surely as she'd understood anything, that one day, whether she liked it or not, Miss Corvus would summon her back.

A week ago in Paris, that day had finally arrived.

Setting her shoulders against the chill, Effie waited for someone to let her in. She'd come straight from the railway station. She was still in her black silk traveling dress, a veiled bonnet perched atop her stylishly arranged ebony hair, and a heavy carpet bag clutched in her gloved hands. Her small black poodle, Franc, was comfortably ensconced within.

Seeming to sense her anxiety, he poked his beribboned head out of the bag's opening. He looked at her briefly, as if to reassure himself she had the situation in hand, before turning to peer through the gates. His lip twitched in a preemptive snarl.

Effie gave him an absent scratch.

Miss Corvus employed no gentleman porter. During Effie's time as a student, the gates had been manned by the junior teachers. Several minutes passed before a door at the side of the house opened and one of them finally emerged. The young woman advanced slowly down the pebbled drive, a heavy shawl drawn around her narrow shoulders, and a large ring of keys in her hand. A pronounced limp marred her gait.

It was Penelope Trewlove. Nell, as she was called by her intimates. There was no mistaking that glossy flaxen hair and beguiling heart-shaped face.

Catching sight of Effie, Nell's angelic countenance was transformed by a roguishly dimpled smile. "I confess, I didn't truly believe you'd come," she said as she limped closer. "Not even when we received your wire from Calais."

Effie smiled in return. It was genuine, not artifice. A rarity with her. So much of her conduct these past several years had been studied instead of spontaneous.

But this was Nell, not an adversary. A version of Nell remarkably unaltered by the passage of time.

Granted, she may have grown taller, and her cheeks were slightly less plump, but her eyes had retained their mischievous sparkle, and her figure was still something to be envied. Above all, she was familiar. Far more emblematic of home than the cold, unwelcoming structure that loomed behind her.

"Nell," Effie said warmly. "I'd hoped yours would be the first face I saw."

"Never mind *my* face." Nell's gaze swept over Effie in glowing approval as she came to a halt on the opposite side of the gates. "How well you look! Lovelier even than when you left us. That's Paris's doing, I'll wager." Her smile broadened, revealing a glimpse of her crooked front tooth. "And this must be the famous Franc!"

Franc stared back at Nell through the bars. He offered none of his usual grumbles. He seemed to sense she was an ally rather than a foe.

"Franc," Effie said, introducing him as formally as if he were a gentleman acquaintance. "This is Miss Trewlove."

"How do you do, Franc?" Nell's dimples appeared again. "Oh, what a little dear he is. And what a continental air he has about him! I feel as though he's judging the unfashionableness of my gown." Her attention fell to the barren ground at Effie's booted feet. "But where are all the rest of your things? Have you not brought any trunks with you from Paris?"

"I left them at the station. I shall send for them directly after I speak with Miss Corvus." Effie paused. "Providing, that is, you let me in."

Nell gave an eloquent grimace. "Yes, yes. Of course. I'm sorry I kept you waiting. Especially in this weather. It's bound to rain any moment." She shuffled through the key ring, selecting a large, black iron key. "I trust you haven't been standing down here long?"

"The hackney cab set me down not ten minutes ago."

"Ten minutes? Upon my word. I'm surprised you didn't pick the lock."

Effie's smile dimmed. "Is that what the Academy's students have been reduced to in my absence? Parlor tricks?"

Nell slid the heavy iron key into the lock, opening the tall gates with a grating scrape of metal on metal. "What you call parlor tricks, I call useful skills."

Effie didn't doubt it. Nell had always believed in Miss Corvus's questionable aims. It's one of the primary reasons Nell had agreed to stay on as a junior teacher. Indeed, on coming of age, Nell and Effie had both been given that option—a five-year contract, after which, they could either remain at the Academy permanently or depart, with a small stipend, to seek their fortunes.

Miss Corvus liked to keep her special girls close. And, as the first and second members of the inaugural class of the charity school, Nell and Effie had been the most special of all.

The gates swung open with a creaking groan. Effie walked through them to embrace her old schoolmate. "Some skills are more useful than others," she said.

Nell hugged her tight in return. "Had you no cause to pick any locks while you were companion to Madame Dalhousie?"

"Not a one, thank heaven." Effie's duties had been confined to accompanying the eccentric widowed madame to art and literary salons, lavish balls, stately dinners, and other social events of both the respectable and unrespectable variety. Such was the life of a lady's companion, even one lucky enough to live in the City of Light.

"Pity," Nell said. "You'll be out of practice for what lies ahead."

Effie drew back, brows notched in a frown. She searched Nell's face. "It's like that, is it?"

"Naturally." Nell released her. "You must have realized it when you received my sampler." She moved to lock the gates behind them, visibly proud of herself. "Clever, was it not?"

The sewing sampler had arrived at Madame Dalhousie's house in Paris last week. A masterpiece of advanced embroidery, it had been composed of delicate, colored threads stitched into a rectangle of coarse cloth, depicting a stately stone house and gardens, a jumbled alphabet, and a flock of birds circling above. Four ravens, to be precise, one of which had a white-tipped wing. The latter was the unofficial symbol of the Academy, and a necessary component of any secret message. Taken altogether, it had been a simple enough code.

Effie had used it to spell out the unmistakable command: FLY HOME.

"Ridiculous, more like." Effie's tone held no malice. Among all the residents of the Academy, Nell was the only one whom Effie counted as a friend. They had corresponded semi-regularly during Effie's exile.

Together, they returned up the pebbled path to the house. Nell's leg hitched with every step. Effie felt the motion as much as saw it. The guilt she nurtured over her part in the childhood accident that had caused Nell's injury sprang anew. It never really left her, that guilt, despite the fact that Nell professed to hold no resentment over the past.

"You might simply have written a letter to me, you know," Effie pointed out, "rather than making a riddle of it."

"How dull that would have been." Nell linked her arm through Effie's. "It was far more amusing to practice my stitchery."

Their full skirts pushed against each other as they walked. It was impossible for them not to, given the respective size of their wire crinolines. Miss Corvus wasn't a lady to entertain the whims of fashion, but she had made an exception for the controversial, and seemingly impractical, cage-like undergarment. All of her teachers donned them, and most of the older orphans, too. Both Effie and Nell wore theirs like armor.

No one could easily get close to a girl wearing a wire crinoline, not without thoroughly disarranging her. Its sheer circumference provided a modicum of protection. But its daunting size had another purpose. A crinoline made even the smallest female an intimidating creature. She took up space for herself—*demanded* space—in a world where ladies were too often diminished and ignored.

"People never trouble to examine samplers too closely, I find," Nell continued. "And when they do, they're only searching for the flaws, never the meaning. It makes them an ideal vehicle for sending secret messages."

"You're a modern-day Madame Defarge," Effie remarked.

Nell's eyes twinkled. "Except that my messages are all for the good."

Effie gave Nell a speaking glance as they ascended the front steps to the house. "*That* remains to be seen."

Like the exterior of the house, the interior of the formal entry hall was composed of aged stone, worn over the centuries to a buttery sheen. Faded carpets covered the floor and moth-eaten tapestries adorned the walls, along with two large, gilt-framed oil paintings. One was an excellent reproduction of Gentileschi's *Judith Slaying Holofernes*. It had been there since Effie had first arrived at the Academy as a girl. A terrifying painting for a child to behold.

The other painting had been there as well. It was a portrait of a dark-haired woman in a lusterless black dress, standing tall and strong in the silhouette of a doorway. But it was no ordinary rendering, made to flatter its subject. The woman in this portrait had her back to the viewer. Her face was completely hidden from view.

Effie had once heard Miss Corvus offer an explanation of the portrait to a questioning gentleman who had come to inspect the premises on behalf of the parish council. "The modest woman conceals her face," she'd told him.

It was as good a story as any, and one that had well satisfied the pious man. But it wasn't the truth, as Effie would learn.

She deftly removed her bonnet with one hand, still holding her carpetbag in the other. Franc scanned the hall, his liquid brown eyes unblinking as he took in his strange surroundings. He offered another low growl.

There was no one about to inspire it. At this time of day, the inmates of the Academy would all be in their classes, sectioned off into the various rooms of the house like busy little bees in a hive.

But what of the Queen Bee?

When last Effie had faced her, Artemesia Corvus had been in her fourth-floor study—a remote tower room filled with books, antiquated papers corded with ribbons, and a bewildering filing system, the secret of which was known only to its equally secretive inventor.

"Where is she?" Effie asked, moving toward the broad, blackened oak staircase at the edge of the hall. "In her study?"

"Not there." Nell set a hand on Effie's sleeve, gently arresting her step. "She's in her private quarters."

Effie's brows lifted. Miss Corvus never received any of the girls in her private rooms. Not even the teachers. At least, she hadn't during Effie's tenure. Miss Corvus's rooms had always been sealed off, as impenetrable as a tomb, behind an impassable set of tall, iron-banded wooden doors. Not even the canniest members of the Academy had dared attempt entry.

Nell directed Effie down the hall. "She caught a fever some months ago. It weakened her considerably. Stairs have become difficult."

Effie's already uneasy stomach jolted at the news. She couldn't fathom Miss Corvus being weakened by anything. To Effie, the Academy's proprietress had always seemed invincible. "Is she—?"

"She's recovering," Nell said. "But slowly." She guided Effie down the long corridor, and through the high, stone archways that led past the library and the old conservatory. A right turn into a narrow passage brought them to the very set of iron-banded doors that separated the public rooms from the private.

Nell's expression sobered as she stopped in front of them. "I won't go in. Miss Corvus insists on speaking with you alone."

"Does she, indeed?" Effie lifted Franc from the carpetbag and set him down on the stone floor. He gave a perfunctory shake before springing into motion. Effie caught hold of his lead before he could gallop off. Franc was a loyal companion, but he was also a rogue. He couldn't resist wandering.

She handed the lead to Nell. "If you would be so good as to take him for an airing? And pray don't let him loose. He's swift as a greyhound when he chooses to be. You'd never catch him."

Nell didn't ask any questions. She knew all about Franc's little foibles from Effie's letters. "I shall take him to visit the hedgerow," she said. "Look for me when you're done."

Effie waited until Nell had gone before rapping twice on the door. There was a taut moment of silence before Miss Corvus answered from within.

"Come," she said.

The clipped, frost-edged voice had its usual effect on Effie. It was a reaction borne from a memory too distant to recall as anything more than primitive emotion. It made Effie long to shrink back into herself. To make herself invisible. Maybe then Miss Corvus wouldn't see her. Wouldn't take her away.

But Effie had never excelled at being invisible.

Stiffening her spine, she opened the door.

Photo by Vickie Hahn

USA Today bestselling author **Mimi Matthews** writes both historical nonfiction and award-winning Victorian romances. Her novels have received starred reviews in *Publishers Weekly, Library Journal, Booklist, Kirkus Reviews,* and Shelf Awareness, and her articles have been featured on the Victorian Web, in the *Journal of Victorian Culture,* and in syndication at *BUST* magazine. In her other life, Mimi is an attorney. She resides in California with her family, which includes an Andalusian dressage horse, a Sheltie, a miniature poodle, and two Siamese cats.

Ready to find
your next great read?

Let us help.

Visit prh.com/nextread

Penguin
Random
House